MH

chani's
karmic
collision

'A funny, compelling and sometimes poignant story of a three-tier generation gap, complicated by the North/South divide. Ultimately, though, this clever novel reveals how the things we think separate us can also bring us together. Told with wry humour, gentle satire and deft plotting.'

David Chadwick, '*Liberty Bazaar*'

'As the characters in this first novel fumble through the aftermath of death, divorce and abandonment, collisions are manifold, relationships blossom and some unlikely alliances are found. Davis's keenly observed comedy of manners offers real insight into ways the family unit can reconfigure itself after it has been blown apart.

Really funny.'

Nicky Harlow, '*Amelia and the Virgin*'

chani's karmic collision

ros davis

First published in the United Kingdom in 2015 by The Cloister House Press

ISBN 978 1- 909465-35-0

Cover design by Phil Davis
(philxdavis@hotmail.com)

To Bettina, with love and gratitude

1

Chani hadn't taken Annabel Fforbes seriously, horrifying though her letter had been – well, really, who would? A girl who couldn't write a letter that made sense? Who called herself a social worker but came to Yorkshire at the end of November wearing only a short, thin jacket, skin-tight jeans and ankle boots, plus two scarves draped around her neck that were useless at keeping her warm but made her look like a lollipop? Whose aura, furthermore, was beige?

She had disturbed Chani's chi, upset her chakras, but still Chani hadn't taken Lollipop Annabel seriously – not nearly seriously enough – when the girl had persuaded her – manipulated, actually – into agreeing to this meeting in, of all places, Welwyn Garden City.

And all because of Celandine. And somebody called Jamie.

It was, in this unimpressive Social Services room, all about to get worse. Much worse.

Annabel looked even more like a lollipop, with her long legs squeezed into tight jeans, thin feet in high heels, close-fitting fine-knit top and blonde bob.

'So, Jamie,' she said in her irritating aristocratic voice, crossing her legs, her fingers pushing hair behind one ear, 'here's the position, yes?'

Jamie wasn't looking at her. Even sitting down he gave the impression of a Roman emperor sparing the merest glance from a great height at the minions under his command. Minions, it appeared, who bored him. His father, Chani remembered, stood like that at the wedding, the one and only time she met him. Why on earth had Celandine ever married that crushingly boring lawyer? His aura had been beige, like Lollipop Woman's. Actually, though, his was probably more magnolia.

Pushing the chi-disturbing thoughts away Chani studied what she could see of Jamie's features. He looked just like Celandine, her daughter and, it seemed now, his mother. He had the same uncontrollable tangle of hair as Celandine, only it was dark, more like Chani's than Celandine's blonde froth.

He'd arrived after Chani and when Annabel brought him into the room, she introduced him by saying, not to Chani, but to him, 'Jamie, I don't believe you've met.' Chani felt like a minor dignity from a very minor country meeting the ruler of the known world. 'This is your granny,' Annabel continued, as if pointing out a new species.

Chani shuddered. 'Oh no, it's Chani, call me Chani.'

Evidently, he wasn't going to call her anything. Or even acknowledge her existence.

'She's come all the way from …. the North to see you,' Annabel said, in a bright voice.

'Hebden Bridge, actually.' Chani tried and failed to catch his eye. 'Yorkshire.'

He made some kind of sound and allowed Annabel to persuade him to a chair, from which he fixed his eyes on the remains of a Lego construction on the floor: a tower crane surrounded by Lego people. He hadn't stopped looking at it since.

No wonder he was bored. Chani tried to concentrate on what Annabel, now holding tight to a clipboard, was saying.

'You're in the house alone, Jamie, yes, apart from your housekeeper, er, Magda?'

What? A housekeeper?

'At the moment she's living in, but that is temporary, right?'

'Well, ...' Jamie said, to the Lego people, his voice sounding much deeper and more masculine than the sixteen Annabel had said he was.

'It's temporary.' Annabel said it again. 'For ...' she consulted her notes, 'another two weeks. And then she's going back to Poland, isn't she. So it is quite urgent—' her head swivelling to Chani, 'that you, Ms Caladan, as Jamie's next of kin, his gran—'

Chani stiffened. 'Gran' was it? She'd had time to think since Annabel's visit, when she'd suggested that, as Jamie's next of kin, Chani was the ideal person to look after him. Chani still hadn't got over the idea of being a grandmother, never mind the fact that Annabel expected her to do this 'looking after' in Jamie's home, here, in Welwyn Garden City.

'Look, Ms Fforbes,' she said, through tight lips, 'I might be his next of kin, if, as you say, there's absolutely no one on his father's side, but why can't Jamie come to live with me? You can come as soon as you like, Jamie.'

Jamie didn't react.

3

Maybe she should tell the Lego people. Have his people fix it up with her people. She struggled not to laugh and couldn't look at Annabel. She focused instead on Annabel's clipboard, which was definitely not funny.

'My house is plenty big enough,' she was now able to say without laughing, and remembered the point she urgently needed to make before Annabel could burst in. 'I'm a therapist, you know, I'm needed there, at the Mind and Body Centre.'

'Oh, sure, totally, yes I'm sure you are,' Annabel said, unfazed, 'but you see, Jamie is at school here, aren't you Jamie? At Stokeley Manor. OK?' Her grip on the clipboard had tightened even more.

'Yes,' Jamie told the plastic people.

What the hell was Stokeley Manor? 'We have schools in Hebden Bridge,' she said.

'Well yes, I suppose you do,' Annabel said, though she seemed to have some doubts. 'But Stokeley Manor is an excellent school. And Jamie's father particularly wanted Jamie to attend there, going forward, didn't he, Jamie?'

'Yes.'

He bloody would, Chani thought, realising what sort of school it must be. Why didn't Annabel tell her about this before?

'Mr Pomfret-Jones put it in his will,' Annabel explained to her, as if describing air travel to a peasant. 'and made financial arrangements. Right? So it's not possible for Jamie to move, is it, Jamie, even if you wanted to.' She raised the board slightly and glanced at the clock.

4

Chani was beginning to feel dizzy watching Annabel's head turning.

'Yes.'

Did Jamie know any other words? And how did he manage to put so much sneer, boredom and dismissal into a one-syllable word?

'OK, right?' Clearly, for Annabel, checking the clock again, this was the clincher.

'No.' Chani drew on all she had learned about assertiveness. 'No, it's not OK. I can't just give everything up and move down here.'

'But Mrs, er, Ms Caladan, you're his next of kin.' As if that explained everything.

'See, Ms Fforbes, as I told you before, I didn't even know he existed till six years ago, and then I hadn't the foggiest who he was.'

Annabel's knuckles went white as she tilted the clipboard towards herself.

At that point it seemed Jamie did know some more words. And that he agreed with Chani.

'I don't need anybody,' he told the plastic tower crane. 'I'm fine.' He didn't sound bored now. And rather more like a sixteen-year-old boy than a Roman emperor.

But they were both up against a tough opponent.

'Right, look,' said Annabel, placing the clipboard on the desk beside her in a very final gesture. Could she ever manage without it? 'What I suggest is we try it out. For a week, yes? A trial period, starting on Friday next, OK – one week.'

She stood. Implacable.

The meeting was over.

Chani opened her mouth to protest but the door opened with some urgency and a plump, harassed-looking woman appeared.

'Annabel, your three-fifteen is here,' she said, the deep significance she put into the words 'three-fifteen' unmissable. 'You'd better hurry, he's, er …' She was making frantic distress signals with her face and sideways jerks of her head. Her hands fluttered.

'Right.' Annabel nodded, grabbed her board and, clutching it like a shield in front of her, moved swiftly to the door. 'Delia will look after you,' she said over her shoulder. 'We'll be writing to you in the next day or so. Thank you so much for coming in.' And she had gone.

Jamie walked past Chani, ignoring her and Delia and disappeared.

'Er,' Delia said.

'Can you just show me the way out?' Chani asked her, remembering the maze of identical corridors.

It was a long way home. Chani fumed, her mind going over and over what Annabel considered to be a meeting, the way Jamie had behaved, and how Annabel could think it was Chani's responsibility to resolve a problem she'd had no part in creating.

Vanessa, she needed Vanessa. She was a social worker, she'd never have carried on like Lollipop Woman. But then bits of the conversation she'd had with her closest friend recently landed in her memory like thrown snowballs.

'…either that, Chani, love, or she had a lover. She is your daughter after all,' she'd said when Chani hadn't been able to believe that Celandine's uptight husband

6

had actually fathered a child.

Granted, Vanessa had made more sense of Annabel Fforbes' letter than Chani could. 'Jamie's mother's gone away, with a man. No one knows where they are. Not even her son, this Jamie, who she's left on his own,' she'd explained.

'Really?' Chani had felt a very unusual maternal twinge. 'That's the first exciting thing she's ever done. I wonder if she's gone through a re-balancing.'

And all Vanessa had been able to say was, 'I can't believe you said that.' Which was no help at all.

Nor had she shown the slightest sympathy when Chani had said, 'I bet it's a horrible house. Anything that man chose would be. His chakras were never balanced, you know.'

And again, when Chani struggled to understand why Jamie couldn't be left by himself at sixteen, when she herself had been perfectly happy to be left on her own at that age, Vanessa had been a bit sharp.

Chani still hadn't forgotten that conversation. 'You were in a commune,' Vanessa had said.

'Yes, it was fabulous.'

'You were pregnant at seventeen.'

'Van, I chose to get pregnant. You can't be worried about Jamie getting pregnant.'

'I'm trying to explain why the social worker wants to come and see you.'

Not a good idea to talk to Vanessa then.

Chani drove on. She shivered. It was December now and so cold that, even in her warm hemp boots and thick Peruvian felt skirt and jacket she still couldn't get warm. If only the stupid social worker had given

7

her enough time for Mike's garage to fix Patricia's heating system.

From her iPod Otis Redding sang 'Mr Pitiful'. It spurred Chani to carry on. It was bloody cold. How could she face doing this again? How could she possibly spend a week with that awful boy? She had to find out where Celandine had gone, but how? Might she find her if she Googled her name? What if ...? Or ...? Ohh, she was too tired to think.

By the time she was approaching Chesterfield she was so cold and weary she had to stop and find some food and a hot drink before she fell asleep at the wheel. The only choice was a motorway services. She was charged so much for a tasteless sandwich, an even more tasteless chocolate chip muffin with what was described as peppermint tea, that she had to tell somebody. Anybody.

She rang Vanessa. 'They should be ashamed,' she told her, and raged about Roman emperor Jamie, Lollipop Annabel, that man's bloody will, the bloody flaming Stokeley Manor school and the ludicrous trial period. 'I'm expected to go down there again and stay for a week! A bloody week! With an arrogant kid who can only talk to Lego people.'

'Lego people?'

'Don't ask.'

'God, how awful. How did Jamie react to the trial period thing?'

'I think he'd rather have nits.'

2

Jamie was appalled; even more appalled than he already was at the idea of having to have a social worker. At least she wasn't *that* bad. But his first sight of that weird woman had increased his horror by the power of ten. She couldn't possibly be his mother's mother.

Sophie was eager to hear all. He could hardly bring himself to tell her, but with her excitement shining through those amazing green eyes, almost on a level with his own, she was difficult to ignore. As well, there were more people he knew in the shop, which was really embarrassing. His shoulders rose and tensed. Sophie didn't like this shop, she never came with him, but today she'd wanted to. He had to get her out of there, but he'd just found the Wagner CD he'd been looking for for ever, was already imagining how it would sound on his Bang and Olufsen – so much better than downloaded music. He couldn't leave, someone else was bound to pick the CD up. He had to tell her something that would keep her happy long enough for him to buy it.

He pitched his voice as low as he could. What came out was, 'I have one week to get rid of her.'

But he didn't get the sympathy he expected. Far from it.

'Is she a witch?' she asked. She was so excited it reminded Jamie of the time her father bought her tickets for a One Direction gig.

Some people nearby turned to look.

He stationed himself between them and her, trying for his most chilling, quiet voice.

'She's seriously weird, Sophs,' he said.

But the strength of his emotions took him over. 'She's like those hippies you see on TV. Weird red hair, all, like, tatty, and her clothes? They were, like, felt? Like we made in art? Really weird boots and her legs were, like, *yellow*?'

More people were looking and Sophie was almost dancing. She clapped her hands.

'Jamie – she's a hippie! Fantastic! Hippie-chic is so-o cool!'

Jamie stared at her. 'Shh,' he whispered. 'Fashionable? She looks like she should be begging on the street.'

'Jamie, I so want to meet her. When's she coming?' She snuggled into his arm and tried to urge him from the displays.

He glared at her, pulled his arm away and turned back to the CD he wanted.

'Oh, there's Anya, look,' she said, waving madly at a group of people he didn't recognise. 'I wonder what she's doing in here? I must go and say hi.

'And then we can go, yes? Mwah!'

'Oh, God,' he muttered under his breath. If only she wouldn't do that.

He grabbed the CD, checking it was the right one, spotted a Schönberg recording the music teacher had recommended, snatched it up and took both to the till, managing to head Sophie off before she told this Anya person all about hippie-chic, whatever the hell that was.

She was nearly hyper as they left the shop.

'Tell me all about her,' she said. 'I can't wait. And I have to meet Mummy in half an hour.'

'Half an hour! You didn't tell me that?'

'Oh, Jamie, I did. She wants me to look at shoes with her.'

'I don't remember,' he said. But, hang on, that was good, wasn't it? 'Where are you meeting?'

'At Cranleigh's, they've got some new stock in from Milan, apparently.'

'Cranleigh's! It'll take half an hour to get there.'

She frowned. 'I suppose it will. Well, you can tell me on the way.'

'There's too much. I'll ring you later.'

Even so, he couldn't get away without describing the woman's weird clothes all over again, with even more detail.

Magda served Jamie his favourite meal, Boeuf Bourgignon, following it with a chocolate pudding.
'I have made Polish-style,' she told him, beaming.

She looked like she might pat his head and he had to stop himself ducking out of her way. He'd no idea what 'Polish-style' was, but it tasted all right.

Even Magda's motherly concern for him didn't lift his gloom about the prospect of that weird woman, a gloom which listening to the Wagner CD, sublime though the sound was, made him feel worse.

It didn't help when he spent the evening playing chess online and was beaten in all three games. That, on top of everything else, annoyed him so much he stayed up until two re-reading all he could about chess moves and fell asleep with the screen still glowing.

Next morning the sight of the sports bag full of the rugby kit Magda had laundered lightened things up. Should be a good game.

At school, he looked for Sophie at their usual place in the trophy corridor but there was no sign of her.

He didn't see her until morning break. She was sitting in the common room with two of her friends.

He strode across and said, 'Hello,' so that it included them all.

The three heads bent closer together.

Must be a project, he decided. Yes, Sophie had mentioned a drama project.

'Sophs,' he said, but she didn't seem to have heard. He said her name again, louder.

She looked up for an instant, her hand making a gesture that clearly told him she was busy.

All right, fine. He turned away and there, coming into the room behind two Year Ten boys, he spotted the bony shoulders, narrow face and geeky round glasses of Alastair Westhouse, his chess partner, the nearest thing to a friend he had.

Jamie performed what he hoped would be a drama project of his own, striding across to Alastair in the role of chess intellectual, sports hero and all-round popular guy.

'Alastair,' he greeted him as if they were good friends.

'Oh, Jamie,' Alastair said, his half-closed eyelids lifting a fraction, 'hi, er, what?'

'Chess, lunchtime, match,' Jamie said, standing right in front of him to get his full attention and doing his best to radiate bonhomie.

'Chess, yes, great,' Alastair said as if waking up and was off on one of his favourite subjects. 'I've been reading up on Spassky's moves—'

Jamie managed to nudge him away and walk with him, deep in discussion, past the group of girls - just as Sophie looked up again - and out of the room. At least his late night studies were coming in useful.

He was in absolutely the right mood that afternoon to take on the Drake House School team, but no matter what the Manor team did Drake pulled further and further ahead. At last the Manor team grabbed points, closing the gap.

The opposition centre crashed through Davenport's hopeless tackle and Jamie groaned. He tensed, ready for their winger, Rhys to get him, but he was swatted aside leaving Jamie as the last line of defence. As the centre charged for the try line Jamie thought fast. If he were to stop a score he had to do more than just bring him down. He hurled himself straight at the solid mass hurtling towards him, hoping to avoid a knee in the face. The impact sent shockwaves down his spine before everything went black.

Through a strange buzzing noise he thought he heard a sort of chanting that came and went. Cheering? Had Harry scored a try? But it sounded more like 'Jamie, Jamie' than 'Harry, Harry.'

His eyes were full of flashing lights, but they were fading. He tasted blood in his mouth, and when he moved his head he realised the buzzing was coming from his ears. He was on his knees in the mud, swaying and feeling sick.

He wanted to stay there but someone was dragging

13

him to his feet.

He was surrounded by grinning teammates. 'Great stuff, mate,' he heard, through dim echoes. Rhys.

Each slap on his back sent sharp pain through his head, electric shocks seemed to be passing down his arms. He lifted his head and saw his opponent flat on his back and forgot the pain as Rhys and Harry helped him to the sidelines, waves of cheering all round him.

It was worth it.

Sophie, who'd been a bit cool since he'd swept past her with Alastair, was waiting for him. She smiled when she saw him and clapped her hands. But when he reached her, her face changed.

'Jamie!' she gasped. 'Your face!'

She flung her arm through his and he winced. 'Bit of a bump,' he said and tried a manly not-quite-limp.

'Jamie, you poor thing.' She gazed into his eyes. 'They're saying you won the match for us. You're a hero.'

'It's nothing,' he said, not-quite-limping a bit more.

'I'll get Mum to give you a lift home.'

As they walked, a couple of fathers of his team mates congratulated him. 'Heroic tackle, that,' one said.

'Think you won the day for us,' the other added. Both were beaming, his teammates hanging back from their embarrassing fathers but flashing him sympathetic grins.

He affected to brush it all off as a hero should and forgot about not-quite-limping.

Sophie's mum was sitting in her Jeep, scanning the crowd. Her mass of rust-red hair always made him think of Boudicca as she had appeared in the film the school had shown them, the open-topped Jeep adding even more to the image. She spotted them and waved.

Like Sophie, when she saw Jamie close up her welcoming smile changed to a frown. 'Surely you haven't been fighting?'

'No, Mum,' Sophie said in a voice full of scorn. 'He was injured winning the match.'

'Oh, Jamie,' her mum said. 'What a hero!'

It was all wonderful. Except that Sophie was going out that evening with some friends of her parents from France and, as they didn't know Jamie, he hadn't been invited. It didn't help that Sophie didn't want to go.

By nine that evening Jamie had finished his homework. The match he'd been looking forward to watching on TV had been cancelled due to flooding in Wales. Magda was out at the Polish Club and the house felt very empty.

He texted Rhys and Harry from the rugby team, the only guys in the team he thought were all right, and though they weren't friends they joined in a few satisfying congratulatory minutes about the afternoon's game, Davenport's missed tackle and his game-saving effort. Their congratulations made the pain from his injuries fade as they looked forward to doing it all again on Saturday.

After that the house felt even more empty. He played the Wagner, lying flat out on the long settee and enjoying the superb sound - so much better than downloaded stuff - and tried to come up with a plan for how to deal with that weird woman who was supposed to be his grandmother.

Nothing came.

All right, he'd have to work out some tactics to help him get through the coming week.

It was still term time, so no chance of going off anywhere. There were no school trips on and no competitions or challenges that would take up the evenings, not even after-school rugby, either practice or match. No concerts, no film club. There might be a debate or something on - anything he could escape to would do - but he couldn't check the various society lists till he was at school tomorrow.

He could always go to a movie with Sophie of course, but she'd want to see stuff he hated. Still, it could be worth it.

By the time he trudged up to bed he was in deep gloom again.

*

Chani was having an uncomfortable interview with Melissa, the owner of the Mind and Body Centre.

'Chani,' she'd said, all smiles, at Chani's request for 'a word'. Now her smiles had gone. 'A week?' she said. 'At such short notice? I don't think —'

'I'm really sorry,' Chani said. 'It's an emergency, you see. I have to go and help my daughter out, she's had to go away, suddenly, and there's her young son. She couldn't take him with her. It's only for a week.'

'Young son?' Her eyes gleamed. Scoop of the week, this would be wouldn't it. 'I didn't know you were a grandma.'

Chani stretched her face into as near a smile as she could get. 'Neither did I. Er, well, not till recently.'

'Oh?' Melissa waited, leaning forward, lips parted.

You didn't tell Melissa anything of your private life if you could avoid it.

The staff had helped each other develop avoidance techniques and Chani used them now to divert her. 'I'll leave everything organised,' she said. 'Amber Bridgeman's in on Tuesday, at two: I told her all about the new facial treatments and she's going for the Young Skin one, with the full body aromatherapy massage. Seline said she can do it.'

'That's wonderful, Chani.' Melissa smiled. Good, she'd be thinking of money instead of the young son. 'Amber's skin could certainly do, I mean benefit from the Young Skin treatment. Well done. What else have you got down for the week?'

Chani ran through the appointments and which of the staff would be doing what.

'All right,' Melissa said, clearly reluctant. 'But I'll need you to use some holiday leave, Chani. I know it's an emergency, a family emergency, but I could only cover two of the days.'

The arrival of three clients all at the same time saved Chani from more grovelling and Melissa's probing.

Later, over drinks in the pub Chani passed all this on to Vanessa.

'So I have to lose three of my holiday days for that stupid boy.'

'How awful for you, Chani, love,' Vanessa said in her full social worker sympathy voice, going straight into cynicism, 'Is business not too good at the Centre, then?'

Chani giggled.

'Business is booming, she's just mean. I think she sits up at night counting her money.'

'Awful, yes. But at least Mike's sorting out the heater for you in Patricia. You should be a bit warmer this time. And, listen, don't worry about your herb plants, I'll make sure they're watered. I'll talk to them too.'

'Thanks, Van.' She gave her friend an appreciative smile and boosted herself with gin and tonic.

'Make sure you take your phone charger. And email me.'

'Right, yes.' Van was all right, she should never have doubted her. But she had been exhausted hadn't she, and frozen. Well, she could confide in her now. 'I'm dreading it, Van,' she said. 'I can just imagine what the house'll be like.'

'You'll have all your soul music, won't you?' Vanessa picked up the empty glasses and made for the bar.

Chani stood with her hand on Patricia's open boot checking all her essentials were there. Aromatherapy oils, burner, two hanging crystals, the little Buddha she meditated to, her Tibetan temple bells, silver teapot and her herb teas. Her iPod was filled with relaxation music, meditation sounds, yoga commentary and, of course, all her soul music.

She had expected to be able to find a pub that had bed and breakfast accommodation somewhere near where Jamie lived, a place to retreat to. But Annabel, curse her, had written to 'set out what was agreed at our meeting'. According to her they'd agreed that Chani would stay in Jamie's house. This Chani had no memory of. She hated the idea but, as she'd told

Vanessa, bloody Lollipop Annabel had effectively trapped her.

'It would seem so,' Van had agreed.

Chani hadn't liked the appreciative look on Van's face. Recalling all this, she went back in the house again and picked up four bottles of wine – hang on, make that six. Two of them were Vanessa's home-made – a gooseberry and a rhubarb – and, just in case, a corkscrew. That should help her face the horrors she was sure would be there, especially if, as she suspected, escaping to a pub would be blocked. She sighed. Ah well, at least she had plenty of herb tea as well as the wine.

At last she drove off, hoping Patricia's heater, after three days in Mike's care, would now work properly. He'd done everything he could, he'd told her, but had only managed to get it to work intermittently. Still, she told herself, better than no heat at all. She turned up the volume of her iPod to hear Aretha over the noise of the engine. '*I say a little prayer*,' Aretha sang.

The long, tiring journey wasn't helped by Patricia being only intermittently warm. The directions Annabel had given her helped her cope with all the roundabouts so she only got lost twice. She drove along a wide main road, with woodland along one side of it, huge detached houses on the other, turned into a side road and there was Marlowe Drive. It was big, with big houses set on three sides of a big square green. All had large frontages and long drives, each was a different, modern-looking design. Serious money, clearly.

She found number five and stopped to take it in. And remembered that so-called letter she'd had, six

19

years ago. More like a circular, it had been. The first communication she'd had from her daughter since the wedding. Not that there'd been much before it, not since Celandine had changed her name to Linda and gone down south to be an accountant. Totally against her karma, but then, she never would listen.

She remembered every word of the thing. 'To whom it may concern,' it began. 'This is to inform you that, following the death of Tim Pomfret-Jones, in an accident on the Gross Glockner Pass, Linda and Jamie Pomfret-Jones will continue to reside at 5 Marlowe Drive, Welwyn Garden City, Herts.'

'*Under the Boardwalk, down by the sea,*' came through the iPod. If only, she thought, wishing she were there and not here.

3

Chani wound down Patricia's window and felt a cold wind. A single magpie landed on the landscaped rectangle of slate backed by huge, spiky-leaved plants and glared at her, like a malign presence. Celandine's, would it be? Or the dead Tim's?

Everything in sight was dark gunmetal grey and black, rigid straight lines, sharp angles, hard surfaces. It was even worse than she'd feared. She felt her chi shrivel.

This was not going to be good. She eased herself out of the car, hung her bag on her shoulder, and stood and looked.

Apart from the magpie there was no sign of life. She felt like a specimen under a microscope and had to turn back and lock up Patricia's doors, something she never did at home. She should drive through the big black metal gates but no, she couldn't do that to Patricia, she would be so out of place.

The sharp angles even included the bell press. There was no sound when she pressed it but after a minute or two the door opened.

She had prepared herself for a grey, angular person to match the house but the woman who stood there was, well, round. Her shape was round, so was her face, especially with her pine-coloured hair pulled back from it. Even her feet were in rounded clogs.

'Mrs Caladan?' she said.

'Chani, call me Chani. You must be Magda.'

The woman beamed. 'I am.' She seemed delighted that Chani knew her name. 'Do come in.' She peered past Chani. 'Where is your car?'

'I left her on the road.'

'On the road? Oh, so, OK, you can put in garage later. Come, I will show you house. Let me take your bag.' She led Chani into a hall you could have held a meeting in. 'Would you like cup of tea first, or coffee?'

'Thank you, I'd love one. Do you have herb tea?'

"Sorry,' Magda said. 'There is no herb tea.' She put Chani's bag in the hall. 'Come into kitchen,' she said, 'you can see what there is.'

She showed Chani into a large, cold, harsh space of stainless steel and glass, the floor, of course, dark grey. 'Is it not wonderful?' she said.

'Mmm,' Chani murmured, shuddering. This wasn't a kitchen, it was a surgery. She ached for her own kitchen, for the buttercup yellow and soft blue.

Magda opened a cupboard. 'Here is tea, come and look what you like.'

Chani settled on green tea. Magda made one cup only, handed it to Chani and busied herself at the sink.

'Oh, but aren't you having one?' Chani asked.

Magda's hands stopped moving. 'Oh, no.' She gave Chani a quick, sideways glance before returning to the sink. 'Sorry,' she added.

Not knowing what else to do, Chani sipped the tea. Too uncomfortable to sit down she stood, shifting her weight from foot to foot.

At least it was nice and warm in there. She took off her coat. Very warm, she thought, halfway down her tea, having to take off two more layers. She finished the tea and put her cup on the drainer.

'Come and see rest of house,' Magda said and scooped up Chani's layers, carrying them as she led the way.

The rooms were many and large. Magda opened some of the doors to show the same hard, grey angular theme: not one soft surface, no colour other than grey, lightened only occasionally, and then by a paler grey. The whole thing was harsh, disturbing and completely soulless.

Finally Magda said, 'This is your room.'

Chani knew how it would be. She stood in the doorway drooping with tiredness, despair and heat.

'I will go for bag,' Magda said and disappeared.

Chani found her Rescue Remedy, let the drops fall on to her tongue and sank onto the enormous grey bed, too far gone and too hot to argue that she could bring her bag herself.

It was stifling in here. The whole house was overheated. She needed air, she had to open a window. There were two, quite large.

Seconds later she had them open and was wafting the cold December air onto herself with the first suitable thing she found – a small shiny, almost black cushion.

She looked out over the rear garden, if you could actually call it that. There was a selection of black metal obelisks, but no plants there to soften the edges, though there were some things she supposed must be plants – five, all of them identical – big, brittle, spiky things like alien life forms.

So that was what hard landscaping was.

A vision of her house in Hebden Bridge appeared in a golden glow in her mind. She saw its layout and aspects – all fully Feng Shuid years ago by Han Lo Chen, her lover at the time.

She saw her warm, friendly, blue and yellow kitchen, its windowsill filled with pots of herbs and sprouting seeds. But instead of the usual bustle of friends around the table, or joining in the cooking, she saw Lollipop-Annabel sitting there. The golden glow was replaced by the beige of Annabel's aura.

Magda reappeared with her bag.

'Thank you, Magda,' she said, putting it on the bed and opening it. But Magda didn't go away, instead she demonstrated how to open the fitted wardrobes that lined one wall, pointing out each drawer.

'This your bathroom,' she said, opening a door. A wave of hot air poured out.

'Magda,' Chani said, her clothes sticking to her. 'Is it possible to turn the heating down?'

'But yes, is here.' Magda demonstrated how to turn down a radiator's thermostat.

'Ah, yes, thanks, but I know how to do that. I was thinking about the rest of the house, it's really very hot.'

Magda nodded. 'I know. Mrs Pomfret-Jones likes for to be warm.'

'She does?' Where had that come from?

'Always that I have working here.'

'Well, she's not here now. Could you possibly ... I mean, it must be unbearable in that laundry room?'

Looking around as if Celandine might be secretly watching, Magda said, 'I will do now.'

As Magda left Chani sank on to the bed. She couldn't live like this. Her stress levels had reached critical mass. Her chi was terribly disturbed.

The room did at last begin to cool. Chani took a deep breath and set about organising things, first pouring drops of geranium oil in her burner, placing it on a windowsill and putting a match to the tea light. Next, she climbed on a metal chair that ought really to have been in a garden centre and secured the threads of her crystals so they hung from the window frame ready to catch the light. She put an aromatherapy candle on each of the bedside chests of drawers and lit them, closed one of the windows, leaving the other slightly open so the scent could fill the room.

She lay on the bed in the warm glow of candlelight, breathing in soothing aromatherapy oil.

She woke with a start, remembered where she was and leapt to her feet. Her phone told her it was nearly seven. Damn, Jamie must have been back ages. Her stomach rumbled and she remembered she'd only eaten a couple of biscuits since breakfast time. What happened about meals? Better go and see Magda and find out what she needed to do.

How many hours a day did being a housekeeper involve? And how much was she paid?

But never mind all that, what she absolutely had to do was persuade Magda not to leave. The first thing was to talk to her and find out why she wanted to go. Obviously, she must want to get away from Jamie, Chani couldn't blame her. Probably things would have been just as bad with his mother there, but now she

25

wasn't, Magda had to put up with him one hundred per cent. How could she possibly persuade her to carry on in that situation? But she must.

In the kitchen, Magda turned from what she was doing. 'Oh, Mrs Chani. Is everything all right for you?'

'Chani, call me Chani. Yes, it's OK, thanks.'

'Would you like dinner?'

The question threw her. She'd been expecting to cook for herself.

'Er, what time do you usually have it?'

'I suppose around half past seven, maybe later. What would you like to eat?'

'But what does Jamie want? Where is he, by the way, do you know?'

'He's at Sophie's house. He will have dinner there.'

That made no sense. 'Oh,' Chani said. 'I thought I would be cooking for him. I didn't know he'd be out.'

'He sends text,' Magda said, matter of fact. 'He is often there. And you have no need cook – I do it.'

'Oh.' This needed thinking about. 'Who's Sophie?'

'She is friend of Jamie – girlfriend.'

'He has a girlfriend?' Whatever sort of girl would put up with Jamie?

Magda's face softened. 'Sophie is very nice.'

'She is?'

'So, Mrs …'

'Chani.'

'Mrs Chani, what would you like to eat?'

'Please, just Chani.' She took a breath. 'What do you have?'

'I show' Magda led the way and opened the huge double-sided fridge.

26

Chani stared. She'd never seen anything like it. The fridge was full of square plastic boxes, on every shelf. Her mouth had fallen open. She shut it.

Magda stepped forward. 'The top shelf is meals. This one is ...' She pulled a box out and peered at the label. 'Cannelloni. The others are chicken curry, Beef Wellington, braised steak and a fish tagine. Here are different kinds rice, here stuffed mushrooms, this tomato gratine, this mashed sweet potatoes and this creamed leeks.'

Chani had to close her mouth again before she could speak. 'How ... how do you know what they all are?'

Magda beamed with obvious pride. 'I made today. Later I can label and put in freezer all you don't want today. All are in portions for one. There are salads also on lower shelf, also dips and other things. And on bottom shelf are desserts.' She took a breath, still beaming. 'You see, if Jamie comes here to eat with himself or with Sophie, I know he likes everything. They can choose and in microwave is very quick.' Her face radiated pride.

This was, Chani understood, her great idea, her creation and she had presented it as if for the camera. Chani lifted her hands to applaud but stopped herself.

She felt slightly faint. She made a vague sort of sound, feeling like someone who had found a noxious weed in Magda's perfect garden. Even that *she* was the noxious weed. 'Do you have any vegetables?'

'Yes, mushrooms, tomatoes, leeks ...'

'Fresh, I mean, not cooked.'

'Ah. No. So sorry, I used them all.'

'You see,' Chani felt awful after all Magda's efforts, but she had to tell her. 'I'm vegetarian, I'm sorry.'

Magda sat down. Rather suddenly. She seemed to be thinking. 'So,' she said, after some time. 'What do you eat?'

Chani did her best to explain and, with an increasingly flustered Magda, found a sort of meal, which she ate alone: white toast with French strawberry jam. She added two glasses of Vanessa's rhubarb wine. When she had finished she took everything to the kitchen, to Magda's anxious protests.

'You would like coffee?' Magda asked.

Chani, too tired to try for anything else, accepted coffee.

'I bring,' Magda said, with a wide smile.

'I'll be in the lounge,' Chani told her, hoping it would be more comfortable there.

Magda's coffee surprised her by being very good, but the only word to describe the lounge – huge, with an enormous grey slate fireplace, three black leather couches, a big smoked glass coffee table and an immense black television – was soulless. Very likely Jamie would stay out for hours. Ahead of her stretched an evening alone, nothing to do but watch the hideous television. She couldn't do it. No, she decided, she would find a pub. She remembered passing one on the main road. It wasn't that far, she could walk.

'I'm going out,' she told Magda, moments later. 'Is there a key I can use?'

The pub was further away than she thought and not that appealing, but it looked better inside. It was crowded when she walked in but she soon found a less packed area at the back, with an empty space in one corner. She was hot after the walk so she dumped her jacket, scarf and gloves on a seat and went to the bar.

They were busy but she didn't mind. She leaned on the bar, glancing around, and saw a woman nearby who looked interesting. She had long black hair and was dressed in all black, with silver rings, a crystal pendant and crystal earrings. Just as Chani was thinking she would talk to her one of the bar staff, a young girl in a vest top, appeared in front of her.

Before she could move away Chani began, 'Campari—' She was too late, the man next to her had already asked for vodka.

The girl shot her an apologetic glance and moved to the optics.

'Oh, I'm sorry,' the man said. 'Let me get yours. What are you having?'

He had a long nose and firm chin, a mobile face and mouth. Judging by the crinkles round his smiling lips and at the side of his eyes, he smiled and laughed a lot. There was some grey in his thick black hair, but not much.

She smiled back. 'Thank you. It's Campari soda.'

The hand holding her glass was slim and strong-looking. Their fingers touched as she took the glass, his were long and agile.

'I feel your sensitivity,' he said.

'Yes.' She smiled. 'People usually do. Are you a therapist, or a counsellor? Hypnotherapist, maybe?'

He had a great smile. 'I can see we're in tune. Hypnotherapist, yes. Reiki, too.'

29

Cynicism kicked in. She waited for the line about healing hands but it didn't come. Instead, he said, 'Actually, I'm a homeopathic doctor.'

That was impressive. 'Ah. Where's your practice?'

'Here. My surgery's two streets away, I live on the premises.' There was a pause before he said, 'And you? Are you a therapist?'

'I do some therapy, and counselling.' Her job description said Receptionist, though Melissa always introduced her as 'Chani, our Practice Manager', but she did lots of counselling, didn't she, and she helped with the therapies all the time. All the girls asked her advice didn't they: all the regular clients did too. Having convinced herself, as she had many times before, she gave him a warm smile.

'Here, in Welwyn?'

'No, in the north.'

'Ah, so you're visiting.'

'You could say that.'

His eyes were crinkling, dancing with amused interest. 'Where are you sitting?' he asked and it felt natural that he should join her.

'I'm Damien,' he said.

'Chani.'

She bought the next round.

'When did you get into homeopathy?' she asked him.

'Well, now,' he said, 'it was a long road. I did some travelling after A levels, didn't know what I wanted to do. India decided me. After that I knew I wanted to be a doctor.' He shrugged. 'Fifteen years later I went back to India and came back changed. So – homeopathy.'

'How interesting,' Chani said. 'I was in India myself.'

'Really! I left in 1981.'

She smiled. 'I was just wandering around then, drifting, I suppose, working for a bit and moving on. It was a well-worn trail, but I loved it. And you're right, it changes the way you look at things, India probably the most.'

'I knew we were connected,' Damien said.

Chani nodded, she already knew.

They were on to Buddhism, the Celtic heritage and Tolkien when closing time arrived and Welwyn Garden City was feeling less hostile and definitely more interesting. They exchanged phone numbers.

He keyed hers into his phone, then pressed some buttons. 'I'll get you a taxi,' he said, and, into the phone, 'Yes, thank you. Going to …?'

She told him.

When the taxi came he escorted her to it. 'Would you like me to see you safely home?' he asked, opening the door for her.

'Thanks,' she said. 'That's very kind, but I'll be fine.' She didn't believe in rushing things.

There were lights on in the entrance, the hallway, up the stairs and on the landing, but the house felt far from welcoming. No concern for the environment either. No light showed under the rooms Chani knew were Magda's and Jamie's, and there was no sound. She went to bed.

Next morning, Saturday, she had breakfast alone, in the dining room, where Magda brought her white toast. Chani started a shopping list. Wholemeal bread, eggs and muesli. Probably cheese, and maybe honey. The cost was mounting and she wasn't being paid for three of the days. But what else could she do? She needed something to brighten her room too, what could she find that was cheap? Perhaps Magda could direct her to some suitable shops after she'd seen Jamie. In the meantime, she had to find something to do or she'd go mad.

She went to the kitchen and found Magda.

'Shall I empty the dishwasher?' she suggested, but had to retreat from Magda's worried face. She had looked just like that when Chani hadn't wanted to put Patricia into the dark cavern of the garage, it had been enough to push Chani to give in. Something stirred in Chani's mind, something had struck a chord, but what was it? Nothing came.

The shops. She opened her mouth to ask Magda for directions but was interrupted by her first sight of Jamie. Of his head, that was, peering round the door.

'Do you know where my PE kit is?' he asked, not looking at Chani.

Magda seemed unfazed by this. 'Jamie, good morning,' she greeted him. 'It's all ready, in utility room. Are you ready for breakfast now? And Jamie, your grandmother is here.'

'Yeah. Thanks.' He disappeared.

'Well,' Chani said, 'that seems to cover everything. Is his conversation always so full and interesting?'

Magda smiled. Chani couldn't be sure if she was being polite, indulgent or was amused. She was busy moving fast to take a plastic box out of the freezer, remove its lid and put it in the microwave. Must be

Jamie's breakfast.

Magda was soon taking away a plate heaped with sausages, fried tomatoes, some brown stuff and what looked like steak. She reappeared after a minute and began making toast.

'Would you like some coffee?' she asked Chani. 'I can make another cafetiere for you while I do one for Jamie.'

'Where is he?' Chani asked, determined. Enough of this.

'He is having breakfast, in dining room.'

'I'll go and sit with him. And yes, please, to the coffee. This, she now knew, would be freshly ground and delicious.

'Morning, Jamie,' she said, as she took a seat across the table from him.

He grunted through a mouthful of toast, not looking up.

She tried again. 'So what's the kit for?' She waited for him to answer. He had a bruise on his face, had someone thumped him?

He finished chewing and swallowed. 'Rugby,' he said. Before she could link that to the bruise he'd buttered three more pieces of toast, picked up the plate, and was pushing his chair back. Moving a bit stiffly he stood, muttering, 'Taking it to my room.'

'I see,' Chani said to empty space. What the hell was the point of her being there?

Magda appeared with coffee. 'Oh,' she said, stopping.

'He took his toast to his room,' Chani told her, crisp-to-brusque.

Magda frowned.

Chani pushed Jamie's odd behaviour out of her mind for now. 'I was wondering, Magda, if you could tell me how to get to the shops. Oh, and a supermarket.'

Magda's eyes grew big. 'Supermarket? You need food?'

'I need food, yes. Like wholemeal bread and cheese and things.'

Another worried look. Magda, it was plain, was shocked. Chani felt a pang of guilt she couldn't explain.

'But I will buy. I will go this morning. You don't need buy for yourself.'

Chani hadn't expected that. Of course, shopping for food was Magda's job, she should let her do it. But the thought of what Magda might choose made her hesitate. No. 'How about if I buy some things and then I give you the bill and you can pay me back?'

Magda appeared to consider this. At least she didn't look worried. Not very worried.

Oh dear, she should have thought about this. 'Excuse my asking, Magda, but do you have money to pay for food? Not your own money, I mean.'

Magda's face cleared. She was like the shipping forecast, 'Rain later, clearing.'

'I do,' Magda said. 'Mrs Pomfret-Jones made arrangements so there is money for Jamie and also money come into my bank for me and for the house.'

Ah,' Chani said, seizing this chance to find out whatever she could. 'Was that before she went away?'

'Yes, the day she went. She asked if I would stay here to look after Jamie. I thought she was going only

34

for week or two weeks. I said yes. I found out that arrangement was for long time. Maybe for permanent. But I can't do that. I have to go back to Poland.'

Chani poured coffee while she worked out what to say.

'Oh. Yes. Do you really have to go back?' Not good, but it would do.

'Yes.'

'Is it something —' But before she could go any further there was a loud galloping down the stairs.

'Excuse me,' Magda turned swiftly. 'I must make sure he has right things.'

Some hours later, having found the shopping centre Magda had directed her to, Chani stood in her bedroom feeling, if not happy, at least less unhappy. The room now had two small soft rugs in tangerine and grape and a pine bedside lamp with a shade that toned with the grape colour – she'd found them all in a big supermarket – and her bedding was a warm shade of amber. She'd also found, in a shop selling mostly cheap tat, a cushion in a deep rose Indian fabric with embroidery and lots of tiny mirrors sewn on. The supermarket had also provided some essential foods that would last for several days. She hadn't wanted to spend the money but her well-being depended on it. And she could take everything home at the end of the week.

Magda had exclaimed over the food and packed each item neatly away.

So far so good. She could give herself over to meditation, followed by soul music.

Eventually, over the music, the front door banged and heavy footsteps came up the stairs. It had to be Jamie, back from the rugby match. All right, she would go straight away and talk to him. But when she reached his door, through the gap he'd left there was the sound of his shower running. She would have to wait. Her meditative mood was broken, she would try again to talk to Magda.

She found her in the utility room; this time she was ironing.

The room was full of racks of ironed shirts and other items of Jamie's clothing and – she gasped at the sight – a row of ironed towels. And Magda was now ironing bedding! What on earth did Celandine pay her?

From behind her came the sound of Jamie's feet down the stairs, followed by the crash of the front door. Chani just managed a glimpse of his back as he disappeared.

'He goes to Sophie's house,' Magda said.

'Why on earth do you worry about him being alone?' Chani asked. 'He's always at Sophie's house.'

Magda gave a tiny shrug. 'Not always, usually not so much as now.'

Chani understood. Clearly Jamie was avoiding her. She couldn't help but admire him, but at the same time she wanted to scream. She'd had to take time off work, lose money, travel all this way, live in this awful house, spend money she couldn't afford, and for what?

She forgot about talking to Magda. Taking the bottle of rhubarb wine up to her room, she spent the rest of the evening struggling to stay calm. As the level in the wine bottle neared the bottom she poured her frustration into emailing Vanessa, getting more careless as she went along.

'*Bugger's never here. Obvious he's avoiding me. After all Ive had to do to be in this terrible place. Youll never believe he has a girlfriend! What sort of girl can she be? Must be soft in head. Housekeeper works like a slave, wont let me do anything. Cant stand it. At least hous not now incresng globle warming. Not talking abt its atmospier wich is arctik.*
Chani'

4

'Daddy's at the golf club,' Sophie said, opening the door to Jamie.

Jamie kissed her. It was good, more than good. But she pulled away.

'Come and say hello,' she said, 'Mummy's in the sitting room.'

'Hello darlings,' Sophie's mum looked up from the magazine she was reading. 'Did Sophie tell you Daddy's going to be late? So I thought, how about takeaway for you this evening, special treat?'

'Great, thanks,' Jamie said. Just what he'd been hoping for, her mum would wait to eat till her dad came home, which meant he and Sophie would have more time on their own.

'Oh, good, thanks, Mum,' Sophie went to a little cupboard and came back with a handful of menus. 'What shall we have, Jamie? How about pizza? Mmm,' she murmured, scanning one of the menus. 'Chicken and asparagus, or *quattro staggione*. I can't decide. What do you think?'

As she gave him the menu her phone rang.

'Oh, hi.' As Jamie studied the various choices her voice faded to background sound, until,

'Bethany, that's … No, you don't mean …?'

Shit, Bethany. He couldn't stand her.

'Oh, cool,' Sophie said. 'Yes, Jamie's here.'

Why had she said that?

'Yes, of course, bring Edward.'

Oh, crap. Bloody Edward. They were both coming here. It couldn't be worse. All those two ever talked about was horses. Bloody boring horses. What was Sophie thinking – she really didn't care about all that riding stuff, why did she keep being friends with Bethany?

'Right. Cool. See you soon.' Sophie looked up. 'It's Bethany,' she told them 'She's coming round with Edward.'

Jamie groaned, he couldn't help it, but her mum's enthusiastic 'Darling! Would they like pizza too?' covered the sound.

Bethany bounced into the room, shedding wax-coated clothes as she moved. She and Sophie hugged and squealed and Jamie tried not to look at her big, squelchy bottom and the fat thighs that were almost bursting out of her jeans.

Edward, as usual, looked like Jamie's memories of Grandfather Pomfret-Jones – probably bought his clothes from the same place Already Jamie wanted to hit him. He sort of nodded to Jamie and grunted, Jamie grunted back. Please let them not stay long.

'We're ordering pizza,' Sophie said.

'Cool,' Bethany said.

'Pizza, yes thanks,' Edward said.

Jamie went to hide in the loo.

When he came back the kitchen table was laid and Edward, holding plates, was passing them to Sophie who put them in the warming oven.

The pizzas came. Sophie and Bethany giggled over them, handing pieces out and Jamie was stuck with

Edward, who just stood there and said nothing. Getting in fast before he could start on about horses, Jamie mentioned the All Black's tour and left Edward to pretend to know all about it.

When Edward stopped talking Jamie could think of nothing else to say and looked for help at Sophie but she was still involved in something with Bethany. Edward looked at them too, then at the empty plates on the table. He cleared his throat.

'You don't ride, Jamie, do you?' he asked.

Jamie closed his eyes. Would Edward never stop asking that same bloody thing?

'I don't, no.' He had become a recorded message. It was like Edward couldn't believe it and had to keep having it confirmed.

'Have you ever?' Bethany said. She sounded genuinely interested.

How could she not know? He forced out the only word that would come. 'Never.'

'He's simply not interested,' Sophie told them. She made it sound perfectly normal. Which of course it was, for normal people.

'Oh, shame,' Edward said. 'We got a good gallop on Sunday, didn't we, Beth.' Bethany gazed at him like he was some sort of god. 'Brilliant, it was a great day.'

Probably fell off her first pony aged three. It was such a great mental picture Jamie moved on to imagine Edward being chased by a pack of hounds, being mown down by them, his flailing arms all that could be seen above the mass of squirming bodies. It was terrific.

Bethany's breathless voice shattered the image.

'I've just remembered, Jamie. Isn't your grandmother with you?'

What? Jamie felt hunted. 'Oh, ah, few days.' His voice was all croaky.

'How nice,' she said, like a soppy old lady. 'Have you met her?' she asked Sophie, back to being stupid Bethany.

'No, not yet,' Sophie said. 'She hasn't been here long. She's a hippie, apparently. I can't wait to meet her.'

Jamie groaned aloud.

'Oh,' Edward said, looking down his nose.

'Really?' Bethany's eyes bulged and her mouth had gone oo-shaped. He tried to ignore her. 'Is she really, Jamie?'

How could he shut her up? 'I don't know. I haven't seen her much.' That should do it.

It didn't. 'Oh? Why not? Isn't she supposed to be looking after you?'

'No.' He glared at her.

She frowned and turned away to find Edward. At last, she'd given up. Now perhaps they'd go.

'We should be going, d'you think?' Edward said as Bethany clung to him.

'Oh, should you?' Sophie sounded disappointed. Jamie held his breath and hoped she was just being polite.

'We should, actually,' Bethany said. 'Mummy's expecting us. It's been lovely, Sophie.'

Jamie smiled.

But when Sophie brought the coats Edward said, 'We're going your way, Jamie, can I give you a lift?'

'Oh, no, I don't —'

'Are you in the new car, Edward?' Sophie asked.

Car. Right. For a moment he'd ... well, they could have been on horseback.

'It's an Audi,' Bethany said and threw her arms round Sophie. 'Lovely evening,' she gushed. 'See you soon.'

'Oh, thanks,' he had to say to Edward. Quickly he moved to a strategic position behind Sophie where Bethany couldn't reach him, but Edward was already swinging his car keys.

'OK, Jamie?' he said, and waited.

Jamie forced a smile and stayed where he was.

'See you tomorrow,' Sophie said.

It was no good. He had to go. It had been a horrible evening and now it was worse.

*

Next morning Chani woke to a quiet house. There was no sign of Jamie, where the hell was he? Probably stayed at the girlfriend's all night.

There was no trace of Magda either. Strange, did she have Sundays off? She'd never said anything.

Chani made herself breakfast in the weirdly deserted kitchen. Decent food at last. With no one there to stop her, she took it up to her room, revelling in the temporary freedom.

But hang on, *was* this temporary? Or had Magda gone for good, back to Poland? Oh, please, no. She ran downstairs again, and searched every room in the house, but Magda was not there. Chani even went outside, in case Magda might be crazy enough to be putting out washing in the December cold. She wasn't.

Chani couldn't think straight. What had Lollipop Annabel said? Two weeks, wasn't it, till Magda would leave for Poland. When did that two weeks begin? She rushed to find her diary, turned to the day of the meeting and calculated. Exactly two weeks from that Friday would mean she'd go on Thursday, this week.

So she hadn't gone yet. Her breath pushed out in a whoosh of relief. But where was Magda? Had she gone early? Surely she wouldn't do that, not without saying anything.

She felt as if she'd lost her footing and actually reached out for support. Thursday was the the day before Chani's week ended. If Magda went then, she'd be left on her own with him, not able to get away. The Lollipop had trapped her!

She counted on fingers that shook. Four days. She had four days to persuade Magda to stay. It was time for the last resort, she had to find her.

She knocked on Magda's bedroom door, but there was no answer. She waited a couple of seconds and turned the handle. The door wasn't locked.

The room was identical to Chani's – before she had modified it – except that it was immaculate. The only thing on any surface was a book beside the bed, but as it was in what she assumed was Polish Chani could learn nothing about either her taste in reading or of her state of mind.

She tried the wardrobe. And let out the breath she hadn't realised she'd been holding. Clothes. And a suitcase. Weak with relief, she closed the wardrobe door and heard a car engine, the first time since she'd been in the house that she'd heard anything outside.

She ran to the window. She was looking out at the drive, the gates were closing behind a very small black car which was coming up to the house. She watched as it came nearer, stopped briefly, moved again and disappeared.

Could it be Celandine? Please, let it be her. Chani rushed out of the room, just remembering to close the door. She had one foot on the top step when there was the sound of a door opening. She remembered the door that connected the garage to the house, it led into the corridor beside the kitchen.

And that was where she found Magda, dressed in a black coat and a grey felt hat.

'Hello, Mrs Chani,' she said, a wide smile pushing her cheeks into rosy apples, like in a child's storybook.

'Oh, it's you, Magda.'

The smile disappeared. 'I go to church,' Magda said. 'Sorry, I didn't tell you.' She took off her black gloves and her hat. 'I get your breakfast now.'

'No, that's all right, I did it myself. I put the dishes in the dishwasher.'

There was that worried look again.

'It was no trouble,' Chani rushed to tell her. 'None at all. There's no sign of Jamie,' she went on, changing the subject.

'No,' Magda said. 'He sleeps late when there is no school.'

'Ah.' Chani wondered how to start the conversation she was desperate to have. 'Magda …'

Magda made an apologetic gesture. 'I must put my things away,' she said. 'Do you need something?'

Chani grasped the nettle. 'I need to talk to you.'

44

'Oh.' Magda nodded. 'I will be quick.'

Why hadn't she looked worried at that? Chani waited until Magda reappeared, praying Jamie would go on sleeping. The second he made a sound Magda would rush to attend to him.

'Shall we go and sit in the lounge?' she said.

Magda's eyebrows rose then fell into a wavy line. Not too happy with that, then.

Chani strode to the room before Magda could protest and went in, standing just inside until a clearly reluctant Magda joined her. She waved her to a seat, this time Magda would sit with her, she'd made sure of it, never mind that the room was sending out all the wrong vibrations. Hardness, they said, harshness, conflict.

Ignore them. Rise above it. Be assertive. Breathing carefully, she grounded herself and visualised a calm, peaceful atmosphere.

'I know you're planning on going back to Poland very soon,' she said, keeping her voice as pleasant as possible. Did she imagine it, or had Magda's aura shimmered?

'Yes.' Magda sat with her feet together, her hands clasped in her lap.

Chani plunged in. 'Would it not be better for you to stay here? I mean, where you have this house, and money. And a car?' she added, making the connection.

Magda looked down at her hands, gulped and took a breath. 'Because I am here,' she said, her eyes meeting Chani's. 'I do not see my husband, I do not look after him, or our flat, he must do himself. And his job.'

'Your husband? I didn't know. So he's here as well?'

'He is for now. But you see, Mrs Chani, when we come here, at first money was good, better as in Poland. And many Polski people here, Polski shops. Now money is not good, is better in Poland. Polski people go home, many. My husband can get more money there as here, and all there is cheaper as here. He want to go before Mrs Pomfret-Jones go away, but I have to stay with Jamie. I tell my husband it will be for one week, or two, but now it might be permanent my husband say no, he will buy tickets for Thursday, this week. I tell him how you are coming, if we wait some more days, maybe you will decide to stay. So he buy tickets for next week, for Tuesday.'

'Shit!' What a mess. It was like being blackmailed.

Magda was shaking her head. 'You will not decide to stay,' she said, drooping with sadness.

'I can't stay here.' Hell's teeth, there was no way. 'I live somewhere else, in the north, miles away. I've a house and a job there and I have to go back to it. Hell, it's not as if Jamie and I …' There were no words.

'No,' murmured Magda. 'I see that.'

'I didn't even know he existed till a couple of weeks ago.'

'No?'

'You're surprised! Well, look, Magda, has Jamie ever said he had a … that I … did Cel, er, Linda ever mention me? I mean, what was her first thought when she was buggering off with this guy? Not to ask me to have Jamie, was it? She asked you to live in.'

Magda had reared back, the expression of worry she showed so much had intensified and she gave a little gasp.

Back-pedalling, Chani said, 'Sorry, Magda, of course you didn't know. But, you see how it is. I really can't stay here. I wish there was a way you could stay, you and your husband. Maybe you could both live here? Actually, I don't see why not. There's plenty of food and everything. Why don't you get him to come here now?'

Magda was twisting her fingers. 'It, he … there is not enough money.' She looked cornered.

'But you wouldn't be paying for your flat.'

'No, but … Oh, Mrs Chani, we have to send money home. For months we have not. For our son, he is … not able, he cannot walk, he does not … not like other children. He needs special looking after, it costs lot of money. Now English money not good so much as before and everythings here cost more.' She spread her arms in a gesture of hopelessness, her shoulders almost up to her ears. 'My mother cannot look after him, she too old, my husband mother is dead. We have to go.'

Chani had run out of arguments. She had nothing that would counter Magda's reasoning. She couldn't deny Magda's need was greater than hers. Fleetingly, she wondered if the not-able son had been invented, but no, she was thinking like a spoiled child. Magda couldn't possibly be putting on how upset she was. Hell and buggeration!

'I'm sorry.' This was horrendous. What the hell was she going to do? Pull herself together, or try to, otherwise she would collapse.

Magda stirred. 'Mrs Chani?'

She looked up. God, what was wrong now? 'Mmm?'

'Would you mind if Tomasz come here today?'

'Mind? Why would I mind? Look, I don't see why he can't live here all the time till you go. Or you can go to him if you want to.'

'Thank you, you are very kind. It will be wonderful. But I must be here for Jamie and for you, better for Tomasz to come here. I will ring him. Thank you.' Her eyes shone, as if she'd been offered a fantastic gift.

'You're welcome. Go on, ring him now.' She'd never persuade Magda she was perfectly able to see to Jamie herself. Even though, and the realisation almost made her laugh, she obviously expected her to do just that once she'd gone back to Poland. Well, she certainly wouldn't wait on him hand and foot.

Tomasz arrived very quickly. Magda brought him to Chani immediately.

'Here is my husband, Tomasz,' she said, standing beside him. 'Here is Mrs ... Chani, Tomasz.'

He was a stocky, muscular man in worn jeans and a thick grey jumper. His almost black hair was thinning, the lines on his face made him seem old but he didn't look old. Maybe it was the anxious smile.

'Hello,' Chani said and held out her hand. 'It's good to meet you.'

His smile widened. 'Thank you,' he said, gripping her hand with his much bigger one. 'Is good for meet you, also.'

When Magda put a hand on his arm, he released Chani's hand and turned to follow his wife out.

As they disappeared she heard him say, 'Is a big house, is it.' As if he'd never seen it before. Probably hadn't.

5

When Magda and Thomas had gone Chani felt too restless and on edge to sit down anywhere, couldn't even relax in her bedroom. She had to do something. Vanessa. Had she replied to the email?

But she couldn't disturb the atmosphere in here. Where, then?

What about one of the other rooms up here? She wouldn't affect anything, all she needed was somewhere to sit. In moments she had commandeered the room next door and was online. There were no new emails. She felt like an abandoned child. She waited but no message came. What could Van be doing on a Sunday?

What would she be doing herself if she were at home? Up in the hills with Van, perhaps, or walking along the canal towpath; perhaps tending herb plants to keep them going through the winter, or making a rich soup for whoever dropped in over the afternoon. Instead, she was here, where everything was wrong: all the chi disrupted, all harmony stifled, all creative flow blocked. Really, had Celandine learned nothing about Feng Shui?

She fled back to her room, where she tried to meditate, but couldn't shut out the turmoil the house created in her mind. Not just the house – what was just as bad was Jamie's non-presence, the not knowing whether he was in or out, or when, or if, he would appear.

Even yoga didn't help, she couldn't switch her mind off.

This was the end of the line, she wouldn't play this game any more, she'd go home. No, she was not going to be beaten. Somehow she would force Jamie to talk to her, make him stay in the same room with her for more than two minutes. It wasn't going to happen, was it. Give up, go home, sod Annabel. No, she couldn't let a stupid boy get the better of her.

A soft knock on her door interrupted the argument.

'Lunch is ready, Mrs Chani,' came Magda's voice. 'Will you come?'

Oh dear. She'd wanted to make her own lunch. Trying not to upset Magda she turned the sigh into a cough, opened the door, forced a smile and said, 'Thanks, I'll be there in a minute.'

Magda had put together a light meal, beautifully presented, at the dining table, where a place was laid for one. It looked very good.

'Do join me,' Chani tried, hating all this servant and mistress stuff. 'You and Tomasz.'

'Oh no, we have eaten. What would you like to drink?'

Chani gave up. She wouldn't have to endure this feudal life much longer.

Feudal. It came back to her – the servant and mistress thing – of course. It had been when she was travelling, she'd been invited by that couple she'd met in Bangkok to stay with them in Jakarta. He was working on contract for two years, he'd talked about how great the expat life was. She didn't work, spent her time at the Country Club, entertaining other expats and being entertained by them. It sounded pretty boring, but, hey, go with the flow.

When Chani got there she'd found the house was run, and the two children were looked after by servants, who seemed to live in a tiny building at the bottom of the garden. She'd been shocked to learn their pay was a fraction of what the couple spent on their social life. They were offering this idle life to her as if it were a precious gift. The servants would provide whatever she needed whenever she needed it.

Chani couldn't stand it. She hated the whole set-up, she hated her part in what she saw as oppressing the poor servants. And she was bored silly. Desperate for something to do, she had hidden some clothes that needed washing, sneaking them into a bathroom to wash them herself. She'd arranged them around her bedroom to dry – very quickly, she expected, in the heat – but of course one of the servants had found them. Chani had gone to her room for something and discovered the poor woman snatching the clothes up and looking terrified.

'She would be terrified,' the woman expat had said, laughing, when Chani told her about this. 'She'd expect to be in trouble and that I'd throw her out so she wouldn't be able to support her family.'

'You wouldn't do that, would you?' Chani cried.

'No, of course not. But a lot of people would, that's what all the servants expect to happen.'

Chani shuddered now at the memory. But surely Magda's worried looks and refusal to even have a cup of tea with her couldn't be the same? But Magda did seem to be very worried about money.

There was a thundering noise and she cried out, reared up like a startled horse and ran out of the room. It was Jamie, of course, thudding down the stairs. Magda had hurried out to see what he needed. Chani also raced to catch him but before she could he had gone, the door slamming behind him. Chani leant against the wall and cursed quietly. Had she ever felt this tense?

Moments after that Magda appeared with Chani's tea. 'Jamie has gone to Sophie's house,' she said.

Chani grimaced. 'Will he be back for a meal later?'

Magda half-shrugged, it felt apologetic. 'He said no. I will make for you only, yes?'

Chani could only nod and try to smile.

She didn't taste her lunch. All she knew was she wanted to go home. Being here was pointless. Well, she would. She would run away. Tomorrow.

As the coffee hit things began to clear a bit. If she did run away she would have broken the agreement to the bloody trial week and Annabel would very likely come after her like the sheriff with a posse. If she stuck it out Jamie would go on avoiding her, nothing surer. She had no way to change that. But she'd be able to tell Annabel she'd done the week, she'd done everything she could and it was no good, it would then be up to Annabel to sort out. She could go home and forget about the stupid boy.

Right.

She felt sick. She couldn't hang around this awful house for another minute. She would go out, it wasn't raining, she would go for a walk.

Outside, dressed in warm clothes, she considered going to the pub again but decided to walk in the opposite direction. She would find a pub she hadn't been to.

It was not a good idea. She left the side road and turned onto the bigger road, looking forward to seeing the lovely woodland along the side of it, but very soon there were no more houses, the woodland was on both sides. That was nice, but there were no pavements, which was not nice. She trudged along, properly facing the oncoming traffic. Huge four-wheel-drives shot past, part of a stream of gleaming BMWs, Audis and Volvos. Mixed in with them, and driving as if on a race course, were rattly, scrappy old bangers, the fumes from their exhausts making her cough. She constantly had to flatten herself into the fencing to avoid being squashed. Shaking and badly needing a drink, she stared ahead but all she could see was un-pavemented road. A battered old Range Rover pulling a horse box appeared and she had to dive into the trees.

Shaking even more she turned, dashed to the opposite side of the road and walked – mostly crabwise –as fast as she could back the way she had come. At last the houses and pavements reappeared. She had to stop for a while to recover before she could go into the pub.

It was full of very tall men with huge shoulders and thick necks, who all seemed to be talking about rugby. The back of the pub was full of darts players: serious, silent darts players.

She bought two whiskies, one with ginger, drank the straight one at the bar to calm her nerves before taking the other and squeezing into a corner to watch the darts.

She was in a pocket of hushed breathing as dart after dart thudded into the board, each hit followed by escapes of breath. There was a polite round of applause, the four players withdrew, and for a few minutes people talked quietly but no one moved, until everything fell silent and four new players appeared.

She recognised the game, it was 501, she'd played it herself in the pub at home with friends. They had thought they were quite good at it. What she now knew was that they were rubbish at it. These people were experts. She felt herself being drawn in, holding her breath and letting it out as the crowd held and let out their breaths. She was gripped until the final match was over and there was a pack move to the bar. As everyone at the bar was at least two feet taller than her, Chani waited. She checked her watch and saw with a jolt that it was almost half past six. She'd been out for four and a half hours.

Walking back would take about half an hour, so even if she left immediately it would be seven when she reached the house. Would Magda worry if she was later than that? What was she doing, being bothered about Magda worrying? Hell, she hadn't been this restricted in her whole life.

Magda welcomed Chani with obvious relief. And what she called a special meal.

Chani tried to look pleased, but the meal wasn't very successful.

After it she could find nothing to do.

She watched some boring TV, drinking wine and then herbal tea. If only she could have stayed in the pub. Around ten she went up to her room to listen to music but was too restless. Sod it, she would go downstairs and wait till Jamie came home, however late that was. She took her iPod and as she put in the ear buds Marvin Gaye sang, '... just about to lose my mind...' and she moaned.

At last, after what felt like hours the house door opened and closed quietly, and soft footsteps sounded in the hall.

She was ready. 'Jamie,' she called, moving fast across the room. 'Is that you?'

'Just going upstairs.' She could barely hear him.

She opened the lounge door. 'Have you been at Sophie's again?' she asked his retreating figure, in what she hoped was a friendly, interested voice.

He stopped and made the smallest possible turn. 'Mmm,' he muttered. His onward momentum slowed by a fraction.

'I was making you a meal,' Chani lied.

'Oh.' He hesitated. 'Sorry.' He was still facing away from her.

'Did you eat at Sophie's?' she pressed. 'Do you need anything now?'

The way he turned his head a little more towards her, managing not to move the rest of himself was fascinating. His body strained to be away like a fish on the end of an angler's line.

'I'm OK,' he said, his voice gruff. 'Er, thanks.' His feet, seemingly of their own accord, started towards the stairs.

It was hopeless. 'Goodnight then,' Chani said, giving up.

He didn't answer.

She desperately needed to talk to Vanessa. In her room she took out her phone but realised it was too late, Van would have gone to bed. Email, then.

'House terrible, no soul, my chi very disturbed. Jamie spends all his time at his girlfriend's place. Can't imagine what she's like, must be desperate. Don't think I can last a week. Magda definitely going back to Poland next Tuesday. What's supposed to happen when my week ends? Hoping he'll stay at girlfriend's permanently. I'm definitely going home when I've done my week. Chani'

*

At half past three on Monday afternoon Jamie wandered out of school, praying Sophie's parents would let him stay to dinner again. If he could somehow avoid that awful woman for the rest of the week she'd go away on Friday and he could ... he could ... something. He would think of something. But he'd have done what social worker Annabel insisted, she couldn't ask him to do any more.

He neared the end of the corridor and there was Josh Palmersby with Madison Bloomingdale, she was gazing up into his eyes. Mamby Pamby, they were known as. Jamie half-smirked but couldn't shake off the wish that Sophie would gaze up at him with the same adoration. Except that Mamby might look good and have loads of money but all she was interested in was looking good and spending loads of money.

A boy he recognised as Year Eight raced past Jamie and dropped his rucksack. Books fell out and scattered in Jamie's path and two quite heavy ones hit his left foot.

'Shit!' Jamie kicked them away and glowered at the boy, who was scrabbling around frantically, trying to pick everything up. Jamie's foot narrowly missed him.

'Sorry, Pomfret-Jones, really sorry.' The boy grovelled, head bowed so his words disappeared into his chest.

'What's your name?' Jamie demanded, through the pain in his foot. That was the badly bruised leg too, now he'd be limping again, but without a heroic reason.

'Peter Frankland, Sir, er, Pomfret-Jones.' The boy cowered away, still trying to rescue his books from the crowd of feet.

'Get this mess cleared up, now,' Jamie barked, oblivious to the wave of students surging past them, like a river round a boulder.

He stood, stiff and fuming as the cowering boy rushed to do his bidding but dropped nearly as many books and papers as he managed to stuff into his bag. He was bright red before he finally crammed the last one in.

'Useless bugger,' Jamie growled, as Peter Frankland retreated, backwards, into the mass, his bag still gaping open. 'Fasten that thing properly, idiot!'

As the idiot was swept away Jamie moved to the wall so he could lean down and massage his ankle. Sodding books were sodding heavy.

Sophie found him there. 'Jamie? What are you doing down there?'

Hell, she'd seen him, in this embarrassing position. He went hot.

'What happened? Are you all right?'

He straightened up. 'Yeah, I'm fine. Some stupid kid dropped his books on my foot, damn fool.'

'Oh, Jamie, that must've hurt.'

He glanced at her, checking for sarcasm, but saw only concern in her face. He shrugged. 'It's nothing.'

Her face cleared. 'Oh, good.' She pulled her bag further up her shoulder and moved with him to the door, talking about the lesson she'd just left.

'You should have heard Elisha,' she said. 'She was so desperate to show how much work she'd done she couldn't get it out fast enough, so all her words were mixed up. Of course One-Direction-Ewan couldn't see how we were trying to help her and he was like, "oh, but, what do you mean? I can't understand you."' She rolled her eyes and mimicked how he'd waved his arms around.

'He would,' said Jamie.

'And poor Emma Jane, I can't believe she spends about six weeks a year in Spain and her pronunciation's so bad. Everyone was laughing at her. But,' and the sympathy faded from her voice and her eyes brightened, 'she's so funny.'

Jamie switched off at that point, until her voice changed again, alerting him just in time as she said, 'So how're things with your grandmother?'

He winced.

'That bad?'

'She pounced on me last night when I got in. Waiting, like a bloody spider.'

Sophie's eyes went big. 'So did she kick off?'

The anger that had flared at being ambushed blazed

again, and some more anger because, unless he lied, which wouldn't work because Sophie would find out, he had to say, 'Not really.' Of course, she didn't let it go.

'What did she say?'

He tried to shrug it off. 'Just, had I eaten.'

'Oh, right. So that's OK.'

He should have been relieved but something made him argue how it wasn't OK at all. He opened his mouth to speak but bit back the words when a brilliant idea came into his head. Before Sophie could move on to some new topic he said, 'Listen, Sophs, it's just an idea, right, but how about if I lived at yours?'

To his delight her face lit up. 'Oh, cool,' she said, almost dancing. 'Would you really?'

Wonderful. The awful woman could go back where she came from. Grinning, he said, 'Absolutely,' but a possible snag occurred to him. 'Would your parents be cool with that?'

'Of course they will. Totes. I'll ask them tonight, after you go home.'

He let her take his arm. 'Let's go to yours now, then, and download that album you wanted.'

*

It was six before Magda told Chani that Jamie had gone to Sophie's and would be eating there.

Chani made a growling sound in her throat, went up to her room and, swearing heavily, let herself go in a long, low-voiced tirade about bloody stupid boys and bloody stupid lollipop social workers. She stamped around for a bit before trying her emails again, in the other bedroom. If Van hadn't got back to her, she would bloody well phone her. And she'd bloody well better be in.

And there was a reply, at last.

'Chani love, it must be awful for you. The house must seem worse if you're stuck in it all the time. Why don't you contact the social worker and see what she says about Jamie never being there? It's good news about him having a girlfriend isn't it, he must have something that appeals to a girl so he can't be all bad? Thinking about you, take care, Love, Vanessa.'

Well, that didn't help.

'Van,' she growled, keeping her voice down but not bothering to tone down her frustration. 'There is nothing good about Jamie. This girl obviously has something seriously wrong with her and obviously no other guy'll look at her. And as for contacting Annabel Fforbes with two Fs ...!' She struggled not to say what she was thinking, not sure why she was bothered about being overheard. She swore again.

But there was one thing that Van was right about – being stuck in the house was crap. And what for? She paced around the room, went back into her own and paced some more. It was all too much. She had to get out. All right then, she would. She'd go to the pub. Before Magda could make another so-called vegetarian meal. But could she find anything at the pub?

Yes, she'd seen the words 'Vegetarian Menu' there, hadn't she? What would it cost? There was thirty-five pounds left in her bank balance till she was paid, and that wouldn't be for another ... she worked it out. Shit, another ten days. Oh dammit, she could pay with her credit card and she could walk there again. Surely she could afford a taxi back.

She sighed, couldn't hold it back, and used her online banking to move money from her savings account, reducing it to an amount that was hardly worth keeping in there.

She felt awful telling Magda she was eating out. 'Why don't you cook for Tomasz instead?' she suggested and Magda seemed pleased. Which plastic box contents would Magda microwave and would Tomasz would like it?

It was pouring down when she was ready to go out. Sod it. She rang the taxi number. Tomorrow she would go to the shopping centre and find a cash machine.

The pub was quieter than before. She opened a tab at the bar using her card and ordered a glass of wine while she waited for her meal. She ate in the bar. Her mushroom starter and vegetable risotto weren't wonderful, but a million times better than Magda's effort had been. The wine was good, good enough for her to have a third glass after her coffee, which wasn't as good as Magda's.

Maybe Damien would be in. She felt a small shiver of anticipation. But he didn't appear. Nor did the woman she'd seen before and who'd looked interesting. There were still only a few people in all evening, all couples, none of them at all interesting.

She took a taxi back and went to bed. Tomorrow she'd see about finding a charity shop and buying something to read. What a thing to look forward to.

Chani had been lying awake for what felt like hours. She'd tried every relaxation trick she knew but nothing worked. She was about to go and make some calming tea when she heard Jamie's soft tread on the stairs and along the landing and the tiniest click as he closed his door. Bugger it, she needed sleep.

It was no good. She thumped the pillow, changed her position and once more started the yoga relaxation exercise beginning with her right foot, tensing and relaxing the muscles up her right side to her face and down to the left.

The process reached her left shoulder. Three more days. She must empty her mind. She carried on, clenching her arm muscles then letting them relax. It had been three days since Damien had taken her phone number, she hadn't seen him in the pub and he hadn't rung. Stop thinking about him. Normally she'd have written him off by day two. So write him off. But she was so bored and frustrated. She really needed a sympathetic ear. Ring him.

Wrong! No! She'd put herself in a weak position.

She threw back the duvet, switched on the light, wrapped herself in her dressing gown and went to make tea.

In bed, as she sipped tea, the room was filling with calming aromas from her oil burner but her mind was still spinning. There were only three days left, it was too late, there was no point phoning him at this stage.

Right, she'd go with that. Forget Damien, he was history. Don't waste any more time on him.

History. Magda would be history, as from next week, history. What the hell was she going to do? She went back over what Magda had said and how final it had all felt. Could she find some chink in her argument? She lay back into the pillows and tried to analyse what Magda had actually said.

The not-able son, needing money for his care.

The husband, earnings here now less than in Poland.

Magda, having to live-in, not able to look after husband or not-able son.

Celandine, how long was she going to be away? Something about the bank ... they'd told Magda it might be permanent, was that what she'd said?

There was a connection between all these things but she couldn't find it. It was there, floating somewhere in the distance, out of sight.

She didn't wake up till ten o clock next morning, coming to with a jolt when she saw the time. She sat up in a rush to shower and dress but stopped when she discovered that she had a plan. A plan. In her sleep her mind had pulled everything together and located a key, a connection that she might be able to use.

Excited, she found paper and a pen and scribbled it down, before rushing to be ready and go downstairs.

Magda was out. Shopping, a note on the dining room table told her. Damn, Chani could have gone with her.

But Magda was soon back.

'I have some things for you,' she said, her face bright and eager like a child's. She lifted items from shopping bags, listing them as she went.

'Organic cheese, organic celery, organic wholemeal rolls, savoury butter beans and rye crackers – all from Polski deli. And I got pasta and pasta sauce and more fresh vegetables, all organic.'

'Magda, that's fantastic. You're wonderful. Thank you.'

Magda stepped back, blushing. 'Oh, is nothing.'

Encouraged, Chani started on Step One of her Plan. 'I'll help you put them away, and then we can have a coffee together.'

Magda made the coffee as they dealt with the shopping. 'I put in lounge for you,' she said, producing a Polish cake with caraway seeds in it.

'Lovely,' Chani said, persevering. 'But it's for both of us. In the lounge.'

'But …'

Chani held up a hand. 'Both of us.'

With the coffee poured and Magda sitting in an easy chair, but not easily, Chani moved on to Step Two.

'Have you worked for Linda for long?' she asked, stopping herself just in time from saying 'Celandine'.

'Long, yes. I came here after her husband pass away. She needed help so she can go to work.'

'Right. So, six years then.'

Magda considered. 'Six years. Jamie was ten.'

Chani knew that, would never forget the 'To Whom It May Concern' missive. Concentrate. Get to the money. But, 'Do you know when this man came on the scene?' she asked. 'The guy she went away with?'

Magda frowned and became solemn. 'Him, yes. Mr Smith.'

'Mr Smith!' It came out with a snort of disbelief.

'Yes.' Magda's face hadn't changed. 'He came to the house, he came for, er, weeks. More, a few months. Maybe in the spring he came first. But he was not much here, not much in the house. He came to the door and Mrs Pomfret-Jones went with him. They go out, she say to me. I never saw when she came back.' She frowned and her mouth tightened. 'In the morning, I saw him.'

'Yes,' Chani said. 'You weren't living in then. What was he like?'

Magda frowned more and said nothing.

'You said you saw him,' Chani prompted.

'But, you don't mind?'

'Mind? Mind what?'

Magda fidgeted with the crumbs on her plate. 'That he ... he stay. Here, at night.' Her face twisted as if she'd eaten something bad.

How old-fashioned she was. 'Why would I mind that?'

Magda gave her a startled look, her eyes big before she frowned and concentrated again on the crumbs.

'So.' Chani ignored it. 'What was he like?'

Magda's shrug was resigned. 'He wore black shirts. And tight jeans. He has gold rings and a jewel in his ear, a diamond.' She sniffed.

'How exciting,' Chani said, to another sniff. 'Did she tell you she was going away? Or where she was going?'

Magda nodded. 'Not where she go, but yes, she told me she was going away and she say about money and

65

what she has arranged.'

'Ah, yes, you told me that.' If only she'd said where, but at least Magda had got to the money herself. Time for Step Three. Chani sat up straighter, composed her face into what she hoped was a sympathetic expression and said, 'I'm not sure how to say this.'

Magda's worried look rushed back.

'Oh,' Chani said, quickly. 'No, I just wondered, I mean, I think that Cel— I mean, Linda might not have paid you enough. She might not have left you with enough money either.'

Magda tried to smile but she was clearly troubled. 'You're very kind,' she said, setting off in Chani a disturbing flare of guilt. She stared at nothing for a moment before sighing. 'Mrs Pomfret-Jones always say she can not pay good money to me, but she is so generous other ways. I do not have to pay for my meals and she let me use a car.'

Chani ramped up the concern she was trying to project. Actually, it wasn't difficult, she was beginning to feel quite angry with Celandine.

'Magda, I think my daughter should have paid you more. Probably a lot more. I think you should have had proper holidays, with pay, and proper time off. I think she should have left you much more money than she has, so that you and your husband would be able to send enough to pay for your son's care. And I think she should have said that your husband could live here with you while she's away, and you wouldn't have to pay any rent for that.'

She paused, not sure how to say what she was leading up to. Surprised, also, that, though she'd

66

dreamed up all this in an attempt to bribe Magda into staying, she now actually believed it.

Magda's face glowed. 'You are very kind lady. I know, God should look after you.'

'Oh, well, I don't know about that. But look, Magda, I don't know how much Linda's expecting you to, I mean, how much money she left you, but I, well, if there's any way I can help to get it increased so that you'll have enough so you don't need to go back to Poland, well, I will. Maybe if I went with you to the bank and explained …?'

Magda's expression changed, her eyes narrowed. 'Mrs Chani,' she began, her hands clasped with her fingers twined together. 'I see you want help me and my family. Maybe you are right, maybe it can be made so I have more money and Tomasz can live here with me. And I would like to have more money, we both, too.

'I know it will help you if we can be here, I understand you need to go to your home. But you see, I work as housekeeper. In day time. Tomasz and me, we like to have our life on our selves, in our place, not in this place. We miss our son and we miss Poland and our friends and our families. If I stay here, and we live here, and we don't know where is Mrs Pomfret-Jones, and Jamie is alone with me and Tomasz only, is big responsible for us. Like parent. He is sixteen only.' She spread her hands out in a despairing gesture. 'What if he wants party? Lot of young people, maybe drinking, maybe drugging. What if he drugging in this house? Or other bad things? What if he do bad things? I think he could do, no? What can we do? If police come, we are

67

Polski, who they believe?' Her flushed face and more and more mixed up English told Chani how hard she was finding it to explain.

Magda took a deep breath. 'You see we have talked about, me and Tomasz. We have talked very much. We want to help Jamie, and you. But is too difficult.' Now she was wringing her hands, Chani realised, the first time she'd ever seen anyone do it. The poor woman was nearly in tears.

'Yes, I see,' she said, wanting to wring her own hands. 'I can see what you mean.' She felt strongly tempted to let poor Magda off the hook, to pat her hands and tell her everything was all right. Except it wasn't all right, she just couldn't let Magda think it was.

So she told her, holding nothing back. 'It applies to me too. I don't want that kind of responsibility either. Especially when it means I'd have to give up my home and my life and live in this awful house with a snobby kid who doesn't want me here. And I don't get paid anything! I'm just expected to do it. And if I lose my job I'll have no income at all.'

Magda looked stricken. 'I'm sorry. Really sorry.' Her face was squeezed up and her fingers tangled together. 'You know we go on Tuesday, next week, yes?.'

Tuesday. Next week. Chani couldn't speak. The awful house was closing in on her, she could feel the walls pressing in, pushing out the air. She gasped, sucked in air and coughed. Magda jumped up and patted her back. 'Would you like more coffee?' she asked.

Chani waved her away, shaking her head, the coughing slowing.

'I'm all right,' she managed. She had never needed Vanessa more.

But Vanessa was unreachable. Chani rang her – as soon as she had calmed Magda down and escaped her strenuous efforts to make yet more coffee, or tea – four times at work, and on her mobile. Twice the office said she was in a meeting, once she was on her way to a meeting and the fourth time with a client. Her mobile went straight to voicemail.

It was a long time before Chani calmed down and was able to think.

The only person who could help was Annabel Fforbes. She would have to find someone to replace Magda. If, that was, Chani could convince her it was the only thing to do.

Surely, anyone could see how pointless it was for her to be there herself. It was crystal clear Jamie didn't want her there, was avoiding her by staying away from the place as long as he possibly could. The girlfriend's parents had to be helping him do that, she couldn't be wandering the streets with him till midnight or later every night. They were feeding him, weren't they? Their daughter must be a real liability for them to be doing so much for such a horrible boy. They had to be desperate to keep him and the girl together. Even so, they must be drawing the line at having him actually live there, or he wouldn't be coming back to sleep and collect clean clothes from Magda. Whatever, she'd never know.

Apart from that, Annabel must see how impossible it was for Chani: her home, her job and her income were in Hebden Bridge. She'd offered to have Jamie there, couldn't see why that wasn't possible. All right, he didn't want to go, and there was all that about the school and his stupid father's will, but surely that could be ignored under the circumstances.

So, yes, she actually had two possibilities to present to Ffrosty Fface Lollipop: either find a replacement for Magda or let Jamie come and live with her.

She took a long, slow breath and let it all out in a huge sigh of relief. It was sorted. Now she could … what? She couldn't go to the pub again, she had no money. Not shopping either. Staying here would drive her mad. Going for a walk round here wasn't on either.

What if she went into the town, she could go and have a look round. Charity shop? Window shopping at least. Well, it was better than nothing. Wasn't it?

*

'So, Jamie, who do you think Shakespeare meant to gain the sympathy of the audience: King Henry or Williams?'

But Jamie was miles away. The letter had come that morning, he'd recognised the Social Services logo and grabbed it before that awful woman could see it. He'd pushed it into his bag but hadn't had a chance to read it till lunchtime, when he'd hidden himself in a study booth at the back of the library, with a random pile of books in case anyone looked through the glass. He'd just ripped it open when Sophie had found him.

'Hi,' she'd whispered, opening the door. She'd ignored his frown and brought in another chair, closing herself in with him. 'The History of Mr Polly?' she'd said, staring at his choice of books.

He'd frowned more, put his finger to his lips and shaken his head. It had no effect.

'Jamie, what are you doing?' 'Ah,' she'd added, spotting the torn envelope and examining it. And she'd sat and stared at him with her eyebrows raised until he'd given in and told her.

'Thursday. After school.'

'At the office, or at yours?'

'The office.'

She'd taken his hand and squeezed it.

He was remembering that now. It had meant a lot.

'Jamie.' Mrs Forrester's voice penetrated. 'Are you with us?'

'Oh, ah,' he mumbled, startled, as someone sniggered, followed by more, abruptly cut off by Mrs Forrester's glare. 'I was thinking,' he said, trying to salvage the situation.

'And what did you think?'

His mind raced over the lesson on *Henry the Fifth*, searching for the last thing he'd heard. 'Er, Williams,' he said, beginning to sweat.

Mrs Forester was showing signs of impatience, but he'd obviously got the right name. Now what had she asked him?

'Tell me how he does it.'

He arranged his face into as bright an intelligence as he could. The English teacher liked him, she was softening, he could see.

'What arguments does Williams use, that might sway the audience of the time more than the King's arguments? Come on now.'

He could breathe. He knew this. 'He shows how war affects the soldiers. He talks about the people at home when the soldiers are killed, or badly injured.'

71

'At last. Yes. Bryn, what effect would it have had on the audience when Williams says "... their children rawly left"?'

Jamie didn't hear Bryn's answer, something strange was happening to his insides, a weird sort of churning, and, even more strange, he'd developed a stitch in his side.

Mrs Forrester cornered him at the end of the lesson, saying something about his last piece of work. When the others had all gone she said, 'Is everything all right?'

He swallowed. She could be very motherly when she chose to. 'Yes, fine,' he said.

'Nothing bothering you?'

'No, nothing.'

She scrutinised his face, doubt in hers, but must have decided to let it go. 'All right then.'

He reached the safety of the corridor feeling like an escapee from Colditz. Mrs Forrester's probing was the last thing he wanted. He knew Social Services had told the school about his mother and he wished with all he had that they hadn't.

He was too busy after that, especially with rugby practice after school, to think about it, or the letter. But he did remember to slip it to Magda when he reached the house.

'Can you give this to ... her?' he asked. 'I'm going out.'

7

Chani found an area of green and parked Patricia so she could walk. The area wasn't fenced. There were goalposts for soccer and another lot for rugby. There were tennis courts and after that an area that might be a cricket pitch in the summer. Would they play rounders down here? Probably not. No one was playing anything at the moment. The only people she met were dog-walkers, ready with plastic bags, their dogs on leads. Most of them nodded to her, a sort of greeting, several looked beyond her as they did it. This puzzled her until she worked it out – they expected her to have a dog, they were looking for it. Did nobody walk here without a dog? It wasn't the sort of place she would have expected to be used for that.

But she was outside in the fresh air and the dog walkers were friendly. She began to feel marginally better, enough anyway to drive back to the house.

Now to talk to Annabel. No matter how frosty she was. Chani would talk about finding a replacement for Magda.

What was that Magda had said about the financial arrangements Celandine had set up? Via a bank account, weren't they. It would be Magda's bank account, wouldn't it – which meant no one else would be able to draw on it. Why hadn't she realised that before? Celandine, stupid girl, must have worked on the assumption that Magda would stay indefinitely: obviously she'd never talked to Magda, never bothered to find out what she thought about the idea, just gone blithely on her way running off with this Mr Smith and abandoning her son.

But there was some consolation. When Ffrosty Fface talked to Jamie it would stand out a mile that he didn't want Chani to be there. Annabel would have to sort out someone to stay with him then. And if not … well, all she'd be left with would be putting him into care and that wasn't going to happen, was it. No.

She drove Patricia into the garage and, wincing, locked her away. In the house she overrode Magda's attempts – mid-ironing – to make a cup of tea for her and did it herself, as part of psyching herself up to ring up Social Services for Annabel. And if she got nowhere with that, she'd bloody well go to the police and insist they search for Celandine. She was walking out of the kitchen when the doorbell rang. Still holding the mug Chani went to open the door.

In front of her stood a young girl, tall and slim, with long, glossy hair and green, star-quality eyes. She could have walked straight out of a shampoo advert. Except it was obvious she would never be in any kind of advert. This girl would probably never need to work.

Her clothes were casual and clearly very expensive. They fitted her perfectly and hung beautifully. Her skin shone with health and well-being, Chani's professional eye noted, and, further, that she had put on just enough make-up with a very skilled hand.

She smiled a charming and confident smile, showing perfect white teeth. 'Hallo,' she said. 'I'm Sophie. I came to see Jamie.'

'Oh? Jamie Pomfret-Jones?'

'Jamie, yes. I'm Sophie. He has mentioned me, hasn't he?' Clearly she had no doubt that he had.

'You're Sophie?' This couldn't possibly be the girlfriend. Chani made a supreme effort. 'Ah, yes, I see. Well, hello, I'm pleased to meet you. But I'm sorry, Jamie's out.'

'Oh, yes, of course.' Sophie still smiled, still confident and charming. 'He's at rugby practice.' She stood quite still, no sign of fidgeting or uncertainty.

This made no sense. 'Rugby practice, right. But … you've come to see him, even so?'

'Actually, I came to see you.' It was like being presented with a gift. 'You're his gran, aren't you?' It sounded like, 'you're the most interesting, lovely person I've ever heard of and it's fabulous to meet you.'

Chani suppressed a sigh. Why did all these people think she was a grandmother? 'Actually, no. I'm Chani. You just call me Chani.'

There was a slight shift in Sophie's bearing. 'Oh, I'm sorry,' she said. 'I thought …'

'Yes, I'm sure.'

But how rude the girl must think she was, still standing on the doorstep like this. 'Look, come in,' she said. 'Do come in.'

She waved her hand towards the lounge, aware of a surging tide of curiosity. She wanted to know about this girl.

Magda was hovering.

'Hello, Magda,' Sophie said and Magda beamed at her.

'Would you like a drink?' Chani asked the girl. 'Tea, coffee?'

'Thank you, no.' She managed to thank Chani and Magda in one warm, polite move.

Using her best professional manner, Chani waved Sophie in and followed her, sat down facing her and, trying to sound friendly but at the same time businesslike, took the initiative. 'So you wanted to see me?'

Sophie was perfectly relaxed. 'I thought it would be good to meet you.'

Ah. Now Chani saw. 'I gather this isn't Jamie's idea.'

Sophie's lips curved a fraction more upwards but she said nothing.

'Yes, I see.' It was time to seize her opportunity. 'Look, Sophie,' she said, noting the spark of interest in Sophie's face. 'Do you mind if I ask you, what has Jamie told you? About his mother … what happened … me …?' She had a strong feeling Sophie had been expecting the question.

'You mean, when she left? Or about his mum and you?'

'Both, I suppose.' So she knew quite a lot. Which meant Jamie had talked to her about quite a lot. Hmmm.

'He said you and his mum weren't speaking. He didn't actually say much, it had something to do with her changing her name?'

Ah. Was Sophie trying to find out more? That was interesting.

'Well, she did. But then, *I* changed *my* name.' And that had been no big deal, but she hadn't gone against her karma, had she? But she wouldn't go into all that.

Sophie had become animated. 'Really? You did?'

76

'Absolutely. It was my karma.'

The girl stared for a second before a tiny sound came from her throat, like a not-quite-cough and she covered her mouth with her hand. She made the sound again and said, 'Excuse me. Chani is an unusual name, isn't it?'

'It's from the *Dune* books,' Chani told her, adding, as Sophie was only young. 'They were big in the seventies.'

'Sort of fantasy books? Wasn't there a movie?'

So she knew about them, what a surprise.

'The movie.' Chani shuddered. 'The movie was ... well, never mind. No, you see, Celandine couldn't accept her own karma. She went off and – I still can't believe it – she did accountancy. Of all things. Such an utterly soulless thing to do.'

Sophie's eyes – blue/green they were – widened and her beautifully-shaped brows rose, then bent into a puzzled frown. 'She's very good at it,' she said. 'She's made lots of money.'

'Exactly,' Chani said, her point made. '*And*,' she added, wanting the girl to understand. 'She married a guy whose chakras weren't balanced.' She sighed. 'I'm glad her father never knew.'

Sophie leant forward, excitement showing. 'Her father. Who ... er, what does he do?'

'He was a folk singer, a vegan.' Chani frowned, remembering. 'I heard he went electric.'

Sophie's bewildered eyebrow furrows were practically meeting. 'Electric?'

'Folk music. Supposed to sound natural, real.'

'Oh.' The furrows levelled somewhat.

All at once her face changed to a new recognition of something and she nearly bounced out of her chair. 'You heard? You mean, you … Did you split up?'

'After the conception, yes,' Chani nodded. 'That was what we'd arranged.'

'Wow!' Sophie was on the edge of her seat, her eyes shone. 'You really are a hippie, Jamie said …'

She was interrupted by the door opening. Jamie stood there, taut and stiff, his expression grim. 'Sophs?' It was a warning.

Sophie didn't seem to notice. 'Jamie, hi. I'm talking to Chani, you were out.'

'I see.' Jamie didn't move, his mouth was a tight line, his eyes shuttered. 'So, we can go to my room.'

Sophie turned her charming smile on Chani as she rose like a dancer to her feet. 'Lovely to meet you, Chani.' She tripped across the room to join Jamie, as though he were offering her flowers. 'See you later,' she added.

Jamie, Chani saw with great interest, was tapping his foot.

The door closed behind them, leaving Chani with much to think about.

Moments later she had even more to think about, after Magda, flushed and apologetic, had tapped on the door and come in.

'Mrs Chani,' she said. 'I'm sorry, I forgot to give you this letter. Jamie ask me to give you, I forgot. I'm so sorry.'

'It's all right, Magda. Don't worry about it.'

It would be something from the school. But it was addressed to her. Here. She saw the Social Services logo and groaned.

Magda left, still apologising. Chani barely noticed. The letter had been opened. Jamie, obviously She looked again. It was addressed to both of them.

There would be a meeting, it said. On Thursday, at four fifteen.

At the Social Services offices.

*

Jamie strode up the stairs, looking straight ahead, his back stiff. How could she? He thrust open the door to his room and went in, waited for her to enter then firmly closed the door behind her.

Sophie was smiling.

'I didn't know you were coming,' he said, spitting the words out like bullets.

'But it's good to see me, isn't it?'

Her voice was soft and warm, like honey on a baked banana. She was so close the citrus scent of her hair filled his nostrils and she was sliding her arms round him. Her eyes smiled up at him, her mouth invited him.

He had to kiss her. 'Of course it is,' he muttered, coming up for air and struggling to hang on to his anger.

She urged his head down to kiss again and, when they drew away from each other he managed, his voice even more hoarse, 'See?'

Some time later, she pulled away, but her fingers still fiddled with the neckline of his sweater, so that he had to fight to calm himself down.

'Jamie,' she said, her eyes shielded by long, curling lashes. 'I came to tell you, I talked to Mummy last night, after you'd gone, about you coming to ours.'

79

'Oh, yes?' His voice broke as a different kind of excitement increased the way he already felt.

Her lips turned down. 'Yes, but, I'm sorry, she's not keen.'

He slumped. It had been his last resort.

She stroked his arm and gave him an encouraging smile. 'She said, would I remind you about Christmas? They're expecting you.'

'Christmas?' How had she got on to Christmas?

'It's not long. Two weeks.'

He gazed at her. And remembered. 'Oh, like last year, you mean? In France?'

'Yes.' Her eyes sparkled, showing how excited she was about it. 'Skiing, at the chateau.' A little frown appeared between her eyes, the green turning a stronger colour. 'You are going to come, aren't you?'

'Cool, yeah, great.' Two weeks till Christmas, he consoled himself. That wasn't long.

*

In her room, Chani, not caring any more who she disturbed, had her iPod in its dock, the room filled with Wilson Pickett.

She pushed the buttons for Vanessa's number, inured now to receiving no response, but this time Vanessa answered.

'Van!' Chani said. 'At last.'

She found the remote and turned the sound down as Vanessa said, 'Have you been trying to get me?'

'For ages. But listen, I've just met The Girlfriend.' She gave the words extra emphasis.

'Really?'Well, that had Van interested, almost panting to know more, clearly.

80

'Really,' she confirmed.

'What's she like?'

Chani paused, to work out how to put it. 'Actually, she's quite something. Very confident, stacks of money, I'd say. And brains. And looks. The lot – what on earth she sees in Jamie …'

Vanessa cut across her. 'That's great. Sounds like she could be a good influence on him.'

Trust Van to think of that. 'He could certainly do with it.'

'How did you come to meet her? Did Jamie actually bring her to the house?'

'He did not! She just turned up, this afternoon, by herself. Said she'd come to see me. I suppose that'd be the only way she would. See me, that is.'

'So Jamie's still keeping out of the way?'

'He's never here.'

'Does he know she's been?'

'He arrived while she was talking to me, strangely enough. He wasn't too pleased, whisked her off to his room, well away from me and my evil influence.' She couldn't stop the bitterness coming into her voice.

'Oh, Chani love, it must be awful for you. When's the meeting with the social worker?'

'Thursday. Day after tomorrow. Four fifteen.' She had no need to check any of this.

'Is she coming to the house?'

'No, she reckons the office is what she calls Neutral Ground. More like No Man's Land.'

'I see. After school, then.'

'Right. So he can go straight there from school, not even travelling with me.'

'Whose idea was that? Hers, or his?'

'His, do you need to ask?'

She heard Vanessa give a little sigh, or it might just have been a deep breath. 'Let's hope something gets resolved,' she said.

'Let's hope I can go home. I mean, nobody could say this is working.'

'No, I suppose … not at the moment, no.'

What did she mean, not at the moment? 'Van, it's not going to get any better, is it? Magda's definitely going back to Poland on Tuesday, I've tried everything I can think of to get her to stay but it's hopeless.' She poured it all out, Magda's circumstances, the money, Celandine being so tight and mean, her worries about losing her job at the Mind and Body Centre.

'Chani love, how truly awful for you.' Van sounded really concerned. 'Do you want me to have a word with Melissa?'

Chani, moved that Van would think of that, considered it. 'I don't know,' she said. 'I really don't know if it's better she knows or if I keep it from her as long as I can. Thanks for offering though.'

Concern still in her voice, Vanessa said, 'All right, I'll leave it for now, then. But I really think you should tell the social worker about the money problems, and about your job, I'm sure she doesn't realise.'

'I'm going to, I worked out a plan, I'm not waiting till the meeting, I'm going to talk to her before then, I've already tried but she wasn't there. A bit like you, really. I've left a message but I'll keep trying tomorrow.'

'Good. And as for Jamie, well, he can't stay at his girlfriend's for ever, can he? I mean, her parents, they'll get fed up with him being there all the time, won't they? And she seems to have a mind of her own, if she's already been to see you. She might start pushing him.'

'She might. She might well, but whether she'll succeed … What you said about his parents, I thought that myself. I don't know how they've stuck him this long. I don't know how anybody would.'

'You know, Chani love, he might be a completely different person with them.'

'Oh yes?' A huge sigh escaped her. 'I don't know what to think.'

Vanessa sighed too. 'No, I can't say I know myself.'

The concern Van was obviously feeling wasn't like her and it worried Chani. She made an effort to push it away and to be positive and assertive. 'I know. But it can't be my worry, it's Annabel's. She'll have to find some way out of it.'

Vanessa didn't respond and the silence pushed Chani's stress levels up so she felt like a volcano about to erupt. Especially when Van just murmured a non-committal sound and added, 'I'll ring you about half past six, seven o clock on Thursday, shall I? See how it went.'

After that, even listening to Aretha did little to lighten Chani's mood.

8

'Shall we go to yours?' Jamie asked At Sophie's puzzled frown his stomach muscles clenched. They had to get out of here.

'I thought,' she said, 'as we're here, and Magda loves to cook for us, I thought we'd eat here. We can go back to mine later, if you like, Mummy's out with her friends and Daddy's at some business thing.'

Shit, there was no escape. He checked the time, almost five. If they went down now Magda should be able to sort something out for them before that awful woman would even think about having a meal, and then they could go.

'Isn't it Magda's night out tonight?' Sophie said.

He gave her a blank look before he remembered. 'You mean the Polish club thing? Is it today?'

'Yes, doesn't she go on Tuesdays?'

'I think she does, yes, why?'

'She likes to make us a meal early,' Sophie reminded him. 'We should go and ask her now, I think.'

'I suppose.' He leapt up as hope began to rise. 'Come on then.'

They found Magda in the kitchen. She smiled when she saw them. 'I can make your meal now, yes?'

'Oh, Magda, could you?' Sophie said. 'Is that all right for you, we should have said earlier?'

'Is not a problem. What you like to eat?'

Jamie didn't care, for once. 'You choose, Sophs,' he said. But what if she went for something that would take ages? He should have picked something. But Sophie worked it out with Magda so she could make something quickly.

'I go and tell Mrs Chani,' Magda said.

'She won't want to eat yet,' Jamie rushed to say. 'We'll have ours now, we're going out afterwards.'

'OK.'

Jamie breathed properly again. He was even more relieved when they were able to leave the house without seeing that awful woman, and without Sophie seeming even to notice. Would he have enough money to take her out for a meal the next day, there was that noodle bar she liked?

*

Although Chani tried all day on Wednesday she couldn't speak to Annabel. She had a dreadful day, stuck in the house the whole time. She checked her bank account again but her financial position was just as bad as the last time she'd checked. She couldn't afford to go out. At least she'd found some novels in a charity shop the day before, she could sit and read.

So she read. She meditated. She rang three of her friends in Hebden Bridge and caught up with their news. Every forty minutes or so she tried to speak to Annabel.

She didn't think she'd ever been so bored in her whole life. She was even driven to surfing the net. She saw Jamie at about half past four as he flashed past on the way to his room, and heard him go out shortly afterwards.

In the evening, after another of Magda's attempts at vegetarian cooking, she tried watching the telly but gave up, took the two novels she'd bought and sat in bed to read. By the time she at last fell asleep she'd read both of them.

Next morning Chani tried again to reach Annabel.

'I'm sorry,' she was told. 'She's out all morning but she did leave a message for you in case you rang again. Just let me… yes, here it is. She says she'll see you at the meeting on Thursday. Oh, that's today, isn't it?'

Chani groaned and gave up. Back into online banking she moved money recklessly, emptying her savings account, logged out, closed it down and went into the town centre.

She had a coffee before meandering round the shops, blew some of her precious money on three more novels, a *Guardian* and a *Mirror*, found a café that looked reasonable and ate a panini that wasn't at all bad, with a scone that wasn't at all good. While she ate she worked through some of the *Mirror's* puzzle page and wondered about what would happen if she ran away.

She thought of the fabulous places she'd been to on her travels in the seventies. India had been wonderful, fascinating, but hard work. It would be difficult, she imagined, to disappear there. She wouldn't need much money but without a job what money she had wouldn't last for ever. Thailand would be even more difficult, she remembered its lovely people who'd seemed so gentle but who'd loved violent sports like kick-boxing. And the police, strung about with guns and bullets. Were they still like that? Working there would be impossible without knowing the language and she'd never be able to learn it.

She thought of the oppressive, energy-sapping humidity and heat of Malaysia, Sumatra and Java. Of the bribes that had had to be paid in some of those places. Of the tight entry regulations and their strict enforcement in others.

Her dreamy bubble burst, Chani moved her imaginings to Britain. How about Scotland? Far north Scotland, the Highlands. Beautiful, remote. No, not easy to disappear there, easier in big cities, like Edinburgh or Glasgow. Or Ireland. Now that was a possibility. Didn't she have some distant relatives there? Or maybe she could join up with a group of travellers. Now, that would be an adventure. Ah – soft, velvety night skies studded with stars, the smell of wood smoke in woodland glades, music probably, played on fiddles; journeying through beautiful countryside during the day. Ffrosty Fface Lollipop would never find her there.

'Did you want anything else?' The nasal voice broke into her idyll, the Australian accent throwing her so she couldn't think where she was. She blinked and peered at a plump figure, black pinny tied like a sack round lumpy hips, fat, leggings-clad legs beneath, muffin top bulging above. A sulky, double-chinned face frowned down at her. She badly needed a good stylist, if she even washed her hair it'd look better. That bright green tinsel tied round her head did her no favours either. What the hell was the tinsel for, surely it was too early for Christmas?

She didn't look like any Aussies Chani had met. But of course, that had been in the seventies, people were a lot thinner then.

Yes, not the seventies now, was it, she was here in bloody Welwyn Garden City.

She blinked, as her second lovely dream floated away.

'D'you want me to get yer somefink else?' the girl asked, as if to a very old, stupid, deaf, and probably foreign person.

Not Australian. That was, of course, the local accent, wasn't it, the worst version of it. It just sounded Aussie.

'No thanks,' she said, choking back the 'love' that would have followed naturally if she'd been in the north. Or anywhere or with anyone friendly.

'D'yer want the bill, then?'

Chani nodded. Thanks.' How on earth could this reasonable-seeming café have employed someone so totally unsuitable? There were other waitresses around who looked clean and neat and efficient. A waiter too. All wearing green tinsel. She shook her head, looked at her watch and was surprised at how long she'd been sitting there. She'd better go back and prepare herself for this sodding meeting.

Chani was late.

Delia, still looking harassed, took her name as if they'd never met before. Murmuring things Chani couldn't hear she led her through the maze of corridors while Chani wondered about the woman's sanity. With some sympathy.

They reached a door which looked like all the others, Delia stopped and opened it, making the slightest of gestures. That must mean she should go in.

Chani walked through. She recognised the room – now Lego-free. There was Jamie, sitting rigidly facing Annabel. Only his lips were moving as he said, 'I don't need her,' directly to the social worker. 'I'm going to live at Sophie's,' he went on, ignoring Chani's entrance.

Hope burst in Chani like popped champagne. '*Are* you?' she cried.

Lifting her head from her clipboard Annabel acknowledged her with a sideways glance. An odd sideways glance.

'Sorry,' Chani said. 'I got lost.'

Annabel's attention returned to Jamie, and the clipboard. 'Sophie … ah, your girlfriend, yes? So, have her parents invited you? I will need to talk to them, OK?'

Chani opened her mouth to say she was sure there wouldn't be a problem but stopped. Jamie was speaking. Or, rather, mumbling.

'It, um, it isn't all sorted out yet.'

Annabel didn't hesitate. 'If you'll give me the name and address and a phone number I'll contact them, OK.'

'Ngh…' Jamie said, to the empty floor.

Annabel placed the clipboard on her lap, a decisive move, and held it tight with both hands. 'They haven't agreed to it, have they?'

This was all new to Chani, but she couldn't help admiring Annabel's technique. At the same time she felt a swoop of disappointment that almost stopped her breathing.

'No,' Jamie said, lifting his head and looking directly at the social worker.

Chani felt a flutter of sympathy for Jamie – it was an oddly moving sensation. She had no time to ponder over it.

'OK, right,' Annabel said, professionally brisk. 'I think we can forget that.' Chani wanted to hit her. 'But should the situation change, Jamie, do let me know. Now, the housekeeper leaves on Tuesday, yes? So, Granny, it's up to you, right?' Holding on to the board almost as if it was a lifeline.

Chani gasped. This was too much. 'Don't call me Granny!' she snapped, incensed. 'I'm not a granny and I never will be.' She pulled in on herself, drew the deepest breath she could and worked to ground herself. She was only slightly calmer when she said, 'Just because my daughter, who I haven't seen since she got married, decides to run off with some guy it doesn't make me into a granny.' She took another quick breath, her brain working now. 'And I don't see how it's up to me? Why is nobody looking for Celandine?'

Annabel, still gripping the clipboard, lifted her head with a jerk. 'Cel ... I'm sorry, Celandine? Oh, you mean Mrs Pomfret-Jones.'

'Jamie's mother.' Chani's voice was icy. 'Who it *is* up to.'

Jamie his lower lip jutting, came to mutinous life. 'She's Linda. *She* called her Celandine.' Under heavy brows his eyes, not meeting Chani's, smouldered.

Annabel's eyes narrowed as she looked from Chani to Jamie and back. 'Right. Whatever.' She shuffled the papers on the clipboard. 'Here's the thing, Gra ... Chani, we don't know where Jamie's mother is. Nobody knows.'

'So why is nobody looking for her?' Chani repeated. 'Like the police, for example?'

Annabel made a coughing sort of sound. 'As Mrs Pomfret-Jones made arrangements for Jamie's, that is, for the housekeeper to live in and look after him, with financial arrangements for her and for Jamie, it's clear that she went intentionally, and so isn't classed as a missing person of concern to the police.'

'But she abandoned her son who's only sixteen,' Chani said. Why wasn't this being taken seriously, never mind that she hadn't herself taken it seriously up to that moment, surely social workers couldn't just shrug it off?

'She made arrangements for him,' Annabel said. 'And we are involved. Mrs Maszenski is police-checked. The problem is now that she can't stay, so we turn to you, Mrs, er, Caladan, as the next of kin.'

'I don't need her,' Jamie burst in.

'Can you not find a replacement for Magda?' Chani asked. 'Clearly, I can't stay here any longer. I agreed to a week, I've been able to take a week off work – *and* I've had to use three of my holiday days – and I have to be back there on Monday. If I lose my job how am I supposed to live, I'll have no money?'

'Would you like me to contact your employers?'

'What? No, I would not.'

'I don't see what the alternative is.'

Annabel checked the time, started to lift the clipboard and to turn towards the desk behind her.

'The alternative, Ms Fforbes, is for you to find someone to replace Magda. I have to go back to my home and my job on Monday.'

'I am sorry, Mrs … Chani, I can't do that. We're not an employment agency.'

'Well I can't arrange for anybody myself, I can't pay them and I can't change Celandine's Financial Arrangements. So it *is* up to you.' Chani was so angry she could hardly breathe, but she was doing her best to stay calm. What made her even angrier was that bloody Ffrosty Fface was so unconcerned. As if none of this mattered.

Except, a fleeting thought suggested, she was clutching that bloody clipboard as if she couldn't let go. But Annabel stood and the thought faded.

'Look,' Annabel said. 'I do see your problem and I sympathise.' She didn't sound sympathetic. 'But, clearly, we can't do anything at the moment. If you can give Jamie a few more days I'll have a word with my manager. That's all I can do. So – a few more days, all right. Jamie, I'll come and see you next week.' She was already glancing at her watch and picking up some files. 'I have to go, I'm afraid. OK?' She moved to the door and held it open.

Chani was hot with fury. Jamie hurled himself between her and Annabel and was gone.

Chani found the determination to stand her ground. She put herself in the doorway, physically preventing Annabel from leaving, the clipboard and the files were like a wall between them. 'This will not do,' she said, ignoring the wall, her hands in fists. 'It simply will not do. How am I supposed to look after a boy who so much doesn't want me there that he stays at his girlfriend's all the time? And when I have no money to pay for anything. How?'

'I can only have a word with my manager. That really is all I can do. I'll try to come and see you next week. I do have to go, I'm sorry.'

She had failed. There was nothing more she could do. She watched the social worker's rigid retreating back and knew that if she didn't leave the place that minute she would tear it to shreds.

*

Jamie's hands clenched into rock hard fists, ready to knock senseless anything his wildly swerving eyes found. He punched doors, hurled them out of his way and stormed out of the building. Blind and deaf to his surroundings, driven by a fierce internal urge, he hit the street.

His feet thumped out hatred with each racing beat, stamping on all the people who'd put him into this horror story. Stamp – Chani Caladan. Stamp – Annabel Fforbes. Stamp – his father for dying. Stamp – and causing this situation. Stamp – his mother. Stamp – the selfish bitch, she didn't care about him at all. Stamp! None of them cared about him. None of them listened to him. Not even Sophie's parents, they didn't want him either. He hated Sophie too, she wasn't bothered in the least that he had to stay with that bloody woman, she'd even been to see her, behind his back! 'Lovely to meet you.' Stamp. Oh yes. Stamp. Bitch!

He came to a sudden halt when a door blocked his progress but he was moving with such force that he rammed into it and the door moved with him, crashed open and hit an inside wall so hard it swung straight back. Jamie's onward rush was slowing but not enough to stop his shoulder from colliding with the door.

The sickening jolt made him cry out.

A figure came running from inside the building and skidded to a halt.

'Jamie!' shouted a voice he recognised. 'What on earth? ... Are you all right?'

Jamie could only gape, his mind struggling to make sense of what was happening. Was that Mr Morris, his PE teacher? How could it be?

He leant his good shoulder against the wall, gasping for breath, his hand clutching the hurt one in an instinctive but useless attempt to hold back the pain.

The guy reached out to him. 'What's wrong?' he demanded. 'Is somebody after you?' It was Mr Morris, wasn't it?

Jamie tried to shake his head, to say no and also to clear the mist inside it.

'Come on,' the man said, some of the urgency leaving his voice. 'I'll make you a cup of tea.'

A cup of tea? He knew all the words but what did they mean? PE teachers didn't make cups of tea.

'Sorry,' he croaked. It didn't seem enough. 'Door,' he added.

'Right. In here, Jamie. Good. Right, sit down there, I'm just putting the kettle on.'

Jamie sat. His shoulder still throbbed. He heard water gurgle and stop, followed by a light thud and a click. He was aware of the man moving, of a door opening and closing, and another. More water running.

'OK, Jamie, get that top off while I have a shufti at that shoulder.'

Must have tackled somebody, Jamie's confused mind told him and he obediently took off his jacket, pulled the shirt over his head – and winced. The pain of prodding fingers, then the shock of the cold, moist sponge were familiar and the smell of the embrocation, as was the initial sting that slowed to something almost soothing.

'You'll live,' Mr Morris said.

There was a pause. Jamie leaned back against the wall and closed his eyes.

'There you are, lad. Tea. Black and sweet, do wonders for you. Drink up.'

It was black, and strong, and very sweet. And hot. It was a few minutes before it had an effect. He opened his eyes, the mist had gone. He was in the sports centre. The rugby pitches were just outside.

'Feel like a bit of a kick-about?' Mr Morris stood in the doorway, a rugby ball in his hands. He had his boots on.

A kick-about? But, yeah, that was exactly what he felt like. He reached for his shirt.

'Go and put some practice gear on, you know where the spare stuff is. Should be boots in your size.'

An hour or so later, glowing from the exercise and a brisk shower, warmed inside by the teacher's skilful coaching and some rare, bluff praise, Jamie set off for home. He pulled out his phone and found he had three messages.

They were all from Sophie. 'Where are you?' they said.

Jamie didn't mention the sports centre.

They were on their own, Sophie's mum had gone out.

'You just missed her,' Sophie said. 'She won't be back for ages. She left us some money to order take-away, we can get Thai if we want.'

She was really sympathetic about the meeting as well. Once she'd made sense of his account of it that was. He had to admit - to himself - his account hadn't been all that coherent.

'So Chani asked the social worker to find a replacement for Magda?' Sophie said.

'Yes.'

'And the social worker wouldn't do it?'

'No.'

'Why not? I mean, that would solve everything, wouldn't it?'

This hadn't occurred to Jamie and he had to think about it.

'I suppose it would,' he growled, not wanting to give Chani credit for anything at all.

'So why would she not do it?'

'Who?'

'The social worker.'

'She said they weren't an employment agency.'

'Hnh!' Sophie dismissed the argument. 'They can ring one up, can't they? It's not difficult, there's loads of them. In fact, Chani could ring one up. Has she thought of that?'

'How would I know?' The odd, sideways look Sophie gave him made him uncomfortable. 'I don't know, do I?'

'Did she say anything that might have told you?'

Jamie shrugged. What the hell was she on about? He didn't want to know what the woman said, or thought, he just wanted rid of her. He could live perfectly well on his own.

'I don't need anybody,' he said. 'I don't need a replacement for Magda and I don't need that awful woman.'

'What, you mean, like, live by yourself?'

It was like he'd suggested something totally weird, like going on *Big Brother*, or living in a tent in the Arctic. 'So what's wrong with that?'

Sophie took a breath. 'You'd be OK with shopping and cooking? And washing up? And washing your stuff? Ironing and all that? What about cleaning?'

'Why not? I can do it if I want to.'

'Jamie, you can't even make toast.'

Stung by her derision, he opened his mouth to defend himself but stopped and gave her a withering look instead. 'You do remember when I got the Duke of Edinburgh Award, don't you? And when I was camping with the school in Spain in the winter and I led an expedition up a mountain and we bivouacked overnight and it was snowing.'

'I know,' Sophie said. 'But you still can't make toast.'

'I don't need bloody toast.'

'Chips then. Or cauliflower cheese. Or pasta. Bacon and eggs. Can you make them?'

'I could if I wanted to.'

She half-smiled, frowning at the same time, took a quick breath and let it out slowly. 'Oh, Jamie, this is silly.'

'You started it,' he sulked.

Sophie's smile grew. 'Look, we could ring an employment agency ourselves. Mum has all their numbers. I'll ask her and we'll get somebody tomorrow.'

'Right,' Jamie said, but he didn't believe it would happen. Actually, he felt like he'd been flattened in a tackle.

That night he lay awake for hours, trying to work it all out. Even if he was the world's best chef, even if he'd won all the scout badges for housekeeping or whatever, even if he'd spent his work experience assisting surgeons to fix broken bones, they still wouldn't let him be here on his own, would they. They'd still force him to have that dreadful woman who insisted on being his grandmother living here. It bloody well wasn't fair.

9

Chani's emotions were boiling so much that she couldn't face going back to the house. She was almost choking on the anger and frustration she was feeling: that she couldn't unleash it on to anything or anyone made it much worse. Here, outside in the street, she was in the cold urban air but she was as much a prisoner as if she'd been banged up in Strangeways. Worse, because she hadn't committed a crime.

How could she go on living in that dreadful house, with that dreadful lad, without even Magda to talk to? And she'd have to look after him, all the cooking and cleaning and washing and shopping, with no job and no money. How could she do it?

The situation was so terrifying and so unreal she couldn't even think about it, everything had gone numb.

There, across the road was a pub. She would have one drink while she tried to work out what to do.

Taking no notice of her surroundings she bought a Campari soda and carried it to a seat by a window.

She was there for some time, telling herself she must think of a way out, but her brain simply wouldn't function.

A barmaid drifted towards her, holding stacked glasses.

'Is this dead?' she asked, reaching out for Chani's empty glass.

Chani nodded. Dead. Too right.

She drove back on automatic pilot, through the gates that clanged behind her like prison gates and up to the garage.

'Afraid you'll have to get used to this,' she told Patricia as she locked her up too. She had to find Celandine, this had to be sorted out and the only person who could do that was Celandine. Or Magda? What could Magda tell her? She must have been there when Celandine ran off. She'd told her she was going and they'd organised money and things.

Magda was waiting for her, rushing out of the kitchen as Chani came through the door.

'Mrs ... Chani,' she said, face and hands twisted with anxiety. 'You have the meeting today? With Social Serves?'

'Oh no,' Chani groaned. 'They don't serve.'

Magda's face crumpled from anxious to downcast. 'It was bad?'

'Bad, yes. She won't do anything to help. She won't organise another person to take over when you go, she expects me to stay and look after Jamie with no money. I don't know how I can do it.' She was about to ask what happened when Celandine left but Magda was already speaking.

'I did something today, it will help you,' she said. 'Come have cup of tea and I tell you.'

She urged Chani into the kitchen, sat her down and made the soothing tea that Chani chose.

'I went to bank,' she said, sitting down as well, her eyes bright in a now-eager face. 'I explain them about Jamie and you and every thing. The lady said, they can arrange so money that is paid to me, that is, paid to my account, by Mrs Pomfret-Jones, it can be paid from my account to you. If you can come to bank with me on Monday, you can have account there, special account, for this money. So you will have money for food and every thing. That is good, is it?'

'Magda, that's … I can't take it in. It's good, yes. Thank you for doing that. Thank you for thinking of it.'

'It's one worry less,' she told Vanessa on the phone later, only just able to talk about the horrific meeting. 'I'll be able to pay for stuff, but I'll still have no money for myself.'

'I can't believe it,' Vanessa said again. 'How can she call herself a social worker?'

'No idea.'

'What a cow!'

'Don't demean cows, they do some good. Even if they do produce all that gas.'

'They produce a lot of shit too,' Vanessa said. She must be really upset.

There was something Chani hadn't told her. 'It seems Jamie's been angling to go and live at Sophie's.'

'Has he? Did it come to anything?'

'Apparently not. Frosty Face pressed him on it and he had to admit they hadn't agreed to it.'

'Pity. That could have been the best – maybe not *the best* – but a good, temporary thing. It must be truly awful for you, Chani love, how are you coping?'

Chani sucked in air, though her lungs seemed to have shrunk.

'I don't suppose I am. I do feel a bit better since Magda's news. But I'm still a prisoner. I'll tell you something though, Van, there's no way I'm running round after Jamie like she does. He'll have to learn to do masses more than he does now.'

'Good. So he should. Listen, Chani love, I've a few phone calls to make, I'll have to go. I'll ring you again as soon as I can. Don't let the buggers grind you down.'

Too late, they already had.

Van rang again, in the middle of the next morning 'I've arranged to take a week off next week so I can come and stay with you, if you'd like me to.'

'Really? Really really?'

'Yes, of course really!'

'Van, you're an absolute star! Do you need this hand I'm biting off?'

Vanessa laughed. 'I think it's going to come in handy, don't you? We have some sorting out to do.'

'I like the sound of that. Especially that "we". How are you going to get down here?'

'Train. I'll let you know the time, I'll book it either today or tomorrow.'

'Fantastic, I'll come and meet you.'

'Great, thanks. It'll be Tuesday, I've covered it with the boss and I spent last night on the phone with the team. They've all agreed to cover anything I can't put off till I go back, but there's a case conference on Monday I have to be at. I'd get the train on Monday afternoon but I daren't risk it, this is a biggie and it could run on and on. But it means I won't need to come back here till the following Monday.'

'That's fantastic. I really appreciate this, Van. And your team. You will thank them for me, won't you.' It felt like light had come back into Chani's life. Some light anyway. She had three more days and the rest of that day to get through, but knowing Van would be with her would make it a lot easier. 'Do you really think you can help me sort all this out?' she asked.

'I shall have a damn good try.'

Chani smiled and felt herself relax for the first time since all this had started. People got out of the way of Van's damn good tries.

*

When Jamie arrived at school on Friday Sophie was waiting for him.

'There's a slight snag,' she said. 'I told Mum about our plan and she was all for it.'

'So what's the snag?'

'It's the money part.' She frowned. 'I don't know if it's a problem or not, actually. Do you have enough money to pay this person, when we find her? Or him?'

'Shit,' he said. 'Slight snag! It's a bit more than that.'

Her frown deepened. 'So you haven't any money?'

'No. I mean, I do, but only for myself, not enough to pay someone.'

'So how does Magda get paid?'

Jamie shook his head. That wasn't something he'd ever thought about. 'No idea. So we're stuck, aren't we.' He hadn't realised how much he'd wanted this idea to work until now it couldn't. He felt totally deflated as it sank in, even though he'd never believed it would work.

He couldn't believe Sophie wasn't deflated as well. 'No, it's just something we didn't think about and that we have to find out. Could you …? No, you wouldn't … Look, we'll go straight to yours after school and ask

Magda. Then we can work out what to do. Right?'

Jamie gazed at her almost in awe. She always knew what to do, nothing ever fazed her.

'Oh, God,' she said. 'Everybody's gone in, we'll have to run.'

'See you later,' he said and ran.

Sophie came with Jamie after school. They went straight to find Magda.

She was in the utility room, ironing. She looked up and gave them a wide smile.

'Shall I make a snack?' she asked.

'Thanks, we're OK,' Sophie said, to Jamie's disappointment. He was starving. 'We'd like to talk to you, actually.'

'OK, I can leave this. We can go in kitchen. I have some Polish cake, Jamie will like.'

He brightened. 'Yes, please.'

He had to wait until Magda had piled two plates with food before she could pay attention. Jamie left the talking to Sophie and concentrated on the Polish cake. It was good.

'You see, Magda,' Sophie said. 'Because you're going – which is very sad, we'll miss you a lot – but Jamie will need somebody to take over from you. So we're going to contact some employment agencies that my mother uses but we need to ask you something personal, if you don't mind.'

'Personal?' Magda, looking worried, stopped putting the cake away and stared.

'Well, sort of personal. You see, we'll have to make financial arrangements, I mean, Jamie will, to pay the agency, so we need to change whatever's been arranged about your pay. We need you to tell us ...'

'Ah, but no,' Magda said, waving her hands around. 'It is changed. Today, with Mrs ... Chani. We have been at bank and changed so Mrs Chani have money. So you have no need, Jamie. You have no worry.' She smiled.

Jamie saw how pleased she was and felt sick. This was the worst news.

'I see.' Even Sophie looked crestfallen. She actually ate a piece of cake.

'All right,' she said, in her usual voice. 'So we need to talk to Chani. She won't know about the agencies. Do you know where she is, please, Magda?'

'She is out, she does shopping. For her friend, who comes next week. I must finish iron, so I can make room ready for friend. Excuse me, please.'

'What friend?' Jamie asked.

'She is friend from where Mrs Chani lives. She comes to stay.'

As Magda left Jamie groaned. 'Two of them,' he said, despairing. 'And she gets the money.'

'Oh, Jamie, don't you see? When we tell Chani about the agencies she'll get someone and she can pay for it. And then she'll go home. That's what you want, isn't it? Though I like her, actually.'

'I bet she doesn't go,' he moaned.

'Wait and see what she says when she comes in.'

'We can't,' he said, with a grin he couldn't hold back. 'We're meeting Adam and Tamara aren't we? Was it at Tamara's or at Adam's?' He hadn't wanted to go when Sophie arranged it, now it seemed a brilliant idea.

'Oh, right, yes. We're meeting them at Den's place, at half six. I need to go home and change.'

'Give me ten minutes,' Jamie said. 'And I'll come with you.' Sophie gave him a big smile, believing, he could see, that he was being helpful. Good, let her think that.

*

Chani put Patricia away and came in to find Magda waiting for her.

'Come,' Magda greeted her. 'I put your friend next to you. Will she like?'

'Oh, good, thank you.' Chani followed her upstairs and Magda, with obvious pride, opened what would be Van's door. The room was identical to Chani's – what Chani's had been like before she'd made it liveable, that was. But what could she say? 'It's beautifully done,' she tried. 'Very neat.'

Magda beamed. 'Also I made many meals – I make more now – and I freeze. I think I cannot freeze your vegetable food?'

'That's right,' Chani lied, relieved Magda hadn't tried. 'You can't. But it's fine, I can make them myself. I like cooking, but I'm glad you made things Jamie likes.'

Magda beamed even more. 'I will do more,' she said, before tripping off, looking happier and more relaxed than Chani had yet seen her.

Chani was not happy or relaxed. She had changed her mind about shopping for Vanessa and instead had spent the day so far researching how to find Celandine. She should have done it ages ago, but stuff had happened and it had filled up her mind, not to mention disturbing her chi. Ignoring that, she'd started online by Googling Linda Pomfret-Jones, but found her only as Senior Partner at her firm of accountants. She rang the firm.

'Sorry, Ms Caladan,' a snooty receptionist told her, 'Mrs Pomfret-Jones is no longer with us.'

'Do you mean she's left? She isn't, sort of, on leave?'

'She is no longer with us.' And that was all she could find out there.

When she tried phoning the police they just told her what Ffrosty-Face had said.

'But her son doesn't know where she is,' she'd said.

'Maybe, but his mother has made arrangements for his care. And, her son hasn't contacted us himself, has he? I'm afraid there's nothing we can do, given the way things are at the moment.'

Celandine wasn't on Facebook or anything else online Chani knew about and the electoral roll was less than helpful. She already knew the address in Marlowe Drive. She wanted to scream.

She'd stamped around for a bit, swearing, until she'd gone and sat in Patricia for some sort of comfort, started the engine and driven off with no idea of where she was going. She'd got totally lost and it had taken nearly an hour to find her way back. By then, all she could think about was finding out what Magda knew about when Celandine went away. Nothing was going to get in her way, nothing.

Magda was in the utility room.

'I need to ask you something, Magda, if you don't mind.'

Magda stopped folding laundry. 'I don't mind.'

'I've been trying to find out where Cel, I mean, Jamie's mother, where she's gone. I'm getting nowhere, so I wondered if you had any idea. Did she say anything to you about that?'

'No, she did not say, she did not tell me she was going, she left a note. It was in her room, I find it, it say to me, to me, not to Jamie. It say she has gone away, but not where she goes. She say about arrangements for Jamie and can I stay in house, look after Jamie, stay at night.' Her English had gone again, she must be upset. Not surprising.

'That's all she did, left a note? She didn't talk to you, she didn't discuss with you about if you could stay all the time?'

Magda still held the towel she hadn't finished folding. She shook her head. 'No.'

'That's ... that's so ... I can't believe it, that's just shameful. I'm sorry, Magda, she shouldn't have treated you like that.'

'Yes, but the day, the before day, I think she have a, a fall-out with Jamie. I don't know what about, but they both shout, they both angry. I don't know if that was reason, they angry and shouting on other times.'

'Did they? Did they get angry and shout at each other at lot?'

'A lot, I think, yes. Many. But that time, I see her, and she was sad. I notice it.'

'Sad? Not angry?'

'Sad, yes. Angry before, angry that time too but as well, sad.'

That was interesting. What about Jamie?

'Did she leave a note for Jamie?'

Magda's eyebrows furrowed her forehead and pushed her eyes almost closed. 'I don't know, I think she did not. It was, when Mrs Pomfret-Jones ... it was, she went when I was not here, I came and she was not ... I found note, I take it to Jamie, I can see, he shock, I know he no idea, he very very shock. So I think she did not say to him.' It didn't seem possible her eyebrows could frown any more but they did. 'There was another thing, I did not think before, I see him and I know he ... is like he afraid. He say, but quiet, I can't hear all, "Oh, God, I didn't mean ..." I can't explain good. I think what he say to his mother? How he make her sad? I remember now. But Tomasz say you must speak Social Serves, you should not be, is too much responsible.'

Chani could have cried at such concern.

*

Jamie managed to avoid the awful woman all weekend, by hanging around after the Saturday rugby match, then going straight on to Sophie's, and by spending the day with her on Sunday. It was a pretty boring day, lounging around watching TV, doing homework and playing computer games, but at least he was spending it with her. They had some fun with her Wii, especially when she fell over trying to play tennis like Serena Williams. She laughed as much as he did but insisted on putting it away after that. Her parents had hardly been in. He and Sophie had had pizza on Saturday so on Sunday he suggested going out. It was a good idea, they met several of Sophie's friends and went with them for burgers.

It all helped him to avoid thinking about the future

after Magda went away and Chani's friend came. Two of them. It couldn't get worse.

Their friends had already arranged to go on to the cinema. 'Are you coming?' they asked.

'Great,' Jamie said, not even asking what the movie was.

But Sophie stepped in. 'Sorry,' she said. 'We'd've loved to, but there's something we have to do. If you're going next week we could come with you, couldn't we, Jamie.'

'What?'

'Go next week.'

And he'd thought it couldn't get worse. 'Oh. Er…'

'Right.' Sophie gave him her warmest smile before turning it on the others. She was very close to him all at once.

To a chorus of, 'Cool, cool, see you then,' the friends moved away.

'What do we have to do?' Jamie asked, more than a bit miffed.

10

All weekend Chani was in a state of turmoil. It was wonderful that Vanessa was coming, but all she could think about was Ffrosty Fface's callous treatment of her. Anger came in waves, big waves. Bloody Ffrosty Fface. Because of her she would have to stay here with Jamie. She felt sick and ill, heavy with lost hope. And soon Van would go home again, how could she cope then? She couldn't bear it.

All she could do was try to be positive. Could she do it? Try to think of positive things. What things, there were no positive things? At least she would have some money, there was that, but how much it would be? Would there be enough for her to buy a drink, or a meal out, or anything? And all her friends were in Hebden Bridge, she would lose all that, her friends and her job were her life. She'd have no life down here. The thought of being stuck in that dreadful house all day, alone and lonely tore at her. At home she was never lonely. At home she mattered to people, and people mattered to her. How could she lose that?

Of course, her job would go. Melissa would finish her without a qualm.

And her house. Hell's teeth, her house. Could she somehow keep it? She'd never be able to pay the bills on it, even if she could ever get a weekend, or even a week in it. Could she rent it out? That would help pay the bills. But whatever rent she might get wouldn't cover very much besides the bills and there'd be upkeep, repairs, who knew what to pay for. Despair rained down like volcanic ash.

She loved that house. It was ironic, wasn't it, she'd spent her life believing in not being attached to possessions, in travelling light, going with the flow, in being defined by who and what you were, not by what you owned. And here she was, distraught at the idea of losing a house.

She had to sit down, it was as if someone had punched her.

It was some time before she could get near to reasoning it out. It wasn't the house itself, was it, it was what the house *meant*. She'd never be able to recreate that down here, even if she somehow managed the impossible feat of getting her and Jamie out of this awful house and into something more human.

Which of course, without Celandine's agreement, she couldn't do.

Bloody Celandine, she'd behaved like a selfish child, only thinking about her own pleasure. Not even leaving a contact phone number. And, it seemed, storming off because of a row with Jamie. A heat like an acetylene flame raged inside her. So, Magda thought she'd looked sad, well, kids made you sad, get on with it. Have rows, be sad, but don't dump the problems on other people. Especially when it meant Chani having to give everything up for this, this terrible place. Curse the stupid girl!

She slept badly that night, but when she woke on Sunday she felt a shade more relaxed, a shade less despairing, maybe because it was almost ten and she'd slept for over ten hours.

Holding on to this tiny bit of upbeat mood, she went downstairs in her dressing gown to an empty kitchen. Yes, Magda went to church the previous Sunday didn't she. With the house to herself Chani made herself breakfast on a tray and took it back to bed, listening to her music as she ate, taking her time. A long session of yoga, a soak in the bath with soothing aromatherapy candles burning and a relaxing meditation and she began to feel she could perhaps cope.

And on Tuesday Vanessa was coming.

Tuesday. What did she need to do on Tuesday? She stood and pushed herself into organising mode. Magda would be going after breakfast on Tuesday to her own home and would leave with her husband later in the day. Jamie would be at school. Vanessa's train was due at three fifteen, so Chani should set off for the station at quarter to, as she wasn't sure about parking.

A knock at her door interrupted her.

'Come in,' she called, expecting it to be Magda.

It was Sophie.

'Oh, Sophie,' she said, surprised but pleased. 'How nice. Do come in. Are you on your own?'

'Jamie's downstairs,' Sophie said. Her eyes flickered round the room and her polite expression changed to raised eyebrows and a hurriedly cut-off 'Oh'. Her hand went to her mouth as she gave a little cough. She turned to face Chani and smiled. 'We wanted to talk to you, but one of Jamie's friends just called him – something about rugby, he'll be ages – so I came myself.'

So Jamie had refused to come with her.

113

'You don't mind?' Sophie was saying.

'Of course not. Talk away.'

Chani sat on the bed, leaving Sophie to choose one of the uncomfortable chairs.

Sophie joined her on the bed. 'Jamie told me the social worker wouldn't do anything about finding a replacement for Magda,' she began.

Chani nodded. So Jamie had actually told her about that dreadful meeting. How much had he told her?

Sophie tossed her hair back. 'I don't know why she wouldn't. It's simple enough. So I got some phone numbers of agencies from my mother. Jamie and I were going to ring them and organise someone but we found out about the arrangement, the financial arrangement, that is.'

'Ah,' Chani said. 'Have you talked to Magda?'

'We talked to her, yes.' Sophie explained what Magda had told them about the bank. Chani confirmed it and Sophie smiled. 'So,' she said. 'Would you like the phone numbers? So you can ring up?'

Something shifted in Chani's mind, like curtains opening to let in the daylight. If she could actually find someone to take over from Magda she'd be free. Free to leave, to go home.

'Sophie, you're a treasure.' Excitement rose. 'Phone numbers are exactly what I'd like. You don't know, I suppose, whether these agencies might deal with live-in help?'

'I assume they do, but Mummy has only ever had dailies.'

Imagine a life that involved daily help with household chores! 'That's really helpful,' she said. 'I'm so pleased you thought of it. Are you having a meal here?'

Sophie lowered her eyes. 'We've eaten, actually.'

She looked uncomfortable and Chani wanted to go and yell at Jamie. But hey, she had some phone numbers. First thing tomorrow, she could contact these agencies.

'No problem,' she said. 'I've eaten too.'

This lovely girl. Surely she wouldn't even think of going out with Jamie if there was the slightest possibility of him doing the 'bad things' Magda had worried about.

As Magda and Tomasz were leaving very early on Tuesday morning Chani insisted Magda took everything she needed from the house on Monday afternoon so she could spend that night with Tomasz in their own home.

'Forget about making breakfast or anything else here on Tuesday morning,' she insisted.

She had to insist quite a lot before Magda finally agreed.

Chani had a strong sense of virtue at her selflessness, however abandoned it meant she was – the one who was being helpful – at her own great expense – when Magda could have stayed longer, at least till Jamie went off to France. It was all Celandine's bloody fault.

For some reason she thought about the washing machine. And the tumble dryer. She would have to use them but how the hell did they work? They all looked incredibly complicated. She needed Magda to show her.

It took most of the evening. They were incredibly complicated.

'This for cotton,' Magda said, demonstrating. 'This for, not cotton, like acryilthing. And for Jamie's rugby things you do this.'

'Why does anyone need machines that do so much stuff?' Chani said, panicking, there was no way she'd remember all this. And as for the tumble dryer—

'I always dry stuff outside,' she said and Magda, pink-faced and struggling with her English, took a deep breath.

'I also, before. But here, outside is not for putting laundry. Mrs Pomfret-Jones say it's not to do.'

'Not done?'

'Yes. No, not done. You can't do it.'

Of course. She should have known. Lower the tone, wouldn't it.

Chani had another restless night, tried next morning when Magda had gone to operate the dishwasher, but had to give up because she was late going to meet Vanessa.

Van was standing there, looking resigned, though patient, her bags beside her.

'Sorry, I'm really late,' Chani panted, having run from where she'd had to park Patricia.

'No problem,' Vanessa said.

Chani flung her arms round her. 'It's brilliant to see you. I've been struggling with the damned machines, I'll never understand them.'

Van hugged her back, and laughed. 'What a welcome! Did you have to pay for parking? Some of these machines are a bit fiendish.'

'No, it was free for fifteen minutes.'

Light dawned. 'No, not that sort of machine. It's the washing machine and the tumble dryer, they're so complicated. I'll have to do it by hand. Or find a laundrette.'

Vanessa's amusement became a puzzled frown. She sort of shook herself, stopped frowning and said, 'Sounds awful, Chani love.' She stood back and gave her a scrutinising look, not saying anything but pursing her lips. 'Your fifteen minutes'll be up if we don't move soon,' she added.

Her look, combined with the silence, worried Chani. Did she look that bad? 'Sorry,' she said again. 'I must sound like a lunatic. Come on, it's this way.' She grabbed one of her friend's bags and marched towards the car park. 'It's fantastic you could come,' she said as they walked. 'I owe you. And your team.'

'They're a great team,' Van agreed. It seemed a bit enigmatic to Chani, still thrown by that odd look.

'How are things at home?' she asked, starting the engine.

Van wrestled with the seatbelt as she always did – it was an early design – until she got to grips with it. 'Much the same.' She passed on what little gossip there was. 'You've only been gone just over a week.'

'A week?' Chani almost missed the red light. 'Is that all? It feels like months.'

She pulled up outside the house. 'Here it is,' she announced. 'Castle Doom, with me now in sole charge.'

'Not sole charge,' Van reminded her. 'There's two of us now.'

Chani smiled, but she was thinking about what was going to happen when Van went home again.

She had planned how she would show her the house. She opened the door, carrying one of Vanessa's bags which she put on the hall floor. 'We'll leave your stuff here for now while I give you the grand tour.'

She'd been watching her friend carefully, had seen how her eyes had widened at her first sight of the house. Now she saw them narrow as Van walked into the hall. She went quiet and seemed to close in on herself when Chani showed her the ground floor rooms. But the kitchen shocked her into speech.

'My God! It's like a hospital!'

'Isn't it. You can see why I hate it. I've been in cosier dentists' surgeries.'

'I can. It's ... a bit stark.' Van moved around, eyes narrowing as her frown grew. 'It doesn't feel like a home, more like a show kitchen. I suppose this is what they call minimalist.'

Chani led her away. 'Come and see upstairs. I'll show you the bathroom, you've got an en-suite as well.'

'Really?'

'Really, I think every bedroom has one.'

Vanessa was again stunned to silence by the main bathroom. Chani moved her on to the bedroom Magda had made up for her. 'I'm sorry about this,' she said. All the rooms are identical. I searched through all the bedding for something a bit less grim but this pale grey is the best I could do.'

Van draped her coat on the bed, its warm blue brightened the room instantly. 'Nnn, she murmured through clenched teeth, as if she'd found she was biting

118

a lemon when she'd expected a peach. 'I don't know how you're sleeping, it's like the grave.'

Chani had kept her own room till last. 'I know. I had to spend some money I can't really afford before I could stand it. Come and see.' She was gratified when Vanessa stopped dead in the doorway and said, 'Ah,' in a tight voice, before moving slowly round it, as if in a daze.

Chani lit her aromatherapy burner. 'I've put one of these in your room,' she said. 'I thought it might help.'

'Oh ...' Vanessa's voice trailed off and she sat on the bed. 'I see what ... this room's more, sort of, you. You've ... I mean, you've gone for, well, soft fabrics, haven't you. And, erm, bright colours, I mean, warm. Like that orange and purple rug.'

'It's called tangerine and grape.' Chani perched on the metal chair, on which she'd put her Indian fabric cushion, but remembered the little mirrors and stood up again, to replace it with the one that matched the rug. 'I had to do something, I couldn't meditate.'

Van's eyebrows rose, creating ridges in her forehead. 'And you can now?'

'Oh yes, mostly. And I need to, believe me.'

Vanessa said nothing, just gazed around until she made a small sound in her throat, lifted her head as if pulling herself out of the stunned state she was in and said, 'How will you manage now Magda's gone? It was today, wasn't it?'

'This morning, early. She left here last night, actually. I don't know how I'll manage. At least, the food side's more or less sorted out, Magda made lots of meals for Jamie and froze them – I didn't show you her

119

system, you won't believe it, but it's the best way to cope with the way he is. Mind you, if he keeps on eating at Sophie's I won't need to even microwave stuff for him. So it shouldn't run out for ages. By which time I hope I'll have organised someone else to be here!'

'I'm sure that makes perfect sense if I just give it time to sink in,' Vanessa said, pulling a face. 'But you look as if you have some news?'

'Not news, but a possibility.' She told Vanessa about Sophie's phone numbers. 'I tried some this morning but they didn't have anyone at the moment. I might be able to ring more of them later today.'

'Good, I hope it works. You'd be asking a lot, though. I presume you'd want this person to live in? And if you find someone who'll do it, they'll have to be checked out by Social Services and the police.'

'Will they?'

'Yes, of course. To work with children.'

'What, even sixteen-year-olds?'

Vanessa sighed. 'Absolutely.'

Chani groaned. 'How long would that take?'

'It depends how busy they are. A week or two at least.'

Chani groaned again. 'Bloody hell. This whole thing's impossible.'

'I'm sure we can sort something out. I gather things with Jamie are still the same?'

'The same.' Chani rolled her eyes and gave a hopeless shrug.

Vanessa put on what Chani recognised as her concerned social worker face. 'Well, Chani love, think what he's been through.'

120

Chani felt herself snap. 'Oh, don't give me all that social worker stuff. I know it.'

Vanessa leaned forward, frowning and held up a hand. 'Chani love, the lad must be *grieving*.'

'Yes.' She had to admit it. But she was still aggrieved. 'All right, but it still doesn't mean he has to carry on like a spoiled brat. And after I've had to just dump my life and come all the way down here – for him! You'd think I'd *chosen* to come here and *force* myself on him!'

'Yes, I suppose … it must be really awful for you, I know.'

Chani's built-up frustration smouldered at this supposedly soothing social worker speak, but then Van had gone to so much trouble in order to come and support her, hadn't she. She gritted her teeth to hold back the bitter words but she couldn't stop a huff of breath bursting out. 'Well, all I can say is, thank God for Sophie,' she said, to try and cover it up. 'At least she talks to me. And she's pleasant, and well-mannered.'

At that moment they heard the front door open and close and the sound of voices.

It was almost as if she'd conjured her up. 'Wow!' Chani said. 'That's her now. And Jamie, would you believe it!'

'That's them?' Vanessa sat up, her face lighting up.

'It is, let's go down.' Let battle commence.

11

The television was on in the lounge – already – it sounded like football. Chani opened the door and showed Vanessa in. Immediately Sophie's head turned and she gave a delighted smile.

'Chani, hi.'

Jamie was still concentrating on the screen. There was a roar from the watching crowd and the commentator's voice went high with excitement. 'What a try! he cried.

Rugby then.

'Hello, Sophie, Jamie,' Chani said. 'This is my friend, Vanessa. She's come to stay for a few days. I think Magda told you, Jamie.'

'Hello, Vanessa,' Sophie said, standing up and coming towards them. As if she were welcoming them to her own house, she said to Vanessa, 'Have you just arrived?' The perfect hostess, she engaged her in professionally-timed welcoming small talk, before moving to sit next to Jamie who was still totally focussed on the game.

Vanessa smiled and sat opposite them. 'Hello, Jamie,' she said. 'I see you're keen on rugby.'

'Yes.' He didn't move.

'Do you play for the school team?' Vanessa asked as if he were paying her polite attention.

'He's good,' Sophie enthused. 'He's done loads of scoring.'

Jamie groaned but still didn't move.

'Do you go and watch, then, Sophie?' Vanessa asked, including her in the conversation she was pretending to be having with Jamie.

'Sometimes.' Sophie smiled. 'There are parties afterwards sometimes, aren't there, Jamie?' She touched him as she spoke.

Chani could only see his back, but it looked uncomfortable. On the screen the crowd was going mad again as the try was converted. The commentator was hoarse with joy. Jamie's back seemed to lower and loosen, conveying a sort of release of tension, he appeared to be thumping his knee with his hand.

'That's good,' Vanessa was saying. 'You can't study all the time. I suppose you're in the middle of GCSEs.'

'Actually,' Sophie confided. 'We did most of them last year. We're doing A levels now.'

'Oh,' Vanessa said. 'Not AS levels, then?'

'In a way, AS is sort of the first year. We'll finish half the A levels next year and the rest the year after, before we go up.'

Her hand, Chani noticed was resting on something on the seat cushion by her side. It was a CD.

'What's the CD you've got there, Sophie?' she asked. Did Sophie still use them?

Sophie turned to her, animated. 'Emeli Sandé, I just bought it, Jamie's going to use his sound system to put it on my iPod, it's better quality than what I can download, isn't it, Jamie.' Jamie's shoulders lifted slightly. 'Do you know her stuff?' she said.

'Not really,' Chani said. 'I'm into soul music myself.'

'That's what she does – soul,' Sophie said, looking surprised.

'Really? I don't know her.'

'Oh, right. She's fairly new, I suppose. Do you like Angie Stone? Or Amy Winehouse?'

Chani perched where she could talk to Sophie. She could see Jamie's side now as well as his back. 'I don't know the Angie one, but I thought Amy Winehouse was quite good. Actually, I prefer Aretha Franklin and Sam Cooke, Booker T, that kind of stuff.' Out of the corner of her eye she noticed the rugby match had finished and jumped when Jamie spoke.

'The dead old stuff,' he said, or, rather, sneered, his upper lip lifting slightly.

'It is old,' Sophie said. 'But I've heard Aretha Franklin, she's good.'

'You liked her?' Chani's head jerked round and she smiled, only just stopping herself from saying 'Wow!' 'What have you heard her sing?'

Sophie closed her eyes and went still. 'Oh, I know,' she said, coming back to life. 'It was 'Sisters Are Doing It For Themselves'. She was with a group, I can't remember the name.'

'The Eurythmics,' Chani said. 'That's one of her later ones. I think her earlier songs were best – like 'Respect' and 'You Make Me Feel Like a Natural Woman'.'

'Yes,' Sophie said, full of lively interest. 'I've heard that one too, 'Natural Woman', it's cool.'

Chani beamed at her. 'Those are all on my iPod if you want to listen again.'

'Cool, I'd like to, thanks.' There was real enthusiasm there, not polite pretend enthusiasm. 'You can listen to Angie Stone on mine some time, I think you'd like her.'

'What groups do you listen to, Jamie?' Vanessa was trying again, as Chani thanked Sophie.

'I listen to opera, actually,' the Roman emperor told his pushy slaves.

'Ah,' Vanessa said, 'I don't know a lot about that myself. Have you been to opera performances? In London maybe, it's not far from here is it?'

Chani watched with awe, especially when Jamie said, 'I used to go a lot.'

'With your mother?' Vanessa asked and Chani held her breath.

'Yeah.' Jamie's back, along with his side and his front, stiffened. 'We should go, Sophs.' He started to stand up. 'We can do your CD another time.' His feet were already moving.

'Oh,' Sophie said, unconcerned. 'Cool.' She moved in a leisurely way to follow him, turning charming smiles on Chani and Vanessa. 'Bye, then, Chani. Bye, Vanessa.'

The two women exchanged looks when the door had closed.

'I see what you mean,' Vanessa said. 'He just clammed up, didn't he, the minute I mentioned his mum.' Her eyes were bright with interest.

Chani felt wrung out. 'Absolutely. But you got far more out of him than I've managed in all this time.'

'Honestly? But that wasn't much.'

Chani's shrug was huge, it included her arms and hands stretched out wide. Vanessa grinned.

Time to change the subject. Poor Vanessa hadn't even had chance to get her bags upstairs. 'Did you get anything to eat on the train?' she asked.

'I had a sandwich. I could murder a cup of tea, is there any?'

'Ordinary, caffeine tea?'

'Preferably.'

'I'll have a look.'

'I'll come with you.'

While they waited for the kettle Chani showed Vanessa Magda's food filing system, grinning when Vanessa just stared, speechless and had to sit down.

'I know,' Chani said.

Refreshed by the tea Vanessa went to unpack and Chani quickly rinsed their mugs. Before she could go up to talk to Van, Sophie appeared.

'Hi, Chani,' she said, coming in.

'Sophie, hello again.' There was no sign of Jamie. 'Are you by yourself?'

'Jamie's gone to get changed.' Sophie pulled out a chair and sat down, so that Chani felt bound to join her. 'My parents are taking us out for a meal.'

'Ah – he didn't say,' Chani said. No wonder, her parents must be tired of all that cooking for him.

'I'm sorry,' Sophie said, 'he probably forgot.'

Chani couldn't say what she wanted to. 'It's nice of your parents to do that,' she said instead.

Sophie considered that, briefly. 'Yes,' she said. It held an edge of surprise and an undertone of boredom, both covered by a charming smile.

Interesting, but keep to the agenda. 'What do they do, your parents? Work, I mean.'

'Daddy's a consultant neurologist.'

'Ah.' He would be. 'At the hospital here?' Chani remembered the road signs.

'Yes. He has a private practice in London as well.'

Of course. It would be Harley Street, wouldn't it. 'Busy man,' she said.

Sophie nodded. 'He is, he's always working. He might not make it this evening.'

Chani offered a sympathetic smile. 'Does your mum work?'

Sophie nodded again. 'She does some translating sometimes. She's half French.'

'Is she, how interesting.' Chani filed the information away. She had thought of something else. 'That must explain the changing colours of your aura.'

Sophie's eyes startled to wide. 'My ... oh. Really?' She frowned. 'Is that bad?'

'No. No, it's brilliant.'

'Is it?'

Chani opened her mouth to explain, but Sophie carried on. 'Jamie said you're from the north somewhere.'

'Yes, that's right. Hebden Bridge.' Of course Sophie would never have heard of the place. 'It's in Yorkshire, just, not far from the border with Lancashire.'

There was no flicker of recognition in Sophie's eyes, but there was interest.

'Is it a good place?' Sophie asked.

'It's a very creative place, positive; very healing, actually. I'm at the Mind and Body Centre there, therapy.'

'Yeah?' Her face had lit up. 'My mum's into all that. There's this spa hotel she goes to, with her friends.'

'That's great. Empowering, a group of women together.'

Somewhere in Chani's mind a bright light flashed. 'You and Jamie should do that, you know.'

Sophie's brows drew together. Chani ignored it. 'Maybe you could go over Christmas. I could arrange it for you if you were interested, unless of course you'd want to go where your mum's been.'

'Oh, no,' Sophie said, her face clearing before she frowned again. 'Did Jamie not tell you?'

Chani felt a pang of alarm, but Sophie's frown went as she said, 'We're going to France, skiing with my parents, we have a chateau there.'

'France?'

'Yes, Jamie came last year.'

'Ah, yes, you said, your mother's half French.'

'You don't mind, do you? Jamie should have told you.'

Chani pulled a face. 'Yes, well.' None of Jamie's rudeness was Sophie's fault. But if she ever laid eyes on Celandine again she would have a lot to say to her. An awful lot.

'Do you mind, Chani?' That was the second time she'd said it. And her eyes searched Chani's while her fingers twined into the chain round her neck. Did she think Chani would refuse? Or ...?

'Mind that he didn't tell me?'

'Well ... I meant about him coming to France with us. Over Christmas. Especially when you've come all this way and you didn't know about it.'

'Oh. God, no, I don't mind at all. You'll have a wonderful time, I'm sure.' She was only just stopping herself dancing and whooping with joy.

Sophie gave a warm smile.

Chani smiled too, trying to keep at least half her jubilation hidden.

As soon as Sophie went she dashed up to tell Vanessa. 'Van,' she said, panting from the speed at which she'd moved. 'I can go home for Christmas!'

'You can? How?'

Chani explained, finishing with, 'Three weeks they're going for. Three weeks!'

'Wonderful. Did Sophie say when exactly?'

'No. She didn't. I didn't think to ask.'

'Only, if you're going to try for a live-in housekeeper you'll need to know. You won't want them here when the place is empty, and you won't want to be paying them for three weeks when you don't need. In fact, it's probably best if they didn't start till he comes back, nobody'll want to move in for such a short time and then move out again, just for three weeks.'

Chani could almost see the dark cloud descend. 'No. I suppose not. I hadn't thought of that.' Trust Van to be the practical one. 'I'll see if I can catch them …' She heard the front door close. 'Hell and damnation, that'll be them going. I'll have to wait now. God knows when he'll appear again.'

'Let's have a think,' Vanessa suggested. 'I'll get the wine I brought.'

'Wonderful.'

'White or red?' In one hand she held a bottle of Merlot, in the other Chablis.

'Chablis! Fantastic! But it won't be cold, I'll put it in the freezer and put some glasses in the fridge.'

Wine in hand, nibbling cheese and olives, Vanessa opened the Think.

'What's today?' she began. 'The fourteenth. That's ten days before Christmas Eve. They'd surely travel to France before then. Do you know when school finishes?'

'No idea.'

Vanessa found her dairy and did some quick calculations. 'Right,' she said, surfacing. 'Unless the new term starts on the third of January, which I'd say is unlikely, they'll break up next Tuesday or Wednesday. That doesn't give them a lot of time to get to France, Wednesday's the twenty-second. But that's when the schools finish in Hebden, so until Jamie tells us I think we're best working on that.'

Chani had lost interest. 'So what are you saying?'

Vanessa's sigh was brief. 'I'm trying to work out how much time we have to get Jamie organised to go away, to France, for a skiing trip.'

'I see.' She wasn't at all used to thinking about what Jamie needed. She hadn't done it for Celandine, who'd been able to think for herself from an early age, Chani had made sure of that. She really didn't want to have to start doing all that now.

Vanessa had found a notebook and a pen.

'What're you writing?'

'A list. Of what he'll need, so we can find out if he has those things, where they are and if they're ready to take. You said they're going for three weeks, didn't you? And did you say it was to the family chateau?'

Chani nodded.

'OK, we can assume there'll be facilities, like for washing clothes, so he won't need three weeks' worth of everything.'

Chani gaped at her.

Van gave a tight smile. 'Like underpants and socks.'

'Ah.'

'He'll need warm clothes, thick woollies for outside and thinner ones for inside. And skiing gear, we need to know what he has.'

'Sophie said he went last year,' Chani remembered. Was Van leading up to a search of Jamie's wardrobes and drawers? Hell's teeth!

But Vanessa was putting the notebook away. 'We can't do any more till we speak to him. I don't suppose you have his mobile number?'

Chani laughed.

'Or Sophie's home number?'

'No.'

'OK. We just wait, then. What are we doing about a meal?'

Chani, realising she was starving, led her to the kitchen, and the wine.

12

The only sign Chani and Vanessa found of Jamie next day was the mess he left in the kitchen, where he'd clearly made himself cereal, leaving the packet on its side, dribbling what was left in it on to the table and overflowing to the floor, and an empty milk carton, doing the same. The dish he'd used was on the counter near the door.

'Hmmm.' Chani pointed towards the utility room, its door wide open. 'You don't need to be a detective to see he's taken some clean clothes.'

'What do you mean?' Vanessa peered round her. 'Oh I see. You're referring to the shirts he's pulled off the rail and left in a heap on the floor, no doubt?'

'That Magda ironed, yes. And what used to be a neat pile of underwear. I know she took loads of stuff to his room to put away, I saw her going up with them. Everything in here was airing, she said.'

'She did everything for him, then?'

'Van, she probably dressed him. Except I think she was too pious to do that.'

'Maybe we establish some ground rules here.'

'I'm not sure how, if he's never here to be told them.'

'He has to be here some time.'

'That's being optimistic.'

'All right then. I suggest that after breakfast we ring the school and find out when they're finishing. At least we'll know that. What's the school called?'

But Chani couldn't remember. In the end they had to Google independent schools to find it.

Chani rang, wincing and pulling a face when she had to explain that she was Jamie's grandmother. But she found out the date. 'They finish on the seventeenth,' she announced.

'Friday,' Vanessa said.

Next morning when Chani went down for breakfast she found Vanessa pacing, shrugging and making little grunting sounds.

'Morning, Van.'

There was no return greeting. Instead, Vanessa demanded, 'Whatever time does he leave the house in the morning?'

Forcing back the words 'I told you so', Chani said, 'Why? What's happened?'

Vanessa made a sound somewhere between a snort and a sigh. 'I was up at half seven, I was determined to talk to him. I heard the shower going in his room so I came downstairs and all I found was the same mess as he left yesterday. He'd just gone off and left it.'

Chani nodded, wondering where Van was going with this all too familiar stuff.

'I cleared it up of course. I was just finishing when I heard him on the stairs so I rushed out. All I saw was the front door closing. He must move at the speed of light.'

She couldn't hold it back. 'Welcome to my world.'

Vanessa's lips thinned even more.

'Sorry, couldn't resist. But that's what's been happening all this time.'

'Yes, I realise. But look, how does he get to school?'

'No idea.'

'He must get there incredibly early.'

'Maybe he walks. I've never thought about it.' And she didn't want to. 'I need a cup of tea. Have you had your breakfast?'

Vanessa shook her head.

Vanessa's interrogation continued during breakfast, mostly questions, like had Magda made Jamie packed lunches, that Chani couldn't answer. Vanessa's frowns grew until they turned into a huge sigh. Finally, she pushed her plate away, leaned her elbows on the table, fixed Chani with determined eyes and said, 'If we don't talk to him very soon we're just going to go on with this mess and he'll never learn and we'll get nowhere with him.'

Chani poured a second cup of tea. With Van in this mood, she needed it. But what could she say? Hadn't she been over and over this already?'

'Beyond leaving him a note, which wouldn't be much use, I don't know. I've racked my brains but I can't think of anything. One thing I do know,' and Chani banged her still half-full mug down, spilling some. 'I am not going to pick up anything he leaves on the floor, either in there or in his room. It'll stay where he's left it. Maybe if he has to wear creased and dirty stuff he'll make the connection between heap on the floor and creased and dirty clothes. Or – and this is what we want – he'll come charging to us to complain. We've got him then.'

Yes, that would work, why hadn't she thought of it before?

'Yes,' Vanessa said, in a tone so dry she might have been in the Sahara for weeks. 'At half past six in the morning?'

Chani grinned through her self-satisfied glow. 'If that's what it takes.'

Vanessa frowned. 'Chani love, I have to say, you seem to be seeing this like a war.'

'Isn't it?'

The frown deepened, overlaid now with concern. 'You can't blame him for the way he's been brought up, you know. He's always had Magda, or somebody, doing everything for him. He doesn't know any other way.'

'Well, it's time he learned. He shouldn't expect me to do what Magda did. He surely didn't expect his mother to.'

'I bet he did. But look, there's no point you and me arguing, is there, we need to work out a plan.'

Chani finished her tea and leaned back. 'We have all day to do it in. And I don't know about you, but I'd rather do thinking and planning somewhere away from here.'

Vanessa nodded. 'The place is like a heavy grey blanket on the mind, isn't it.'

'I couldn't have put it better.' Chani gazed out of the window. 'It doesn't look too bad a day, let's find somewhere to walk.'

She drove until they found some woodland, happy to spend the morning walking through it, even though the area was so small they had to keep doubling back and going round a different way. Around midday she drove them to the shops, with a detour to the pub for lunch. She felt much better when they arrived at the house in time for Jamie coming home from school. If he did.

Of course, he didn't.

'Doesn't he let you know?' Vanessa sounded surprised.

'No. He never let Magda know, it wasn't just me, though I thought at first it was.' She watched Vanessa move to Plan B, could almost see the switches go off and on. But what Van said came as a surprise.

'OK, Chani, I'm going to treat you to a meal out. Let's go and find a decent restaurant. In a taxi.'

'Van —' Chani began but Van was in full flow.

'And tomorrow morning I'm going to be up at six. I'm going to catch Jamie and I'm going to insist he comes home from school – straight from school – and sits down and talks to us. I'll say we have to organise his stuff for the skiing trip – which we do. We'll develop on from there into our plan.'

'Van —'

'Don't argue. I'm treating you, and I'm the one getting up early.'

Chani shrugged. 'I owe you.'

She had a brief thought about getting up at six herself but let it slide into oblivion. There were limits.

Next morning Vanessa greeted Chani with a smile.

'You did it?'

'I did. I think he was quite shocked when he found me there in the kitchen.'

*

Jamie was in shock.

136

He'd crept, as usual, downstairs just before six, foraged through cupboards and the fridge for food, assembled the combination of cereal, milk, bread, butter and jam he'd found, and eaten them. He couldn't find a big enough bowl and had to use a small one, it held the bread OK but he had to eat that first or the milk would have made it soggy, as he had found out the previous morning.

He was about to go into the utility room in search of clothes when he heard, 'Ah, good morning, Jamie.'

He froze. Shit, what the hell was that awful woman doing here? She never got up this early.

He whirled round and froze again. Not her. Shit. Her weird friend. 'Er...'

The woman smiled. 'Chani was telling me you're going to France soon, skiing.' She paused. She was still smiling, a pleasant expression on her face.

She reminded him of the women who ran stalls selling things at the Summer Fete held on the school fields and which all the students were pressured to attend. He felt the same mild resentment he always experienced at having to buy stuff from them, and the same guilt because they were so helpful and unthreatening.

So he said, 'I am, yes.'

'Sounds terrific,' she said. 'The thing is, we – Chani and I – we need to make sure, with you, that everything you need for your trip will be organised and ready. So it's absolutely vital that we have a chat with you about what you'll need.'

'Oh, er ...' There was no time now, he had to get to school and do his homework.

'Not now, of course,' she said. 'When you get home from school today. Four o' clock? We'll be here then. All right?'

He was impaled where he stood by her smile that never moved and her voice that stayed mild whatever she said.

'Right,' he muttered and released himself enough to shuffle to the door.

'Just pop your dishes in the sink, Jamie, would you?'

He turned, surprised into reaction. She had her back to him, filling the kettle. He picked up the dishes he'd used and carried them to the sink.

'If you could just run some water over them.'

He turned to glare at her. She flashed him a smile and seemed not to notice, just said, 'Thanks, Jamie, that's a great help. You'll find clean clothes in your room, I believe.'

Later, when Sophie suggested going into town after school he had to say, 'I can't today, Sophs. Something I have to, er, get from home.'

'Oh, right. Shall I come?'

'It's homework stuff,' he lied. 'I might be an hour or so. Tell you what, I'll meet you at McDonald's at six, right? OK?'

'OK. Though, no, can you make it half past seven? I might as well do some homework too. I'll give you a ring when I'm ready.'

'Right.' It didn't sound like a put down but it had the same effect on him as if it had been.

He felt Sophie take his hand and looked into her smiling face. He squeezed her hand and she reached up to give him a quick kiss. As they parted at the gates she said, 'See you later, then,' and turned towards her bus, linking up seamlessly with a group of girls.

He felt better, but was still cringing at the pathetic excuse he'd come up with. He couldn't have told her about the morning's encounter. No way.

He was in no hurry to reach the house, so, once he'd left the school he slowed down and took the long way round, making sure no one going his way could join him.

When he walked in Chani came out of the kitchen to meet him. 'We're in here,' she said. 'We've been shopping. Would you like a drink?'

So he had to join them in the kitchen.

'What would you like?' her friend asked.

'Coke, please.' Certain they wouldn't have bought any. But she opened the fridge door and took out a can.

'You know where the glasses are,' she said.

He frowned, trying to remember. He had seen them while he'd been looking for a bowl … now which cupboard was it? He had to try four cupboards. Neither of the women helped him.

'So,' Chani said. She was facing him. Somehow they had all sat round the table. 'Your skiing trip. I think Sophie said it's for three weeks. Have I got that right?'

'Did she?' When the hell had that been?

'Yes, but I'm not sure I've remembered it right. Is it three weeks?'

He had no idea. 'I don't know.'

'Not to worry,' the other woman said. 'Is it less than that?'

He frowned.

'More?'

It didn't help. 'I don't know. Sophie didn't say.'

Unfazed, she went on, 'OK. How long were you there last year?'

He tried to remember.

'You're going before Christmas, aren't you?'

'Yes.' At least he could answer that. 'On the twenty second.'

The other woman wrote that down, speaking as she wrote. 'And did you do that last year?'

'Yes.' He'd been glad to, he remembered, it had saved him from having to spend it with that Smith man.

'And did you stay for New Year then?'

Jamie shook his head. 'I can't remember.'

The looks on their faces, like they saw him as stupid, drove him to explain. 'They don't bother with New Year. It's Sophie's relations, they don't do it.'

Chani nodded. 'All right. We'll work on three weeks. Do you have all the clothes you'll need?'

What were they talking about? He saw those looks again. 'Er…' he tried.

'We need to know, Jamie,' Chani's friend said. 'Because if there's anything you need we haven't got long to buy it. And if you need to take anything that has to be washed we must get it washed and dried.' Her voice faded. 'You have no idea, have you? Did Magda just sort it all out for you before? You were just given a packed bag and you took it and took stuff out of it when you were there as you needed it?'

Jamie was still adrift. 'Somebody unpacked it when I got there,' he said. Why didn't they understand?

The women exchanged glances and again it was plain to see what they were thinking.

'Yes, I see,' the other one said and took a breath. 'What you have to understand, Jamie, is that – here, at this end of things – that's not going to happen this time. Magda isn't here, we have no one instead of her and, though we are trying, there won't be anyone to replace her until January at least. That's if we can find anyone willing to do that kind of slave— um, job.'

She took a deep breath before going on. 'Chani and I don't mind washing whatever needs doing. We might even iron it. But you have to help us. We're not servants, and we're not being paid – I have to say that so you understand what you can and can't expect of us.

'So, what we need from you is, one: that you go through all the clothes in your room and find the stuff that you need to take to France. Two: when you've done that, we need you to tell us what's missing, what things you need but haven't got. And, three: you have to go and buy those things for yourself because we would obviously find it very difficult to do that for you. And anyway, I'm sure you're used to buying your own clothes at your age.'

Jamie could only stare at her. His mouth was open.

'We need you to do the first two things today,' she continued. 'I have a list here, a list of suggested things. I'll go through it, you might be able to say now if you have them.' She began reading from the list, starting with things like skis and ski jackets, hat, gloves and boots.

'Skis are in France,' he said, in a strained voice. Surely that was obvious. 'I have gear, jackets and stuff,

I mean.'

'Good.' She moved on to clothes. 'Sweaters?'

He nodded.

'How many?'

How many? He made a wild guess. 'Five.'

The woman made a note and handed him the piece of paper. 'These are the things you need to check. Take a pen and jot down how many of each you have, please. That is, the things that aren't crossed out, if they're crossed out that means you have them already. All right?'

'Think so,' he muttered.

'Brilliant. Can you go and do it now, please?'

Jamie rose, moving as if under a spell.

He was searching for nearly three quarters of an hour, mainly because it took so long to find where Magda had put his things. Why couldn't she have labelled the drawers? But finally he had a completed list. Feeling like a small child, he took it down.

They weren't in the kitchen. Why had they moved? Not pleased, he found them in the lounge and handed the list to the other woman, ready to race off to Sophie's as soon as he had changed out of his uniform.

'Thank you, that's great,' she said and both women smiled.

He fled.

His welcome at Sophie's was warm. Her mum smiled and offered him a drink. 'Nibbles?' she asked. 'I'm going out but your meal will only be about twenty minutes. You haven't eaten, have you?'

'No. Thanks,' he said. He was ravenous.

Sophie's welcome was even warmer.

'Did you sort out your homework?' she asked, as they ate.

'Yes,' he lied.

'What about that geography question?' she asked, geography being the only subject they did together. 'I'm not sure what Mr Bowles wanted us to research. What did you do?'

'He thought fast. 'I didn't get to geography,' he said. Well, it wasn't a lie. 'We could have a think about it now, if you want.'

'Would you mind?'

Of course he minded. She snuggled up to him and he melted. 'Course not.'

*

'Van,' Chani said, as Jamie left the house. 'How did you know all that about skiing gear? And all the stuff he'll need?'

'Kids in care, holidays.'

'Ah.' Chani leaned back. 'You're Wonder Woman. You deserve a drink.'

'One of mine,' Vanessa said.

Just after two the following afternoon, social worker Annabel rang Chani.

'I can call and see you and Jamie next week,' she said. 'On the twenty-second. Jamie should be there, shouldn't he, it's school holidays.'

'Actually,' Chani said. 'He's going away on that day. We've only just found out.'

'I see,' Annabel said, very frosty. 'With his girlfriend's parents, yes? I will need to talk to them, do you have their address? And their phone number?'

A small thrill of pleasure shivered up Chani's spine. 'I don't have either. He doesn't give out information. It's been bad enough trying to find out what he needs to take with him for the trip, so we can get it ready.'

'In terms of ski gear, you mean?'

'No, we've sorted that out, thanks to Vanessa. No, clothes in general. Not to mention trying to find out how long he's going for.'

'Who's Vanessa? That's not his girlfriend, is it?'

'She's my friend, from Hebden Bridge.' Smiling to herself, Chani added, 'She's a social worker.'

'Really?' Frosty-Fface sounded astonished. 'So,' she added, 'she'll be police-checked.'

'What?'

'Police-checked. To work with children.'

'Oh, CRB'd,' Chani said, remembering what Van had called it. 'Of course.'

'Oh, right.' Chani heard her puff of breath, and the quick in-breath. 'I can tell you what he'll need to take with him. Do you have a pen and paper there?'

'Paper?' Chani said. 'Oh, I see, yes.'

Annabel reeled off a comprehensive list of all the things he would need, most of which they already knew but also some they hadn't thought of.

'Thank you,' Chani said, busy writing and hating having to say it.

'It'll be helpful to you to have your friend there, won't it,' Annabel said, chattily.

As if the comment weren't bad enough in itself, the tone in which it was made inflamed Chani's resentment. 'Absolutely, it's company for me,' she snapped. 'So I'm not alone all the time.'

144

Across the room Vanessa's eyebrows arched and her lips formed an 'ooh!'

Annabel seemed to have missed Chani's snap altogether. 'Could you possibly get the address and phone number from Jamie?' she asked. Business as usual. 'Tell him I have to have them or I can't let him go. I'll need to talk to her parents before Wednesday, so it's fairly urgent.'

Amazing! Amazing what she considers urgent. And what's not urgent – like me. Her resentment now a fierce blaze, her next remark came out in a tight, sarcastic voice. 'All I can say is, I'll try, but I have to see Jamie, or Sophie, in order to find out, and as you know that is not easy.'

Before the social worker could say any more she put the phone down and turned to Van, her breathing fast and shallow.

'There's steam coming out of your ears,' Vanessa said. 'What did she say?'

Chani told her. Van's lips went thinner and thinner. 'How could she stop him going?' Chani demanded.

'Turn up here with documents to prevent it,' Vanessa said. 'But if he's at Sophie's when she arrives and we still don't know the address there won't be anything she can do. Beyond camping out here until he puts in an appearance. Do you even know Sophie's last name?'

Chani shook her head. 'Not the faintest.'

'What were you writing down?'

Chani told her.

'Stuff he needs?' Vanessa's lips parted, her eyes widened , then narrowed. 'Aah,' she said, her lips now twitching. 'Supervisor must've had a word with her. She's actually trying to be helpful.'

'Helpful! That's being helpful?' But Chani was busy working out how they could be sure to avoid seeing either her or Jamie before he left for France. It was ironic, wasn't it. For the first time since she'd come here she actively wanted Jamie to stay away. Even though she knew it was far too long a time until the twenty-second.

She was right. It came much sooner than she'd expected. Five minutes later, just as Vanessa had made a cup of tea to help Chani come round and to help them think, the doorbell went.

Chani opened it. Sophie stood there, still in uniform but with one of her trendy bags slung over her shoulder.

'Hi, Chani.'

'Hello, Sophie,' Chani smiled. 'Are you on your own?'

Sophie made a movement with her head that was almost a nod and, in a delayed reaction, Chani's mind replayed her voice. Something was wrong. Sophie was not herself. Subdued. 'Are you all right, love? You look a bit ... pale.'

'Mmm, yes.' But she clearly wasn't.

'Come in. Come and have some tea with us.' She led her into the lounge. 'It's Sophie,' she told Vanessa. 'She needs a cup of tea.'

'I'll get another cup.' Vanessa sprang up and headed for the kitchen, returning speedily with a small mug.

Sophie took the tea and sipped. Vanessa lifted an eyebrow at Chani, who could only give a tiny shake of her head, at which point they heard a key turn and the front door open. Sophie turned her head to the sound.

'Jamie,' Chani called and Vanessa raced to catch him.

'Sophie's here,' Chani heard her say and, after a moment, 'in here.'

Jamie appeared in the doorway, frowning, Vanessa behind him. 'Sophs?'

Sophie was clearly upset about something; she seemed to have shrunk. 'It's –' she stammered. 'I've just found out … Jamie, we can't go to France.' Her voice had risen almost to a wail.

Chani reached out to take the mug from her before it fell. Jamie was staring at Sophie with a baffled expression.

Vanessa propelled him gently forward. 'Why not, Sophie?' she asked, at the same time as Chani. Jamie still gaped, as though he couldn't understand the language.

Sophie lifted up her hands then let them drop, as if she had no control of them. She began twisting them together. 'It's … it's Mummy and Daddy.' Her voice sounded clotted. 'We've just had this, like, talk.' She turned tragic eyes to Chani and on to Vanessa, then dropped her head. 'It's a bit …' Her hands clenched into fists and she gave a few little gasps, as if trying to squeeze air into her lungs. 'They said they need to be on their own for a while so they can sort out their relationship.' The words were pushed out on one shaky breath and now she had run out of voice.

There was a heavy silence when no one seemed to be breathing. Chani couldn't think what to say to comfort the poor girl, her own desperation, that she couldn't, after all, go home, was so huge it was blocking out everything else.

Jamie took a step towards Sophie. 'We could go to France on our own,' he said.

Chani gasped. Had he really said that? She stared at him and then at Sophie's agonised face, tears clearly not far away.

'We can't.' Sophie's voice trembled. Swallowing hard, she tried to explain. 'Mummy wouldn't ... hear of it.' At that she crumpled.

Vanessa was there, her arm found the sobbing girl and held her. She had the ideal figure for that, Chani had always thought the phrase 'ample bosom' could have been invented for her. 'It must be awful for you, Sophie, love,' she was saying in her most soothing voice 'Poor girl. Awful.'

Chani shot a dark look at Jamie, who hadn't moved. The only feeling she could read there was of being thwarted. Selfish swine. All right, her first reaction had been disappointment for herself, but he wasn't showing any concern for poor Sophie at all.

'Chani love,' came Vanessa's voice. 'Why don't we take these things away and make some coffee.' She had helped Sophie to slide into a chair.

'Coffee?'

Vanessa jerked her head in the direction of the door. 'In the kitchen,' she said. 'Here,' and she handed Chani two mugs before picking up the other and the teapot and moving, so that Chani had to go in front of her.

'What?' Chani asked her when they were in the kitchen, with the door closed.

Vanessa tutted. 'They need to be alone. Sort it out themselves.'

'Oh.'

13

The door closed behind the two women. Jamie didn't move, couldn't move. Inside him all his frustration boiled, he wanted to howl, to kick things and smash things and he fought to stop himself doing anything like that in front of Sophie. But he couldn't hold all the frustration back, it came out as a growling sound in his throat, which he tried to cover up by pretending to clear his throat but the words came anyway. 'Great. Now I'm stuck with the ugly sisters.'

'Jamie!' He couldn't miss the shock. 'You so can't say that. They're being really nice.'

She sounded weird. All shaky. He wanted to rush over to her and bury his face in her hair, to hold her till she felt better. But his voice said, 'You're so not living with them.' It was like he had no control over himself.

'Oh, Jamie.' Her low, sad voice cut through him. He couldn't look at her. 'They're looking after you now Magda's gone, aren't they?' The weirdness of her voice reminded him of *Sean of the Dead*. 'And Vanessa's going home soon, you can't complain about her.' He heard her gulp and swallow. 'And, actually …' A bit stronger now. 'What about me? When my parents are separating.' Her voice cracked on the word and he moved a step towards her.

And stopped. 'I can't stand her.' Like he had a death wish. What was wrong with him?

'Just chill, yeah.' Utterly weary, like she was never going to speak to him again. He wouldn't blame her.

His hands balled into tight fists. He needed several deep breaths before he could force out the word. 'Sorry.' It took a huge effort to go on. 'It's just ... I was looking forward to it. To going. With you.' There was something in the way of his voice, something in his throat, in his chest. He coughed and managed another, 'Sorry.'

He made himself look away from the rain streaming down the window and face her. Her head was bent so her hair hid her face, but he knew she was crying. Her breath came in short bursts. He still couldn't move. 'Are you OK?' he gasped, past the tightness and berated himself for saying something so fucking stupid. Of course she wasn't OK.

'I suppose.' It was so quiet he wasn't sure she had actually said it.

He moved. To the window. It was still pissing down. He turned and edged towards her, watching her.

He felt a desperate need for air. 'Do you want to go out?'

At last she raised her head, lifted a hand that seemed too heavy and dabbed her eyes. Her shoulders still drooped.

'Cool,' she said, barely above a whisper.

Now he could hold her.

*

Chani and Vanessa hadn't made coffee. Vanessa had rinsed the mugs they had used, not taking much care, and banged them down on the drainer. As one they'd left the kitchen and walked into the dining room where they stood at the window and stared at the thick, heavy rain. It matched Chani's mood exactly.

151

'I'm going to the loo,' Vanessa said after they had done this for far too long for Chani's mental health.

She could only nod. When Vanessa had gone she turned her back on the window, switched on every light in the room and positioned herself at the table where she couldn't see outside. The depression she'd pushed down in concern for Sophie was back in full force. Having to stay here felt a million times worse now that she'd had a chance to escape and it had been taken away. Damn Sophie's parents. Why couldn't they have separated after Christmas? Surely it would have been better for Sophie if they'd left it. Could she find out where they lived and go and talk to them?

The door opened and she started to tell Van about this idea, but it was Sophie who came in, looking pinched and very pale. Her aura was wavering, her usual air of assurance entirely missing. Chani felt wrung by this new, pitiful Sophie.

'Sophie, love,' she said. 'Are you all right?'

Sophie's lips twitched and she attempted a smile and to straighten herself up. 'Yes, I think so.' It was a brave try, but her voice sounded choked. She swallowed. 'I just wanted to ask you,' she went on, a little stronger. 'Would you mind if I stayed here tonight?'

Chani stood and went to her, put her arm round her and guided her to a chair, sat herself next to her. 'Of course I wouldn't mind.'

'Thanks.' She was making knots with her fingers.

Chani's mind flew to bedding and towels and whether Sophie had anything with her or would need toiletries and things. 'Are you in with Jamie?' she asked.

'In with …?'

'In his room?' She might need to borrow a dressing gown and slippers, what size were her feet?

'Oh no.'

Sophie's shocked voice jerked Chani out of housekeeper mode. 'Oh,' she said, surprised. She'd assumed Sophie was sixteen, like Jamie. 'You don't sleep together, then?'

Sophie still looked shocked. How old-fashioned.

'No. It's too ... we're only sixteen.'

OK, go along with it. 'I suppose so.'

Sophie lifted her chin. She'd been crying. 'We decided. We're into celibacy.'

Wow, that was a shock. 'Celibacy? Really?' She pulled herself up. Better let it go, get back to housekeeping. 'All right, Van'll help me sort out a bed for you. I'll go and find her.'

'Thank you. We're going out for a bit now.'

'Out?' Chani's eyes moved to the rain.

'We just feel like going out.'

'Well ... all right then, fine. Will you be having a meal here?'

'Please.'

Chani reached out to pat Sophie's hands, found them still knotted together. She started to get up and go in search of Vanessa when an idea struck her and without stopping to think she said, 'Look, I've had an idea. Since your trip isn't on now, why don't you come to Hebden Bridge with me over Christmas?'

Another, much less happy thought occurred to her, one she wanted to keep to herself. But of course she couldn't. 'Unless, that is, Sophie, you'd rather be with your mum and dad. I mean ... your mum or ...'

153

Sophie's fingers were practically plaiting themselves, her face one big frown. Staring at her knees she said, 'I don't want to be with them, no.' When she lifted her head her eyes were moist. 'It's really nice of you to ask me, Chani, thank you.'

A strange look passed across her face, it could almost have been defiance. Her chin rose. 'I would like to come, yes. Thank you.'

'That's great,' Chani said. Her excitement was rising. 'I'm so pleased. I'll go and get that bed sorted.' She should speak to Sophie's mother, or possibly her father, she knew that. She should ask Sophie for the number. But what if they said no? 'Er,' she said. 'Yes.' And left.

*

Jamie waited for Sophie to come back from talking to Chani and when she didn't he peered round the door to try and see where she was. But Chani walked out of the dining room, Sophie didn't. He hung on and when Chani disappeared he went in.

Sophie was there, sitting beside the table, her back to him. He closed the door carefully and moved so he was in front of her, stood by the fireplace, restless hands fiddling with the heavy black glass cubes on the slate mantle shelf.

'You're staying, then, are you?' he asked. 'She couldn't have said no.'

'Of course she didn't say no.' She seemed impatient. 'She's gone to sort out a room for me.'

'Oh, right.' He felt oddly uncomfortable. They were supposed to be going out, weren't they, but Sophie didn't look as though she wanted to move.

'You shouldn't keep dissing Chani,' she said. 'It's not fair.'

'What?' It felt like a blow, but what she said next was like being hit from behind.

'She invited me to Hebden Bridge.'

He couldn't speak. What was she talking about? 'Who?' he managed, when he could actually form words.

'Chani.' Like she was talking to an idiot. 'She invited me to Hebden Bridge.'

It didn't make any sense. 'Where?'

'Hebden Bridge. Where she comes from.'

Ah, now he understood. He gave a snort of laughter. 'Oh, yeah, right. Like you'd go!'

It was clear immediately that was the wrong thing to say. Sophie's eyes flashed and her chin came up. 'I am going. It sounds cool, it's a spa.'

This was ridiculous. 'A spa! Yeah, like, come on!'

'There's a Mind and Body Centre,' she said, and he began to sense danger. 'She's a therapist there. It's really nice of her to ask us.'

Too late, Jamie picked up on her tone of voice. And one of the words she'd just used. 'Us?'

'Yes. Because we can't go to France.'

'She expects me to go?'

'Of course she does. It'll be good.'

A deep, dark chasm was opening up between them. 'Oh, God,' Jamie gasped in total horror.

'Jamie, really.'

She'd turned into her mother. This was a nightmare.

She tossed her head. 'Daddy'll give me loads of money. We can have a great time.'

'It'll be freezing up there.' Grasping for arguments. 'It's ... north.'

'We can take warm clothes. Our skiing clothes, they're warm. I've got these fabulous boots.'

He scrutinized her carefully. Oh, shit. She meant it. She wasn't taking the piss. But why ... how could she want to —

He was interrupted by a voice from the opening door. 'Is the skiing trip on again?'

They both jerked their heads round at the sound of Vanessa's voice. Jamie groaned. No, this was all too much. As the woman came into the room he made for the door.

'I'm going to watch the rugby,' he said.

'Not skiing, no,' he heard Sophie say. 'We're going to Hebden Bridge.'

He fled.

*

'*Are* you?'

Ah – there Vanessa was. Good. But when Chani reached the door and realised the other voice was Sophie's she hesitated.

'Yes, 'Sophie was saying. 'Chani invited us. It sounds great. Chani said it's a spa.'

'She did?' There was a brief pause before Vanessa said, in a strange, low voice, 'I wonder why she said that?'

She had to hear this.

She reached out a hand but something stopped her. Not a good idea to go in. To stop herself moving she held on to the door jamb instead of pushing the door further open.

'Well,' Sophie said, 'she said about mind and body and healing.'

'Ah. Mmm. The Mind and Body Centre. I see.' Chani flinched.

'Yes. And she's a therapist there, isn't she.'

Chani flinched again when Vanessa cleared her throat. 'Did she say that?'

'Yes.'

There was another pause before Vanessa said, 'She … actually, she helps run the Centre.'

'So, is that a spa?'

Chani had to smile. What a great job Sophie would do on *Newsnight*. She would pit her against Jeremy Paxman any time.

'They, er, they do all sorts of therapies.' It was all right. Chani stopped holding her breath.

'Ri-ight.' Doubt had crept into Sophie's voice.

In a rather brisker voice Vanessa said. 'And is Jamie going too?'

'Yes.'

Chani heard it in bold. So was Vanessa's reply. 'You persuaded him?'

Sophie gave a startled giggle.

It really was all right, Chani could go in. But the question in Vanessa's voice as she said, 'Sophie,' stopped the foot she was about to move. And when Van said, 'I suppose you met Jamie's mother?' she grabbed at the door jamb and held her breath again.

'Oh yes. All the time.' Said with Sophie's usual charm.

'What happened, exactly? If you don't mind me asking?'

'You mean, when she went away?'

'Yes. With a man, I gather.' It took all Chani's will to stay where she was, and stay as quiet as possible.

'You mean John Smith.'

For what felt like ages no one spoke and Chani tensed even more.

At last Sophie said, 'He was ... sort of good-looking, for an older man. I thought he was a bit creepy, but she really liked him.' Chani could almost see a 'can-you-believe-it' shrug.

'She must have,' Vanessa said.

Sophie giggled. 'I suppose.'

'Did Jamie? I mean, he never talks about his mother. Was he very upset when she went?' Great, at last they were getting somewhere. Please, don't let Sophie clam up.

'I don't know, really.' She spoke slowly. 'He didn't get on with her.'

'Oh?'

'They had quite a few rows.'

'Did they?' A second's pause before Vanessa said, 'What about?'

'Sort of, um, things she made him do, I think.' Chani heard sounds she couldn't recognise. If only she could see. 'Like the school,' Sophie said. 'He hates it, you know.'

'The school he's at now?' Vanessa sounded as surprised as Chani was. She couldn't stop the gasp, choking it back with both hands over her mouth she listened as hard as she could.

'Yes,' Sophie was saying. 'I mean, it's all right, I suppose, but Jamie's never liked it.'

158

'I see,' Vanessa said.

This was awful. How much longer could she stand there like this?

But instead of going on Sophie said, 'I think I'd better phone my mum and tell her I'm staying here. Will you excuse me?'

Chani couldn't wait another second. As she walked in Vanessa was saying, 'Of course, love.'

'There you are, Van,' Chani said, trying for casual. 'I've been looking for you. Oh, hi, Sophie.'

Sophie was already moving. 'Excuse me, Chani,' she said. 'I have to go and phone my mum.'

It was no good. Chani sank into a chair as a little moan pushed up her throat.

Vanessa said, 'Sophie's just been telling me —'

Chani held up a hand to stop her and turned to make sure Sophie had gone before she moved to the chair Sophie had just left and said in a low voice, 'I know. I was listening, you'd left the door open a bit. Very interesting, isn't it?'

'Certainly is,' Vanessa said, drily. 'So when were you thinking of going to Hebden Bridge?'

Exhausted, Chani slumped. 'I hadn't got that far. It's all spur of the moment.'

'Mmm,' Vanessa murmured, with an almost smile.

As Chani leaned back, taking deep breaths, an idea began to trickle into her mind. 'Why don't we go on Monday? You have to go back then, don't you? We could all go together.'

Vanessa was clearly torn between smiling and frowning. 'You mean in Patricia?'

'Of course in Patricia.'

Chani stretched one leg at a time, letting her foot tighten and drop, then circling it from the ankle.

'How about going on Sunday?' Vanessa said and Chani relaxed. 'Just in case. I'll go and buy some warm clothes in the morning. Where's the best place?'

They had started on making a meal, celebratory glasses of wine beside them, when Vanessa said, 'Did Sophie get her parents' permission to go to Hebden Bridge?'

'Permission?'

'Chani, love, they need to know.'

'They don't seem to care much, do they? Doing this to her at Christmas.'

'Yes, I know. But I think they'd still ... I mean, how old is she?'

'Sixteen.'

'She looks older. But she definitely needs their permission at that age.'

'She did go to talk to her mum about it,' Chani said.

'We must remember to ask her. And we'll have to let the social worker know about Jamie going there.'

'Oh, hell!' Chani swore, adding, 'Hell's teeth!' And had a worse thought. 'She won't be at work now, will she? Does that mean we can't go till Monday? Assuming we can get hold of her then.'

Vanessa considered. 'No, I'm sure we can go, you can ring her number and leave a message. He's going to your home, not out of the country.'

Chani pulled a face. 'It's out of the country to Ffrosty Fface.'

Vanessa laughed. Chani didn't

14

Jamie stared at the match on the TV screen, but he felt too numb to take it in.

What had just happened?

He stumbled to his feet, moved two or three steps and came to a halt. What was he doing? He stared, unseeing, around him. Nothing made sense. He wanted to go to France, with Sophie. He still couldn't really see why not. But if Sophie's parents were ... what had she said? Separating? They couldn't ... they'd never ... they were ... He couldn't get his mind round it. All the time he'd spent there, it had always been so, so all right.

They were the only actual parents, like a mother and a father, he knew. The only family he knew. And now, now they weren't.

He felt weird, like he was empty, but also sort of heavy. As if he were in water, lots of water around him and above him, pressing him down.

He heard a sound behind him. The door opening.

'I've rung Mummy.' Sophie.

He turned. Sophie, yes, it was.

'She asked me a lot of questions about Chani and where Hebden Bridge is but it's all right, we can go.'

'Go?'

'Yes.'

'Hebden Bridge?'

'Yes. With Chani. We just talked about it.'

'Chani? Chani!'

'God, Jamie, what's wrong with you?'

He gaped at her. 'Wrong? With me? Me?'

'Don't keep saying what I've just said!'

'What?' He was shouting. Why couldn't she understand? 'What you've just said is ridiculous. Going to Hebden Bridge – why the hell would we go there?'

'You've just said you would.'

'No, I didn't.'

There was a long, heavy silence. He couldn't cope with it, didn't know what to do, what to say, or not say, where to look. He couldn't look at Sophie.

'Jamie.' A very small voice. A trying-to-be-patient voice. He wanted to put his hands over his ears so he wouldn't hear the tremble in it. 'I've told Mummy we're going, I've given her Chani's phone number.'

Shit. 'Why?' He was furious, wasn't he? So why did his voice sound so whiny, when he ought to sound furious and, like, masterful?

'Oh, Jamie, really. Chani invited us, because we can't go to France. And if we don't go to Hebden Bridge, I'll have to be at home with my parents while they work out ... separating... they'll be ... Christmas ... I can't ...'

Jamie had already opened his mouth to argue, knew he shouldn't, but it came out anyway. 'But—' Too late – she had spun round and was rushing out of the room, leaving him stranded.

What could he do? Sophie had never done that before, rushing off and not saying why she'd thought they would go, not saying anything.

He couldn't understand, would he ever understand anything? All he knew was he didn't want to go to Chani's house. That bloody awful woman, it was all her fault. Why couldn't they all leave him alone?

But not Sophie. Why couldn't she stay here? Shit. Everything was shit. He sank onto the sofa and turned on his side, letting the fog in his head take him over. Somebody would have to sort this out.

When Vanessa came to say the meal was ready he said he was tired and there was an important match on that he really wanted to watch. 'Can I eat here?' he asked.

Vanessa's eyes probed him. 'What's happened with you and Sophie?'

'What?'

'She doesn't want anything to eat, she's staying in her room, says she's tired.'

'Nothing's happened. I'll come and get mine.'

*

'He's upset her,' Chani said as soon as Jamie had gone off with his meal on a tray.

'He may well have,' Vanessa said. 'Shall we eat in here or in the dining room?'

'What a choice – sterile clinic or baronial bleak.'

'Let's have some good wine, then, with the baronial bleak.'

*

Sophie still didn't want to eat anything, Jamie learnt when he turned up for breakfast, not having slept much. His eyes felt full of grit and when he'd seen himself in the mirror he'd been horrified at the black marks under them. What was wrong?

'Tell you what,' Vanessa said. 'I'll make her a tray of nice little things and you can take it up to her, Jamie, while we make you some porridge and toast. Or scrambled eggs? Which would you like?'

163

'Er,' he said. The woman was already laying out a tray with a white cloth, little bowls of fruit and stuff.

'Porridge?' she asked, glancing up at him. 'Or eggs?'

His stomach rumbled.

'How about all of them?' Chani asked.

'Er, well ...'

'No problem. I'll start the porridge.'

Vanessa indicated the tray. 'You take that up, Jamie, love, I'll get going on the eggs.'

He groaned.

Upstairs there was a line of light round the door of Sophie's room. He did not want to do this. Could he leave the tray on the floor and just say it was there? He put it on the floor, stared at it and moaned to himself.

Lifting a hand that felt heavier than he was he bent it into shape, knuckles fixed ready. It shook. The smells of porridge and eggs shimmered towards his nose.

All right, knock on the bloody door. No answer. Shit. He picked up the tray and opened the door.

'They sent you this,' he said, searching for somewhere to put it and not looking at the bed.

'Thank you,' Sophie said, like a stranger.

He could find nowhere to put the tray.

'What is it?'

He moved to the bed and held it out. Her hands reached out to take it. She was sitting up and she had on a dressing gown that could not be hers. All up the front of his body muscles tensed.

'Thank you,' she said again.

He had to look at her. The muscles tightened more and he had to swallow. She was pale, her face looked thin and she sort of drooped.

164

'OK,' he said, through the constriction in his throat.

'OK what?' She seemed too tired and ill to move.

'OK Hebden Bridge.'

*

The further north Chani drove the colder it felt. Patricia's heating system had battled noisily for a while until settling into a pattern of belching out ten minutes or so of heat before packing up. After resting for half an hour or so it would repeat the pattern.

'I gather Mike at the garage installed climate control,' Vanessa said. She sat in the passenger seat muffled up in three scarves, with layers of fleece under her thick wool coat, warm trousers and big boots. She'd treated herself – upsetting Chani's veggie principles, though she could hardly complain under the circumstances - to sheepskin-lined gloves and hadn't taken them off since they left Welwyn Garden City.

Chani, to Sophie's evident delight, was in her warm winter clothes. Sophie had been very interested in her knitted yellow tights and wanted to know all about Maisie Cate, who had made them for the boutique she ran. Jamie of course had winced and scowled through the whole conversation. He and Sophie were in expensive down-filled ski gear. Sophie's wedge-heeled boots seemed to Chani to be more après-ski. She did like their woolly beanies and said so, with a malicious flash of enjoyment at Jamie's embarrassed reaction. He deserved it, after all that fuss he'd made about coming, only finally giving in when he'd upset Sophie so much. She'd heard him wandering round the house at night, having trouble sleeping, wasn't he? Not surprising. Maybe he'd realise the effect he had on other people.

But he was here. And four people in the car could generate more heat than two or three. Especially with all the impatient shuffling in the back seat that had to be Jamie. The downside of course to four people in the car was that one of them was Jamie. But that was because she'd escaped, she was on her way home.

'Where are we now?' Jamie demanded, as he had about fifty times already. Clearly, he was reaching for his inner child. A child who couldn't read the motorway signs.

But Vanessa, who had far more patience, pulled the road map from the side of her seat and consulted it.

'Kegworth,' she said. 'Not far from Nottingham.'

'Oh, God,' Jamie moaned. 'It's miles yet. Why is it taking so long? Can't you go faster?'

Chani's patience had worn out ages before. 'Only downhill, I'm afraid.'

'What?'

'She only has a small engine.'

'So?'

'So,' she said, gritting her teeth, 'this is as fast as she can go. We'll stop soon and you can stretch your legs.' And she could go somewhere and scream.

'But that'll make it even longer,' Jamie said.

Vanessa stepped in. 'I wouldn't mind stopping soon, actually. I'd love a cup of tea.'

'Where's the next services?' Chani asked her quietly. And gratefully.

Vanessa studied the map. 'Not far, it's Nottingham.'

There was another groan from the back.

'Chani,' came Sophie's voice, not moaning. 'Could I listen to some of your music, please?'

Chani let herself dream for a second that there had been some sort of mistake and it was actually Sophie who was Celandine's child. Huh, fat chance of that. Not that she wanted this situation, but if she had to have it, well, how much better if it had been Sophie.

'I'll put a cassette in,' she said, so Sophie could hear her. 'I'd give you my iPod but I can't get at it till we stop.'

'What sort of car doesn't play CDs!' Jamie muttered to Sophie.

Chani heard him and had a – very quiet – mutter to herself, featuring Emperor Jamie and what she would like to do to him.

'If you listen to your iPod you won't hear it,' came the voice of sweet reason from next to him and Chani had to choke back a shout of laughter.

Vanessa, meanwhile, had been going through the cassettes in the glove compartment and offered one to Chani. 'Aretha Franklin OK?'

'Great.' Chani inserted it and Aretha began with 'Chain of Fools'. Very apt, she thought.

Jamie groaned again but Chani concentrated on Aretha. Whenever there was a break in the music her ears caught the tinny but unmistakeable echoes of opera-singing. Good. He'd followed Sophie's advice.

And here was another upside – she could listen to Aretha. Van liked her too.

15

The sleet began at Barnsley, forcing Chani to drive even more slowly. When they finally arrived in the early evening at Vanessa's house, Chani was exhausted. At least the sleet had stopped before they'd turned off the motorway. She felt stiff and weary when she climbed out of the car to help Van struggle her bag out of the crammed-full boot.

'Thanks, Chani love,' Vanessa said, adding, in a low voice, 'Best of luck.'

'Thank you Van, for coming. You've been a fantastic help.'

'Listen,' Vanessa said, louder, as Chani banged the boot shut. 'Why don't you all come to me on Friday, we'll have a Christmas Eve supper.'

'That sounds wonderful, thanks.' Chani gave her a tired, strained and very grateful smile and climbed back in the car. It had been a terrible journey but she was nearly home. She had left the awful dark grey tomb behind.

*

Jamie had been stunned into silence by the darkness, the great mass of darkness beyond the road and the weirdness of driving inside the funnel the car's headlights created on the unlit roads between the towns and villages. They'd passed some small settlements of buildings that huddled into the dark masses as if for safety, people presumably shut away behind curtained windows, or in the pubs they passed every now and then, their bizarre Christmas lights and fairy-lit trees like sentries at the edge of the known world, before they were plunged back into the darkness. He'd almost fallen asleep a few times, tired out from not sleeping. And the nightmares, like horror films where his dad came out of his grave and pushed him into Army recruiting offices, or the RAF College and Sophie dumped him.

Sophie chattered away about the names of places – where she could see them. 'Oh, look there's a place called Friendly, what a cool name.' Luddenden, she liked and Luddenden Foot even more, and she was fascinated by Mytholmroyd. 'How do you say that?' she asked, but even when Vanessa had pronounced it for her Sophie still couldn't say it. She kept on trying and Jamie turned up the volume of his music.

'Hebden Bridge,' Chani suddenly announced and Sophie went quiet. They drove along streets of dark buildings, making crazy sharp turns to drive up unbelievably steep, narrow roads, all lined with dark grey houses. The car turned onto another narrow road that ran more or less level and seemed to cling to the hillside it crossed. Jamie caught glimpses of side streets whose near-vertical ravine-like drops were marked by lines of dim street lights.

Vanessa's house and everything round it had been totally dark. So, when they reached it, was Chani's, but there was a street lamp nearby.

'I'll go and open the door,' Chani said. 'Hang on till I've put some lights on and you can see where you're going.'

*

Chani had never been so pleased to see her own house. She stood in the hall hugging its welcome to herself until she felt able to go outside again.

'Can you two bring in the stuff from the car while I sort out beds and things?' she said, opening the boot and picking things up at random.

Inside she rushed to turn up the heating which she'd left on low and to make sure the water was heating up. She stood in her kitchen and sighed with pleasure. She was home. Upstairs she quickly made up her two spare beds. She couldn't wait to snuggle into her own.

When she walked downstairs the house felt freezing. Was something wrong with the heating system? That was all she needed. She gasped when she saw the front door was wide open. Had someone followed them in? She moved faster but stopped when she spotted the piles of things in the hall. Ah. Jamie and Sophie. They'd been bringing the stuff in from the car, hadn't they. Judging by the freezing cold, they'd had the door wide the whole time and just left it. Had they no sense at all? She ran out to check they weren't still outside, to find Patricia's boot lid still up, the boot empty, as was the inside of the car, and no sign of Jamie or Sophie.

As fast as she could she closed up the car, ran back in the house, shutting the door firmly. Damn, the living room door was fully open.

Inside, Jamie and Sophie were clinging to the big radiator. No, they didn't have any sense. None whatsoever.

It was pointless to make a fuss. She made hot drinking chocolate for them all, showed them quickly round the house so they would know where things were. Reluctant though they were to leave the heat of the radiator Chani wanted to be sure they could look after themselves in the morning. There was no way she was going to get up early.

'If you're cold in bed,' she told Sophie. 'There's hot-water-bottles in that drawer. You know how to do them, don't you?'

Sophie nodded. 'Thank you, yes, we use them in France.' A shadow crossed her face, but she blinked, swallowed and said, 'And you showed us the kettle.'

Best to push on. Chani still had to show Jamie his room. 'Good,' she said.

By the time she'd done that she was exhausted. All she wanted to do was fall into bed and sleep. But instead of taking their drinks upstairs her guests went into the living room. All right, she'd sit with them for a few minutes and unwind.

But Jamie had found the remote control and, without saying a word, he was soon channel-hopping. Chani needed stillness and quiet. The constantly-changing sound and picture were driving her mad.

Could Celandine really have set out to create a monster? He had no manners at all. What could have been on her mind?

'Jamie,' she said, raising her voice. 'If you'll give me the control I'll show you how to get the guide to what's on.'

'It's OK,' he said. 'I can see what's on.'

'I'd still like you to give me the control.'

His scowl as he handed it to her was like an approaching force nine gale. She ignored it, muted the sound and went to the programme guide.

171

Eventually, they settled on an American police drama which was halfway through and Jamie's scowl faded. Chani went to bed, leaving them with the television and a promise to keep the sound low.

'I'm shattered,' she said. 'You know where everything is now, don't you?'

'Yes, thanks, we do.' Sophie again.

'Night, then.'

'Goodnight, Chani,' Sophie said, with a smile. Jamie grunted, his eyes on the screen.

Chani gave the control to Sophie.

After a blissful night in her own bed and a long lie-in with a cup of tea, luxuriating in the novel she'd had to abandon to go to Welwyn Garden City, Chani drifted downstairs and made herself breakfast. It was well after eleven by the time she finished and there was still no sign of Jamie or Sophie.

Well, whatever. She got up and looked in the fridge and the small pantry. Yes, as she'd thought, she'd have to go shopping.

Chani had put the shopping away and was preparing a veggie moussaka for them to eat that evening when Sophie, all bright and fresh, appeared, followed by Jamie, who was not.

'Hi, Chani,' Sophie said and came to see what she was doing.

Jamie sat at the table.

'What can we eat for breakfast?' Sophie asked.

Chani ignored the fact that it was lunchtime. 'There's muesli and yoghurt and you can have toast if you want.'

Jamie mumbled something and went to open the fridge. 'Where's the toast?' he asked, pushing the door with his knee. It didn't quite close.

'Well, you won't find it in there,' Chani said, struggling not to laugh.

Jamie glowered at her, but she'd learned a thing or two from Vanessa. She told them where everything was, finishing, 'could you make sure the fridge door's shut, please?'

Jamie's eyebrows registered amazement, followed by annoyance. Chani enjoyed watching the interaction of his eyebrows with his nose. Part of her felt sorry for him, but she made no move to help him.

'Here.' Sophie, unfazed, collected all the items. She demonstrated cutting the unsliced, wholemeal loaf, passed him two slices. 'Pop these in the toaster.'

Chani concentrated on layering the moussaka.

'Oh, Jamie,' she heard and looked up to see Sophie take the bread and show him what to do.

'Magda must have always done that,' Chani said.

Sophie actually tutted.

Chani left them to it. She was clearing things away when her doorbell rang.

Brian, her neighbour, stood there.

'Brian,' she said, with a big smile. 'How lovely to see you.'

'I saw the car,' he said. 'So obviously you're back. Mum asked me to give you your Christmas present. And this is a bit of something from me.'

He handed her a carefully-wrapped and decorated package and a smaller, undecorated and far less neat one.

173

'That's lovely, thank you. I'll get yours to you when I've sorted myself out.' Actually, when she'd bought them. 'Come and meet my guests.' She took him in.

'This is Jamie, Celandine's son, and Sophie,' she said. 'My neighbour, Brian.'

Brian straightened after ducking his broad, six foot five frame to come through the doorway. His craggy thirty-something-year-old face beamed and he crushed Jamie's hand in his, taking a more gentle hold of Sophie's. 'Hiya, good to meet you. Here for Christmas, then?'

'Jamie's a rugby player,' Chani told him, to avoid anyone having to answer that.

'Oh yes?' Brian's beam radiated enthusiasm. 'Who do you play for?'

'For school,' Jamie said. There might have been a spark of interest there.

'I'm off to a match this afternoon, actually. Well, quite soon, one o clock. You could come with me if you like, I've room for two in the car. It's Castleford and Wakefield, be a good match.'

'Oh, er …' Jamie fumbled with the remains of his toast.

'You go,' Sophie said to him. 'You'll enjoy that. I don't really feel like a rugby match today, but thanks very much, Brian, for the invitation.'

Brian smiled and shrugged a good-humoured response.

'Great stuff,' he said. 'See you shortly, Jamie. One o clock.'

'You have time for a coffee, do you?' Chani asked him.

'Actually, no, not this time, thanks. I'll see you later, I'll let myself out.'

Jamie, looking as though he didn't know what had hit him, went for suitable clothes Why hadn't she told Jamie he was a university lecturer? She knew why – he worked for the Open University and Jamie would probably only rate Oxford and Cambridge. Oh dear, did thinking like that make her more or less snobbish than Jamie?

She shrugged and turned to Sophie. 'Would you like to have a look round the village?

'Oh, cool, yes please. I'll get my jacket.'

Chani's phone rang.

It was Social Services. 'You left a message for Ms Fforbes – Annabel Fforbes?' a woman's voice said.

'Oh, yes, I did.'

'What it is, she isn't here just at present. My name's Nicola Harrison, I've taken over her caseload. I've had a look through the file for Jamie Pomfret-Jones and I understand you're staying with him, Ms Caladan.'

Chani tried to fight off the Ffrosty Fface image she knew. This woman sounded, if she could let herself believe it, a bit more human. A bit older too. Still, better be careful.

What should she say? It needed some care. 'I was. I rang you, I mean, Ms Fforbes, because things, well, changed.'

'Oh?'

'I'm not sure how much you know,' Chani said and plunged into as brief a summary as she could manage of how and why they were now in Hebden Bridge, adding, 'Sophie's parents, I mean, we made sure Sophie had their permission to come here.'

'I see. Jamie and his girlfriend have gone with you to your house for Christmas.'

'That's right.' Was that really friendliness in the woman's voice?

'And Jamie is happy with that, is he?'

How did she answer that? 'Well,' she tried. Oh, hell, may as well be honest. 'Jamie has some trouble with happy. Mainly he's come because Sophie wanted to and because they can't go to France.' Inspiration came. 'And, you see, it helps me keep my job and not lose quite so much money.' More inspiration. 'And I can give them both a much better Christmas here than I could there, given the circumstances.' Though how?

'Yes, of course you can.' Chani nearly dropped the phone. 'I'm sure you understand our primary concern is for Jamie and what he wants and needs. It sounds as though you're doing your best for him but I do need to talk to him. Is he there?'

'No.' Chani had to cough to make her voice work. 'Not at the moment.' She explained about the rugby match.

'That sounds splendid. I'll ring again in the morning, if you could possibly make sure he can speak to me then.'

'Yes, I will.'

'Bye then, and thanks for letting us know.'

She had to sit down. Nicola Harrison. Was she real? Had she just dreamed all that? Her eyes drifted to the phone in her hand. How much easier everything would be if she was dealing with Nicola and not Ffrosty Fface. How long would she be away? Please let it be a long

176

time. It was only then she realised she hadn't ended the call.

Sophie was waiting.

'Ready?' Chani said, and smiled.

They walked down to the area where the shops, cafes and pubs were, passing artists' studios and two galleries on the way. The air felt damp and the wind that gusted through every opening they passed was arctic but Chani was warmed and cheered by being home and, however wary she felt about it, by the change of social worker.

Sophie didn't seem to mind the chill. 'What wonderful views,' she said, having enthused about all the stone-built houses.

'They are, aren't they?' Chani agreed, but her mind had gone back to Melissa and the Mind and Body Centre. Really, she should call in and say she was back. Really, she should have gone back to work that morning, but how could she have left Jamie and Sophie on their own? She didn't want to call in because Melissa would complain about her not working. Why hadn't she thought to phone? Sophie would want to see the Centre, wouldn't she, but she would have to wait for another day.

'There are some good shops here,' she said, to divert her.

Sophie looked pleased and smiled. 'Like Gap? Or Monsoon?'

Chani smiled and shook her head.

'Oh, right. What about Warehouse? Zara?'

'Sorry, no.'

There were crease lines on her forehead.

'I'm afraid not. We keep all the shops local. So no national names, no chains, not even M and S.'

'Oh.' Sophie gave the word two syllables, her voice dropping on the second.

'It was a community decision some time ago. We do have the Co-op but that's it. There's loads of interesting little shops, locally-run, you'll like them.'

'I know,' Sophie said, brightening. 'The Mind and Body Centre. I'd love to see that, is it near here?'

'Well ...' Chani hesitated. What could she say? Ah— 'Actually, I need to look for Christmas presents. And I know we don't have Gap and so on, but would you like to see my friend Maisie Cate's boutique? She has some fabulous clothes, from all over the world. She's just round the corner.'

'Oh, cool.'

Maisie Cate was serving someone when they walked in, but she spotted Chani straight away, with a wide smile.

'Be with you in a moment,' she said. Today she was wearing a fluffy sea-green sweater that reached her hips, brick-red embroidered trousers and thick-soled blue, embroidered Mary-Janes. The outfit looked great with her mass of hennaed curls.

Sophie was already going through the racks of clothes.

The customer hadn't finished putting her card away before Maisie Cate was round the counter, her bracelets jangling, and asking Chani, 'Are you back now, then? How did it go?'

Chani checked that Sophie wasn't looking and grimaced. 'Euch,' she mouthed. Sophie was engrossed, so she added, in a whisper, 'Apart from Sophie – Jamie's girlfriend.'

Maisie Cate's eyes gleamed. 'Very nice too,' she whispered back, giving the girl a thorough scrutiny.

Sophie, hearing her name, turned and Chani introduced them. 'Jamie's gone to watch rugby with Brian, from next door,' she added.

'Brian ...' Maisie Cate pondered. 'Is he the OU guy, used to live with Ellie? Photographer Ellie?'

'Yes,' Chani said, 'I didn't know you knew him.'

'I don't, but Ellie comes in here, she used to rave about him. Anyway, Sophie, lovely to meet you.' She put her head on one side and continued her brazen appraisal. 'I know exactly what'd suit you. We haven't had them in long, I think I've got your size – an eight, are you?' She bustled into the inner recesses of the shop, past all the racks of thick sweaters made from yak hair, the woven llama-hair tunics, the ikat-patterned tops and skirts and the Peruvian knitted hats.

Sophie followed. 'I didn't realise there was all this,' she was saying, as she reached the Tibetan pants. 'I can't take it all in.'

Maisie Cate pulled out a jacket. It was indigo with panels and buttons of lime green, hand-knitted lime green cuffs and a deep collar. 'It's lined,' she said, opening it up to show a pale blue, knitted lining. 'It's lovely and warm, and it's long enough to cover your hips.'

'It's gorgeous.' Within seconds Maisie Cate was holding Sophie's jacket while Sophie admired herself in front of the long mirror. Maisie Cate showed her how she could double the collar over to display its knitted lime-green lining, and either fasten it up cosily or pull it up and fix it so it covered her ears.

'I'll take it,' Sophie said, entranced. 'I love it.'

As she took it off she spotted the jewellery and stopped to study it. 'Where does this come from?' she asked, holding up a silver bangle set with a purple stone and Maisie Cate gave a pleased smile.

'I make it.'

'You do? Here?'

'At the back of the shop, I have a little workshop.'

Sophie picked up a silver pendant, an unusual shape, almost futuristic but traditional at the same time, with a jade green stone at its tip. 'How did you do this?' she asked.

'Ah, that's from my fusion range.'

Another customer entered at that point and was quickly followed by a group of four.

'I can't show you now,' Maisie Cate said. 'But if you'd like to come round when I close, around half past four, I'll show you then. Maybe you'd like to have a go yourself, would you?'

'Oh,' Sophie breathed. 'Could I?'

Hopefully all the excitement would have taken Sophie's mind off the Mind and Body Centre but, to be safe, Chani led her into a number of shops so she could buy the Christmas gifts she still needed. She would have to find something for Sophie and Jamie, maybe while Sophie was with Maisie Cate later on.

Sophie was a little bored with the vintage shops but Chani came across some real finds. There were a couple more in one of the charity shops, which meant she had all she needed, and she hadn't made too big a hole in her credit card. She knew Sophie was just being polite and didn't want to be in these places at all, so she showed her two of the trendiest places for shoes and boots. Sophie seemed keen to look but didn't find anything she liked.

'How about some refreshment?' Chani suggested, spotting a good vegetarian café. 'They do brilliant carrot cake in here. And a whole range of coffees, the real, ground stuff, lots of it's Fairtrade.'

'Cake made with carrots?'

'It has grated carrot in it,' Chani explained. 'Gives it a lovely taste, sort of sweet but not too much, and it adds to the texture. It has gorgeous icing. But there's lots of other cakes and buns, flapjacks and things if you prefer.'

'No, you've got me interested. I'll try the carrot cake.'

In case Sophie didn't like it, Chani shared a piece with her, the portions were generous. She was pleased when Sophie loved it.

Finishing her lavender and honeybush tea Chani glanced at the clock on the wall and saw they had half an hour before Sophie's meeting with Maisie Cate. What could they do for half an hour?

'Do we have time to go to the Mind and Body Centre?' Sophie's voice had a pleading sound. 'I would really, really like to see it.'

Chani gave in. She'd have to show it to Sophie some time and it was probably better now than when she was actually working. Especially as they didn't have very long.

Chani opened the door of the Centre as if it were Pandora's Box. They were busy. Melissa wasn't her usual perfectly made-up and turned-out self. Her face showed signs of perspiration and she badly needed to do something with her hair. Not a good sign.

There were four women waiting at reception, one of them was pacing up and down and kept looking at her watch, another stood stiffly at the desk, her foot tapping. The pot pourri needed replacing and the little fountain that trickled over a bowl of polished blue stones hadn't been switched on.

Melissa was pouring over the appointment book, flicking pages back and forth. 'I'm so sorry,' she was saying. 'I can't find it. Are you sure it was today?'

'I have it written down,' the woman said in a tight voice. Hmm, must have said it several times already.

'I can't wait any longer,' the pacing woman said, spun away from Melissa and strode to the door.

'Oh, Caroline, no, Sherella will only be another minute,' Melissa said, rushing frantically round the desk after the departing Caroline.

'Chani!' she cried, like a besieged general spotting the cavalry. '*Can* you sort this out? I've had to leave my client, I *must* go back to her.'

'Chani,' the waiting women's relieved voices chorused.

Chani made a not-at-all-resigned sound in her throat, pretended to cough and picked up the appointment book, scanning it quickly. What a mess.

Notes all jumbled up and some crossed out. 'One fifteen, she said. 'Er, I'm sorry, I can't read this, Ms ...? It looks like Ms Pigmore?'

Melissa rushed back, grabbed the book and peered where Chani was pointing. 'Ms Denver,' she snapped, handing it back. 'Oh, oh, that's you, isn't it?' She looked at the woman standing there. 'I'm so sorry. Do forgive me. I'm a bit ... er ...'

'Yes,' Ms Denver said, without parting her teeth.

'You're with Delores, Ms Denver, I'm afraid she's running a little late, we had to squeeze someone in earlier, you see. I'm so sorry.'

'How long?'

'Oh, mm...'

'I'll go and find out,' Chani said, glancing at the sheepskin-clad woman standing behind her. 'Siobhan, you're at quarter to two, with Anise, isn't it, and,' she turned to the woman sitting down. 'Is it Ms Clayton? You're quarter to two as well, with, ah, Melissa. Can you manage to wait a little while? I'll sort out a drink for you in a second.' She remembered Sophie. 'Sorry, Sophie, can you give me a second?'

'They don't seem to know what they're doing, do they?' Sophie said, as Chani, having sorted out a second lot of confusion over appointment times was at last able to show her some of the treatment areas. 'Do you usually have to sort it out like that?'

Chani forced a laugh. 'They're short-staffed and it's busy. I manage the Therapy Programmes.' she spoke fast, moving briskly on. 'Now, we do Indian head massage here, and in there is the Beauty Therapy suite. We've just started a new deep massage facial treatment.'

'Do you do the stones thing?' Sophie asked, gazing around.

'That's the one you always see on publicity shots for spas, isn't it, the Hot Stones Therapy? Yes, we do. I can't show you in there at the moment, there's a client in treatment. I can't show you the Reiki either, or some of the more private therapies. I'm sure you don't need any of our treatments, Sophie, your aura tells me you're totally balanced.'

'Really? How do you see that?' Her eyes were wide with interest.

'I sense it. I'm very sensitive to auras.'

'Wow,' Sophie breathed. 'Cool.'

As they left Chani had a quick word with Sherella, who was showing her client into a treatment area. 'Could you tell Melissa I'll ring her about half past five?'

'Sure,' Sherella nodded, looking harassed. 'Are you in tomorrow?' She was almost begging.

'Sorry, I can't tomorrow,' Chani said in a snap decision. 'I'll talk to Melissa later, OK?'

She got away with only five minutes left before Sophie needed to be at Maisie Cate's.

What bliss to have the house to herself after what felt like months of being away, in that awful place. She set the iPod on shuffle, placed it in its dock and wandered from room to room, reacquainting herself with each one.

She had at least an hour before Sophie came back, she could relax. She put her feet up and leaned back in a contented glow. She was free, and she had the unbelievable bonus of Sophie.

But, like the serpent in Paradise – not that she'd ever believed in that – the niggling thought intruded. What was she going to do with them? They were strangers here, she couldn't expect them to amuse themselves. She would have to show them round, not just the town but the area around as well. Sophie would be interested in everything, but Jamie ... the contented glow had gone.

She closed her eyes to think. What was there to see? The canal?. Where it went through the town it was all done up for tourists, she could take them there, they could walk along the towpath and she could tell them about the canal's history and show them the craft places and the workshops. There were usually some boats moored up. That would involve a fair amount of walking, which was good, Jamie needed exercise. Actually, so did she, which gave her another idea: she could take them for a good tramp on the fells, it would be great for views as well as fresh air and exercise.

Would that be enough so they could find things to do themselves while she was at work?

A deep groan escaped her. Work. She loved her job and wanted to get back to it, but what would Jamie and Sophie do? She really didn't want to ring Melissa but the thing was, the longer she left it the longer she would have to go with no money. Worse than that, if she were to have any hope that Melissa would pay her for the coming Christmas break, as she always had in the past, and, maybe, even pay for some of the time she had been away, she would also have to be nice to Melissa. Smarmy with her in fact, because Melissa could well knock some money off because of how long

Chani had been away. But hang on, she realised, it hadn't been that much time, it may have felt like a life sentence but it had actually been … she reckoned it up. Twelve working days. It was bad, but it could have been worse. She picked up the phone.

'Chani, thanks for helping this afternoon.'

Wow! Far from the cool reception she'd expected from Melissa this was almost warm. 'No problem,' she said, going for a safe response.

'Can you get in tomorrow?' There it was. 'We're terribly busy, with the run-up to Christmas.' Melissa sounded desperate.

Chani had no choice. She took a deep breath. 'I could do the afternoon. You see, Melissa, I have these two young people to look after, I need some time to show them round, so when I leave them on their own …'

'Yes, oh dear, well, I suppose so.' There was the briefest of pauses. 'Actually, tomorrow we're opening till seven, so let's see, if you came at one, you'd actually get a full day in.'

Chani covered the phone and allowed herself a quiet moan, but the bad news didn't end there. It seemed the Centre would be open till seven on Wednesday and Thursday as well. As Friday was Christmas Eve, the Centre would close at lunchtime, which meant Chani would have to work in the morning that day. Oh, well, maybe it would work out all right. She agreed to one till seven, plus Friday morning. It would give her three mornings to show her guests around, organise food and sort things out domestically. Quite what that would involve she still had to think about. There was actually quite a lot she still had to think about as a result of her impulse decision to bring Jamie and Sophie here.

She felt tired already. She clenched her fists and stamped her feet. Pull yourself together! She was here and not there. That had to be worth a bit of organisation. As she calmed down something else came to her. Melissa'd made no mention of going out anywhere when they closed on Christmas Eve. For the last few years she had tried to organise some sort of festive staff get-together but Melissa was the last person any of them wanted to celebrate with and last year they'd ended up at the last minute just going to the pub for a sandwich and a drink. Maybe this year Melissa had given up the idea.

But Christmas now, that was another thing. Chani poured herself a glass of wine and sat at the kitchen table to do some planning before she would be interrupted.

On her own, as she usually was, she made very little fuss of Christmas. She didn't believe in all the religious stuff, or the pagan stuff it had replaced. She preferred to spend the time with her friends, usually in the pub. Sometimes one or more of her friends invited her for what they called an Un-Christmas Day. But this year she had Jamie and Sophie and she had no idea what they might want to do. Most teenagers she knew avoided all the family stuff and did their own thing together. They'd expect something, though, some sort of Christmas meal. What would that involve?

By the time Sophie appeared Chani had made several lists and was chewing the end of her pen. Sophie was bubbling over with excitement.

'Look, I made these,' she said, handing two pairs of earrings to Chani, with great ceremony. One pair was made of beads threaded on wire, done, Chani thought, with real imagination. The other was created from shapes cut out of some sort of metal, enamelled in beautiful colours. They were lovely.

'They're gorgeous,' Chani said, admiring them. 'I love how you've put these colours together, I'd never have thought of that. And these seem to glow.'

'I'm not responsible for that, Maisie Cate had already done the enamelling, but I designed the shapes and I cut them out and everything. Maisie Cate thinks I have real talent.'

'So do I. I really do. And this is your first go?'

'Oh yes, I've never done this before. Do you really think so?'

'I do. And if Maisie Cate thinks so, you do. She doesn't say things like that if she doesn't mean it.'

'Really? Oh, brill. I can go back tomorrow, the same time, if it's all right with you.'

'It's more than all right, I'll be working till seven for the next three days.'

'Oh, will you?' Sympathy filled Sophie's voice and her face, not at all what Chani would have expected. Then she brightened. 'You like your job, though, don't you?'

'I do. And I need to get back to it. I'm just a bit concerned about leaving you two on your own.'

'Don't worry about that. We're used to being on our own.'

It was said in a totally matter-of-fact way, but Chani didn't know what to say. When she'd been a child in the communes there'd always been someone there - sometimes her mother, occasionally her father, always someone - she'd never been alone. It had felt normal and when, later on, she had left that way of life, she hadn't been able to cope with being alone and had always managed to find company. When she'd decided to do her own thing it had been hard at first, but actually, she'd found being alone such a positive thing that from then on, she'd travelled by herself, mostly, and lived by herself, whenever she could afford it. She'd made a deliberate decision to have a child by herself – apart, of course, from the conception – and to be a single parent. Though that wasn't actually being alone, was it, she'd had Celandine there, until *she'd* gone off to do *her* own thing.

Yes, that was what Celandine had done – her own thing. Like she had herself. She'd never seen it like that before, it was as if she'd been struck by lightning,

'Anyway,' Sophie was saying. 'I'll be with Maisie Cate some of the time.'

Chani pulled herself back to earth. 'Yes, I know. But I was thinking, I need to show you both round the place, all of it, not just the shops. I can do that in the mornings, before I go to work.'

Sophie smiled. Grinned, more like. 'That means starting early,' she said, a gleam in her eyes. Chani ignored it.

'It will,' was all she said, knowing exactly who Sophie was grinning about and couldn't stop herself grinning back.

Brian came in with Jamie, flushed and wind-blown.

'Brilliant match,' Brian enthused as he came through the door.

He and Jamie filled the hall with maleness, a mixture of the scent of sharp outside air, the fug of the car and a lingering pub smell of male sweat, beer and chips.

'I'm taking this lad off again tomorrow, Chani, if that's all right. So he can join our lads at the club practice. Show him some proper rugby!' Brian laughed and thumped Jamie's shoulder. Jamie didn't seem to mind.

Brian lifted his head, sniffed and smiled. 'By,' he said. 'Is that your scones?'

When Brian left, some time later, arrangements for the next day's rugby practice made, all the scones had gone.

Chani saw him out. 'Thanks for looking after him, Brian,' she said.

'No thanks needed, Chani. I enjoyed having him there, good lad, that. Likes his rugby. Good to see, somebody keen like that.'

Chani closed the door feeling dazed. Could Brian be talking about the same lad?

Voices sounded in.the living room. Jamie and Sophie. What were they talking about? She had to know. Luckily they hadn't closed the door. With the kitchen door left open, creeping around like a burglar, she started on the evening meal.

'How was the match?' came Sophie's voice.

'Not bad.' Jamie's sounded surprised. 'I should've realised it wouldn't be Union.'

Chani held back the sniff. Trust him to find something to complain about.

'Ah,' Sophie said.

One day Sophie would work for the Diplomatic Service.

'They were good teams, though.' Well, that was a surprise.

Chani put the moussaka in the oven as Sophie, her voice light, almost teasing, said, 'So you enjoyed it?'

Jamie's reply was muffled. Chani, rinsing salad leaves, turned off the tap to hear better. 'Well ...' Had he moved away? He sounded further away.

'Come on, admit it, you did.'

'Probably better than looking round this place.'

Typical Jamie get-out. What would Sophie say to that? Sophie laughed.

Chani stood still, the salad abandoned, and waited. But they weren't saying anything. Had they fallen out? There were some small sounds, followed by 'mmm' and a little giggle from Sophie. Not fallen out, then.

Chani went back to salad leaves. She had put them in a bowl when Sophie spoke again.

'How did you get on with Brian?'

Chani held her breath. Had Brian told him what his job was?

'OK. Actually, he seemed pretty intelligent.' There was wonder in his voice.

This was where Chani got involved. From the doorway, holding the bowl of salad, she said, casually, 'Brian? He's a university lecturer. Earth Sciences.'

Jamie's eyes widened as he jerked round to stare at her. All he could say was, 'Oh.'

'Science,' Sophie said. 'That's your best subject. Didn't you talk about that?'

Still looking dumbstruck, Jamie said, 'No. Just about rugby.'

Time to move on. 'I thought we could go for a walk round tomorrow. See where everything is, so you can find your way to places yourselves.' Giving Jamie the chance to object she said, 'I'm working from one o'clock for the next three days, till seven in the evening, so we'll have to go out in the morning, early, no later than ten.' She avoided looking at Sophie, couldn't look at Jamie either. Don't think about how he could get up insanely early in Welwyn yet sleep in so late here. 'The other two mornings I thought I'd show you the canal, it's really interesting, and we can walk along the towpath. I thought as well you'd like to walk up on to the fells, there's some fantastic views, though we wouldn't get far in the time. You've got boots with you, haven't you?'

'I brought my après-ski boots,' Sophie said.

'Yes' The heels were quite high. 'Are they what you wore to come here?'

'Yes, they're really warm.'

'They do look warm, but those heels wouldn't be too good up there. I could probably lend you something, what size are you?'

'Six.'

'Oh, good, so am I. I can lend you some good, tough wellies and some lovely warm socks, from Tibet, they are. Nice and soft too. You could try them on, see what you think. What about you, Jamie? Do you have boots for walking? I think those you came in probably are?"

'What?'

'Boots. You have some, don't you? For walking.'

'Yes.'

'Good.' Chani took a breath. 'Dinner should be ready soon, I'll just go and sort it out.' She considered allocating jobs to them but when, as she left the room, Sophie began to tell Jamie about her afternoon she changed her mind and again listened in from the kitchen.

'We went to the spa centre, where Chani works.' Chani held her breath. 'It's got everything, more than that place Mum goes to. They don't seem to be managing very well without her, she had to sort a few things out. And we went to the One World Boutique, it was fabulous, the woman there's really, like, weird but she had this totally cool jewellery. She's called Maisie Cate, I've never met anyone called that before.'

'Oh right.' Bored.

Sophie carried on anyway. 'She's lovely. She's been showing me how to make jewellery, I made two pairs of earrings, she said I have real talent. I'm going to go again and learn some more.'

'Oh.'

'So it's good you're going to this rugby thing. What club is it?'

Chani went to organise the table.

17

Chani waited until everything had been eaten and Jamie seemed to have relaxed, at least a bit, before she told him about the new social worker.

'She needs to talk to you, in the morning, so that'll have to be before ten. Can you manage that?'

He groaned.

'She just wants to make sure you're all right.'

'You can do that, Jamie, it won't take long,' Sophie said, full of confidence.

Well, that wasn't too bad. But that night Chani's mind, instead of closing down for sleep, churned over and over the planning she'd done for Christmas, including what to give Jamie and Sophie to eat. What she hadn't planned for was how to fit in going to buy so much fresh food. It would have to be done tomorow morning, at the same time as showing her guests round the area. She would need a detailed, timed plan.

Half past midnight found her sitting up in bed with paper and pencil, making lists. She'd have to buy a Christmas tree, wouldn't she? And the greenery she usually got because she liked it. She had to start a new list. What about decorations? Were those boxes still in the loft? She added them to the list, as well as time for putting them up.

Jamie and Sophie would just have to help her. They could do the tree in the evening, after work and after the meal, they'd know what to do with it.

She lay down again and closed her eyes, only to jerk awake at the thought that the Christmas tree would have to be fitted in that morning as well. Or perhaps it was the sound of Jamie wandering round that had woken her. What the hell was he doing?

Nicola Harrison rang at quarter to ten, Jamie had just finished breakfast. On edge, Chani waited through his one-word answers to Nicola's questions until he finally said, 'Cool, I suppose,' and, handing the phone to her said, 'she wants to speak to you.'

'Thanks, Ms Caladan,' Nicola said, cheerfully efficient. 'I've had a chance to go through the file a bit more thoroughly and I'm not sure from what it says – it's quite, well, brief – it seems Ms Fforbes thought it would be best if you came to live with Jamie while his mother is, um, away, because of his father's will, which apparently stipulated he should attend Stokeley Manor School. Now, when we spoke the other day I gathered from what you said that doing that left you in some hardship. Have I understood that correctly?'

Chani gulped, forcing back the words she wanted to say and managing only, 'Absolutely.'

'I see. Clearly, that isn't a good outcome for either you or Jamie. What I suggest is that I come up to visit you in the new year, when I've been able to look into things, and we see what can be worked out. Would that be all right for you?'This wasn't happening, it couldn't be happening.

'Of course,' Chani said. She could say no more.

'Good. I'll give you a ring then and make arrangements. Have a good Christmas.'

Chani let out a shaky breath, blew her nose and put the phone in her pocket, her mind in a whirl.

They didn't quite manage to leave the house at ten. Not, in fact, until eleven, so that, instead of walking, as Chani had intended, she had to drive.

By twelve her guests knew how to find their way to the shops, to the canal, where to catch a train and where the buses stopped. Chani wasn't sure this transport knowledge was a good idea, Jamie could well decide to go back to Welwyn Garden City by train; the station people would help him work out the journey. On the other hand, it was knowledge he and Sophie might need. Possibly. She took the risk.

'Now,' she said, as she drove away from the station. 'I have to buy a Christmas tree, so we're going to a place just outside the town. It'll be busy, everybody goes there for Christmas trees.'

'Cool,' Sophie said. 'I've never done that. Ours is always delivered ...' Her voice trailed off and she went quiet.

Oh, hell, she should have realised. No tree delivery for Sophie this year. What could she say?

'I hope you'll enjoy choosing one for me, then,' she tried and as Sophie blew her nose she hurried on, inventing as she went along. 'I need one about five feet high, I haven't space for a really big one. I'm sure you can find a good-shaped one. It'll only take about five minutes to get there.'

Mercer's Nursery was busy. As they turned into it a line of vehicles – two Land Rovers and a big estate car – drove out, each with a big, netted tree strapped to sturdy roof racks.

They were followed by a plumber's van, a tree sticking out of the tied-together rear doors.

As they walked away from the car park Chani glanced at Jamie. Sophie was holding on to his hand and he kept looking at her. Concerned looks.

Norman Mercer, a short, burly man who had just put down a huge spruce, greeted Chani. 'Hiya, Chani, lass. Don't usually see you this time of year. Left it a bit late 'aven't yer?'

'Have I? Do you still have some?' she asked.

Norman laughed. 'Do we still ...? One or two, Chani, one or two.'Ere, Mick,' he yelled, to a much younger, equally burly guy. 'Come and give us an 'and 'ere.'

'Hiya, Chani.' Mick grinned and pushed back his black and green striped woolly hat. 'These ovver 'ere, is it, like?' He pointed towards a large space where rows and rows of trees were growing, spruce, larch, pine, all sorts. The nearer ones on the left were very small; to the right they were around five to six feet tall. Beyond them, the trees increased in height.

'You 'ave a look, I'll get 'saw and I'll be with you.'

'Is this the size you meant?' Sophie asked, as they wandered around. 'About two metres?'

'I mean about like this.' Chani waved her hand towards the middle section.

'About one and a half,' Jamie said, addressing the hoi polloi.

'Is it? Well, yes.'

Sophie seemed to cheer up as she examined the trees, talking with Chani about needle-drop and what was the best shape. Chani hadn't realised it was so complicated. Jamie was physically there but, it was clear, not in any other way.

'This one, then,' Chani was able to say at last.

'Right.' Mick readied himself to start the chainsaw. 'I'll bring it out to Norman. You'll want it brought ovver to 'ouse won't you. I can do it in 'mornin', 'alf eight-ish.'

'That's good, thanks, Mick.' Something else she hadn't thought of. Chani led Jamie and Sophie to the till where she was used to paying for garden plants, on a counter made from an old door set on sturdy trestles, its sheathed cable leading along the ground to a large shed. The shed was only partly effective in cutting down the noise of a diesel generator housed inside.

'There's no one here,' Jamie pointed out, disapproval heavy in his voice and his frown.

'Norman will be pricing it,' Chani told him. 'He'll be here soon, he has to wait for Mick to cut it down. There, look, he's coming.'

It was well after twelve when everything was sorted out. With only half an hour before she had to be at work, Chani did some swift planning.

'I'm going to drop you at a café,' she said. 'It's very good. You can get your lunch there. I need to do this shopping and get to work for one, I'll take my key into Willis's and get two more cut so you have one each, so you can go back to the house when you've eaten. You can pick the new keys up on the way, the shop's three doors down from the café. Remember to take the keys when you go out or you won't be able to get back in. I'll be home about quarter past seven. I'll have paid for the keys, will you be all right to buy your lunch?'

Sophie nodded and Jamie looked pained. Chani hoped they'd understood.

On her own, she moved like a whirlwind. By five past one she had found most of the things she wanted, arranged to pick some of them up early next morning, collected her key and sorted out the bill and for the new ones to be picked up, gone home, put the shopping away, changed and driven to the Centre, eating a fast sandwich on the way.

Tomorrow, she vowed, she would make sure Jamie and Sophie were up and ready much earlier.

*

Jamie had never felt so disoriented. He and Sophie were in the weirdest café he'd ever seen, at a table that seemed to be made of planks, and sitting on heavy wooden chairs. His feet rested on a bare wood floor. He was surrounded by objects he didn't recognise, ranging from large pieces of some sort of machinery to the speckled brown rock in the middle of their table. It had a hole in it, with three feathers sticking out of the hole.

He was so tired from not being able to sleep he couldn't make sense of it. Why did he have to be here? He hated it. Why couldn't he stay in his own house, he'd be fine. He didn't want this weird woman or her weird food, or this weird, cold place. Even Sophie didn't believe he could look after himself. And he was still hungry.

At least he recognised the food, or some of it. His panini had tasted quite good, but he wasn't keen on the peculiar juice Sophie had chosen. Blueberry and something.

He glanced at her, remembering she'd seemed upset, earlier, talking about Christmas trees.

'Would you like to come with me to the rugby club?' he asked her, the only thing he could think of.

Her eyes scanned his face and she smiled and reached out to touch his hand.

'No, but thanks for asking. It's not a match, is it, just a sort of practice.'

'Yes, but you'll be on your own.'

'It's fine, I don't mind. I'll probably do my nails. Though, no, I'll be making jewellery at half past four.'

How did she do it? One day in this weird place where they didn't know anybody and she'd made a contact and got involved in stuff. Whereas he … carted off to a rugby match by this guy, Brian, probably set up by Chani, he seemed to be a mate of hers.

He wasn't a bad guy, though. This 'run-about' Brian had talked about, he'd need stuff. He hadn't brought any of his kit with him, how could he play? He'd need boots that fitted and borrowed ones never did. There was no chance there'd be a shop selling them here.

What sort of players would they be, rubbish, very likely.

He really didn't want to go, how could he get out of it?

But then, if he did, what else would he do? Sophie had arranged this thing and never thought about him. He scowled.

'What time are you being picked up?' Sophie asked, and he jumped.

He looked at his watch. 'We'd better go.' At least he'd get some sort of a game.

'I thought so. We must allow time to pick up those keys on the way.'

Brian was waiting outside when they reached the house. Sophie went to open the door and Jamie stopped at the car.

'I haven't any kit with me,' he said when Brian lowered his window.

'No problem, I've got seven lots of spares in the boot, bound to sort you out with one of them.'

'Do we go anywhere near a shop where I could buy some boots?'

'Buy? But haven't you already got boots at home? They're not cheap, you know. Unless you really need another pair?'

'No, it's...' Oh, hell, no point arguing. 'I really need another pair,' he said.

Brian shrugged. 'Your business. But we'd best be off sharpish if we're going to stop on the way.'

'I'll only be a minute.'

The place Brian took him to was amazingly good.

'They've got the exact same ones,' he said. All the way up here, amazing.

'And they suit you, do they?'

'They're great.'

Even better, they had his size, and the brand of socks he liked. And when the guy clearly knew what he was talking about, so much so that the three of them were soon deep in a discussion about the coming international matches, he had to admit to himself he was impressed.

'Good bloke, that,' Brian said, back in the car. 'I get most of my stuff here. No point going all the way into Leeds.'

But the clubhouse, little more than a large hut with a shower room attached, was not impressive, or the pitch they used. He might have known it'd be like this.

'Can't afford a groundsman,' Brian said. 'We have to rely on members. Their dads, actually, or some of the older brothers, but they're all working or at school or college. Anyway, come and meet Danny, our coach. Used to be half-back for Hull.'

The afternoon was not memorable for the standard of play, or the quality of coaching, whether he'd been half-back for Hull or not. There were only two good players in the whole group, in Jamie's opinion. One of them, a wiry scrum half with lightning reactions, had his head shaved so severely he looked bald. The others called him Terrier Tim; on the pitch he played with fierce determination. That was why, then.

At the end of the practice Tim appeared at Jamie's side as they trooped into the clubhouse. 'Who do you play for?' he demanded, not in the rough accents Jamie had expected but sounding much like the boys at Jamie's school.

'School,' he said, still off-balance.

'What school's that?'

'Stokeley Manor.'

'Never heard of it. It's not round here, is it?'

'It's in Welwyn Garden City.'

'Ah. Well, you're bloody good, even for a soft southerner. We could do with you on the team.'

'Oh, er, thanks.'

Torn between being pleased by the praise and horror at the idea of playing for such a poor team, even though Tim was so good, Jamie couldn't think what to say.

Before he could think any more he was almost knocked over as what felt like an iron girder thumped him across his shoulders. Steadying himself, he heard Tim say, 'Hiya, Tim.'

Coughing, Jamie turned and saw the other player he'd thought was good, a guy built like a bull.

'This is Tank,' the first Tim explained. 'He's Tim as well.'

They began the who-do-you-play-for thing again but Terrier Tim interrupted.

'He's from down south. I said he should play for the team but he doesn't seem too keen.' There was laughter in his eyes that he was clearly struggling to hold in.

'No,' said Tank, between snorts of laughter, and gasps from Tim as his burst out. 'I don't blame you.'

Tank's shoulders were moving as he laughed, but he was so solidly-built that was the only movement he made.

A blast from the coach's whistle cut across him.

'I'll explain later,' Tank promised, still laughing, now at Jamie's puzzled looks.

'Most of the team are away,' Tank told Jamie afterwards, in the cramped changing area. 'Holidays, injuries, or sick. These are all younger, or they haven't been playing long. But Tim's right, you are good. It'll be Union of course, won't it, in the south.' He didn't wait for an answer. 'You did all right, though.'

'Thanks. I do watch League as well as Union. I was at the game yesterday with Brian. Castleford and Wakefield.'

'Were you? Great game, wasn't it.'

He paused. 'Listen, where do you live? Up here, I mean.'

'I'm in Hebden Bridge at the moment.' It felt really strange to say it.

'Right. That'll be how you know Brian, then. I live in Heptonstall. Tim's on the road up to Chiserley. There's some good games coming up, Boxing Day's always good. Why don't you come with us, we're going, aren't we, Tim?'

18

The Centre was the busiest Chani had ever known, with all sorts of problems caused by a chaotic appointments book. Four times in the first couple of hours two women turned up for the same appointment. It was even worse than when Chani had come in the previous day with Sophie.

'We can't manage without you,' Anise said, as she shepherded one client out and simultaneously guided the next one in.

What should have been a calm, therapeutic atmosphere felt more like A and E. Chani could only hold the fort, much too busy to sort things out properly, until, around four, there was a lull. Delores and Sherella had a space between clients and they rushed to make drinks for everyone. Chani took the opportunity to try to sort out the appointments book.

'Just as well I've gone through all this,' she told Delores when she brought Chani's tea. 'I've found another three double bookings between five and seven. Two of them are with you.'

'Oh, God, let's see.' Delores studied the page. It looked as though giant spiders with muddy legs had been running across it. She leaned on the desk. 'Right. We can ask Sheila to come in the morning, I can fit her in at nine, she'll have dropped her little girl at nursery then. And Lucy might be able to come at twelve, I just won't have a break then. You couldn't ring them, could you, Chani?'

'I'll ring them, I'll do it now. If you see Anise can you tell her she's got somebody called Phillips at the same time as Irina?'

It was five past seven before the last client left. Chani had done a crystal therapy and an Indian head massage to help sort out two of the double bookings. Both of the clients were new and said how much they had enjoyed the therapies. But of course, Chani had known they would.

The staff gathered in the reception area to fall into the squashy sofas and stretch out their legs. Even Melissa. Chani carried the appointment book over and insisted Melissa went through it with her.

They found two cancellations that weren't entered in the book and two more double bookings. 'At least there's two spaces if they can swap times,' Chani said.

'I'll ring them,' Melissa offered.

Chani imagined the mess Melissa could make of the changes, left to herself. 'You ring this one – is it Caitlin Houlihan?' she said. 'I'll ring Carola Simms.'

'Chani, you're back.' Carola had been coming to the salon for a long time. 'Actually, I thought I saw you this morning, up at Mercer's.'

'Did you? Were you buying a tree?'

'So it was you. You had two young people with you, are they your visitors?'

'They are, yes, Jamie and Sophie. I was showing them round the place so they can look after themselves while I'm at work.'

'I see. Are you looking for things for them to do?' This was typical Carola, seeing the important issues straight away, almost certainly she would also have thought of a solution.

'I am, actually,' Chani said.

'Do they ride?' Was that a solution?

'Ride? I don't know, why?'

'How old are they?'

'Sixteen, they both are.'

'I thought they were about the same as my Tara. She's at a bit of a loose end, her friend's away visiting family somewhere out east. I'm sure she'd love to show your two her horses. You know where the stables are, don't you?' Yes, a solution. And not only for Chani, even more typically Carola had thought of something which helped her daughter and so herself.

'I don't, Carola, no.'

'They're down Mills Farm Lane, just off Birchcliffe Lane, you can't miss it.'

'I'll ask them, thank you. It's a great idea. Now —'

'I'll give you Tara's number, they can give her a ring and arrange it themselves.'

Chani wrote down the number as Carola said it and, before she could say anything else, explained about the need to change her appointment time.

At twenty past seven Carola had finally stopped talking and Chani could go home. She felt tired, but elated. It was good to be back.

She made sure she had the house to herself before she went to her room and rang Vanessa to tell her about the new social worker.

'Ah,' Vanessa said. 'Just let me check I've got this right: the new social worker actually said Annabel "isn't here at present", those actual words?'

'Yes.'

'That's it — they've got rid of her.' Triumph rang through her voice.

'You think so?'

'Oh yes, I'm sure. I'm amazed she's lasted this long. This Nicola sounds much better, like a proper, professional social worker. I always felt Annabel was unprofessional. Things are looking up, Chani, love.'

'Why didn't you tell me you thought that about Ffrosty Fface?'

'Well, Chani, love, I couldn't really. And I didn't know what constraints she was working under. But I wasn't sure she was putting Jamie's needs first, not like this new one seems to be.'

Chani thought back to the meetings with Ffrosty Fface, remembered the clipboard and the way the receptionist had looked so terrified. 'She did seem pretty stressed,' she said.

'Yes, quite likely. Anyway, things should improve now.'

'I hope you're right, Van.'

*

Jamie returned from his practice more cheerful than he'd felt for a long time.

Sophie was even more cheerful. Bubbling over with the wonderful time she'd had with Maisie Cate she stopped talking long enough only to give him a very brief kiss before insisting he look at more earrings she'd made.

'These are more complicated,' she told him. 'I had to shape the wire to have three lines of beads as well as fixing the ends so the beads don't fall off. Tomorrow we're making chandelier earrings, and after Christmas Maisie Cate's going to show me how to work with silver. She keeps saying what a fast learner I am, and how I have a really good eye, and a flair for design. Isn't that fab!'

'Chandeliers? You're making chandeliers?'

Sophie laughed. 'Not lighting, Jamie, earrings. That's what they're called, it's the shape of them, sort of branching with beads or something hanging down from the branches. Like drops.'

What – branches? Not very interested, he left it there. Sophie was clearly having a great time and wanted to carry on doing it, whatever it was.

'I met these two guys,' he said.

'Oh, yes.' Sophie's attention was still on her earrings, which she was holding up to the light.

'They're all right. Both called Tim so one's Terrier Tim and the other's Tank.'

'Tank?' Now he had her attention.

'They're in this club,' he explained.

Her face relaxed. 'Ah. Rugby.' She looked again at her earrings. 'Was it good?'

'It was awful, except for Tim and Tank, they're the only good players. Very good, actually. They said most of their best players are away. I'm meeting them tomorrow to go to their gym. They're going to pick me up.'

Sophie was smiling. 'Tim and Tank. What are they like?'

'If you're around at half nine in the morning you'll meet them.'

Sophie had a very odd expression on her face.

209

Jamie had no trouble interpreting it.

'Half nine,' she said, 'I'll definitely be around.' She turned away and busied herself with her earrings.

He grinned. He'd never told her how early he'd got up in the mornings to avoid Chani and probably never would. Let her go on thinking he couldn't do it. He went and switched on the television, channel-hopping to find some sports news, not really paying attention, his mind busy with the realisation that he'd made not just one friend but two, on only his second full day in this crummy place. So there.

He was thirsty. 'Do you think there's any Coke?' he asked Sophie.

'You know where it is,' she said. 'I'm going to put these earrings away. You might get me a glass of mineral water, if you don't mind.' And she had gone.

All right, he could manage without a drink, but after only a few minutes knew he really did want one. He lumbered to his feet and into the kitchen, located the fridge but though he found the mineral water there was no sign of Coke, either in bottles or in cans. Where the hell might Chani keep it? He opened every cupboard in sight but found nothing he wanted. Except the biscuit barrel. Grumbling to himself he took it with him and returned to the television. The biscuits were chunky and tasted odd, a bit like peanut butter.

'What have you got there?' Sophie asked as she joined him on the sofa.

'Biscuits. They're a bit odd.'

She peered into the barrel. 'I see there's only one left.'

He swivelled his head to look. 'Is there?'

She smiled. 'They can't be all that odd. Where did you put my drink?'

'Oh, sorry, I forgot. There wasn't any Coke, I looked everywhere.'

'In the fridge?'

'Yeah,' he huffed. 'In there first.'

'Did you try the pantry?'

'The what?'

'All right, I'll show you.' When Jamie didn't move she said, 'Come on, you might need it again.'

Reluctantly he let her lead him to a small cupboard-like room off the kitchen. It was cold because it was against an outside wall, made, as were the pantry's other walls, of unlined stone. Even the shelves and two wider slabs at one end were made of stone.

'Chani showed us this,' Sophie said. 'She stores all sorts in here, potatoes and wine and things. Look, there's a carton of Coke.'

It was as cold as if it had come from the fridge. But why couldn't it have been in the fridge? Why did there have to be this weird pantry thing? It was, like, stone-age. He couldn't suppress the grin. Stone, yeah, funny. He repeated it to Sophie. She grinned too.

He had drunk two Cokes before Chani came home.

'Oh, good,' she said. 'You found the biscuits. I need a cup of tea before I can even think about food. It's been a very tiring day.'

*

It was nearly eight. Chani frowned and pursed her lips. She would have just thrown something easy together for herself but meals now needed more thought and effort than, just then, she had the energy for.

211

'Sophie, Jamie, I need your help,' she said.

'What do you need?' Sophie asked, but Jamie glowered, looking like a tall toddler, working up to a tantrum.

Ridiculous, bloody ridiculous, and just when she really needed help. Why couldn't Celandine have left her with Sophie and not this awful boy?

'Look, I'm really tired, there was no time this morning to leave something ready so I need you to help me make a meal now.'

'Why can't you get something out of the freezer?' Jamie asked.

Clenching every muscle she had, including her brain, Chani said, 'I don't have meals in the freezer. I make everything fresh.'

'Come on,' Sophie urged him.

He followed her as if being forced into slavery. And when Chani handed him a bowl of carrots and asked him to scrub them he stared at them as if they were maggots. He looked so funny she wanted to laugh, but wouldn't that be disastrous!

Struggling to hold it in, she washed potatoes and handed them to Sophie. 'Can you cut these up, on that chopping board, please, into pieces roughly like inch cubes.'

From his great height Jamie said, 'About two and a half centimetres.'

The urge to laugh went. Sophie's lips tightened but she concentrated on her task.

Jamie was hopeless, but Chani needed whatever he could produce. Sophie clearly knew what she was doing but did it very slowly and carefully, stopping every so often to show Jamie what to do. Especially when he moved on to cutting the carrots up.

'All right!' he snapped at her. That was probably not a good idea. Chani opened her mouth to say something.

'I know!' Jamie said, his voice rising.

When he shouted, 'Shit, all *right!*' Chani moved fast to put out a warning hand to Sophie, at the same time trying to place herself between them. She was too late.

'Fuck it!' Jamie yelled, slammed the knife down and stormed out, on his way catching the corner of the chopping board so it hit the floor, scattering large, misshapen pieces of carrot. The knife slid across the floor and, in his wake, doors slammed.

Sophie gasped, wide-eyed.

'Bloody Hell, Jamie!' cried Chani and chased after him.

He was, of course, in his room with the door closed.

Chani had moved as fast as she could so was panting for breath when she reached it. She leant against the wall until she had enough voice to shout over the loud and awful music.

'Jamie,' she yelled. 'Open the door.'

Nothing.

'That was ridiculous, that knife could have hurt one of us, it could have killed us! I won't have behaviour like that in my house. And you can forget about dinner.'

Still nothing.

All Chani wanted to do was smash her way into him, stop the awful noise and — No, she couldn't let herself think like that. Besides, she felt as if she'd just been in a car crash, dizzy, breathless and close to tears.

Sophie, she must be in the same state. Go to her. She was shaking, her legs felt they wouldn't hold her up. Stop it, breathe, calm down, Sophie needs you, breathe.

Sophie was still chopping, slowly, almost as if nothing had happened except that her mouth was pursed, her eyelids narrowed to slits, and her hands shook.

Chani dashed to her. 'Here, love, I'll do that,' she said, 'you'll cut yourself. You need to sit down for a while.'

'I'm all right,' Sophie said, but she let Chani take the knife from her. In this sort of frozen but still shaking state she set about picking up the bits of carrot from the floor.

Chani put down the knife and went to find a colander. Action, yes, probably was the best thing. 'Put them in here, love, I'll give them a good wash under the tap.'

Abandoning any attempt at a decent meal she threw everything into a big pan and made a stew. She was starving. Leaving the stew to cook she got out the cheese and biscuits intended for later and poured some wine. Jamie could bloody well starve.

Sophie sat with her and had a little wine, but as if she were acting. Badly. Shock, Chani knew. Was wine good for that or bad?

'He was mad at me.' Sophie the robot.

'He may well, but he can't do that sort of thing, it's not on, I won't have it. Look, love, try some cheese.'

'I'm not hungry. Thank you.'

She unfroze a bit after a while, nibbled at cheese and sipped at the wine.

Jamie appeared as Chani was serving the food out. Must have smelt the damn stuff, well, he still wasn't having any. He looked uncomfortable and a bit pale.

'Sorry,' he said.

'Oh,' Chani said, rigid.

He turned to Sophie. 'Er, Sophs, are you all right?'

She gave him a sharp look through half-closed eyes. 'That smells good,' she said to Chani, as if to a waitress.

'Could I ... er, could I have some of that, please?'

Chani gaped at him. 'Did you hear what I said?'

'Well, yes. I'm sorry. Really. Wondotagain.'

'You certainly won't.'

He stood there like someone about to be shot.

'Oh, damn it,' Chani said, 'get yourself a big soup bowl and a fork and spoon,'

As he started to eat she said, 'And don't say a word. Not a word.'

Sophie ate about half of hers, he emptied two bowls. Nobody spoke.

Chani's food tasted like shredded rope.

Sophie started to get up. 'Hang on, love,' Chani said. 'There's something I have to tell you. I have to tell you now because it's about tomorrow.' She took a long breath, pushing down her anger, leaned her elbows on the table to give herself strength and told Sophie, not looking at Jamie, about Tara and her horses. 'Might you be interested?'

'I would,' Sophie said, giving the clear impression that Jamie would not be welcome. 'I can ride, but I don't, much but I would like to meet Tara.'

She stopped, into a heavy silence.

'Sophs,' Jamie said eventually, 'could we, er, can you come ...'

She sat very still, looking straight ahead.

'Please,' Jamie managed, not easily.

She turned her head and gave him a long, hard look.

He flushed. 'I'm sorry.' The look stayed. 'Sorry, Chani,' he said.

Chani said nothing, her face stony.

Sophie stood and walked out of the room. Jamie followed her. Chani, having to do something, stacked and rinsed the dishes. She needed to sit in comfort with some more wine. They'd better not be in the living room.

From the hall she heard murmuring and was relieved there was no shouting. As she carried her wine to the blissfully empty living room, they moved upstairs. She sank into a chair and tried to relax but she was too wound up. Was Sophie all right? Stupid, stupid Jamie, he could have killed one or both of them with that knife. What on earth had possessed him? He probably was mad at Sophie, as she'd said, but neither of them had done anything to upset him to that sort of reaction. She shuddered, she'd have to keep him away from knives in future. Bloody stupid boy. He'd bloody well still have to help though, temper or no temper, she wouldn't give in on that.

She was starting to feel drowsy and thinking of going to bed when Sophie appeared, Jamie following and looking a bit stunned, his eyes so deeply shadowed he could have come straight from a disaster zone. What on earth had Sophie said to him?

'Chani, I need to contact Tara about tomorrow,' Sophie said, as if everything was normal. 'Do you have her number?' Maybe not *quite* normal.

Chani checked the time, half past ten. 'I do, but I don't know if she meant the morning or the afternoon.'

'Good, thanks. Jamie won't be able to go, will you, Jamie?'

'No,' he said, head down. 'I'm going out.'

'Oh?' Chani said, trying to make sense of the way they were being with each other. Was all forgiven? She hadn't forgiven him herself, that was for sure. 'Where are you going?'

'I'm, er —'

'Tell her about Tim and Tank,' Sophie urged him.

He stood, awkward, shifting his feet. Really, Sophie might have asked him to address the United Nations. Was this punishment?

'They're just two guys I met. I'm going to the gym with them.' His shoulders were rigid.

Chani stared. 'Two guys? Who are they? Where did you meet them? Somewhere here?'

'At the practice.'

'Oh. So they're rugby players?'

'It's just a, like, Junior League thing.'

'Why is one of them called Tank?' Sophie probed.

'Well if he thumped you, you'd know,' Jamie said, with feeling.

'Did he thump you?' Sophie was clearly shocked. And, Chani felt, a bit amused.

'He was being friendly.' Jamie's sigh was both resigned and proud. 'They're both called Tim so one's known as Tank. They call the other Terrier because he's a scrum half and small and tough like they have to be. And he plays like a terrier. Like, he doesn't give in.' Chani marvelled. She'd never heard him say this much before and wondered if it was because he was stressed out. He'd better be.

'And Tank just rolls over people, does he?' Sophie said, her face giving nothing away.

Jamie glanced at her through narrowed eyes. But yes, everything did seem to be forgiven. How did he manage it? She felt sure Sophie hadn't seen him do anything like that before. Sophie seemed all right, but was she really? She gave up.

'Do they live in Hebden?' she asked instead.

'No.'

'Oh, where then?' She would find out about them if it killed her.

'They told me where, but I don't remember.'

'Do you know their surnames?'

'Tim's called Hepworth. I don't know about Tank.'

'Ah, Tim Hepworth. Does he live out on the way to Chiserley?'

Jamie gaped at her. 'Yes, that's what he said. Is that near here?'

Chani smiled. 'It's not far. I know his mother. They're a nice family. There's a brother, I think he's called Callum.'

Jamie nodded. 'He's driving us.'

'He's picking Jamie up at half past nine in the morning,' Sophie said, glancing at Chani.

'Half past nine?' Chani repeated. 'Do you want me to give you a knock?'

Sophie stifled a laugh.

218

Chani saw the fleeting scowl cross Jamie's face to be replaced by something else she couldn't work out, it could almost have been glee.

'I'll be up long before then. The tree'll be here about half past eight. If that doesn't wake you up I'll knock on your door.' She turned her attention to Sophie. 'Here's Tara's number.'

'I'll ring her now.'

'Mightn't it be a bit late?'

'It'll be fine.

19

Chani's sleep was disrupted by some disturbing dreams that woke her up. It took ages to go back to sleep, only to be woken by the sound of someone moving round the house. Was it Jamie again? She groaned, reached for her dressing gown and, shivering in the night-time cold, crept out to investigate.

From the landing she could see there was a light on in the living room. Managing to avoid the places that creaked she reached the door and listened carefully. She could hear low voices. More than one person. Who the hell was it?

She couldn't move, except for the shaking that wouldn't stop. Until the voices changed. The telly. Someone had changed channels.

She crept back upstairs and checked Jamie's room. The door wasn't quite closed, his room empty. Had he done this in his own house? She didn't think so. What was wrong with him? She slumped against the nearest wall until the pounding in her chest and her shaking body slowed enough for her to stagger to her bed. She had hardly slept at all when Jamie's stumbling on the stairs woke her again.

In the morning, barely awake, she drove Sophie, complete with the wellies she'd tried on in case she needed them, up to Tara's stables. Thank God she had the morning to herself. She could go back to bed, or at least lie on the settee.

The settee was easiest.

What about the tree? What about the evening meal? What about tree decorations?

She groaned and sat up. All right, make another plan. She found a big pot in the garden, wiped as much dirt off it as she could and carried it into the living room. She filled it with sand and covered it with red crepe paper, dragged the still-netted tree in, stuck it into the sand and poured water into the pot until the sand was solid enough to hold the tree in place.

She was pleased with the result but the effort it had taken needed a coffee and several biscuits before she could carry on. She needed to change her clothes too, but before she did there was the loft. Didn't she put some boxes up there, from some ancient celebration many years ago? She found them, stuffed in a corner, covered with dust. One was actually labelled 'Tree decorations'.

She piled the boxes in a corner of the living room, Jamie could help Sophie put them up, she'd allow no excuses.

She needed a shower after all that, leaving enough time to put the meal she'd prepared in the fridge, write out instructions and stick them on to the plastic covering. She could ring Sophie later and ask her to put it in the oven. And, bliss, there was a whole hour left to eat something and relax before she had to leave for work.

She was on the last bite of her sandwich, about to pour herself a first mug of energising tea when Vanessa rang.

'I've got a few minutes free, the usual pre-Christmas mayhem or I'd have rung you before. How's it going?'

Chani took a sip of tea and thought about that. 'Not bad, I suppose.'

'That sounds better than it might have been.'

'Yes, I know. I'm quite surprised. I'll tell you the best part first.' She told Vanessa about Sophie's jewellery-making activities and Jamie's rugby ones.

'That's brilliant,' Vanessa said.

'It might be even better. Jamie seems to have made some friends.'

'Really?'

'Really. One's Tim Hepworth, you know, from out towards Chiserley.'

'Oh yes, nice family.'

'Yes. The other one's Tim as well but they call him Tank. I saw him when they picked Jamie up this morning, he looked familiar but I can't think where I know him from. And guess what time they left. Half past nine!'

'So late?'

'Late? You're joking, neither Sophie nor I thought he'd make it.'

'But he was up and out incredibly early in Welwyn.'

'He was, I know, but he's been sleeping really late here.' She went on to Tara and horse-riding. 'I hope they get on. Tara and Sophie, I mean, not the horse.'

'They will. Two of a kind, I reckon.'

Van had to respond to a message from someone at that point. 'Sorry, if I don't actually leave the building …'

Chani told her about her hours at the Centre and the chaos there. 'That's how this thing with Tara came up,' she explained.

'There you are. Meant to be. But look, Chani, love, it's good Jamie's got involved in stuff, and great if he's actually making friends, but, well, it may not last. I have to warn you to be prepared for him to throw a wobbler or two.'

'Don't I know – that's the worst part, I was about to tell you.' She described the carrot incident. 'Just like a kid's tantrum, except he's a damn big kid.'

'I see.' Vanessa's voice was full of sympathy. 'It must have been awful for you, both of you. But actually, a tantrum's what it was, sorry to go into the psychology but it shows how stressed he is. What did you do?'

Chani told her.

'Good, you did right. How did Sophie take it?'

'She sort of froze him out, for ages, and then went off without him. I don't know what she did or what she said to him after that but I tell you, Van, he was eating out of her hand. Mind you, she seemed to have forgiven him.' She shook her head, as if Van could see her, shrugged and pulled a face.

Good,' Vanessa said. 'that's just what he needs. What?'

'What what?' Chani asked, but Van carried on talking.

Ah, it was somebody else.

'Sorry, Chani, love, I have to go. Not a good time just now. See you on Friday, you are coming, aren't you?'

'Absolutely.'

'Great.'

Chani sat and worried. What might Jamie do next?

What was it Sophie had done that Van thought was so good? Van – she hadn't wrapped her present, had she. Damn, something else to fit in before she could go to work. Better leave everything ready so she could do it when she got back. She'd be a wreck by Christmas.

*

Tim's brother, Callum nineteen and home from Loughborough University where, Tim told Jamie, he was studying sport science.

'He plays for the uni,' Tim said.

'Yeah,' Callum confirmed, turning the car into a parking spot outside the gym. 'So I play Union for them and League back here.'

'Like you, Jamie,' Tim said and Jamie had to explain again about the school team.

'Not easy, is it, switching from one to the other?' Callum said, looking round at Jamie and giving him a nod that Jamie felt good about. 'But Tim said you played well.'

The praise in Callum's voice definitely felt good. What was even better was when, in the gym, Callum took the trouble to make a few suggestions to improve Jamie's weight-training techniques.

They were turning into the road up to Tim's and Callum's house when Tim said, as if he'd just remembered, 'Mum said she was making lunch for us. You can stay, can't you?'

'Oh, great, yes thanks.' Was that too eager-sounding, Jamie worried? He cringed when Callum laughed.

'Mrs Caladan not feeding you, Jamie?'

'I, er, yes, but she's at work,' he muttered. But no one was taking any notice, Callum intent on getting the car straightened up before an oncoming tractor reached them and Tank eager to tell Jamie how good Tim's mother's food was. He was evidently staying for lunch too.

Tim's mum, a cheerful, neat-looking woman, served the four of them huge helpings of steak pie, mashed potatoes and vegetables and left them to it.

'I'm off, boys,' she announced and disappeared. Minutes later Jamie heard a car drive off.

'Going to work,' Tim explained, his mouth full.

The food was as good as Tank had said. He had two helpings. Jamie couldn't manage that but then, Tank had spent the time at the gym lifting far heavier weights than any of the others could.

Once they'd eaten Callum collected all the dishes, put them in the sink and ran water over them. Without anyone saying a word, they all drifted into another room, stretched themselves out on an array of seating and Callum found a sports channel on the television.

No one moved for a long time. Jamie was so tired from not being able to sleep he nodded off. No one seemed to have noticed when he woke up, in time for the next match to cheer and groan through.

That one finished and minutes later Jamie was in the kitchen, holding a tea towel.

'You'll dry won't you,' Tim said.

'Yeah, won't take long with two of us,' Tank said.

Jamie let him start so he could watch him and find out what he was supposed to do. He wasn't sure but it seemed a pretty old-fashioned thing to do.

At the sound of a car outside Callum said, 'Mum's back.'

'Putting the kettle on now,' Tim said and he and Callum grinned at each other.

'It's half past five, she has to have a coffee she gets in from work,' Tim explained.

His mum, her mug of coffee in her hand, exclaimed at her welcome.

'Callum,' she said. 'There's a fruit cake in the tin. Would any of you like coffee, or tea?'

Jamie felt as if he was in a story. His own mum had never behaved like this. Magda, and the women who'd done the job before her had made all the meals. He'd never had a gang of friends round like this, never gone like this to anyone else's house, only Sophie's.

It felt even more like a story when they all sat round the big kitchen table, eating the generous slices of cake Tim's mum cut for them, everyone too busy to say much.

'So, Jamie,' Tim's mum said, putting down her coffee. 'You're Chani Caladan's grandson?'

He winced and stammered something.

She didn't seem to notice. 'I didn't know she had a grandson. And now here you are. It's lovely to meet you.'

Clearly, he would have to offer some sort of explanation. He pushed at the cake left on his plate and thought about what he could say, but all he could come up with was, 'I didn't know either. It was only because my mum, er, had to go away and Mag— er, the housekeeper was going away too.'

Tim's mum frowned and looked concerned. 'Do you mean you didn't know Chani was your grandmother?'

Jamie writhed as everyone's eyes turned to him. If only he hadn't said anything. 'No. She, I mean, she didn't know about me.'

'Chani didn't know about you?' Tim's mum's eyebrows had gone up into her fringe.

Jamie felt himself going hot. 'My mum and her ... they didn't ... they didn't see each other.'

'Oh.' There was a tiny pause before she quickly, 'Oh, right, OK. I see. But anyway, you're here now. And Tim says you're keen on rugby.'

'Yes.' Glad to change the subject, Jamie volunteered the information that he played for school.

Tim carried on for him, explaining about Union and League to his mum. Jamie could see he didn't need to do this, but she still nodded and said, 'Ah' and 'Yes'.

He was relieved to hear another car pull up. Its door clicked shut, a house door opened and a man's voice called, 'Hello.'

'Dad,' said Tim.

Tim's dad. Now he'd have to go through all that about being Chani's grandson again.

But when the big man with the ruddy face walked in, putting his laptop bag on the table, throwing down his briefcase, undoing his tie and pulling off the jacket of his business suit as he moved, Tim's mum just said, 'This is Jamie, darling, Tim's friend.'

'Hello, Jamie. Hi, Tank,' the man said and went to the fridge where he took out a can of beer.

'Piece of fruit cake, love?' his wife asked.

'Definitely.' He gave a wide smile and went to put his arm round her shoulder, lean down and kiss her before joining the group at the table.

'We need to be ready for half past seven,' he reminded her.

She nodded. 'All in hand.'

'I'm meeting Kieran at eight,' Callum said. 'I could give you a lift?'

Jamie sat watching all this happen like it was a dream. Were they like this all the time? He began to notice the little ways Tim's parents looked at each other, glances that asked and answered questions, confirmed things, signalled meanings, some he could interpret, some he couldn't. How was he working that out? Tim and Tank were teasing each other about something, pretending to punch each other while Callum sometimes joined them and sometimes was involved in his parents' conversation just as if he were, like, their age.

He breathed in sweet, yeasty, fruity cake smells; sharp, acid scents of tea; the richness of Tim's dad's coffee. He found the smell of the washing-up liquid still lingering and sensed an earthy tanginess that he traced to some pots of green stuff. He could still taste the warming, meaty pie, overlaid now with the softer sweetness of the cake.

He caught the people smells too: male sweat, after-shave, and lighter female scents, appley and warm.

He felt bathed in sensations, part of the light of the cream and lemon coloured room with its pale wood table.

He longed for it for himself, feeling on the edge of it. It disturbed him, depressed him, he burned with envy, jealousy. He wanted to go. He wanted Sophie. He wanted not to think. He had never felt like this.

He stood. Felt all their eyes on him.

'Could I use the bathroom?'

Everyone smiled. Tim's mum directed him.

In the bathroom, beige tiles, deep blue towels, cool and safe. He leaned against the door and closed his eyes. He'd had a dreadful night, full of bad memories so he'd had to go and watch some rubbish on TV to drive them away.

All today he'd felt good and everything here was so nice. So damned *nice*. So why did he feel so confused? What the hell was wrong with him?

When Callum dropped him off Jamie was still feeling weird and off-balance. So when Chani let him in and told him Sophie was having a shower he couldn't think what to say or do.

'Did you have a good day?' Chani asked. 'Can I get you anything?'

'I don't need anything,' he said. Her expression made him uncomfortable so he added, 'It was OK, thanks.'

She looked down at the sports bag he'd dropped on the floor.

'You must have two days' worth of muddy kit. Can you get yesterday's and put them all in the big sink in the cellar to soak? You'll need to run the cold water into it first, before you put the clothes in, or it'll splash and you'll be covered with water.'

It barely penetrated the weird sort of force field around him.

'Sink?'

'In the cellar, do you not remember?'

229

She shook her head. 'No, I can see not. Look, just bring all your muddy gear and I'll show you.'

Sophie, looking gorgeous, met him as he emerged, fed up and grumpy, from the cellar. She smiled and they were in each other's arms. His world began to steady as he took in the lovely, fresh, clean, familiar smell and feel of her as he held her.

'I helped groom a horse,' she told him a little while later. They were sitting together on the sofa.

'Did you?' He'd forgotten about Tara and horses.

She pulled her face and wrinkled her nose. 'It was, like, good, but the smell was awful.'

'You mean the horse?'

'No, the stables. They have a guy who comes in and cleans it out but not till the afternoon.'

'Did you actually ride?'

'Sort of. Just round the paddock. Tara's nice, she rides, she and her friend do dressage and all that stuff. We walked to her house and made ourselves some lunch. We were talking for ages. She has some gorgeous clothes, Jamie, she showed me all her things, we had a great time trying things on.'

She paused and took a breath. 'We're going to go shopping in Leeds some time. And she's dying to meet you, she wants us to go out together when her boyfriend's up here again. He's been in Venezuela, he's studying languages.' She paused for breath. 'Did you have a good day?'

Jamie was drinking in every word. He was *so* glad to see her. He managed to talk with enthusiasm about the gym, the steak pie and Callum and the TV room.

'Are you ready to eat?' he heard and, turning, saw Chani in the doorway. At last, he could stop talking. 'What do you think of the tree?' Chani asked.

He hadn't noticed a tree, so thought it best to say nothing.

'It looks really good,' Sophie said.

'When we've eaten we can decorate it,' Chani said.

It was only when she led them into the living room after their meal that he saw the tree, a Christmas tree and remembered when it was bought. Slowly, as Chani brought out boxes and unpacked them he realised what she wanted them to do. 'We'll start at the top,' she said, emptying shiny bright baubles, glittery shapes, fancy little birds and sparkly lengths of tinsel until they covered the sofa.

She was talking as she did it – stuff about how Christmas was a pagan festival, when Jesus was really born and the winter solstice.

He was letting it all flow over his head, until he heard, 'So, Jamie, you're the tallest, can you fix this at the top of the tree?'

'Ngh ...' he said, searching for an excuse to leave.

'Oh yes, Jamie,' Sophie said, gazing up at him, her eyes shining.

'I just wanted ...'

'But you're the only one tall enough.'

He hung five things in places it seemed only he could reach. Things seemed to be happening sort of outside him. Chani and Sophie would look on, talk to each other about where stuff should go, he'd put stuff where they said and have to move it when they changed their minds.

It was like someone else was doing all this and he was, he was, he didn't know what he was.

He had an urgent need to be alone. A sharp scent came from the tree, he could almost see it, it came in volleys, surrounding him, entering his skin and his head like darts. 'I'm going to watch the rugby,' he said, coming down the ladder as fast as he could.

'All right,' Chani said. She seemed far away, he was dimly aware that she wasn't at all concerned. 'Do you feel like helping me arrange the greenery when we've finished the tree?' he heard, as if it came from the next room.

'What greenery?' Sophie asked, looking round. This too came from somewhere almost outside his vision.

'I bought some mistletoe, it's in the shed, we can hang it wherever. And I cut some holly and ivy from the garden when I got home,' Chani said. 'It's so much nicer than a lot of artificial glitter. I put it in metal pots I've had for years, they've actually become trendy recently.'

Visions of metal pots, Chani wielding huge scissors and tendrils of ivy floated past his eyes. 'I'm just …' he said, or thought he did, and stumbled from the room.

20

Chani's phone rang. She answered it, Jamie disappeared. No surprise there.

'Zainab, how are you?' she said.

'I'm fine. I left a message for you yesterday, did you not see it?'

'You did? I didn't notice, sorry, I've been really busy.'

'With your visitors?'

'You heard, then?'

'Of course. Anyway, we're all dying to see you and hear all about it. That's what I was ringing about. Can you do a night out?'

A night out. With the girls. Fantastic. 'Can I! When were you thinking?'

'Are you doing anything tomorrow?'

'No, I don't think ... oh, hang on, it's Christmas Eve, isn't it? We're at Vanessa's.'

'No, it's Thursday tomorrow, Christmas Eve's Friday. We're meeting in the pub at eight if you can make it.'

'Sounds wonderful. Who's going?'

'Maggie and Elaine. I just spoke to Maisie Cate, she said she would. Her sister's staying with her, so she'll be there too.'

'Janetta?' Chani said. 'Is she here?'

'She came today. Leanne might come as well, she's not sure if she can make it but she probably will. Couldn't get in touch with Vanessa, could you?'

All her friends. 'Terrific. I'll get hold of Van. See you there.'

Fantastic. Just what she needed. She put down the phone, smiling. Now she truly was home.

She looked up and saw that Sophie was winding the tinsel into rolls and putting them back in a box. The girl was a dream.

Sophie. And Jamie. The pub at eight. Work till seven. Ah.

'Sophie,' she said. 'Tomorrow evening I'm going out, I have to be there for eight. If I leave a meal ready could you put it in the oven, or whatever it needs – I don't know what it'll be yet.'

'Sure. I should be back in time. Will you leave me a note or something?'

'Of course I will. Back from what?'

'Tara's. We're going for a ride.'

'You don't mind doing that?'

'No, I mean, I like Tara, the riding's all right.'

What would Jamie be doing? She didn't ask. He'd been really weird while they'd been doing the tree, but she couldn't put her finger on why she'd felt that. In what way weird? He'd just looked odd. No, more than odd, as if he might fall over. As if he wasn't with them. Dashing off to watch rugby like that, when nothing had been said about rugby before then. He'd done that before, but this time it'd been different. Was he ill? Come to think of it, how many times had she heard him wandering about in the night, like that time he'd been watching TV? Could he not sleep? Something must be disturbing him, was he worried? Had he had a row with Sophie?

There was every chance of that, but surely she'd have been able to tell?

On the other hand, he'd made those two friends, Tim and Tank. And been out with them. She gave up. If there was anything really wrong, it was bound to show sooner or later.

'Hi, Chani.'

Not yet properly awake, Chani was greeted by Sophie, as she had been every morning so far. As usual, Sophie was bright and alert and ready to talk about whatever was attracting her interest; Chani was not bright and alert first thing in the morning. She could function on a sort of automatic level; she could rise to dealing with the occasional frantic phone call from Melissa, or early texts from Vanessa, as long as she could crash out afterwards into near oblivion. Sophie's lively conversation was too challenging. Especially when there was nobody else there to help her out.

Chani was on her third cup of reviving tea when something in Sophie's tone of voice changed. She had asked a question.

'Oh,' Chani said, paying attention. 'Mmm,' she said, hoping that would do for an answer.

'I just wondered,' Sophie said. 'Because you won't have much time, will you?'

'Time?'

'If you have to be there for eight. I mean, you'll have to get ready won't you?'

Eight? Where the hell did she have to be for eight? It must be nearly that now.

'This evening. You said you were going out.'

'Oh, this evening, yes, of course. I will have to hurry, yes.'

'Will you want to eat and then get ready, or the other way round? Only, it affects what time I'll need to start the meal you said you'd leave?'

It was too much this early. 'I'm only going for a drink with some friends.'

'Oh, for Christmas?'

'Well, not really. We often go out together.'

Moments later, not quite sure how it had happened, she was telling Sophie about her friends, with all the added detail that Sophie's enthusiasm demanded.

'There's Vanessa, of course, we've been friends for a long time. And Leanne ... she's Brian's mum, she was the first person I got to know when I moved here.'

'What's she like?'

'She's a nice woman. She does crystals – all sorts, for healing and for jewellery; she makes magnetic jewellery too, she's very talented. We sell them in the Centre. And there's Zainab, she hasn't been here that long, she started a business growing herbs, she sells them all over the place now. She's quite a businesswoman, like Leanne. I've never been into that sort of thing.'

'Four of you, then.'

'Six, actually. There'll be Maggie and Elaine tonight, they don't always come with us.'

'What do they do?'

Chani thought again about her interviewer potential. She would be so good. Somehow, her probing questions didn't seem intrusive, she was clearly fascinated and genuinely wanted to know.

'Maggie's an artist,' she said. 'She does wonderful paintings, huge things, she's always out on the fells, painting. Real moody stuff, quite moving. Very restless aura, Maggie has. Good job she's with Elaine, or she'd starve.'

'Oh. So …?'

'Elaine writes scripts for TV things. She's quite different to Maggie. Organised, very organised.'

'They sound really interesting women.'

'They are. We'll have a good laugh. Specially if Zainab has a bit to drink and does her stand-up stuff.'

'Stand-up? Do you mean stand-up comedy? Really, wow!'

'She does it as an extra. She's very funny. Writes all her own stuff.'

'Brilliant! Where does she do that?'

'Anywhere she's asked, or where she can get herself in.'

Sophie's eyes shone. 'So we could go and see her?'

'You could if you knew where she'd be on, and when. I'll ask her if you like, if she has anything in the next week or so.'

'Oh, yes please, I'd love that.' Her eyes shone even more.

But would Jamie love it? She didn't ask.

Sophie's lift up to Tara's had arrived. 'I'll leave you a note about the meal,' Chani said. 'Have a good time.'

*

Jamie slept later than he'd meant to. When he went downstairs Sophie had already left. Damn, now he'd get all that stuff about how he couldn't get up in the morning.

Chani was busy making something in the kitchen. 'Morning, Jamie,' she said, hardly looking at him. 'Kettle's boiled. There's eggs if you want them.'

Fried eggs. With bacon. But no, of course there'd be no bacon. Scrambled then, he loved that. How the hell did you cook them? He gave up, Chani was moving so fast he felt in the way.

It wasn't a good start and it got worse. He had nothing to do, couldn't find anything to do. Wherever he went in the house Chani seemed to be there, vacuuming, moving things, whatever. He shut himself in his room and listened to opera. He couldn't get into it. Bored, he pulled out the earphones and stared out of the window at rows of grim stone houses, great lumps of dark hills behind them and a sky that made him feel closed in. He needed to move, to get out and do something. The gym had been good, maybe he could join it and do some training. But how would he get there? And back? There were buses, Chani had shown them. Trains too.

Trains. He could get on one and go to Welwyn. He'd have to find a bank with a cash machine. He could be at home, by himself, no one interfering, making him do stuff. Nobody would know he was there, awesome. He should leave a note for Sophie, he supposed.

Better wait till Chani had gone to work. He checked the time, she'd go soon, about half an hour.

Home. All to himself. He could ... he could watch what he wanted on the telly, he could do online stuff, some of the games weren't bad, like online chess. He reached for his iPad.

'Jamie.' Chani's voice. 'I'm making Spanish omelette, would you like some?'

He was starving.

Chani ate hers standing up, very quickly, ran water over her plate in the sink and put on her coat. 'I've made scones, if you want some later, they're in the tin there. Have to go now, see you later.'

He was on his third scone and sitting at the kitchen table, near the stove, deep into a game of online chess when Sophie came in, her skin glowing, her eyes full of excitement.

'I met Tara's boyfriend,' she said, hanging over the stove. 'He's back earlier than they expected. They've asked us to go for a meal with them – you remember, I told you – but it's tonight, they said it's a really good Italian restaurant. Tara's dad's going to pick us up. We need to be ready for half past six.'

Tara? Oh yes, the girl with the horses. He shuddered, it would be just like those friends of Sophie's in Welwyn, Bethany whatsit, another awful evening talking about horses and nothing else.

'You go,' he said. 'I'll stay here.' He moved his bishop.

'What?'

'I was going to watch the rugby,' he said, the first thing he could think of.

'Jamie, you can't. They're so nice, it'll be really good.'

He tore himself away from the chess and saw her face, how her eyes stared and her shoulders drooped. He couldn't miss the disappointment in her voice. Inside, he squirmed.

'You mean I should go and talk about horses all evening?'

He couldn't look at her, he was being a shit but he couldn't stop.

'How can you say that? They won't, they're really interesting. And it's a great restaurant, you like Italian.'

'No I don't.' He tried not to look at her, pretended to concentrate on the chess, but at her little gasp his eyes lifted anyway. The silence that followed made him feel worse than if she'd moaned at him. Still, he wouldn't give in.

'OK,' she said, in a sort of squeezed voice that made his stomach muscles clench.

She was at the door when he realised she'd moved. 'Where are you going?' The whine in his voice was unmistakeable even to him.

'To tell Tara we can't go.' Each word sounded like it was bitten off at the end.

He jerked his head up to see her opening the door. 'Why can't you go without me?' the whiny, brattish kid he'd become said.

'I can't tell them you prefer rugby,' she said and he felt the air between them freeze. 'I'm sure you don't care what they think but I do.'

He stared at the icy, empty space, hating himself and heard her go upstairs. It was all that awful woman's fault, forcing him to come here. And his bloody mother. And Magda, why did she have to go away? All of them, they'd all gone and left him in this shithole and now Sophie wanted to drag him off with yet more stuffy people who'd only talk about bloody horses. He hated bloody horses. Restless, he moved into the living room, where he wandered to and fro, from the door to the window, to the TV, to the door.

It was ages before he heard Sophie walk downstairs. He tensed and waited for her to come into the room but she didn't, she went to the kitchen. He'd been about to go and get himself a drink, now he couldn't, she was stopping him.

Sod her. He could go in the kitchen if he wanted to.

She looked up as he sauntered in, trying to be cool. Her eyes were red. Oh shit, he'd made her cry.

She turned away from him. 'Mummy rang,' she said into the row of plants on the windowsill.

He felt it as a punch in the gut that warned him not to say anything about skiing in France. 'Oh,' he said, floundering, 'are you —'

'Not really.' He could only just hear her.

'Sophs, I'm sorry.' He wrapped himself round her on a rush of guilt, instinct and concern. She pushed him away and reached out to open the fridge.

'I'm all right,' she said.

'No, you're not. It's my fault. I'm sorry, I really am.'

'Oh, right then, so it's all OK now,' she yelled, slamming the fridge shut.

He recoiled, her anger was so ... so big.

'Mummy wanted to know if I was all right. She was upset this had happened at Christmas.' She threw the words at him. 'She was sorry. Daddy's sorry. You're sorry. Well, it's too bloody late.' She put out a hand as if to stop herself falling, her head turning this way and that, her feet following the changing directions.

Jamie, feeling he was falling too, could only pull her into his arms and hold her while her hands scrubbed at her face. Eventually she went limp and gave in to tears. It was worse than if he'd killed her puppy, if she'd had one.

Now what should he do?

At last she calmed down, the sobs turning to sniffles. He grabbed the nearest thing she could use to dry her face.

'What time did you say we'd go?' he asked, hoarse and uncertain.

Her only reply was more tears. Should he offer her a drink? He couldn't speak, something had happened to his throat, and when she recovered and dried her face after only a short time he was so relieved his legs felt weak.

'Oh,' she said, the catch in her voice making him feel ill. 'Jamie, it's the tea towel.'

*

It was getting on for four when Sophie rang Chani at work.

'You don't need to worry about us this evening,' she said. 'We're going out. Tara's boyfriend's come back earlier than they thought, so we're all going for a meal together. Her dad's picking us up and bringing us back, we can let ourselves in.'

And when she'd rushed to make a meal that would only need heating up. But no, this was much better. 'Great,' she told Sophie. 'I'm sure you'll enjoy yourselves.'

She turned a beaming smile on the next client. A whole evening of being a free spirit.

21

At home after work Chani ate a quick sandwich and took a cup of tea with her to have while she lay back and luxuriated in the bath.

She had just finished drying her hair when the phone went. She had to run downstairs to where she'd left it, so her 'Hello' was somewhat breathless.

'Hello?' a male voice answered. 'Who's that?'

Chani clicked her tongue. She still had to get dressed, an idiot on the phone was the last thing she needed. 'This is Chani Caladan,' she snapped. 'You rang me.'

'Ah, of course it is. Sorry, you sounded ... different.'

'And who are you?' She made no attempt to hide her impatience.

'It's Damien.'

Who was ...? No, it couldn't be.

'We met in the Crossley Arms. In Welwyn Garden City.'

It was. By all the ...! How should she deal with this? Whatever 'this'was.

Stay cool, right. 'Damien, hello. How are you?' Yes, cool.

'I'm well, thank you. How are you?'

'Well, yes. Busy.' Quite cool.' Get on with it.

'I wondered if you might make it to the pub in the next day or two. Even tonight?'

She couldn't speak. What a bloody nerve! Just as if they'd seen each other only a few days ago.

'I'm afraid it would take a bit too long to get there,' she said, keeping her voice, now distinctly chilly, steady.

'Ah. Does that mean you've left Welwyn? Have you gone back to ... Heddon something, was it? Yorkshire?'

'I have.' Chilled almost to ice.

'I didn't know, I've been away, I only came back yesterday.'

Where had he been, she wondered, somewhere with no phone signals? Outer Mongolia, perhaps? Though they'd surely have phone signals there. She let a silence happen.

'I've been at an ashram, it's been marvellous. It takes a little, sort of, re-adjusting, to come back from it.'

That was true. She should be impressed that he'd been to an ashram. A few years ago she probably would have been. A few years ago she might have just come back from one herself.

'So you've been to India?' she said, pretending interest.

'No, not India. Wales.'

Wales! Ashram Bach! She had to choke back the giggles. But he was in full flow. 'It was someone I knew who told me about it. He's a druid, fascinating man, you would enjoy meeting him. I spent some time with him, he was going to the ashram so I went at the same time.'

He breathed deeply. 'It's a shame you're not here. Though I had the impression you didn't want to be here anyway.' The tone of his voice had changed, become smoother, as if he'd gone into therapist-mode.

Her tone was flat as she said, 'No, I didn't.'

'I wonder …' He paused. It was amazing, he simply didn't seem affected by how distant she was being. 'Is Heddon something anywhere near Leeds?'

'Hebden Bridge. It's quite near Leeds, but not exactly next door.' She couldn't resist adding, 'Why?' though with an edge of frost.

'I have to be in Leeds in January. It's a meeting of homeopaths, over two days. I could stay longer, maybe come over to see you. If you'd like that?'

'I'm not sure.' Not sure! Of course she was sure – no. The answer was no. 'I can't actually make plans that far ahead, I don't know what's going to happen, if I'll still be here, or … well, I don't know what's going to happen.'

'No, of course. Perhaps I could ring you again, in January, and see?'

'If you like.' Why had she said that?

But … Why not? Why not go with the flow? Let things happen as they might: why not? It was how she'd led most of her life.

But no, that wasn't true, some things she didn't. Some things she didn't want to change, as this business with Jamie had shown her. She wanted to stay here, more than ever now she'd actually got back here. Before, she'd have moved on without a care. There'd be new friends, new jobs, she would have thought, if she'd thought at all.

Before what? What had changed? Why did it matter if she stayed here or not?

The fear that gripped her, that she might have to leave, might not be able to hang on to her life here, convinced her. She had changed. She liked it too. It was important to keep things like friends and home and a job she loved, important to have stability. That was it, stability.

'Good,' he said. 'I'll be in touch.' And the line went dead.

She was standing on her doorstep before she realised what she was doing, taking gulps of refreshing air. Cold air, it was, but it felt good. Her shoulders were almost up to her ears, the muscles set solid. His call had disturbed her more than she'd known, but there was no time to re-balance herself. All she could do was to light relaxing aromatherapy candles in her bedroom – three of them – while she dressed. She stood and took several deep breaths until she could begin to feel the flow from her body to her mind.

Outside and moving, walking to the pub she was at last able to think of the phone call as something to make them all laugh.

Three gin and tonics later they were all laughing. Even if some of it was a bit hysterical. Maisie Cate set them off, with stories about some of her ditzier customers, from the woman who was a size sixteen, trying to squeeze herself into Nepalese-made trousers designed for size six girls with slim legs, to the girl who came in with her boyfriend.

'He was buying her a present, which I thought was nice, you know, like, romantic. She kept picking things up and showing them to him, she had a good idea about what would suit her, but all he wanted to know was where they came from. Every time I told him he'd say, "Where's that? Is it near Birmingham?" Or, "Is that in Cornwall or somewhere down there?" I mean, places like Tibet or Goa or Peru! In the end I found her a sweater from the Orkneys. I was going on about it being hand-knitted from local sheep's wool they gathered and spun and dyed themselves and he said – *"Oh no, we don't want none of that foreign stuff –"!*

Maisie Cate's sister, Janetta had come with her as Zainab had said she would, and she shook with laughter at these stories. She had the sort of laugh studio audience managers would have paid mega-money for: uninhibited, hilarious and so infectious that everyone laughed at the stories and then even more at Janetta.

In this atmosphere Chani had no trouble milking Damien's insensitivity as much as she wanted to.

'Will you meet him, then, when he rings?' Leanne asked, into the laughter.

'Course I bloody will,' Chani said, which set them all off again. But why on earth had she said it?

Van was telling story after hilarious story about red tape and bureaucracy, not to mention health and safety rulings. After that, even Leanne, usually too shy to join in this sort of thing, came up with a tale about someone who'd bought a healing crystal from her.

'Online,' she said, laughing so much she was hardly able to speak. 'And the next day I got this long, furious email about how I'd misled them – both of them, mind – when the thing was far too big to eat.' She was crying with mirth, they had to wait till she calmed herself down enough to get the rest of it out. 'I always send clear instructions with everything but they'd actually tried to grate it over their food and they were complaining because it was too hard and they wanted

247

their money back!'

Janetta's laughter had become great, loud whoops that had others in the small, downstairs room of the bar laughing too. By the time Chani was thinking she couldn't possibly laugh any more Zainab started: her jokes soon morphing into a stand-up performance. Everyone there of course became her audience, the whole room laughing and cheering. Including, at last, Maggie, whose deeply introspective mood had kept her isolated for much of the evening, no matter how much Elaine had nudged her and said things like, 'Oh, Maggie, did you hear that!'

Zainab's stand-up degenerated into more of a fall-over performance, resulting in such loud laughter it brought the manager downstairs. She was soon joining in.

*

Jamie tried hard not to like Tara, but as she turned out to be very much like Sophie it was impossible, pretty much..

'It's lovely to meet you,' she told him, turning round from the passenger seat as he climbed into the back of Tara's dad's car, like she really meant it. Her long, brown hair shone and flared out as she turned her head, smiling. She looked slim, not at all like Bethany whatsit. Didn't smell of horses either. 'I'm so glad you could come. This is Arnie.' She waved a hand in the direction of the person who was moving along to let the two of them in.

'It's from my surname,' said the guy. He was sitting down but Jamie could see he was tall, and that he looked sort of loosely and untidily put together.

'Nobody can pronounce my name, it's Danish.'

'He's back earlier than we expected,' Tara said. 'He's been in Beijing.'

Sophie had told him this, Jamie sort of remembered, but she hadn't said what he'd been doing there. So, for something to say Jamie asked him.

'I'm doing a degree in Business and Management, with languages, Chinese and Spanish. I was on a two month placement. Fascinating.'

'It sounds it,' Sophie said and the conversation went from there, continuing in the car and well into the meal in the Italian restaurant.

Neither Tara nor Arnie had any interest in rugby, but Tara knew both the Tims from school. She was interested in science, like Jamie, she wanted to study the subject at university. And Sophie shared Arnie's love of languages. Jamie relaxed. For the first part of the evening the conversation flowed and he enjoyed himself, especially as Arnie, who was eighteen, ordered some wine.

But then Sophie asked Arnie about his Danish background.

'My mother's English,' he said. 'Dad met her in Manchester, he did an MBA there. He's lived in this country for a long time, but he misses the snow so he likes us to go to Scotland over Christmas and New Year. This is the first time for years we're staying here.'

'His mum would rather go to the Bahamas, wouldn't she,' Tara said and Arnie smiled and nodded. 'She likes the sun. My mum keeps saying we should split up and Arnie's dad and mine go skiing and his mum and mine go somewhere sunny!'

Her voice seemed to Jamie to echo, all the weird sensations he had felt at Tim's and again doing Chani's Christmas tree were back. His hands gripped the seat of his chair, restaurant sounds, voices, rich garlic and tomato smells coming in waves mixed up with onion, cheese, wafts of hot pizza and a sudden cold draught.

He was dimly aware of a swirl of movement next to him, a jarring, scraping noise and a distant voice saying something about Sophie and all right. And Sophie's voice, he couldn't hear what she said except '... fine. Excuse me.'

The whirling around him slowed, things came slowly into focus. The chair next to him had been pushed back and was empty.

Arnie and Tara, across from Jamie, were absorbed with each other.

Jamie fought for control of himself until he thought he could stand.

'Excuse me,' he said and managed to pull himself up. He looked around.

'It's over there,' Arnie said. 'Over in the corner.'

When, with the help of a lot of splashes of cold water, he had recovered enough to go back to the table Sophie was there and talking to Tara and Arnie. They all looked up and smiled at him. It was like he was seeing them on a stage.

'We've got the dessert menu,' Tara told him, handing one to him.

He made as if to study it, still trying to pull himself together.

'Shall we share one?' Sophie asked him. 'There's this gelati, you can choose two from the list.'

'You choose.' Hoping nobody had noticed anything unusual.

It felt like hours before Tara's dad came to pick them up. He had to force himself not to rush out and throw himself into the car without waiting for the others. They moved so slowly he had to push his clenched hands into his pockets, his leg was juddering. When Tara's dad didn't, as he'd dreaded, take them back to Tara's house but dropped them off at Chani's the relief was enormous. Even more when Sophie didn't ask them to come in. Better still, Chani wasn't in.

'They're nice, aren't they?' Sophie said, making for the living room.

'Yes.' They were, but what he was most concerned about was what the hell was happening to him.

*

The Centre was even busier next day, it was Christmas Eve and Chani and all the staff were working hard to fit everyone in before closing at lunch time. The clients were mostly cheerful, festive and free with their tips. Even those who were too frazzled by what they still had to do were soothed by their treatments into being generous with both tips and Christmas wishes.

'You're very quiet this morning, Chani,' Anise said after she'd waved off her client.

'Heavy night,' Chani said.

Anise smiled. 'Was it worth it?'

'Definitely. Just what I needed.'

'Girls' night out?'

'It was. And totally spur of the moment.'

'They can be the best,' Anise said with a laugh before her next client needed her attention.

Chani didn't regret any of the gins. It had been too long since she'd had an evening like that. As they'd all said, some speaking more clearly than others, but all hugging each other in the street outside with extravagant good will before going home. She held on to the memory for as long as she could, smiling to herself.

At last the final client had left, the takings were organised and everything was put away. The staff stood around, sort of hovering and exchanging quick, uneasy glances that said, 'Please don't let her want us to go out somewhere.' So when Melissa appeared with two bottles of wine and a plate of mince pies, announcing, 'They're veggie, so's the wine,' Chani wasn't the only one to let out a relieved breath.

Melissa put everything on the reception counter and went for glasses.

'Now this, this I can cope with,' Delores said quietly as soon as Melissa had disappeared, and they all laughed.

'Hair of the dog, eh, Chani,' Anise said, raising the glass Melissa brought.

'Why not,' Chani said.

'Happy Christmas everybody.' Melissa held her glass high. 'I know it's been madly busy this week, I haven't done a final count yet but it looks like we've made record profits. There'll be a little bonus to come for you all, to thank you for all your hard work.'

This had never happened before. 'Cheers!' everyone said, full of enthusiasm.

'Little bonus,' Irina muttered on the way out. 'What d'you reckon? One pound fifty or two pounds?'

'Oh, two seventy-five,' Delores muttered back. 'Be fair.'

In spite of her hangover Chani was still giggling when she reached Patricia.

22

It was half past two in the afternoon, but the state of the kitchen told Chani Sophie and Jamie hadn't been up long.

She was putting her shopping away when Sophie bounded in. 'We'll clear this away in a minute,' she told Chani. 'We only finished breakfast a few minutes ago.'

'All right,' Chani said. 'I need to sit down for a while, it's been hectic this morning.'

Sophie put the kettle on. 'When are we going to Vanessa's?' she asked.

Chani found a mug and a teabag. She didn't feel ready yet to organise anything. 'I'm not sure. I'll have to think.'

'I'll get Jamie,' Sophie said. 'He can help me with this.'

Hoping 'this' was the kitchen, Chani allowed herself ten minutes alone in the living room with her feet up. She leaned her head back and closed her eyes. In the distance Sophie's quiet footsteps came downstairs, after them, more loudly, Jamie's, followed by muffled sounds. Hopefully they were sorting the kitchen out.

It seemed just seconds before they joined her. Jamie went straight to the television, thankfully he didn't put it on too loud, and Sophie wanted to know how Chani's evening had gone.

Chani gave her an edited account of it, leaving out any mention of Damien. 'How was your evening?' she asked, partly to divert her.

'It was lovely.' Animated and with shining eyes, Sophie told her all about Arnie and the restaurant. 'They're interested in the same sort of things as we are,' she enthused.

How quickly she appeared to have got over the shock of her parents' split. Chani hoped the mood would last but there didn't seem much hope of that if either of her parents rang. And as it was Christmas Eve surely they would.

From the kitchen Chani's phone rang and she had to go and find it – in her coat pocket.

She didn't recognise the woman's voice. 'I'm Stephanie Markham,' she said. 'Sophie's mother.' She had a very slight accent, but what stood out was the sadness in her voice. She'd sounded choked when she said who she was, and Chani couldn't think of anything to say but 'oh, ah, hello.'

'I know I should have spoken to you earlier,' Stephanie said. 'I'm sorry ... it has been ...' She made a strange sound, like a hiccup. 'I wanted to thank you for your so kind invitation to Sophie, she's so very upset, of course, and it would be very hard for her to be here.' Her accent had become stronger. 'We – family, you know, it's so important, we believe it, we both – and you know, we tried, we really did, we tried to leave things until after Christmas, but ...' She trailed into silence.

'You don't have to explain,' Chani said, feeling choked herself. 'She's more than welcome. But I'm very pleased to talk to you.'

'You are so kind. Thank you. I'm ... sorry, I'll have to go. Thank you.'

She had gone.

Chani waited a moment or two before going quietly to stand in the doorway, working out what or even if she should tell Sophie. She sneaked a glance at her and Jamie: it would take a stampede of bison to take his mind off the rugby on the TV. Sophie sat next to him, her eyes on the set, but something about her said her mind was somewhere else. All right, Chani would say nothing about the call, at least, not now.

'Maisie Cate was there last night,' she told Sophie instead. 'She was telling everybody how good your work with the earrings was.'

Sophie turned quickly to her and did her best to smile. 'Really?' She had gone pink, she looked thrilled. It was the first time Chani had seen her look less than totally confident.

She hoped she had avoided a crisis, but she had a lot of things to do.

'I have some wrapping up to do,' she said. 'It's all upstairs. I'll find out when Van wants us too. And if there's time I'd really like to go out and get some fresh air. Would you like to come with me?' She aimed the words at them both but Jamie didn't move.

'Oh, yes please,' Sophie said.

Obviously he hadn't heard. Chani said, 'Do you think Jamie would?'

'I'd say so, yes.'

He must be very bored.

They walked downhill as far as the canal. On the way through the shops, all in their festive finery, Sophie bought a gift for Vanessa of some locally-made pot-pourri and a jar of strawberry jam with cinnamon and ginger, also locally-made and organic. They stopped again to buy wrapping paper – two sheets of hand-made paper and a card.

'She'll love that,' Chani said. It was true, she would.

It was clearly a stop too far for Jamie, who muttered something and wandered off on his own. Fair enough, let him. He knew the way to the house. Apart from unsettling waves of sympathy for Sophie's mother, Chani's head was clearing.

How much might Mellisa's promised bonus be? There was no way it would be in the fantastical realms of bankers' and boardroom ones, but maybe it would help make up for the money she'd lost by having to go and stay with Jamie. Especially after buying all those gins.

She took deep breaths of cold northern air.

Jamie was looking at a bookshop window display further along the street, as if fascinated by it, But Chani had seen how he looked when he was absorbed in a rugby match; also, she knew the books displayed were on things like environmental issues, food miles and macrobiotic diets.

From the way Sophie took his hand and returned his nonchalant look with a smile she wasn't fooled either. He wasn't saying much, though that could be because Sophie talked all the time.

They reached the canal and stood, leaning on a railing to look at the water, dark with a still heaviness. A few canal boats were moored and judging by their battened-down appearance it didn't seem likely anyone was in them, or would be for some time.

The afternoon was already going dark but off to their left lights glowed from buildings that edged the towpath.

'What's in there?' Sophie asked.

'There's a craft shop, I think, and there used to be a couple of workshops, I don't know if they're still there.'

They had a look round but the glass workshop was closed and the crafts didn't have much Sophie-appeal: no Jamie-appeal at all, so Chani showed them the engraved signs telling about work done by the local community. They were interested in that – well, Sophie was – Jamie read a few lines but soon lost interest.

Chani led them along the towpath for a few minutes before letting him off the hook and turning back. As they made their way uphill the sound of a brass band came and grew louder, they were playing Christmas music, interspersed with other pieces.

'There's an orchestra,' Jamie said in tones of wonder. 'The wind section's playing Rossini.'

'I don't think it's an orchestra,' Sophie said. 'I think it's a band.'

'You're both sort of right,' Chani said. 'It's a brass band. I can't see them but they always play at Christmas. Have you heard a brass band before?'

'No,' said Jamie, adding, to her surprise. 'I know about them. I thought they played marches. I didn't know they could do classical music.'

'They do all sorts,' Chani said. 'The traditionalists don't like it though.'

Jamie raised his eyebrows, his disdain for these traditionalists unmissable. At least something had interested him.

Chani wore her long black velvet skirt, her purple velvet top with embroidery down the sleeves and round the hem, and her crystal pendant and earrings. As they would be walking to Vanessa's she put on her warmest boots and her thick wool coat. She had to smile when she saw Jamie had made an effort and had on new-looking jeans with what looked like a trendy shirt and an expensive-looking man's cardigan. Sophie looked fantastic in a tightly-fitting long top over thick black tights and high boots, with a long knitted jacket from Maisie Cate's boutique. Both were pulling on skiing jackets, hats and gloves.

Sophie carried the gifts for Vanessa, Chani her own gift for her. She passed her other bag to Jamie.

'Please will you carry this,' she asked him, ignoring his Roman emperor expression. 'It's a bit heavy, there's some books and my shoes in it.'

'It feels much colder than it did this afternoon,' Sophie said, giving him no chance to say anything. 'Do you think it's going to snow?'

'I think it might be too cold,' Chani said, though she wasn't entirely sure. She was afraid of what they would think of Vanessa's house.

Van didn't bother much about how her home looked. She hadn't changed much of it since her parents died about twenty years ago, when Van had moved in, with her partner at the time, Terry, another social worker. Neither of them had much money, so they did nothing with the house, and when they split up after only a few more years there'd been no spare cash for Van to do anything with it either. Later on promotion had given her enough to put central heating in, for which Chani was glad, and to replace the ancient kitchen appliances. It all meant the place would very likely come as a shock to Jamie and Sophie. Jamie's reactions could easily upset Van.

She was seeing Van's Christmas decorations – the same every year – through Jamie's eyes: the tatty old plastic tree, draped with decorations Chani had long ago decided had been thrown out by some nursery or community centre. The living room would be festooned with paper chains that Van had probably made as a child, the windows decorated with cotton wool snow that was brought out every December and put away in January. Chani loved it, she felt at home surrounded by it all. It was messy and chaotic, but it held the spirits of Van's family and must mean a lot to Van herself.

Sophie wouldn't like the gaudy, clashing colours, or the total lack of design, but she wouldn't show it, Van would never know. But if Jamie ran true to form ... Chani shuddered.

Their arrival was exactly as she had imagined.

Vanessa had made more of an effort than usual, even to the extent of a little make-up and lipstick. She looked good in the red, black and silver top she wore and the black pants that had a bit of a flare suited her.

'Come in,' she said, smiling. 'Happy Christmas Eve.' She stood back so they could all pass through. She shivered. 'I didn't know it was so cold,' she said. 'Just let me close this door then I can take your coats.'

That done, she hugged each of them, even a shocked Jamie, and led them into her living room.

Chani saw Jamie's face - just as she'd feared - and tensed. 'We heard a brass band this afternoon,' Sophie told Vanessa brightly. 'I've never heard one before. Chani said they play every year at Christmas. They were good, weren't they, Jamie?'

Thank God for Sophie.

'Good, yes,' he said.

'We didn't know brass bands played classical music,' Sophie went on.

Vanessa smiled. 'They are good. They've won prizes.'

'Where do they come from?' Jamie asked.

'Oh, here,' Vanessa said.

'Here?'

'Yes, they're all local. And what's good is they have quite a few young members. Anyway, let me get you a drink, I have some lovely elderflower cordial, or fruit juice, or lemonade.'

'I'll try the elderflower cordial, please,' Sophie said.

'It is nice,' Chani said.

'Do you have any Coke?' Jamie asked, his slightly bewildered expression still there.

'I think so, yes. Chani – blackberry or gooseberry wine?'

'Blackberry, please. I'll come and help you.'

When everyone had a drink and a seat Vanessa said, 'Cheers,' lifting her glass. 'Here's to a good Christmas.'

'Cheers,' the others said, even Jamie.

'How do you like the elderflower cordial, Sophie?' Vanessa asked.

'It's lovely,' Sophie smiled.

'She makes it herself,' Chani told her. 'She makes

wine too, this blackberry and the gooseberry. Did you do any more this year, Van?'

'I made elderberry and a rice wine, that's not ready yet.'

'Rice?' Jamie couldn't have looked more disgusted if Van had said 'sewage wine'.

Vanessa smiled. 'Rice wine's really good, the Japanese have made it for a long time, I think they call it sake.'

'Wow!' Clearly, Sophie was impressed.

Jamie became a Roman emperor again and Chani exchanged an amused glance with Van.

'Let them have a taste, Van,' Chani said, happily sipping hers.

Vanessa gave an uncertain frown. 'I don't know, it's pretty potent.'

'They can have a drop, surely,' Chani urged. Really, all this fuss. These two probably drank all the time at home, and why not? Better to do it that way, with adults, than make themselves ill later because they weren't used to it.

Vanessa still seemed uncertain, but then, she was a social worker. 'Well, all right,' she said. 'We'll have some supper in a minute, and you can have a taste with that.'

'Thank you,' Sophie said. 'We've got a little gift for you, first. I hope you like it.' And she handed her the carefully-wrapped package.

'Oh, that's lovely,' Vanessa said, holding it. 'What lovely paper. How nice of you.'

'Do you want her to open it?' Chani asked Sophie, hoping she would say yes.

Sophie smiled. 'Of course.'

Vanessa opened the package taking great care not to tear the special paper. 'It's gorgeous,' she said. 'Really gorgeous. I love it.'

'I brought mine for you too,' Chani said.

'And here's yours from me. Isn't this exciting?'

These gifts received much less care in the opening. Surrounded by torn paper, Vanessa immediately put on the crystal pendant with its fine silver chain from Chani.

'It's perfect with that top,' Sophie said, admiring it. 'It's so unusual, I love the way it catches the light.'

Chani was pleased at that, she'd bought Sophie one very much like it, to give her next day. And thrilled with the Tibetan temple bells Van gave her. Even Jamie agreed what a beautiful sound they made.

'I didn't get presents for you two,' Vanessa said. 'I've made special treats for you instead. Will you be ready to eat in ten minutes?'

'I'm sure Jamie will be,' Chani said, smiling. 'And I definitely will.'

'Great. I just need to see to the things in the oven.'

'I'll come and help.' Chani took her wine with her, ready to top it up.

Vanessa had set out the food in her dining room, every surface was full.

'D'you think there'll be enough?' Vanessa asked. 'There's only the canapés and hors-d'oevres left to bring in, can you help carry them?'

'Van, there's enough here for the whole street without more!'

But Vanessa produced two large trays of the little starters. They were fabulous tiny bites which could easily have been served at the Ritz or Claridge's. There was octopus, smoked salmon, caviar and a couple of things involving meat. These must be the special treats for Jamie and Sophie.

Chani helped herself to veggie things and Jamie piled his plate high. That was a good sign.

When the starters had all been eaten Vanessa gave Sophie and Jamie small taster glasses of blackberry and gooseberry wine.

Sophie liked the gooseberry best. Jamie didn't say but he'd looked more pleased with the blackberry.

'It tastes like real wine,' he said, surprise evident in his voice and his widened eyes.

Chani laughed. 'It is real wine. Better, because it's totally organic and there's nothing bad in it.'

'And it's just blackberries?' he asked, in the same voice.

'And sugar and yeast, so it ferments,' Vanessa said. She topped up her own and Chani's wine and gave more cordial and Coke to the other two.

'Come and help yourself to food,' she said. 'In the dining room. It's a buffet, it's all out on the table.'

For some time no one did anything but eat, except to say how good it all was.

Soon Chani was on to her third glass of wine. Or was it her fourth? So what – she wasn't counting.

All the food they could manage to eat had been eaten. Vanessa had covered what was left or put it in the fridge 'for later' and all four lay back in chairs, too full to move.

Vanessa looked around. 'If anyone wants a drink, they're in the kitchen, help yourself. I've put the Coke in the fridge.'

There wasn't much conversation until Vanessa remembered something Maggie had said in the pub that had made her laugh and it sparked other funny things that had been said, or that had happened that evening.

'That woman trying to eat a healing crystal!' Chani said and they both giggled.

'Yes, and that lad who thought the Orkneys were foreign!' Vanessa remembered, to more giggles. 'And Damien ...' she started.

Quickly, Chani cut across her with, 'What about Maisie Cate's sister? That laugh!'

'God, yes, she brought the house down.'

'No, that was Zainab. Oh, hang on, she fell down, didn't she.'

'Fall down comedy!' Vanessa couldn't stop giggling.

'You have to tell us what you're talking about,' Sophie insisted.

They tried, but as neither of them could recall more than a few words of each story, and as neither of them could talk about it without laughing, they didn't do too well.

Sophie laughed anyway. 'You're so funny,' she said. 'Even though you can't remember it. Or perhaps because of that.'

Jamie had a weird half smile on his face but he seemed miles away.

23

Jamie had been glad to get out and to walk. He'd never seen a canal before, had expected it to be dark and grim and piled with rubbish, but it wasn't. He'd enjoyed the time he'd spent with Sophie when they had gone back to Chani's much more. She'd been wrapping Vanessa's gift but she hadn't minded when he'd interrupted. He smiled to himself, remembering. Might she possibly reconsider this celibacy thing? All the guys at school said they'd done it. He didn't believe them all, but some he did.

Vanessa's house was a bit of a shock, really small and tatty, especially her decorations – kitsch, Mum would have called them, but the food she'd laid on was good, really good, and nobody was asking him to do stuff. It was a bit boring, though, maybe if he and Sophs could go back to Chani's and be on their own, she might ...

In the distance, just outside the awesome picture he was imagining, someone was giggling. They didn't stop, the picture faded and was replaced by Vanessa's living room. It was her doing the giggling, her and Chani, why wouldn't they shut up? What the hell were they talking about? It sounded as if they'd had a good time somewhere. He'd never seen Chani laugh like that, actually she seemed, well, all right.

He went to the kitchen hoping his dream would come back. May as well have a drink while he was there, Vanessa said to, didn't she? He found the elderflower cordial Sophie had liked, next to it in the fridge was the gooseberry wine. He'd quite liked the blackberry stuff, it hadn't tasted like alcohol at all. He poured himself some of the blackberry into the glass Vanessa had insisted he use instead of drinking from the can. Not bad. In fact, the second mouthful was pretty good. For the first time in days the weird feeling that had kept sweeping over him had gone. He drank some more.

Better take some Coke back, he thought, and emptied a can into his glass. He could take some of that elderflower stuff for Sophs too.

Sophie smiled at him when he gave it to her. 'Jamie, that's brilliant,' she said. Her eyes were lovely, all soft and shiny. Her hair too, it fell like a rippling sheet of white gold.

Lucky sod, having her for his girlfriend. He hadn't been appreciating her enough. He smiled at her. 'Pleasure,' he said.

'Are you all right, Jamie?' she asked.

'I'm fine. Absolutely fine.' He drank some Coke, could still taste the blackberry. He drank some more. 'Abso – lute – ly fine.'

He needed the loo.

Vanessa told him where it was. On his way back he noticed the living room door was closed, he didn't remember shutting it but he must have. He could hear their voices but the sound was muffled. As quickly as he could he tiptoed into the kitchen, found a small glass, considered it and changed it for a bigger one which he filled with the blackberry thing, gulping it down. Better wash the glass.

Put it back, yes. Oops, nearly missed the shelf.

*

Was it just Chani's imagination or was he looking a bit less strained? Sophie had told Vanessa about their evening out with Tara and Arnie and Jamie had actually joined in. It would be so good if she could she forget about him for a while and relax.

Now Sophie was telling Vanessa about making earrings with Maisie Cate.

'Yes,' Vanessa said, 'Chani told me. And that Maisie Cate said how good you were.'

Jamie stood up and looked vaguely around. 'Excuse me,' he said, moving towards the door.

'The loo?' Chani said. He seemed to be about to go the wrong way.

'Upstairs, on the right,' Vanessa reminded him. 'Oh, careful,' she added, as he tripped and bumped into the door frame on his way out.

Chani grinned at Vanessa. 'I didn't know your wine was that potent!'

'It must be all that Coke. That's the third time he's gone to the loo. You'd think he'd know the way by now.'

'Fourth time, I think,' Chani said, beginning to wonder.

Sophie's eyes narrowed. 'Yes,' she said, in a tight voice.

Vanessa got to her feet and went over to her stereo. 'I'll find some cheerful music.'

Chani was familiar with Van's music. 'I'm not sure these two will be all that keen on your music, Van.'

'Oh, OK.' Vanessa turned to Sophie.

'Did you bring any with you, Sophie, love?'

'I did, yes, but it's at Chani's. I'm sure yours'll be good.' But she didn't seem too sure.

For a moment Chani thought Sophie was about to go back to her house for her stuff, but Vanessa said, 'Oh, well, never mind.' And as Jamie came through the door, 'There you are Jamie.'

His progress across the room was unsteady.

'Oh, mind that ...' Vanessa warned, too late to stop him banging into her sideboard and setting off jangling noises from inside it. He had only just missed knocking over the antique ormolu clock – the only valuable thing she owned.

Vanessa gave a little gasp. Chani moved fast to take Jamie's arm and guided him back to his seat where Sophie reached out to him.

'Are you OK?' she asked him, a bit sharp.

'Yeh, course.' Jamie waved her away with a grand gesture that brought another gasp from Vanessa, who took a sip of her wine – quite a big sip – and another.

She gave Chani a vague smile. Chani recognised the signs, was about to suggest they make coffee, was totally unprepared for what came next.

Slurring her words a trifle, Vanessa said, as if she'd been thinking about it for some time. 'I wonder what your mum's doing now, Jamie.'

Chani gasped and tensed.

Jamie's head jerked up. His eyes closed and he grabbed at the sides of his chair.

Chani tensed more, ready to catch him, but he appeared to recover, shrugged and said, in a dismissive voice, 'no idea.'

Vanessa, ignoring the warning hand Chani held out, leant forward, reached out to Jamie in a consoling gesture and, in her best concerned social worker style said, 'Have you never heard from her, love?'

'No.' There was no doubt this was all he was going to say.

Neither Chani nor Sophie moved. Sophie's face was a reflection of Chani's own frozen state.

Vanessa clearly hadn't received the same message. 'Oh, how awful for you,' she murmured.

Jamie's hands clenched. 'Don't want to hear,' he said, his teeth snapping, his lower lip jutting and his brows almost meeting. Chani didn't need to examine his aura.

'Really?' Vanessa sounded heartbroken. 'That's so sad.'

By now Chani was gripped. Needing to know, heedless of Jamie's feelings, she said, though a voice in her head screamed at her not to, 'I can't believe she made all those careful arrangements – you know, about Magda and money and everything – and she's never let you know where she is.'

Jamie's jaw still threatened. 'Why would she?'

'Well ...' She was too taken aback to say any more.

'Poor boy,' Vanessa said, in full social worker empathy. 'She's your mother.'

Chani got her voice back. 'She'd never just *abandon* you!'

Jamie turned on her. 'How do *you* know. *You* abandoned *her*!'

'What?' Her voice cracked. 'I did not!' She wasn't having that. 'I never did. She was really happy in the commune. There were umpteen people looking after her and she *always* knew where I was.'

'What?' Vanessa swung round to face her with wide eyes.

'When I went travelling. You know.' Chani threw the explanation at her, surely Van understood.

This was followed by a silence she could feel.

Sophie was white, sort of pulling into herself, her face drawn, her hands spread on her knees as if to hold herself up.

'So ...' Vanessa's voice faltered.

'Oh, hell!' Jamie swore, then gave a great, heavy sigh. 'I got rid of her, all right?'

'Got rid of her?' Chani gasped. 'Whatever do you mean?'

Sophie had turned even paler. 'Jamie?' she said in a faint, shaky voice.

'I set it all up,' he went on, in the same 'so what' voice, standing up but not managing it, nearly missing the chair as he fell back on to it.

'You ... what?' Sophie looked as if she might faint.

'It was my idea, all right?' He was nearly shouting now. 'I paid him, I gave him money to ... to take her away.'

'What?' Chani half rose as the full horror of the words 'got rid of her' hit her. Her hands curved to fit his throat as images of Jamie hurling the knife down on the chopping board whirled into her head and she too had to sink back down.

Vanessa pushed herself forward on her chair and fired questions at him.

'Who? Who did you pay?'

'This guy. This ... John Smith.' He sneered as he said the name.

'This was the man your mother was seeing?' Vanessa said.

Jamie made a sound in his throat. 'Seeing!' His feelings for John Smith were plain.

'So how did he do this, exac—zackly?'

He glared at Vanessa, gestured with an arm he wasn't totally in control of as if swatting away a fly.

'Well?'

He growled. 'He, like, he sort of flattered her and stuff and he persuaded her to go off with him.'

'Jamie!' Sophie again, as if from a distance.

'Yeah. So what.' He sighed. 'Where's the wine?'

Chani had to get away, to sort all this out in her mind. She turned to Vanessa. 'Erm ... I think we need to, er, in the kitchen, Van, to, m-make some ...' Run away, she meant.

'Yes,' Vanessa agreed. 'Some tea ... or coffee. Black coffee.'

Leaving Jamie and Sophie to themselves they stood looking at each other. Neither made a move towards the kettle or anything to do with tea or coffee, they just leaned on things. Chani needed to lean on something, she felt as if she'd survived a major disaster that was still happening outside.

After a while Vanessa said, 'I think he's drunk.'

'He is,' Chani said. 'But he only had a drop.'

Vanessa picked up a bottle from the worktop she was leaning against. 'Look – it's nearly empty. We've not been drinking from this one.' She put it down again, almost missing the counter edge.

Chani, to her surprise, was no more steady. 'Thash why ... all that going to the loo.'

'And taking so long.'

Chani nodded. And remembered. 'Did he just say what I thought he said?'

Vanessa started to nod but lifted one hand to her head, holding on to the counter with the other. She took a breath.

'He said he paid this guy, this John Shmith to romansh his mother and get her to go away with him.' She had to gasp for air.

'That's what I thought he said. After he said he got rid of her.'

'Got rid ... No, no.'

'No, he can't have.'

'No, he can't have. Can't've what?'

'Can't've said it. Can't've done it.' That was clear, wasn't it? But Chani couldn't be sure. 'Can he?'

'No. No-o-o. Shooly not.'

'No. How?'

Still holding her head Vanessa shook it slowly. 'I don't know.'

'No wonder they go in for cebliss ... celabliss ... don't sleep t'geth.'

'What?'

'Shamie and Sofa.'

Vanessa waved her finger in the air. 'They're only sishteen. Anyway, I think thash good. Good thing.'

Chani felt an overwhelming sadness. 'The poor girl.'

'Who? Sophie?'

'No. Celandine. The poor sod.'

'Right, yes.'

Vanessa's face flowed from bewilderment to concern to indignation. 'Yes! Betrayed!'

'Betrayed.' Chani agreed with her. 'By her own son. Oh, poor … By that little …'

'That great big …'

'Him. Yes.'

Chani glared into space. 'Got rid of her' repeated in her head like a recording, mentally filling in the spaces between with more horrifying scenes, many involving sharp knives, that turned her mild dizziness into all out vertigo.

Neither spoke.

Until, 'you're bothered, aren't you?'

Chani focussed, just about, on Vanessa, who seemed to have a ghost behind her. Some ghosts, spinning. Must be her aura. 'Bothered?'

'About Shel … Shelnd …'

'Well, jush think, what might've happened. To her.' She'd said it, the thing she couldn't think about.

'Oh, God.' Vanessa lifted her hands to her head but had to grab at the worktop.

'I know.'

'What c'n we do?'

'I don't know. I can't get my head …'

'No. Nor me.'

'I'll think of something. Tomorrow.'

There was silence again, until Vanessa said, 'Better go back.'

Sophie was sitting all hunched up, her clasped hands held between her knees, her eyes closed. Jamie lay slumped on the settee, snoring.

'He's gone to sleep,' Sophie said, sounding bitter.

'Better leave him there,' Chani said, speaking with care.

'Righ'.' Vanessa held on to a chair.

'Come on, Soffa,' Chani said. She was starting to sway. Van had kept refilling her glass, hadn't she. How many ...? 'We'll go home,' she said, as Sophie sort of shimmered into view.

At the door the cold hit them.

'It's snowing!' Sophie gasped.

'Oh, yes.' Chani scarcely noticed. 'Come on.'

24

Jamie couldn't open his eyes. Or swallow. He wanted to move his head but when he tried it felt like white hot bolts were being hammered into it. Instinctively he lifted his hands to hold on to his head but he couldn't do it, something was stopping him. He couldn't move his feet either and the effort of trying made the hammering in his head worse.

There was another pain, one that was getting worse. In his neck. And shoulder. And down his back. He made a tentative attempt to roll on to his back, it brought waves of vicious pain to his head.

After a while he tried again, with the tiniest of movements, to lift first his hands and then his feet. But something was pinning him down, pinning down his whole body.

He forced his eyes to open just a millimetre – to the shock of glaring bright light and his eyelids slammed shut.

He tried swallowing again. No go. Something told him that if he didn't move his head, even though everything hurt, the pain in his neck would get worse. Whatever it was, it was right. The slight movement he managed made him gasp but it did begin to relieve his neck and shoulder.

He seemed to be lying on lumpy rock. Where the hell was he? He had to know. He opened his eyes very, very slowly, letting the glare of light in one nanosecond at a time, until, at last he could, without lifting his head, sort of look down his body. He gasped in horror. He was bright pink.

It must be a nightmare.

After some time the pinkness became a blanket. A bright pink blanket, tightly wrapped, so tightly he couldn't move. With infinite slowness he managed to push with his feet at the blanket, sweating and gasping, until he had freed himself enough to move his arm and push the blanket away.He rolled on to his back, his head swimming and his stomach lurching even worse than that time the channel ferry hit a fierce gale. He knew now. This had happened before, at Mark's sixteenth birthday party, held when his parents were away. This, though was much much worse.

There was something else now. His arm, the one he had been lying on, had gone dead and now he'd freed it the feeling was slowly coming back, adding to the pain.

Oh, fuck. He knew with vivid clarity what was happening in his arm: they'd done it in Biology. And that there was nothing he could do about it. If he moved any more he'd be sick. He might be sick anyway. He concentrated on not moving.

Where was he? He lifted his eyes as much as they would go and was assaulted by such glittering, bright colours his eyes clamped shut. His mind processed the input and produced an answer: Christmas decorations. He was at Vanessa's. He couldn't remember anything. Oh, God, this was horrendous.

'Jamie,' came a soft voice. 'Are you awake?'

Unable to speak all he could manage was a quiet moan.

'You are. Good. I'll make you some black coffee.'

It was Vanessa. At the thought of coffee he gagged.

'Ah, right,' she said. 'Hang on.' In seconds she was beside him again. 'Here, hold on to this,' she said.

In an instinctive reaction he moved his hands to hold whatever it was and his eyes opened to see a bright orange bucket. Shit, all these terrible colours.

He retched and somehow ended up on his side vomiting into the bucket which had moved to the floor. The effect on his head was dreadful. Whatever the fuck it was he did last night he would never do again. Never ever.

Vanessa was back, making kind sounds. She wiped his mouth with something, then placed something cool on his forehead and pushed him gently back.

'There, there,' she murmured. 'How awful for you.' With the gentlest of movements she took his hand, placed it so he was holding the cool thing himself and manoeuvred his feet down to the floor so he could lean back with his head resting on something soft.

She went away, returning with a fresh cool pad. This one also covered his eyes.

Two fresh pads later she brought black coffee and persuaded him to take a sip. It made him heave but nothing worse happened so he risked another, and another.

After a while Vanessa brought a bowl of warm water and a cloth and bathed his face. He felt very slightly better. At least, he could open his eyes. He swallowed to try to moisten his mouth so he could speak.

'Thank you.' It was a croak, but he had spoken.

Finally, he was able to stand.

With a huge effort, everything around him spinning, he made it to the loo. Thank God she had one downstairs.

'I'll drive you back,' she offered but he didn't think he could cope with that.

'Thanks,' he croaked. 'I'd rather walk.'

'Yes, it's better. Fresh air. How about some toast first?'

'No-oh-oh.'

'No, perhaps not yet. Oh, tell you what, Jamie, love, I'll walk with you. For a bit, anyway.'

He managed to thank her, to put on his jacket with her help and to walk outside. And onto roads and pavements covered with soft, slippery slush.

'It must have thawed,' Vanessa said, taking his arm. He had to cling to her to keep his footing. He was massively embarrassed.

She left him a few houses before Chani's.

'Thank you,' he said again, with an effort. Walking had made his head pound even more. Never. Never again.

*

Chani was in that half-aware state between sleeping and waking, aware of a headache, of the warmth of her bed and that she didn't want to wake up. Into this semi-stupor came very quiet sounds of her door opening.

'Are you awake, Chani?' Also very quiet, but she couldn't shut it out. Sophie. She tried to ignore her, nevertheless, but of course she couldn't. There had to be a reason for this.

She turned her head to the door. 'I am now.' Sophie was in a fluffy, deep blue dressing gown and fluffy boots. Chani started a breath which became a yawn. 'Are you all right?'

'Mummy just rang me.' Sophie's voice put Chani on instant full alert. She sat up, her eyes fully open. Her head pounded. Sophie was upset, really upset.

'It's awful, Chani,' Sophie went on. 'They're getting divorced. Mummy's gone to live in France, they're selling the house and Daddy's getting a flat in London.'

Oh, God, poor girl. What did she do now? And then, almost like a sideline, why now, at Christmas? After what her mother had said about family!

Sophie choked back a sob and carried on, in a breathless little voice. 'They want me to decide which of them I want to live with while I'm at school and which during the holidays.'

'Sophie, that's terrible.' Chani got out of bed and reached for her dressing gown.

Sophie came across the room and sank on to the bed, so Chani sat on it too, next to her. 'Yes, absolutely.' The poor girl looked terrible. 'I don't want to live in France and if I live with Daddy he'll just give me loads of money but he'll be working all the time.' She stopped and gulped in air, which made her hiccup.

Chani put an arm round her and took one of her hands. 'Yes, I see. What would you like to happen?' She'd said it without having to think.

'I don't know.' Sophie had both her hands holding Chani's. 'I know they're not going to get back together. I want to go and talk to Mummy.'

Chani had to work this last bit out. 'In France?' But no, she can't be in France now? Not already, surely not.

'Yes.'

The desolation in Sophie's voice tore at Chani.

She felt a surge of fury which turned her hands into fists. No, not that, channel it to useful action. Biting back the curses she wanted to scream out, she forced some calm into her voice and instead said, 'Then that's what you should do. Come on, I'll get up and make us some coffee.'

As they both stood up, from outside came the peal of church bells. More than one lot of church bells.

'Oh my God,' Chani said. 'It's Christmas Day.' She turned to Sophie and took her hands again. 'I can't really say Happy Christmas, can I? Oh, love, don't cry.'

Dressed and breakfasted, Sophie had recovered somewhat, though she was pale and hovering between listless and twitchy.

Chani was feeling only slightly more capable. She switched on the laptop and went into Flights to France. It was very slow but at last she had done it. At least, she had once she had found her credit card and Sophie her passport. The first available flight was eleven am on Wednesday, four days away.

'Can you wait that long?' Chani asked.

'It's the only one, I'll have to.'

'I'll drive you to the airport,' Chani said, 'I'll take the time off work.'

Sophie hugged her. 'Thank you, Chani. I'll get Daddy to send you the money. I'll ring him now, after I've talked to Mummy.'

They looked at each other as another bell pealed. 'I thought they'd finished,' Chani said, 'Ah—

'It's not — Sophie said. 'I'll get it.'

Chani dagged herself up to follow her but stopped when Sophie's stiff voice said, 'Jamie. Hi.'

Chani moved fast to the door, reaching it as Jamie finished mumbling, 'Hi, Soph.'

'Jamie,' Chani said. 'Come in the kitchen, how are you feeling?' He looked dreadful. His face was drawn and … grey? No, actually, green. He was leaning against the door, his hair a tangled mess and his clothes looked as if he'd slept in them. Of course, he probably had. He groaned and held his head.

'I'll go and phone,' Sophie said, quite brisk, and ran upstairs.

Chani took Jamie's arm. He looked so awful she felt sorry for him, however self-inflicted his state was.

'Come on, Jamie.'

She moved him along towards the kitchen, explaining about Sophie. So how bad he felt, she thought, he really needed to know what had happened to her. 'She's had some bad news. I'll make you some black coffee.'

Jamie staggered through the kitchen door and sank on to a chair, leaning his elbows on the table so he could hold his head up. 'Vanessa did that.' He sounded terrible too, quite croaky.

'Yes, she would. Did she make toast?'

Without moving he croaked, 'Don't want any.'

'I'll make some. You just stay there. Kettle's only just boiled.' She bustled about cutting bread and making coffee.

Jamie groaned. 'My head hurts.'

'Yes.' That was his own fault. 'It will.'

'Have you any painkillers?'

Chani took the mug of coffee to him. 'You can have some with the toast. Otherwise they'll probably make you feel sick.'

'Already do.' He ignored the coffee and clutched at his stomach.

'Yes, you will.'

Jamie groaned again. Chani prayed he wouldn't throw up. Just in case, she located an old bowl under the sink and put it where she could grab it.

'OK,' she told him, when the toast was ready, just a little marge on it. 'There.'

Jamie looked at her as though she was offering him ground-up worms. 'No ... I ...'

'Eat it,' she insisted. 'Just a bit. It will help, honestly.'

He took a bit, chewed for ages but forced it down.

'I think I need to lie down.'

Oh no you don't. Toast, coffee, painkillers. Then lie down. I want to talk to you first.'

Jamie's groan was agonised. Chani ignored it. 'Toast.' She waited till he ate another bite. When he'd swallowed that she said, 'Yes, I suppose you were telling the truth yesterday, about your mother? And this John Smith.' Again, she felt that strange rush of concern for Celandine. And panic. Did he really say 'got rid of her'? Did he mean ...? Her headache was getting worse.

Jamie ate more toast. Chani waited, not taking her eyes off him, wanted to shake him.

He swallowed and sighed, slumping in the chair. 'Yes.' Another sigh. It was like air escaping from a puncture.

'Do you know where he was taking her to?'

Jamie was now holding his head with both hands. 'No.'

Chani had had enough. She needed proper answers. 'I don't believe you.'

Jamie looked up at her, slowly, through hooded eyes. 'It's true.' He groaned again and looked down. 'I didn't want to know.'

How could she get it out of him? Try another tack. 'Eat the rest of the toast.'

Jamie frowned, a puzzled look on what she could see of his face, but he did eat more toast.

Chani's heart was thumping as if it would burst out of her body. 'Have you thought about what might have happened to her?' She had to sit down and take a couple of deep breaths. 'This guy – he could have abandoned her somewhere. He could have taken her abroad and sold her as … well, I'm sure you can work it out. My God, he might have murdered her.' She clamped her teeth together to stop herself asking him direct – *did you kill her? Or arrange it?* Her skin was crawling and cold. She had to calm down, she was terrifying herself, never mind this gormless lad.

Jamie was staring at her, his eyes enormous. 'No.' So quiet he was probably talking to himself. And louder, 'no!'

Well, that got through. 'You didn't think of that, did you?'

He'd gone even paler, but before he could say any more Sophie had run downstairs and burst into the kitchen. She was almost as pale as he was, had obviously been clawing at her hair in some emotion, and was breathing in fast bursts.

'Jamie,' she started and the words poured out in a panting stream. 'I've just been talking to Mummy, it's awful, Jamie, they're getting divorced, she's living in France, I have to go and see her, I'm going on Wednesday.'

'Oh, no, Sophie, I – Jamie, I need to tell you—' It was too late.

'What?' Jamie looked at Chani, his eyes wild, and back at Sophie, 'France? You're going to France? But what about me?'

Sophie burst into noisy tears.

Chani rushed to her. 'Oh, God, Sophie, come here, love.' She took her in her arms, patting and rubbing her back. 'Yes, I know. It's all right, Jamie's a bit, well, a lot hung over.'

'Yes.' Sophie turned on him. 'Jamie – how could you?'

Jamie clutched his head. 'Oh, God,' he moaned. 'Don't you start too.'

Chani tried to soothe Sophie but she stood over Jamie, her breast heaving like a scorned woman in a Victorian melodrama.

'Look,' Chani tried. 'Why don't you both go and sit down in comfort. I'll make some more coffee.'

Jamie groaned, sounding like someone fatally wounded. 'I really need to lie down,' he moaned, faintly.

'Go on then,' Sophie hissed. 'Go and lie down.' And sobbed, falling back into Chani's arms.

'Oh, you poor girl,' Chani said, glaring at Jamie.

He staggered up. 'I ... sorry, I have to ...'

25

A car pulled up outside, music spilling out when its door was opened. 'So this is Christmas ...' Chani groaned. Bloody Christmas Day.

As Sophie sobbed in her arms she stroked her hair and patted her back, her legs trembling, her mind a whirling chaos of worries. How could her sodding parents do this to her, today? Bet they didn't even send her a card. Had she sent cards herself? Cards had come to her – she and Sophie had put them up in lovely fan arrangements on the walls of the hall – but she had no recollection of sending any, except the one she'd taken to Vanessa. She must have bought them, but where were they? Why didn't she think about that when they were putting hers up? What was she going to do about all the Christmas stuff? She had presents for Jamie and Sophie, but they weren't going to be interested now, were they?

Why was she thinking about all this stuff when Sophie ...?

The whirls changed direction. Jamie – he probably wouldn't emerge till Boxing Day, if then. So it would be just her and Sophie. What could they eat?

And on to Sophie – how to cope with the poor girl, who was still sobbing. Maybe if she burned some aromatherapy oil ... which one would be best?

Sophie's sobs were becoming more like sniffles. She was fumbling in her pocket, her head down so her hair was covering her face. Chani loosened her hold on her.

'Do you need a tissue, love? Here, sit down, there's some here.'

She guided Sophie to a chair, reaching for the box of tissues and putting them on the table in front of her. Sophie took one out: it seemed to take a long time.

Chani began to panic. Would aromatherapy make much difference to the state Sophie was in? Her head was still whirling with issues around cards and Christmas dinner, the pain in her head was really bad and she didn't want to think about food. What she really needed was to sit with her feet up, the scent of soothing oil wafting around her, and drink very spicy ginger tea till her chi flowed freely again. Maybe Sophie could be persuaded to join her?

Just thinking about talking Sophie into it left her feeling exhausted.

'Excuse me,' Sophie murmured. 'I need to use the bathroom.'

'You do, love,' Chani said, relieved. 'Try splashing your face with cold water.'

Sophie, head and hair hanging, shuffled out.

Chani took a huge breath, held it and let it out in a slow, tension-relieving huff. She put the kettle on, went into the living room, set two oil burners going and lit two soothing aromatherapy candles, went back to the kitchen and made a big pot of ginger tea, adding extra spice, took it and her best hand-made pottery mugs into the living room.

She had another idea, found two plastic bowls in the kitchen, filled each one with not-too-hot water and stirred soothing herbs and foot balm oil into them. She carried one at a time into the living room, setting one in front of her chair and another alongside it, ready for Sophie, before collecting soap and towels.

When Sophie reappeared, her face made up, but still pale and listless, Chani had sunk into the comfort of soothing aromas, ginger tea and soft warm water.

'What are you doing?' Sophie asked.

After that it was easier, Sophie was soon doing the same.

They stayed like that until the water was going cold and they'd had two mugs each of the tea.

'Don't move for a minute, Sophie,' Chani said. 'I'll dry your feet and do a little massage as soon as I've dried mine.'

Sophie moaned with pleasure as Chani massaged her feet.

'That was wonderful,' she said, when Chani finished. 'I don't want to move.'

'You don't need to move. I'll give you a footstool and take the bowl, there you are.'

Sophie leaned back and closed her eyes. Chani set herself up with a footstool and did the same. Ah, fantastic.

When she woke Sophie hadn't moved. Chani stayed where she was and, now her head was clearer, started on a good think. It was almost six. Jamie had been up there for about two and a half hours. He'd very likely be out for some time yet. Ditching her original plans she visualised the contents of her fridge and her cupboards until some ideas began to form, then moved as quietly as she could to her room and changed into something a bit more appropriate for Christmas Day – a vintage black velvet dress with panels of blue lace over it, and a necklace of lapis lazuli bought in Greece during her time travelling. The face of the Greek hotel owner who had helped her out with the purchase floated into her mind. Very handsome, she remembered, thoughts of him taking her over until some sound outside brought her back to earth.

In the kitchen she found the ingredients she needed to make veggie goulash and a spicy Moroccan couscous. That seemed exotic enough, and she could bake bananas with raisins and honey if Sophie was hungry enough. There was wine but she wasn't sure she wanted any more.

Ten minutes before the food was ready she was about to check on Sophie when she walked in. She was still quite pale and heavy-eyed but seemed calmer.

'What are you cooking?' she asked. 'It smells gorgeous.'

Chani told her and was relieved when Sophie smiled – quite a small smile – and said, 'Shall I set the table?'

'It's all done, love. You can help me serve when it's ready, in about ten minutes. How hungry are you?'

'Actually ...' Sophie looked surprised. 'I'm starving.'

'Good. I'll do baked bananas then. With honey and raisins.'

'Gorgeous.' But a little frown began on her face. Had to be related to Jamie. And when Sophie's eyes looked briefly upwards she knew she was right.

'He's out cold,' she said. 'I can't see him waking up for hours.'

The frown deepened and her mouth formed a pout, but it was fleeting. 'His loss,' she said and nodded to herself.

The meal worked out fine, to Chani's relief. In spite of everything she was longing to find out if Sophie knew anything about what had happened with John Smith, if she'd seen anything or if Jamie had told her anything, but how could she when Sophie was so upset and making such an effort to hold herself together? So she pushed it away.

She'd expected uncomfortable, long silences, nor sure if she should try to fill them or just sit there. But Sophie talked almost as normal. Not normal, of course, more like she was running on nervous energy, but even so, it amazed Chani how easy she and Sophie were with each other.

'What would you be doing now if we weren't here?' Sophie asked, between courses.

'I'd be at Maisie Cate's house, probably, with whoever could be there.'

'So you're missing that.' Sophie looked concerned.

Chani *was* missing that.

Or, at least she had been, earlier. Now she wasn't so sure. Maybe she and Sophie were connected from a previous life. Or maybe they were meant to be connected in this one, maybe they had a karmic connection. Karmic connection, she thought. With Jamie it was more like a karmic collision.

For once she didn't say what she was thinking, going instead for tact.

'It doesn't matter, I can see her and my other friends any time. And anyway, that's the basis we work on, people have other commitments, there's usually at least one of us who can't make it. One year nobody could and we had the day in January, it was a great day.'

'Do you have a lot of friends here? As well as the ones you were with the other night?'

'I suppose I do. And in other places.' But not in Welwyn Garden City.

'But none in Welwyn Garden City,' Sophie echoed the thought. She was almost smiling.

'No,' Chani said, and surprised herself by adding, 'I thought I'd made one but he turned out not to be.'

'Really? He?'

'Just a guy I met in a pub. I thought … he had a good aura, we seemed to be in tune, good vibes. But he never rang. Not while I was there.'

'You mean, for, like, a date?'

For a moment Chani was stunned by Sophie's evident amazement. Bloody hell, she was a woman wasn't she! 'I do have dates,' she said, unable to keep the protest out of her voice. 'With men.'

'Sorry, Chani. I don't know why I … of course you do.' Sophie moved her fork around her empty plate with fierce concentration.

Chani wasn't used to seeing Sophie's poise disturbed. Part of her knew she should try for some poise herself, recognise the shocks Sophie had just had and how disrupted the flow of her chi must be, but she couldn't get past the righteous indignation. Get over it woman, gain some karmic credit, look out for your own chi's flow.

'I'll get the bananas,' she said.

To Sophie's 'Ooh,' when she put the dish on the table she said, able now to put a kinder tone in her voice, 'How about you? Do you like living in Welwyn Garden City?'

Some of the troubled look left Sophie's face. 'Oh, I don't really know. I mean, I have friends there and I ride and stuff, but I have friends in London too, and in France. Welwyn's pretty boring really, but I'm not actually, like, there very much, apart from school. And I spend most of the time with Jamie or in school, or else sort of hanging out.' A new shadow crossed her face, leaving a pinched look. 'I don't know what I'll ... where ...'

'No,' Chani said swiftly. 'You won't know yet. But you'll be with your mum soon. Look, it's Christmas Day, why don't we have some mulled wine? Have you ever had any?'

'Yes, when we've been skiing we have it. I like it.'

'I'll go and do it, it'll only take a few minutes. You can put some music on if you like, or the telly, whatever.'

But Sophie was clearly making an effort to pull herself out of the shadows. 'I'll clear the table as soon as I've eaten this. Oh, it's yummy.' There was no sign of shadow when she laid down her spoon, smiled and sipped the wine that Chani, now busy finishing her banana, had brought. 'Everything in the kitchen?' Sophie said, picking things up with brisk movements.

They spent the evening watching re-runs of *Friends* and sipping mulled wine, Chani answering phone calls from Maisie Cate and her friends wishing her and her guests a happy Christmas, and from Vanessa with the same greeting, concern about Jamie's condition and how she and Sophie were coping.

'Out cold,' Chani said. 'I'll catch up with you tomorrow.'

'Ah, I see. Sophie's there with you.'

'Yes. Give my love to your family.'

'Vanessa's at her sister's,' she explained to Sophie, ending the call. 'There's a whole horde of them – her sister and her sister's in-laws, Van's nephew and niece, an auntie and her daughter. They usually manage to fit in a row, some tears and a big reconciliation as well as lots of silly games. Van seems to like it.'

'She's a very kind person,' Sophie said.

'Oh, yes, I suppose she is,' Chani said.

When, at around midnight, they went up to their rooms Sophie hugged Chani and kissed her goodnight. Chani, her throat unexpectedly tight, didn't quite know what to do.

She was on the verge of falling asleep when it hit her that Sophie hadn't once mentioned the things Jamie had said at Van's. Odd. But then, neither had she. Odd again.

It was the following morning before Chani could take in the full impact of everything that had happened. And how little she had been able to get out of Jamie before Sophie had come in with her dreadful news.

Poor Celandine. Would she ever get used to these pulses of maternal concern? She lay with her eyes closed and thought about it. Well, anyone would be concerned, wouldn't they, not knowing what had happened. She shivered as the words 'got rid of her' ploughed into her mind again. What exactly had Jamie said? She'd had quite a bit to drink by that stage, hadn't she, and now she couldn't remember everything.

He'd paid the guy, John Smith – that couldn't be his real name – to take Celandine away. Assuming that was true: how much? How much did it take? How much was poor Celandine worth?

'He sort of flattered her …' yes, Jamie said that. But he hadn't been very clear. He could have been making it up, trying to put her and Van off the scent. But he'd been drunk by then, well-drunk. So … if he hadn't harmed her … she couldn't think about that. Could it be possible that Celandine didn't know what Jamie had done?

Where was she? Why hadn't she contacted her son? Maybe she did know about the bribe Jamie had given this Smith guy. Suppose she had found out, she'd never want to see Jamie again. She'd be humiliated. The poor girl.

The chances of John-so-called-Smith still being with her were slim, if not zilch, so she'd be on her own, wherever the hell she was.

The more these thoughts boiled up in Chani, the more she wanted to inflict pain on Jamie. Physical pain.

No, no, don't think that, no. Get a grip.

She crept downstairs, made herself a cup of Lapsang Souchong and took it back to bed. The house was quiet and still and the tea helped clear her head but she still wanted to knock Jamie senseless. Of course, she'd never actually do it, she had never hit anyone in her life, but as long as she felt like this she couldn't go and talk to him.

And talk to him she must. Calmly.

The house was still quiet when Chani opened Jamie's door, enough to see if he was still in bed. He was. No surprise there.

'Jamie,' she said, not bothering being quiet, she had to get him moving. 'Are you awake? I've brought you some tea.' She put it on the cupboard at the side of his bed.

'I'm awake.' Jamie's voice emerged from the scrambled bedding, followed, slowly by an arm, then his head. His hair was wild. 'What time is it?'

'Boxing Day. You slept most of Christmas Day and night.'

There was a pause, presumably while Jamie absorbed this.

'Sorry.'

Chani took a breath. 'I think there's a couple of other people you need to say that to.'

That was met by silence, but Chani could take no more. 'Why did you feel you had to set your mother up like you did?'

Jamie didn't move but the atmosphere changed somehow. It was there in the silence.

'Well?'

His voice when he at last spoke was truculent. 'She's a cow.'

Chani could believe this but even so her anger was so strong she burned with it, it flared hot in her face. 'Oh? What did she do?'

'Nothing.'

Oh no, not good enough. Calm, she had to stay calm. 'Something must have driven you to it. I mean, getting some guy to run off with your mum, well, it's not, like, an everyday thing.' That wasn't calm at all.

Jamie's breath caught in a gasp that turned into a coughing spasm as he jerked himself upright. Choking

295

back the cough he said, in a voice that snarled, 'I hate her,' glaring at Chani as if it was all her fault.

The venom in his voice was a big shock, but she held her ground. And hit back.

'So you got rid of her.' Bugger calm, she'd held it back for far too long.

'So?'

Ah, a challenge. 'How? How did you get rid of her?'

'I told you.' He hurled the words at her.

'You said you paid this Smith man to take her away. Honestly, Jamie, can't you think of anything better than that?'

'It's true,' he bellowed, slamming the side of his fist into the cupboard by the bed. The crash knocked the mug over, sending hot tea flying, most of it landing on Jamie's bare arm.

'Fucking hell!' he shrieked.

'Run in the bathroom and hold your arm under cold water,' Chani told him.

Jamie's face screwed up. 'Can't.'

'Why?' Don't be stupid, you need to do it now.'

'Oh, fuck it.' Jamie flung back the bedding and raced past Chani. In a very small pair of underpants.

Chani controlled the hysterical urge to laugh and looked around for his dressing gown. It was, she wasn't surprised to find, on the floor on the other side of the bed. She took it and waited outside the bathroom until the sound of running water stopped.

'I've got your dressing gown,' she told him.

He opened the door just enough to take it from her and slammed it closed.

She waited.

He wasn't going to shut himself up in there was he?

The loo flushed. Maybe not.

When he came out he looked awful, his face pale, his sleeve rolled right up showing a very red arm. It would hurt, of course, but the tea hadn't been hot enough to scald him, not with milk in it.

'Go and sit in the kitchen,' she said, giving him no choice. 'The stove's going. I'll make some fresh tea. Ah, you've nothing on your feet, go and find your slippers.'

'Now,' she said, sitting across the table from him and handing him another tea. Darjeeling, strong. 'You were about to tell me something. What you said to Mr Smith, maybe?'

He glowered at her, pushed his chair back and stood, his face whitening even more.

'No, sit down, you're all shaken up.' She waited as he did, feeling she might start shaking soon and wishing she'd made herself some Darjeeling. 'So, you said—'

He groaned. 'I said I'd give him money if he took her away.'

'What made you think he would?'

'He'd've taken money from anybody.' His mouth tightened.

Chani needed no explanation of that. Magda had clearly had similar thoughts when she'd said about the diamond earring. She pressed on with the questions she'd thought up while waiting for him. 'How much money did you offer him?'

Jamie exploded. 'Shit! Does it matter?'

Chani did some exploding too. She banged her hands flat on the table and half stood. 'Of course it bloody matters! How much? How much was your mother worth?

She watched it hit him, saw how he reared back, his hands lift. Felt satisfaction. Until he dropped his head into his hands and moaned.

'Jamie,' she said, more quietly. 'How much?'

'Five hundred.' The words seemed to come from far away.

She couldn't believe it. He couldn't have said that. 'What? Did you say five hundred?'

Nothing.

'Where would you get that kind of money?'

'Savings.' As if he had his mouth full.

'Savings? Your savings?'

Nothing.

She tried to reason it out. Such a lot of money for a boy to have access to, but still not enough to persuade even a low-level gold digger to take his mother away. And – with some relief – certainly not enough to buy a murderer. Was it?

A sound came from Jamie, his head still in his hands. Could it have been ...? Another. A sob, yes. What the hell?

She reached behind her to the kitchen roll, pulled off a few sheets and pushed them between his elbows.

One hand moved to grab them, followed by some determined nose-blowing.

Chani waited till it stopped. 'Tell me,' she said, gentle now.

She could hear the wall clock ticking. For a long time. She couldn't decide if Jamie meant to hold out until she gave up, but she was not going to give up. She wouldn't move until he told her, however long it took. Her main fear was that Sophie would wake and come down, if she did Jamie would escape. It was amazing Sophie had slept through all the noise, poor thing, she must be worn out. Van would tell her Jamie was probably worn out too, she could hear her say it, but it wouldn't do.

As if he'd read her mind, Jamie slumped, his arms forming a pillow on the table for his head to lie on. No, he couldn't thwart her like that.

'Jamie,' she said. He didn't move.

'Jamie.' Sharper. 'Wake up.' She prodded him.

He raised his head as if it was too heavy for him and blinked.

'You were telling me about giving money to Mr Smith.'

He groaned. 'Shit.'

'What?'

'He's a shit.'

'Mr Smith?'

Another groan.

'So you gave him money – five hundred pounds, from your savings – because he's a shit?'

'He was in the house all the time, at night, both of them. I got rid of them, it was worth it.'

Chani stared. 'You mean, your mother and him, sleeping together. You thought they shouldn't? Your mother shouldn't?'

'With him?' He was glaring at her, contempt in every line of his face. He might have been talking about a child molester, or worse. The effort was apparently too much, his head dropped back onto his arms.

The phone in Chani's pocket rang and buzzed. She couldn't ignore it.

'Are we still on for this afternoon?' Brian.

'Afternoon?'

'The match. Jamie and Sophie. By, you must have had a heavy day yesterday.'

It was coming back to her, but in a sort of mist. 'You could say that. I'll have to find out, get them to ring you back.'

'OK, but they'll have to be quick. See you later.'

She ended the call. Jamie had made this arrangement; he'd have to deal with it.

'That was Brian,' she said. 'About the match this afternoon. What are you going to say to him?'

Jamie didn't move.

She raised her voice. 'Jamie.'

Without lifting his head he said, 'Wha'?'

'Brian. Rugby. Today. What will you say to him?'

His head lifted enough for his barely-open eyes to appear. 'Wha'?'

'Are you going?'

He closed his eyes, gave a huge groan, paused, sighed and propped his head up on one hand.

'I said I would.'

Chani's sigh was immense. 'What about Sophie?'

He frowned. 'Er.'

Chani could see the cogs in his brain making slow connections as the frown gradually faded. 'Oh. She didn't want to go.'

This time it took real effort for her to push it out, every part of her had tensed up. 'I mean, are you going to go off and leave her on her own?'

He regressed in front of her to a sulky child. 'She's going off and leaving me isn't she?'

'Oh God.' Chani turned away and left him, managing, but only just, not to slam the door. She needed to talk to Vanessa.

26

Jamie had actually woken up quite a long time before Chani came into his room. He'd still had traces of hangover. He tried to remember how he'd ended up with it, tried for ages, but all he'd been able to recall was sneaking into Vanessa's kitchen to help himself to the blackberry stuff. What the hell was in it, he'd wondered? He'd had hangovers before, two or three times, like when he and some of the rugby team had shared a bottle of vodka or something somebody had pinched from their parents' stock. He'd never felt that bad before.

The more awake he became, the more a sick, heavy feeling of dread filled him, like he'd done something awful, but he had no idea what it might be.

Until Chani came in and hammered away at him. All those questions. It was bad enough when she went on about people he needed to apologise to. He had to do some quick thinking. Vanessa, he supposed, he must have upset her. She'd seemed all right when he woke up on her settee, he must have upset her the night before. But who else?

And then Chani said that about setting his mother up. He groaned, as it filtered back, then hit him like a jet of freezing water. That's what the dread was all about. He'd let it out, hadn't he? How much had he said? 'Getting some guy to run off with her,' Chani had said. So they knew that.

Did Sophie know?

Had she been there when he'd said – whatever he'd said? He felt sick all over again. He couldn't face her. He buried his face in the pillow and tried to shut it all out, but it wouldn't be shut out.

No wonder Sophs was going off and leaving him. And to France, when she'd said they couldn't go there. It was like he was sinking into a big hole of misery. Deep into it. He was overwhelmed by how everything was against him. All those people he'd met, with their picture perfect parents, their sickeningly cosy houses, no wonder he'd kept feeling weird. They weren't real. They were like you saw on the adverts, eating cheese from smiling cows. Real life wasn't like that, he knew that, none better!

Well, Sophie would know that now. Now her perfect family wasn't so perfect any more.

And it had got worse, Chani interrogating him when he'd felt so awful. He'd had to tell her about that terrible guy, him and his mum, how sickening that was. Chani knew that now. He thought she'd never leave him alone, and when she did, after Brian rang, he'd crawled back to bed, desperate to sleep, even if he missed Brian and the rugby. But he couldn't sleep. He lay there, everything running through his mind like some dreadful film.

He felt a burning in his eyes, a tightening of his throat. Hot tears ran down his face. His throat closed up and he couldn't swallow. He retched but nothing came up. A sob tore its way out, he choked on it and the tears poured out and his nose ran. He fumbled into the mess of pillow for a tissue, pulled something out and swiped at his face. Another sob forced its way out,

303

it felt like his lungs were being torn away. He threw himself down to bury his head, to shut out the sickening, bleak awfulness that was engulfing him. His body shook with sobs, he grabbed at the duvet to pull it over his head to muffle the sounds he couldn't stop.

It went on and on, nightmare images popping up like clay pigeons at a shoot –his father, going on about Stokeley Manor, best school there was, his own father had gone there, as had his grandfather, proud to go there, Jamie should be proud to go there – his mother, telling him he had to make his father proud, even though he was dead, reminding him how much his father had wanted him to be an officer, would want him to stay in the sea cadets and develop good officer qualities – that moron his mother had found, the nauseating way she'd gazed at him like an idiot puppy, that ghastly flashy man with his bloody flashy earring – the school head and the times he'd had to listen to him, with his disappointment and what would Jamie's father have thought – that fucking social worker who wouldn't listen to him, nobody ever listened to him. And Sophie was going away. Everybody went away, even Magda. Except Chani who he wanted to go away.

He woke up feeling terrible, curled up so tensely he didn't think he could straighten himself out. His head ached, his throat was raw, his eyes were swollen shut and his nose was blocked. His whole head felt blocked up, his neck and shoulders were sore, even his teeth ached.

He pulled himself free of the bedding that covered his head and lay on his back, one arm shielding his eyes, until he felt able to move, to do something, to get out of bed. He had to get out of bed, he needed the loo. As quickly as he could he opened his door and peered out. There was no one around. He made it to the bathroom and locked himself in.

The shock of seeing himself in the mirror propelled him into running a bath and lying in it as long as he dared, then, wrapped in a towel, standing at the wash basin and sluicing his face with cold water. Brushing his teeth helped too.

So did clean clothes.

What the hell happened? He felt like somebody had stretched him like a piece of elastic until he had no stretch left. Like he'd been really ill.

He checked the mirror. He still looked bad, but not like before. He hoped he just looked like he'd had a bad hangover.

He picked up his phone, saw the time and, with a jolt, remembered. Brian. It was half past twelve. What time had Brian said?

He crept downstairs. Rugby, he thought. Just what he needed.

*

Vanessa's phone rang a long time before she answered. Chani's hand holding her phone was still trembling.

'Bloody Jamie,' she said, the instant she heard Vanessa's voice. 'I'm going mad.'

'Chani, love—'

'Van, you wouldn't believe.' Struggling to stay calm, Chani brought Vanessa up to date, all her frustration gushing out.

There was a long moment of silence after she stopped.

'So,' Vanessa said, at last. 'You're saying he wanted to get rid of his mother and John Smith because they were having sex and he saw that as his mother lowering herself for such a revolting guy. He used all that money from his savings because he couldn't stand it. Right?'

'That's what he said.'

'You see, Chani, love, I see this situation quite a lot: the teenage child or children disgusted by their parent having sex with their new man or woman friend, it's a pretty normal reaction. Not the money part of it, I mean, but the disgust. But in Jamie's case, he's in a better position than most kids to use money to do something about it, extreme though that was. But I have to say, what I was worried about at the time was, well, he'd got rid of her, like, really got rid of her.'

'Oh, Van, so you thought that too.' She couldn't say it.

'Well, yes. It was the words he used.'

Chani's hand shook even more. 'But you think it's not ... not as bad as that?'

'Not as bad as murder, no. Though I can't actually see Jamie doing that. And now you've told me it was £500 he says he gave this Mr Smith, well, it's not much, is it, to arrange a murder. I don't think it is, not that I've had any experience ...'

'No ... I suppose it's not. Is it enough to make him take her away?'

'Again, I've no experience. But, there are other terrible things besides murder you know, in these relationships, a widowed mother, a young boy who detests the mother's boyfriend ...'

'Van! You mean, a paedophile?'

306

'I'm just saying, if this was a case I was dealing with, it's something I'd have to think about. So I have to ask, did anything Jamie said make you feel, I don't know, like the hairs on your neck stand up? Anything like that?'

'Hell's teeth! I can't think ...'

'Don't push it, just wait and see if anything comes to you. It's just something we need to think about. Jamie doesn't seem to me to be, well, wait and see.'

'You've knocked me for six.' Chani needed support, found a chair and sank into it.

'I'm sorry, Chani, love. Anyway, I assume you didn't get any more out of him?'

'No, because Brian rang.' She felt quite shaky.

'Ah, yes. I gather Jamie's gone with Brian.' Vanessa's voice was perfectly normal. How did she do it? Was she dealing with this sort of thing all the time? 'So he recovered enough to do that?'

Some of her anger was back. 'Oh yes. Did I tell you what he said about Sophie?'

'You did.'

'He's unbelievable. About as sensitive as an iceberg.'

'I'm not sure he's able to do sensitive after everything that's happened to him, you know. I mean, I know he's really upset Sophie but I don't think he can help it.'

This was desperate. How could Vanessa feel all this sympathy for Jamie, when he was so awful with Sophie, who was really suffering? But then, if Mr Smith had, well, interfered with Jamie ...? How could she? What could she? 'What the hell am I going to do with them?'

'When's Sophie going to France?'

'Wednesday. How am I going to get them sorted out before then?'

'Chani, love, how ... I'm not sure you can. Or that you should even try. If he's as self-centred as you say all this could be for the best. It might help Sophie see what he's like so she'll realise she has to ditch him.'

'Omigod! No! She's the only thing that's keeping me going. My God, imagine if I'm left with just him, *and* he's been ditched. There couldn't be anything worse.' Except if Mr Smith ... There could be much worse.

'All right, calm down. It might never come to that. It's quite likely he can't cope with her distress because his own is too much for him. You'll just have to be patient.'

'Patient! '

'I know, I do know. But it's all you can do. Give him time. He has started talking to you, hasn't he? Maybe he'll open up a bit more – it can only help him if he does.'

They were interrupted by a knock on Chani's door. She jumped so much she dropped the phone. Was Jamie wanting to open up to her already? She wasn't ready for that.

Trembling, she found the phone, got it the right way round and spoke, her voice shaky. 'Hang on, Van, somebody's at the door. I'll ring you back, OK?'

It was Sophie, attempting a winning yet apologetic smile. Chani's heart rate slowed.

'I've been going through what I brought with me and ... I really need to go shopping. Today. I need loads of things for France. Could you feel like shopping?'

308

Hell's teeth, what next? Shopping. She hated shopping – the sort Sophie would be meaning – at the best of times, but it was Boxing Day. Where would they find shops open? Halifax? Huddersfield? Bradford? Would they have the sort of shops Sophie liked?

Making a supreme effort to be gentle, she said, 'Sophie, love, I don't know if the shops are open today. It's Boxing Day.'

'It's the Sales, lots of them start today.'

Oh, God. Sales. Could things get worse? She really couldn't do that. She'd rather die. How could she get out of it? Might Brian want her to go to the rugby? Don't be stupid, Chani. Could she ring Vanessa and ask her to pretend she desperately needed her?

She looked at Sophie's still pale, trying-so-hard face and was lost. 'You mean shops like Gap and ...' She couldn't even think which ones.

Sophie nodded and almost smiled and supplied some names, none of which meant anything at all.

But then Chani had an inspiration. 'I don't know where any of those places are. But Tara will, won't she?'

Sophie's smile reached approximately three quarters. 'I'll ring her. My phone's in my room.'

Chani waited, hoping Tara was there and free to go shopping. Sophie was soon back.

'We need to go to Leeds.'

Chani groaned.

'Is that a problem?' Sophie asked, clearly concerned.

'It's quite a long way.' Please let her not have to drive there.

Sophie must have thought fast because very soon her face cleared and she pressed buttons on her phone.

'Hi, Tara,' she said. 'Chani says it's a long way.'

Tara's voice came through clearly – just like her mother's. 'I see – it's a long way in that old car. I'll ask Arnie to take us. Hold on.'

'Sorted,' Sophie said, seconds later, though her, 'Oh, great, cool. See you then,' had already conveyed the welcome message to Chani.

A great weight lifted from Chani. 'What time are they coming?'

'In about half an hour. I'd better get dressed.'

'Have you had any breakfast?'

'No, I forgot.'

'You get ready, I'll make you something.'

Chani took the opportunity while she made Sophie's breakfast to ring Vanessa again.

'What I think you need, Chani, love,' Vanessa's decisive voice said, 'is a good blow on the fells. It'd do me some good to get outside as well. Why don't you text me as soon as they've gone? I'll come and pick you up. Wellies, I think,' she added, without a pause, and thick socks.'

Ten minutes after Jamie and Sophie had left, within minutes of each other, Chani and Vanessa set off to tackle the moorland paths, both in wellies and very thick socks,

Chani talked non-stop about Jamie.

'You did really well there, Chani,' Vanessa said. "You certainly let him have it. Good for you, he needs to face up to what he's done.' She paused and seemed to be thinking, before going on, 'It does seem very odd his mother hasn't contacted him at all.'

And all the fear had rushed back, as if Chani had walked into a thick bank of cloud.

'Suppose she can't,' she said, her teeth chattering.

'Come on now, Chani, love. We've been through that. You can't keep thinking like that.'

'I know, but I do. We don't know where she went, whether she's on her own or still with this guy, how he's treated her or, or anything.' Her voice kept rising.

'Chani, stop it. Let's go and find a cup of tea. It's colder than I thought.'

Chani sat with Vanessa in the wholefood cafe, with plates of warm mince pies and pots of spicy tea in front of them.

'I feel as if I've been run over by a bus,' Chani said.

Vanessa gave her a sympathetic smile. 'Awful, Chani, love. But you've got some time to yourself now, Jamie and Sophie'll be gone hours won't they?'

Chani let some of the tension go in a long breath out. 'It's like being on holiday.' Vanessa smiled, encouraging her to say, 'if I only had Sophie to worry about I wouldn't need this.'

'She is a lovely girl. How awful for her, her parents splitting up.'

'Doing it at Christmas too, and telling her to choose which one she wants to be with while she's at school and which during the holidays. I think that's cruel.'

'You mean if she chooses her mum she'll have to go to school in France?'

'I suppose so. I hadn't thought of that. And go to

school in London, very likely, if she chooses her dad. She said she doesn't want to live in France, or with her dad because he's at work all the time and just gives her money.'

Chani ate another mince pie without tasting it. But the spices, the tea and the warmth of the cafe were helping. People moved round them, some they knew, who said hello. She began to feel a bit less wound up.

Moving on to the pub a little later helped even more.

The gin and tonic must have relaxed her, enough for her to remember snatches of the conversation she'd had with Magda about when Celandine had gone away.

'Magda said Jamie was shocked when he found out his mother had gone away,' she said.

'What? What are you talking about?'

'I was remembering about when I tried to find out what happened to Celandine, what Magda might know about it.' She told Vanessa about the note Celandine had left her, how Jamie clearly hadn't known when Magda told him she'd gone, and how shocked he'd been.

And something else. 'She was worried about being left alone with him, being responsible for him if he had parties, or took drugs, or did bad things. She said he might do bad things, she thought he might. Oh, God, Van, what's he done?'

Vanessa's frowning had become intense. 'Chani, love, I'm having trouble following this. When was it? When did you have this talk with Magda? Was it all at the same time?'

'It's just come back to me, bits at a time.'

She did her best to explain the how and when but it was all jumbled up in her mind.

Vanessa bought more drinks and sat in silence with hers. 'I have to get it sort of straight in my mind,' she said. 'Give me ten minutes.'

There was very little left in her glass when she placed it on the table with a decisive movement. 'OK,' she said. 'I think there's stuff we don't know about, stuff Jamie hasn't told you. I'm going to run through what he has told you and I want you to listen and tell me if I've got it all right. *And* I want you to see if anything else comes to you that might give us a clue, or if you remember anything else he said. Or anything at all that comes to you. All right?'

Chani listened. Vanessa did a pretty good job of listing everything she'd told her and that they'd already gone over.

'I can't think of anything you've missed,' Chani said.

'Hmm.' Vanessa drummed her fingers on the table for a while. When she stopped and lifted her head, the frown had almost gone. 'It's something about the money. Do you think John Smith, from what Magda and Jamie and Sophie have said about him, do you think he'd have taken five hundred pounds from Jamie and been persuaded by it to take his mother away?'

'No,' Chani said. 'Now you put it like that, no. It's not enough, is it? But it's pretty likely he took the money. I don't know what happened after that.'

'Exactly what I think. What happened after that? Did Celandine go off with him because she'd thought of it herself? Or did he skedaddle and she couldn't cope and ran away because she was disturbed and upset? Or did something happen to make her want to run away, on her own or with John Smith?'

Chani couldn't take her eyes off Vanessa. This was compelling stuff. 'Ah,' she said, knowing, though not how she knew, 'that something has to do with Jamie, doesn't it.'

'It has to. How are we going to find out?'

It was freezing again when Chani and Vanessa left the pub at the end of the afternoon and set off in their different directions to walk home. They had talked and talked but were no nearer working out how to get the information they needed from Jamie. She could see lots of stars, even with the light from the street lamps. She liked it like this, sharp and crisp. Her mind veered to Sophie.

How long would she be with her mother? Maybe she would decide to stay there, live in France. Certainly, Jamie wasn't much of an attraction for her to want to come back here, the way he was being with her.

What would she do without Sophie? And when she'd still have Jamie. And she had to find a way to interrogate him. Despair settled round her like a blizzard.

She was putting her key in the lock, still shrouded in bleak despair, when a car pulled up and three people scrambled out, laughing and talking. Sophie, Tara and a guy she didn't know who must be Arnie. He opened the boot and took out bag after bag.

'I'll carry these for you,' he said to Sophie.

Chani invited them in.

'I found everything I wanted,' Sophie said, having introduced Arnie. Her face was full of colour, though her eyes were still dulled and shadowed.

Chani made coffee while Sophie took her bags – five of them – up to her room.

Tara and Arnie talked easily. 'This is great,' they agreed, indicating the coffee. 'We didn't have time for one.'

Chani already liked Tara and she was liking Arnie too. The pair were clearly aligned. They didn't stay long, Tara's mum was expecting them, she said.

As they left, Tara gave Sophie a long hug. Chani thought Sophie had probably told her everything. Good, it was what she needed.

When she closed the door behind them Sophie turned back to Chani and said, 'Come and see what I bought.'

Chani admired everything. 'You had a good time then?' she asked.

'Oh yes. It was busy, lots of people.'

'It would be,' Chani said.

Sophie smiled. 'Not your thing?'

'Not really. But you enjoyed it, didn't you?'

'I did.'

The meal that evening was strained. Jamie had been quiet when he'd returned with Brian, who hadn't seemed to notice.

'No snow tomorrow,' he'd said as he left. 'Just as well, I have to go to Newcastle.'

Chani was glad there wouldn't be snow, hoped it would stay like that till after Wednesday. She wasn't

315

looking forward to driving to Leeds/Bradford airport then, had already wondered if Brian would take them in his Land Rover if it did snow.

Sophie was still being stiff with Jamie, who decided to spend the rest of the evening in his bedroom. Strains of opera music drifted downstairs from time to time – miserable opera music, it would surely block the flow of his chi.

Sophie had put the TV on but clearly wasn't watching it. 'Do you mind if I check the weather forecast?' Chani asked her.

'Mmm?'

'I need to check the weather.'

'Mm.'

Taking that as a yes, Chani checked every station's weather forecasts, to be on the safe side. No one forecast snow but it wasn't enough to lift her mood.

She turned off the television and before she could hold back the words, she said, 'I'm going to miss you, Sophie.'

'Actually,' Sophie said. 'I wanted to ask you. I mean, well, I don't want to stay in France. I'm only going for a few days.'

'Are you going to stay with your father, then?'

'No, I don't want to do that either. I mean, it's like, I want to see them both, of course, but ... Chani, would you let me stay here, with you?'

'Stay with me?' The despair fell away instantly. 'Would your parents agree to that?'

'I can't see why not. You are Jamie's gran. And your friend's a social worker.' How practical she was. Chani would never have thought of that.

316

'Sophie, of course you can stay here. As long as your parents say you can.'

'Cool! I'm so pleased,' Sophie said. 'I feel so much better, now.'

'Good.' She couldn't take it in. The only way she could deal with it was to be businesslike. 'Now, your flight's at eleven so you'll need to be at the airport for nine, which means we'll leave here at eight at the latest, probably half past seven.'

'I'll be ready for seven o'clock,' Sophie promised.

Neither of them mentioned Jamie, Chani couldn't cope with thinking about what might happen with him. Not until she had to.

27

Jamie had a restless night, with more dreams involving his father. In one he ordered Jamie into the army. 'Make a man of you,' he kept saying.

Twice Jamie found himself falling – once from a high cliff, once into a deep hole. Each time his father watched but made no attempt to save him.

When he woke he didn't want to open his eyes, it still felt like the middle of the night. He wanted to go back to sleep but, the images of his father still fresh, was afraid to. He lay there with his eyes closed and made himself think about yesterday, when he'd been in Brian's Land Rover, as Brian was driving them to the match.

Jamie had felt the impulse to talk to him, to ask him what he thought, but the guy had nattered all the time about cheerful, Christmas-related stuff. There never seemed to be the right moment, and when Jamie did, finally get the chance to speak all he'd managed to do was ask for more information on the school Brian had told him about, the Sixth Form College.

'I really want to study science.' Wow, he'd actually said it, never been able to before, always blocked by other people's disapproval.

'They send at least four science students to Oxford and Cambridge,' Brian had said. 'The others tend to choose Leeds – it's a good uni.' He'd gone on to talk about the science teaching, and the teachers who also worked part time for the Open University. 'The school's good for Art and Drama too,' he'd said. 'Isn't that what Sophie's interested in?'

'Yes,' Jamie had muttered and changed the subject, giving way to Brian's mindless cheer. Sophie, yes, well: wasn't going to happen now, was it.

The memory did nothing now to cheer him up, or to banish the bad images of his father. His eyes closed and despite his fear, he dozed off, to be awakened – sort of – by a tapping sound. It was dark, must be the middle of the night. Groggy from his disturbed sleep, he lifted his head. The door opened, allowing a faint light through that had to be coming from the landing. Outlined against the light he could make out a shape – Sophie.

'I'm going in a minute, Jamie,' she said, in that stiff voice she used now.

As his eyes sort of adjusted he thought she was wearing outdoor clothes. He didn't know what to do. Well, he did, but he couldn't. Don't go, he wanted to say.

'Oh, really!' She strode across to the bed and shook his shoulder. Hard. 'Jamie Pomfret-Jones – wake up!'

'I *am* awake,' he moaned. He couldn't see her expression in the dark but he could hear it, and make out the way she was standing. All sort of spiky, rigid, fed up.

'I said I'm going in a minute.' Even more stiff.

'Why do you want to go and live in France?' he demanded from his pillow, like he was five or something.

'What? I don't.' He struggled to a sitting position, struggling also to adjust his mind.

'Why are you going there then?'

'Oh, Jamie, have you heard anything I've been telling you recently? My parents are divorcing, Daddy—'

'Divorcing!'

'My God, I knew you weren't taking any notice.' She snapped on his bedside light, shocking his eyes into squeezing shut. 'Yes, they're getting a divorce. It's mega upsetting, you know.'

'Well ...' He felt terrible. What could he say? He lifted a hand to shield his eyes and squinted through the beam.

'I have to choose. Daddy in England or Mummy in France. That's even worse.'

Oh, crap. 'Er ... yes. What do you ...?'

'I don't know. I don't want to do either. That's why I need to talk to Mummy.'

'Oh. But why do you have to go to France?' There was something he was missing. Apart from not being able to see her.

'Because that's where she is.'

'Oh.'

'I'm only going for a few days.'

He felt faint with relief. For a moment, before he realised how he must be coming across to her.

'I thought you were ...'

'Going for good? Is that why you've been sulking?'

He couldn't cope with her anger. But nor could he admit to sulking.

His eyes were adjusting at last but now, as he opened his mouth to speak he couldn't look at her. 'I haven't.'

'You have. I told you about the divorce, you must remember.'

'I don't, I really don't.'

'No.' The word condemned him. As well as having other meanings, none of them complimentary to him.

Worse came. 'You were drunk, that's why. You must have sneaked into the kitchen at Vanessa's. That was stupid, Jamie.'

That really stung. But what could he do? 'I know,' he admitted. 'I've apologised.'

'Oh, so that's all right then.'

She turned towards the door. She was leaving. His eyes sprang fully open, he had to stop her.

'I'm sorry, Sophs.'

She half turned back to him, but he couldn't miss her anger. 'And what about your mum? I can't believe you did that, didn't you think about what might happen?'

Oh, God, now she was lecturing him about that, when he'd already had Chani on at him. He shivered. It was freezing cold.

He only had on a T shirt but he couldn't get up for his fleece dressing gown while Sophie stood there. He slid down a bit in the bed and pulled the duvet up as much as he could. Being got at while you were in bed was demeaning, especially when it was the second time.

'No,' he admitted. 'I didn't, at the time. But Chani told me … everything that might have happened. I shouldn't have done it, it was stupid. I know it was, I wish I hadn't done it.' He took a breath.

There was no sign that he could make out that she was softening.

Sounds came to his ears from downstairs. He heard footsteps on the stairs, followed by the bathroom door closing. Chani.

'Are you really coming back?' He was miserably aware of the pleading in his voice.

'Yes, I said.' All the indications were that she was about to go.

Something occurred to him. 'To Welwyn?'

Her breathing changed, he wasn't sure what that told him. 'I won't have a home there,' she said. Shit, she was upset.

'Sorry,' he murmured. Home – with no Sophie. Having to go to the school he hated and no Sophie there.

Sophie drew a long breath. 'Chani says I can come back here.'

What? 'Here,' he breathed, but ... 'But you'd have to go to school.'

'There's that sixth form college Brian told you about. It sounded cool.'

'Sophie,' came Chani's voice. 'We need to go. Are you ready?'

'Yes, coming,' she said and moved towards the door. Slowly.

'Hang on, Sophs,' he said and leapt out of bed, lunging for his dressing gown while her back was turned. 'I'm sorry.' He threw it on and pulled the belt into a rough near-knot.

She stopped moving.

He reached her.

'Are you?'

'Yes.' He pulled her into his arms and kissed her,

feeling her response, and trying to hide his own..

'Sophie?' Chani called.

He pulled himself away. 'Wait for me.'

Jamie had to sit in the back with Sophie's bags. He felt a bit like a bag himself, wearing yesterday's clothes, thrown on in a crazy rush. He ran his fingers through his hair in a vain attempt to tidy it. In the front Sophie read out directions to Chani. Printed out from Google, he could see.

'Have you booked the flight back?' he asked.

'No, Mummy'll do it from there. I'll email you.'

'And me, please,' Chani said.

As they neared the airport the day started to lighten. How far were they from the Arctic Circle?

They waited as long as they could with Sophie, in the queue for the check-in, talking in odd bursts about nothing.

'I'm going to find the loo. Give me a hug, Sophie, in case I miss you.'

Jamie watched them, the obvious affection between this weird woman and his Sophie making him feel strangely emotional, and dizzy.

As soon as Chani walked away he put his arm round Sophie's shoulders, steering her bag with his free hand. She rested her head against him.

'Will you work something out with your mum?' he asked.

'I don't know.' She lifted her head to gaze up at him with troubled eyes, a little frown between them. 'I hope so, but I definitely know what I don't want.'

'To live in France?'

323

'Right, or to live with Daddy either, I'd never see him.'

'No.' Jamie felt an odd clutching sensation at the base of his ribs.

The queue moved. He pushed Sophie's bag into the space in front.

'We have to work it out,' Sophie said, her voice tight. 'What we're going to arrange about seeing each other. I want to see them both but I don't want to spend all my holidays with either Daddy or Mummy. I don't know how we'll do it.' She nuzzled herself into him and he tightened his arm round her. The clutching feeling intensified. Was he going to be sick?

They reached the front of the queue. There was just time for a last kiss before he had to come away.

Chani appeared in time to wave to her. Together, he and Chani walked to the car park. Chani said nothing, Jamie was glad, he didn't want to talk. He felt empty, except for the weird clutching sensation.

Neither said much on the drive back, Chani concentrating on where she was going until she reached familiar ground, Jamie concentrating on the navigation instructions, not easy when they kept blurring or when his eyes kept closing. He gripped the page with tense fingers. He felt exhausted, confused and tense.

'You've had no breakfast, have you?' Chani asked when they were inside.

He shook his head. He was starving. That must be why he felt funny. He turned towards the kitchen.

'Sit down,' Chani said. 'I'll make you scrambled eggs, it's the middle of the day. Would you like mushrooms with that?'

'Yes please.' He felt enormously grateful. 'Thanks.'

Chani sat at the table with him, eating a smaller version of the meal she'd given him. 'Tea?' she asked him, reaching for the pot.

'No, thanks. I'll get some water.'

He carried it back with him and rejoined her. She'd pushed the used plates to one side. She looked at her watch.

'She should be taking off soon.'

Jamie had already checked. 'In ten minutes.'

*

Chani's lips twitched. What a fool he was, but maybe he'd finally seen sense.

'So,' she said, hoping she was right. 'You two have made it up.'

He looked down at the table. 'Yes.'

She let the silence lie and thought about what to do with the rest of the day. Jamie sat, hunched over, like someone pulled from the wreckage of a sinking ship. He was pale, the shadows round his eyes dark like bruises.

'You look terrible,' she heard herself say.

'Didn't sleep much,' he muttered.

She scrutinised him more intently than she had before. He did, indeed look terrible, more than from a bad hangover. Even with a guilty conscience as well. Was he ill? He'd eaten everything she'd given him, he couldn't be that bad.

'Do you feel ill at all?' she asked, with a little more concern.

'I don't know.'

'Maybe you should go back to bed?'

'I don't know.'

'How about if I run you a bath and you can have a good soak?'

His eyes half-closed, he considered the idea, his shoulders lifted in a half-hearted shrug. But he raised his head to look at her. 'OK, thanks.'

In the bathroom she lit an oil burner, added a healing oil and left it on the windowsill. Found clean towels. Opened her mouth to call him but thought better of it and went down to him. He hadn't moved.

'It's ready,' she said. He pulled himself up and shambled out of the room. Tired out, must be.

She still felt uneasy. Once she was sure he was in the bathroom she went up to his room. The bed was a mess. More than a mess. She started to straighten it, but as soon as she touched the duvet she knew she couldn't leave it smelling like that. She opened the window; however cold it was the room needed air. She would close it when she'd finished.

She carried the stripped-off bedding downstairs and put it straight in the washing machine, then washed her hands before going back to put clean bedding on his bed.

Jamie slept most of the afternoon. By the time he appeared Chani had cleaned Sophie's room and washed her bedding. Just as well she'd be away for a few days, there was no more clean linen till this lot dried.

She had also had two visitors – Leanne and Zainab. Chani and Leanne had exchanged Christmas presents and had only finished opening them when Zainab arrived. They had sat in the kitchen, talked about their Christmases and gossiped.

'Brian was a bit worried about your Jamie when he took him to the match,' Leanne said. 'Thought he didn't seem too good. Is he all right?'

'He's a bit down,' Chani said, making light of it. 'Sophie's gone to France this morning, she's really upset, her parents have decided to get divorced. Her mum's in France – she's French – and Sophie needed to go and talk to her. I think Jamie got the idea she wasn't coming back but she is.'

'Poor girl,' Leanne said.

'Has it only just happened?' Zainab asked.

'They've only told her about the divorce a couple of days ago. She only knew just before they came here that they were separating, so it's come as a shock.'

'That's bad,' Zainab said. 'Times like that, you need to explain things to your kids. It makes all the difference.'

Leanne agreed. 'Were they a close family?'

'I think so, I've never met them.'

'Haven't you?' Leanne was clearly surprised.

'Well, no. I only met Sophie a few days before they came up here with me. I was only down there just over a week.'

'Was it only a week? It seems ages ago.' Zainab said.

'I know. It felt a lot longer than a week to me.'

They laughed and Chani brought out the mulled wine.

This was great, her friends here with her, having a laugh and a gossip, here in her kitchen.

'I've been thinking about that man you talked about, Chani, when we went to the pub,' Zainab said.

'Yes,' Leanne said, eagerly. 'Tell all.'

327

Man? Oh, Damien. Chani had forgotten about him. 'He's just somebody I met in Welwyn, in a pub. I thought he was interesting, we seemed to have a lot in common, but I only saw him that once. And then he rang me up, out of the blue. That's what I was telling you about. I was annoyed, actually.'

'Yeah,' Leanne said. 'That's what it looked like. Like he thought he could just pick up where he'd left off. I'd've been annoyed too.'

Chani told them about the ashram.

'What an excuse!' Leanne said.

'I doubt he'll ring again,' Chani said. 'But there's no way I'll be seeing him if he does.'

She had the total support of her friends, as she'd known she would.

'Even so,' Zainab said, 'I bet you'd meet up with him.'

Leanne laughed. 'You told me you would.'

Chani grinned. 'I was drinking at the time.'

'Oh, right, whatever,' Zainab said.

'Anyway,' Leanne said, still chuckling. 'Our Brian's got a new girlfriend.'

'Who?' Chani and Zainab asked in chorus.

'She's not from here,' Leanne said, sounding disappointed. So were Zainab and Chani, though Zainab had only lived a short time in the area. 'She's from Huddersfield. I haven't met her yet.'

Over a second mulled wine the three of them enjoyed dissecting Brian's love life and his mother's hopes for him.

'His dad just says, "Yeah, right, whatever",' Leanne said.

'I think he's a bit more interested than that,' Chani said. She knew him well.

'I'm sure he is, but he won't let on to me. I noticed he "just called" on our Brian yesterday!'

28

Chani felt much happier by the time they left, so that when Jamie appeared, in clean clothes and with his hair brushed, she greeted him cheerfully.

'You look much better,' she said. She was rewarded by what could have been taken for a smile.

'I've had a text from Tim,' he said.

'Oh, are they back then?'

His eyes widened. 'How did you know they were away?'

Chani smiled. 'I know his mum. I think I did tell you that.'

'Oh. Well, there's a practice tomorrow. I'll need my stuff.'

'Right. You can sort that out, can't you? I'll be at work tomorrow.'

'Er... '

'Where is it?' She wasn't sure what he meant by 'stuff' but was pretty sure socks, pants and rugby top came into it. At least.

'That's the thing. I don't know.'

'You don't? But haven't you done a practice before, the other day wasn't it?'

'Yes, but ... I've looked, but I don't know where it went. Did somebody ...?'

'No, Jamie. Erm ... what did you do with your, er, stuff, when you'd used it?'

She knew the answer of course, she was trying not to laugh. He would have dropped it somewhere, expecting it would magically be found and magically washed.

Between them, they tracked down the very dirty 'stuff' in a corner of his room, along with all the clothes he'd worn since he'd arrived.

'See,' Chani said. 'This is what you do.'

She led him downstairs, with him carrying all the used clothes and, discovered at the bottom of the pile, a pair of muddy, grass-covered boots, to the cellar.

'You remember this sink, I showed you before?'

Jamie frowned but nodded. 'Oh, er, yes.'

'You can clean your boots in it,' she said. 'I clean my dirty wellies and boots in there. Then let the water out, rinse the sink out, put the plug back, half-fill it with cold water and soak your rugby clothes overnight. Can they all be washed together?'

Jamie looked blank.

'Do any of them run?'

No, that was knowledge he didn't have. Well, they would find out.

'Actually,' she said, 'if you want to wear this stuff tomorrow you need to wash it tonight. So be as quick as you can doing your boots and getting things soaking. I'll show you the washing machine about eight o'clock.' They could hang the things on airers in Sophie's room overnight and, with any luck, the heating in the morning would help them dry, or nearly dry.

'What time's your practice?' she asked.

'Half past one. I'll ask Tim if I can have a lift there.'

'Fine. And when you come back from the practice, you need to do all this again with your kit. You'll be able to leave it to soak properly then.'

Would he, she wondered, ever learn?

When Chani came back from work Jamie had cleaned his boots and put his rugby kit to soak. So, there was hope for him yet.

'Well done!' she said.

He actually smiled.

'Had your kit dried for your practice?'

He gave a little grimace. 'Not quite. But it dried on me. Then we were soaked by rain and then by sleet, so it didn't matter any more.'

It was her turn to grimace. 'You don't go inside when it's sleet, then?'

He shook his head, his mouth turning up at the corners.

'Right,' Chani said. 'I'm going to treat you. I was paid a bonus today, how would you like a pub meal?'

He smiled again, his eyes bright. 'Really?'

'Really. We'll go about seven. I'll even make you a sandwich to keep you going.'

She fed him and left him watching television while she meditated to relax. It had been busy at the Centre, people detoxing after Christmas and before New Year's Eve. The bonus had been the big surprise, forty pounds for each of them.

'Business has been good these last few months,' Melissa said. 'All thanks to you.'

Chani wondered what had happened to transform the woman into a human being. So, she learned, did the rest of the staff.

*

In the pub Jamie accepted a half pint shandy and ate

steak and kidney pie and chips with relish. Let Chani eat her vegetable curry, his meal tasted fantastic.

He'd hardly finished eating when they were joined by a group of women.

'This must be Jamie,' they all said, squashing up so they would fit round the table, the woman next to him so close he was really uncomfortable.

Chani introduced them, but the only name he could remember was Leanne, who Chani said was Brian's mum. She was nice.

They all made a fuss of him. Another shandy appeared, soon followed by meals for the women, each one something vegetarian.

One of the women turned out to be a comedienne.

'I've got a gig on New Year's Eve,' she said, seeming excited about it.

So did the others. 'Where?' they asked.

'The Fiddlers,' she told them. 'I hope you can come, some of you at least.'

It turned out all of them could go.

'You'll enjoy it,' Chani said to him. 'Sophie'll be upset if she misses it.'

He wondered how Sophie knew about this woman. Wondered, too, how he'd cope with being there with the group. They didn't seem quiet women at all. Tomorrow he'd get in touch with Tim and see what he and Tank were doing on New Year's Eve, something he'd never bothered about before.

When they left the pub at about half past ten he had found out that one of the women was the Maisie Cate Sophie had talked about. She was as weird as Chani. The comedienne was called Zainab. She didn't seem at all like the stand-up comic she said she was. He had also drunk four shandies. They must have been mostly lemonade, he didn't feel any different at all.

It snowed that night, and on and off during the day. Chani walked to work.

Jamie emailed Sophie to tell her about the comedy and the snow. He signed off, *'Jamie xx'*

'Snow here too,' came her reply. *'Sorry can't get back for comedy, should know tomorrow what flight I can get. Sophie xx'*

He spent a boring day watching sport on television – at least, what sport he could find when Chani didn't have the sports channels – and listening to his music. The highlight was a text from Tim: 'Will see what we can arrange.'

Sophie emailed the next afternoon. *'Arrive 3.20 pm. Leeds/Bradford, Weds. 5th . Couldn't get on a flight over New Year. Hope you can get to airport if snow still there. Speak soon xx'*

'Sophie's emailed,' he told Chani when she came in. 'She's back on Monday. Can you get there if it's snowing?'

'I'll talk to Brian, if he's free then he'll take us in his Land Rover. I'll look at my emails now. You couldn't make me a cup of tea, could you?'

Jamie managed it. Chani had exactly the same message from Sophie. And remembered the Centre opened on Wednesday. Melissa wouldn't like it but it didn't matter, she would have to take the afternoon off.

'Thanks,' Chani said. 'I'll nip round to Brian as soon as I've drunk it.'

*

'What time does she land?' Brian asked, offering Chani

a glass of wine.

'It's called Merlot,' he said. 'I got it in for Mum.'

Chani took a sip. 'It's good,' she said, and took another.. 'Sophie's supposed to land at three twenty, that's if the flight's not affected by the weather.'

'More likely to be affected by trying to land at Leeds/Bradford. Still, we'll go and if we have to wait we do. If she has to land at Manchester or somewhere, we'll have to see if we can get there. She might have to stay overnight if it's really bad, though it's usually worse up here. Let's hope it clears, eh.'

It seemed a good moment to change the subject. 'I met your mum on Tuesday,' she began.

Brian grinned. 'Yes. So you'll have heard. Talk about the Hebden Bridge Broadcasting Service!'

Chani laughed. 'She's not the only one.'

'No, but I'm her special subject. I can't cough without half Yorkshire knows about it, East Lancashire too, likely.'

'So come on, who is she?'

'You mean you don't know? Didn't she give you the full life story?'

'No. Only that she's from Huddersfield.'

'She's slipping. Yeh, she is. Aisha, she's called, she teaches at Huddersfield Uni, Physical Geography. At the moment she's in Iceland. Went yesterday, she won't be back till the end of January. She's twenty-eight, by the way, and divorced, no kids. Mum'll tell you if I don't!'

'You're right, she would. I look forward to meeting her.'

His grin widened. 'I'll let you know. And

Wednesday, if it's still bad, I think we should set off about two, probably.'

Talking to Brian had reminded Chani of something else Leanne had said, something to do with Brian being concerned about Jamie. It brought back her own concerns about him and some of the things he'd said about Celandine.

Her first chance to bring this up came as they were finishing eating. Jamie helped clear the table and as she washed the dishes he offered to dry them.

'I'll leave them to dry by themselves,' she said. 'It's better. I wondered if you'd like a small glass of mulled wine?'

They took their glasses into the living room and before Jamie could switch on the television Chani said, 'Cheers.'

'Cheers,' he answered.

Encouraged by that, and a sip of the wine, Chani said, 'I've been thinking, Jamie, about something you said. About your mum changing after your dad died.'

An odd expression crossed Jamie's face, it might have been resignation. Had he been expecting her to say something?

'You did say that, didn't you?' she said, to give him a bit of a push. And watched as he took another drink. And a deep breath.

'It was like … like she took over from him.'

She hadn't expected that. 'How do you mean?'

'I hated him.'

She hadn't expected that either.

'I only met him once and I wasn't impressed,' she

336

said. 'But …'

Jamie ignored that. 'I was never good enough.'

'Oh, you poor lad,' she said, shaken by the bitterness in his voice.

His eyebrows rose, fell again. 'I never did anything right, not that he thought was right.' He took another drink of wine. 'He was horrible. I was *glad* when he died. But then he left that will and I still had to do what he said.'

Could that be true? After all she'd gone through so he could stay at that damned school? But she remembered Sophie had said something on those lines, she hadn't really believed it.

'You mean the school? Stokeley Manor?' She had to get this clear.

Jamie screwed up his face. His free hand clenched, his other gripping the wine glass so hard she feared he might break it.

'Not just the school. It was all about how things looked.' His lips curled. 'Fitting in. He was always on about fitting in. I had to be in the cadets and do naval training so I'd be a good officer. I don't want to be an officer, I want to be a scientist.' He gulped the last of the wine and banged the glass down with such force Chani was amazed when it didn't break.

'Did … did your mum want you to do that?' she asked, to try and divert him. 'Be an officer?'
He pulled a face and shrugged. 'She used to stand up for me. But when he died she didn't. It was all "your father would want you to do this" and "your father wouldn't like that". Just like he was still there. Worse.'

He glared at Chani, as if he were angry with her, as

337

if she should know all this.

'I see,' she tried. How useless was that? But what else could she say?

His expression changed again. To worried. 'You don't really think he'd have murdered her, do you?'

'Your dad?' she asked, confused.

'No. John Smith.' Again, as if she should have known.

She had to be honest. 'He might, Jamie, he could have done. I hope he hasn't, I really do, but I don't know. It could be we won't know. Just have to hope she gets in touch with you. You really, really don't know where she is?'

He shook his head. 'No. I really don't.'

She had to leave it at that.

When Jamie went off to watch TV Chani stayed where she was, thinking over what Jamie had said about his father. What sort of relationship must they have had?

She'd detested Tim Pomfret-Jones on sight, could imagine him pushing his son towards being an officer, going to the same school as his male ancestors and all that stuff about fitting in. She was a bit shocked Jamie had been glad when he died, but she could understand it. And then, when he'd expected all that pressure would go only for Celandine to turn into his dad. What a nightmare. He'd have had six years of that, wouldn't he. And what, five years of being at a school he hated? She felt choked. No wonder he wanted rid of her.

A picture of Celandine when she was ten, the age Jamie was when his dad died, came into her mind. Celandine never had a dad of course, except physically.

Some faint process in her mind connected that with Jamie, but she couldn't work out how. Something to do with role models? But Celandine had loads of father figures when she was growing up.

Other images rose to the surface. An older Celandine, unbelievably changed, as if an alien had taken her over.

'I've changed my name, I'm Linda now. I don't like Celandine, you mustn't call me that any more.' Not defiant, just cold.

Another picture. Chani wanted to close it off but it wouldn't go. 'I've signed up, I start in September, Accountancy. I can go anywhere with that.'

Chani wanted to see pictures of Celandine before these things happened, fought to summon them up. The lovely girl she'd been, so alive, sort of glowing, quick, bright. Always smiling, full of ideas, always knew who to ask about what she needed to know, everyone pleased to see her and to help her.

It was like being stabbed. The hurt, the rejection. Her lovely daughter turning her back on everything Chani believed in. She gasped and wrapped her arms round herself for comfort, the pain was so strong.

Through the pain her mind seemed to slow until it sort of jammed. It would free itself for an instant, each time spitting out a memory, or a new idea.

The pain – she'd seen it in Sophie, raw. Sophie's family, they'd seemed supportive, loving. She wasn't used to things breaking down.

Jamie, poor lad, he was a wreck. Pain there too, she hadn't recognised it before. He was used to the breaking down stuff. Didn't know how to cope. Never been able to decide anything for himself had he?

Whoa! She'd never seen that, never realised.

Sophie now, used to taking control. Was that why this split had hit her so hard?

Her pain was not as bad now; the chaos in her head was clearing. She knew all this stuff meant something, but she couldn't see the connections. She felt confused and sort of unsteady. She wanted to think, to work all this new stuff out, but she was too muzzy. She remembered the Merlot, and the wine just now.

Her chi was blocked, that was it. She needed to get its flow going again.

That was what Jamie needed too. How could she start the flow for him? Did he even have any chi? Was there anything she could do, or did he have to go through what he seemed to be experiencing, sort of like rehab? Poor boy.

29

Jamie slept without nightmares that night, slept so deeply that when he came to it was a long time before he felt fully awake. The house was empty, the day, also empty, stretched ahead of him.

He wished again he could go to the gym, but, on top of the problems he'd thought of before, like how to get there, he realised he'd need either Tank or Callum to use their guest pass for him. Was there any chance one of them might want to go? Was the gym within walking distance? Even if it was, and he could find the way, whoever was with him would have to walk there too. He checked the state of the snow and saw it hadn't changed. His brain felt so sluggish it was really hard to think about this.

Maybe he could just go out and walk by himself somewhere.

His phone went. He grabbed it and pushed the answer button as fast as he could. It was Brian.

'Hi, mate,' he said. 'Listen. I've just had a thought. I have to go to a meeting at Leeds Uni on Tuesday, how'd you like to come with me and I can get one of the technicians to show you round the labs?'

'That would be great. Thanks, Brian.'

'Fine. Sorted. I'll pick you up at half nine, all right?'

'Yes, that's good.'

'Great. See you then.'

Tuesday. He'd better make a note of that. What day was it today? Chani had a calendar in the kitchen, he remembered and went to look. Friday. The thirty-first. He groaned, New Year's Eve. Tim hadn't got back to him, he was going to have to go to this women's comedy thing with Chani and her friends and be embarrassed for hours.

He would go out, even if he had to walk round the streets. It would be boring, but not as boring as staying in the house; or watching Chani's midget TV.

He put on his boots and his ski gear, made sure he had a key and left the house. He walked to the end of the road and stopped. Up or down?

His phone vibrated in his pocket. His inside pocket of course, he only just managed to find it and answer before the call went to voicemail.

Tim. Great.

'Are you doing anything right now?' Tim asked.

'Not really, I've just walked to the end of the road, why?'

'We're going sledging, do you want to come?'

Sledging – brilliant.

Tim's instructions involved walking up the hill till he reached a lane which led to what Tim called 'the Sledging Place'. 'You can't miss it,' he said. 'It'll be packed. You'll hear the screaming!'

He did hear screaming, as well as shouting and laughter. The place was at the base of the fell, a long stretch of sloping land, dotted with low bushes, that flattened out at the bottom. This was edged by clumps of bushes and a few low, scrubby trees with fencing beyond them which marked off rows of houses. It was ideal. Jamie envied Tim, there was nothing in Welwyn like this.

He studied the slope, looking for Tim. The place was, as Tim had said it would be, packed. He saw queues at the top and, as he watched sledges on their way down he realised it was similar to ski runs; some were much steeper than others. He noticed the little kids on the equivalent of the nursery slopes. They were still quite tough for kids though, with the run so long. Impressive.

Tim spotted him long before Jamie could pick him out of the crowd. He was with Tank and they were covered with snow.

They led him up to the top, where Callum was about to push off, alongside a girl whose long black hair streamed back from her bright red hat.

'That's Rachel,' Tim explained. 'She's his girlfriend. She's staying with us, she's from Nottingham.'

'How did you get here?' Jamie asked. 'in all the snow?'

'Rachel,' Tim said with a grin. 'She has a four wheel drive. Tank walked. He's staying the night too, and you as well if you'd like to. Rachel said she'll drive us down so you can pick up your stuff and come back with us.'

'Great,' Jamie enthused, not just, he realised, because he wouldn't have to go to the comedy thing. He was really pleased to be asked, was looking forward to it.

He had a great time sledging and throwing snowballs, just him, Tim and Tank at first but soon they were including Callum and Rachel, who, it turned out, had a terrific sense of humour and gave as good as she got. She also handled the big four wheel drive like a professional.

'Chani's at work,' Jamie said, when she pulled up outside the house.

'OK,' she said. 'You go and pick up your stuff, I'll get this thing turned round. We'll wait here till you're ready.'

He was very wet, he'd have to change everything he had on. He moved fast, throwing stuff into his small bag, changing as he went and actually thinking to put in a toilet bag. He added shoes, remembering he'd need his boots again for outside.

Ready, he was about to leave when he realised he'd have to let Chani know what he was doing. He didn't have her phone number, Sophie always did that. He'd have to leave her a note.

It took ages to find paper and a pen.

'Staying night at Tim's,' he wrote. 'Back tomorrow.' And added, without thinking, 'Have a good time at the comedy. Jamie.'

He put the note by the kettle and dashed to the door, only remembering to take his key at the last moment.

The big vehicle was parked on the other side of the road, its engine running. He raced to it as fast as the snow would allow.

Tim opened the rear door to let him in. 'You were quick,' he said.

'I thought I'd been ages,' Jamie said. 'I couldn't find anything to write Chani a note.'

'Wow!' Tank teased him. 'That's old-fashioned!'

Tim's parents greeted him and Tank with hugs.

'Lovely you could come,' his mother said.

Tim showed them to the bedroom they were to share. It was just big enough to hold twin beds, with a wall of fitted wardrobes, drawers and shelves.

'Bathroom's next door,' Tim said. 'You'll have it to yourselves, the other rooms have en-suites.'

Jamie went to bed around three after the best New Year's Eve he'd ever had.

It had all been sort of ad hoc. Food was a running buffet, a mixture of hot and cold, like hot soup in flasks and things like Indian snacks and mini pizzas whenever someone decided to heat them up. The reason for this became clear as the evening went on.

'We pace ourselves,' Callum explained. 'As soon as it's midnight people start first footing.'

'Start what?'

'First footing.' He grinned. 'You probably don't do that down south. It's an old tradition, Scottish, I believe, originally, where people call on each other to bring in the New Year. Putting the first foot over the doorstep, it's meant to bring luck on the house. You have to take the means to live with you, that's bread and salt and something to make a fire, like wood or a piece of coal. I think that's so you'll always be able to manage, even in hard times, but I'm not too sure about it.

'And of course,' he went on and Jamie thought he would never stop, though it was interesting. 'When somebody first foots you, you have to offer them hospitality, that's food and drink. We're usually the first houses to be visited at this end of the street and after that we visit the others. It can go on all night but we

345

don't do that so much now.'

'Amazing,' Jamie said. 'So who, I mean, which people do this?'

'Everybody in our street, that's twenty houses.'

'Wow!' Imagine anything like that happening in Marlowe Drive. There were people there he'd never met, nor, he was sure, had his parents.

Pacing themselves, he found out, meant not doing an awful lot, eating and drinking only sparingly, but somehow having a great time. Every now and then there'd be a silly game, the most strenuous being Charades. Jamie couldn't believe how much he enjoyed it. He was even able to recognise an Aretha Franklin song: 'I Say A Little Prayer'.

'Jamie!' Tank cried. 'How on earth do you know that?'

'Chani. She plays it all the time.'

'Really?' Tim's dad said. 'Bet you didn't know that, did you, love? Something you and Chani have in common, isn't it?'

'I did know, actually,' his wife said.

Jamie scored again with a Justin Bieber song, courtesy this time of Sophie's musical taste. Or what used to be her taste.

'She'll be pleased you take so much notice of her music,' Callum teased him.

'Course he does,' Rachel fired back. 'He knows what's good for him.' She paused for the laughter before saying, 'Shame she couldn't be here.'

'Yes,' Jamie said, but he was thinking he'd probably have been at the comedy thing if she hadn't been away.

'She's back soon, isn't she?' Tim asked.

'Yes, on the fifth.'

'Hope the snow will have gone, then,' Tim's dad said.

'We'll be in Brian's Land Rover,' Jamie said. 'As long as the plane can land, that is.'

'Well, let me know if you need a back-up four wheel drive,' Rachel said.

'Oh.' He felt overwhelmed. 'Thank you.'

As midnight approached Tim's dad opened the back door and at twelve they heard bells as well as a clock somewhere chiming.

'The church,' Tim's mum said. 'They do it every year.'

Their first foot was only minutes later, a group of people who were introduced as the next-door neighbours, a middle-aged couple with their daughter and an aunt, uncle and cousin who were staying there. They presented their gift – a small parcel of bread, salt and a piece of firewood, as they came in.

Hot food appeared as well as the buffet and drinks all round. Mostly, it seemed, whisky. Jamie, shuddering at the memory of Christmas Eve, stuck to soft drinks with the occasional shandy, as more and more people appeared while others left.

He had no idea what time it was when everyone moved to put on boots and jackets and, because she had the darkest hair, Rachel was given the small parcel of bread and so on for their first foot. What dark hair had to do with it no one could explain.

'Just tradition,' Tim said.

They went to a house further up the street and here they were given champagne.

'Do we go to all the houses?' Jamie asked Tim who laughed.

'Not all of them. You won't get champagne again, though, it's only for the first one you do. After that we're just seeing the New Year in.'

New Year's Day, what Jamie saw of it, was a calm, quiet time of winding down. It was afternoon when Chani, still in her dressing gown and carrying a cup of tea, came into the living room where Jamie was idly thinking of sending Sophie a text.

'How was your evening?' she asked, settling herself into the chair she usually sat in.

'Good,' Jamie said. 'They did something called first footing.'

'Good,' she echoed. 'You'd enjoy that. We do it here, but we were out. We can catch up later on, probably.'

'How was the comedy?' He'd better ask.

'It was great. There were some really good comedians and Zainab was very funny, she always is. I was hurting from laughing so much.'

She was smiling, but, as she sipped at her tea the smile died. 'There was a message on the phone yesterday, from the morning. Were you out all day?'

'Well, from about half past ten or eleven, we were sledging.'

'Oh, were you. With Tim?' At his nod, she asked, 'Did somebody drive them over from Chiserley? The snow's bad up there.'

Jamie explained about Rachel, adding her offer to be back-up for the airport.

348

'That's nice of her. I don't think I've met her. Anyway, it was the social worker, the new one, Nicola.'

Jamie went cold. 'What ... er, what ...?'

'She wants me to ring her back on Tuesday. Monday's a bank holiday, isn't it?'

'Why? What does she want?'

'She didn't say. I should think it's to talk about you and Sophie being here.'

'Oh.' Jamie stared down at his knees. He didn't know what to think. Or what he felt, except that it wasn't good.

'I'm going to make some more tea,' Chani said. 'Would you like one?'

'Yes, please.' It was an automatic response.

Quite a bit later he remembered Tuesday. Chani was in the kitchen, watering the herb plants on the windowsill.

'Brian asked me to go to Leeds with him on Tuesday,' he said. 'He has a meeting at the university and he's organising for me to look at the science labs.'

'Is he?' A strange expression flitted across her face. 'The science labs. At Leeds.'

'He wants to go about nine thirty, in the morning.'

'Well, that'll take all day, won't it.'

*

All day. What if the social worker rang? Well, she would miss Jamie, there was nothing Chani could do about it. It might even be useful, actually, to talk to this new woman, Nicola when Jamie wasn't there.

The forecast for Sunday had been exactly right. What it hadn't said was that it would last the whole day, which

Chani had set aside to do laundry. Monday's forecast was little better.

Chani set up clothes airers in Sophie's empty room and everywhere else she could find space, filled them with clean, drying laundry and the house with warm, damp air.

Jamie just seemed to lounge around, watching TV and texting.

If only it would clear up, there could even be time before Wednesday for it to start to thaw. Might even thaw tomorrow, for this trip to Leeds.

Brian, when he called to wish her and Jamie happy New Year, was optimistic.

'Roads are clear,' he said. 'Should be all right tomorrow.'

She had just ended Brian's call when the phone rang again.

'May I wish you a very happy New Year,' Damien's voice said.

So there it was. How should she do this? Playing for time she said, 'Thank you very much. And the same to you.'

'Thank you. But look, I'll have to say this fast, I'm on a train and if it goes through another tunnel I'll be cut off. I'm on my way to that conference I told you about, in Leeds. It starts tomorrow, but not till six, so I'll have most of the day free. Which means, I hope, and I'm sorry for the short notice, we may be able to see each other. If you're free, of course. What would you think about meeting for lunch?'

Chani's mind replayed her 'course I bloody will' answer. It seemed flippant now.

Oh well, might as well be reckless as well as flippant. 'Why not?' she said.

'Great. Is it far from Leeds to you?'

Not wanting to seem too eager, and certainly not wanting to drive to Leeds, however clear Brian said the roads were, she said, 'It's a fair distance. What could be a problem is the snow.'

'Snow? There isn't any here.'

'Or here, but there could be tomorrow.'

'No problem, I'm hiring a car, so I'll get a four wheel drive. So, will you be there, say late morning?'

He was being very considerate, with the four wheel drive, wasn't he, so she gave him directions to her house.

30

Chani wore her black velvet, her purple embroidered waistcoat, crystal pendant, thick purple socks and Doc Martens.

He stood at the door in a big heavy black overcoat, a chunky red and grey scarf covering his ears and the lower part of his face, so his eyes, and the crinkles that said he was smiling, only just showed. He lifted a gloved hand to pull the scarf down.

'Chani,' he said. 'It's good to see you.' His lips on her cheek were cold.

They sat in her living room with the rosehip and ginger tea she'd made. For a while they talked about his journey from Leeds; he said what an interesting place Hebden Bridge looked, she held her mug in both hands and said it was. They might have just met.

'Much more interesting than Welwyn Garden City,' he said, lifting his left eyebrow, his mouth turning up at the corner and the crinkles by his eyes very clear.

That was better. She smiled her appreciation. 'So,' she said. 'Tell me about the ashram.'

He leaned back, took a sip of tea and put the mug down. 'I think I mentioned a druid?'

'You did.' She mirrored his moves with the mug and the leaning back.

'Fascinating man. He told me he came from a line of druids, I don't know if it's actually passed on but he certainly had a gift for story-telling, he could make the most ordinary thing seem magical.'

'Like the ashram?'

'I knew it as soon as I saw it, from what he'd said. It's not easy to get to, in the middle of nowhere in the mountains. The air is so clear and fresh, everything's slowed down, quiet, perfect for peaceful meditation but if you want to be with other people it's good too. I stayed longer than I meant to, especially with no contact at all with the outside world.' He fell silent, his eyes shuttering.

Chani said nothing. So he *had* been somewhere with no mobile signal.

Damien opened his eyes and shook his head. 'Sorry.'

'You were there, weren't you?'

'I was, yes. But how rude of me. I came to see you, not to drift off to another place altogether. So, you – when did you leave Welwyn? You never did tell me what you were doing there. I wouldn't have thought it was your sort of place. Especially now I've seen your home.'

'It's not.'

His eyebrows shot up. 'You said that with a lot of feeling.'

'I know.' She told him about Jamie, not meaning to say much at all but finding there was only so much she could leave out.

'So you got him to come here, and his girlfriend too,' Damien said when she'd reached that part. 'What an achievement!'

'I'm not so sure.' He wouldn't be able to miss the feeling that was said with.

'Difficult?'

'Teenage angst. And Sophie's parents splitting up.'

353

She hadn't meant to say anything about that.

Very soon he had the whole story. He was turning out to be even easier to talk to than Vanessa.

'It sounds horrendous,' he said.

'I'm quite angry with Celandine,' Chani said. Where had that come from? 'She can't have any idea of the position she's put me in. She must know what she's done to Jamie, though.'

She shook her head. 'The state his chakras are in. And she doesn't seem to have taught him anything useful, he can't do a thing for himself. And the way she treated Magda – that woman never stopped working, for slave wages too, *and* having to run round after Jamie.' She stopped, horrified that she'd let all that pour out.

'You are angry,' Damien said, in full therapist mode. 'It's good you can talk about it.' But he stiffened, as if something had startled him. 'Celandine?' he said. 'That's your daughter's name?'

'Yes.' How had they got to that?

'Lovely name.'

What could she say? 'Yes.'

His eyes got that shuttered look again and he went still, looked down at his hands and murmured, 'how odd' as if he were talking to himself.

Chani resisted the urge to ask what was odd, moving instead to take his mug and her own.

He looked up, almost as if she'd woken him. 'Thank you for that,' he said. 'It was lovely, just right.' He shifted his position, inching forward. 'How about we go and find some lunch, I'd like to buy you a drink and something nice to eat. Is there somewhere near here?'

'Great,' she said, itching to know what had affected him but leaving it to him to tell her, or not. 'Would you prefer pub or wholefood cafe?'

'Does the cafe have alcohol?'

'Of course. We can walk there too.'

Conversation lightened up over lunch and a bottle of organic wine, most of which Chani drank as Damien was driving later on.

By the coffee stage the ease between them was back. Damien glanced at the clock on the wall. 'I'm very sorry, but I do need to keep an eye on the time, I have to be back for about quarter to six. I'd better get the bill.'

As they waited Damien took a breath and looked at her. 'Your daughter, Celandine. Does she look like you?'

The teaspoon Channi had been playing absently with fell from her hand. 'Like me?'

'I just wondered.'

'Well...' She had to think about it. 'She used to look like me, except that she's blonde. I don't know about now, I haven't seen her for sixteen or seventeen years.'

'Ah.' He nodded. 'It's just, there was a woman at the ashram. A youngish woman. Her name was Celandine. There can't be that many Celandines around. And she did look quite a lot like you.' His eyes seemed to scan her. 'Yes, same build and height, bone structure, similar hair, red too – henna-red.'

'No, it couldn't be her,' Chani said, no doubt in her mind at all. 'She changed her name to Linda and went off to be an accountant, down south. Years ago.'

She felt quite a lot of warm satisfaction at the horror on his face and the way he said, 'No!' It helped to soften the hurtful memories that rushed back.

'Quite.'

He frowned. 'This woman certainly didn't look like an accountant.'

'There's no way,' Chani said. 'An ashram! Not unless she was their accountant. And then she'd have been in a business suit.'

He smiled and shook his head. 'Nothing like that. She had lots of tinkly bracelets and crystal jewellery, long velvet and patchwork-type skirts, that sort of thing. Very, sort of, New Age, talked about her karma, being in the flow, Gaia, ley lines – that sort of thing.'

Chani almost laughed, though it wasn't funny. 'No. And anyway, I can't see the guy she went off with being there either, from what I've heard about him.'

'She was on her own,' Damien said. Chani felt a sort of flutter in her stomach. She pushed it away, glad of the business of putting coats on and setting off back.

As they walked Damien asked if she would be free so they could meet again before he left. 'It's a three-day conference. We finish at one on Friday, my train is on Saturday morning, so if you had any time on Friday from about two?'

He took her hand, those long fingers twined into hers, his thumb gently stroking the base of hers, setting tremors running up her body. The message was clear.

Friday. Three days, anything could happen in three days. The social worker – she dismissed the social worker. Sophie – who knew what? Jamie – term must start very soon – probably not yet. Well, why not?

356

'I think so. But, well, it's possible I might not be here.' She did *not* want to think about that.

'Ah, your young charges. But I hope you will be. Look, how about if I ring you, say on Thursday, see how things are then?'

'Fine, yes, do that.'

Damien followed her into the house. Jamie still wasn't back. Damien was very close, his male presence stirring feelings she hadn't had for ages. Was there time?

'I'll have to go very soon,' he said. In the narrow hall she felt his breath on her ear, and a strong pang of disappointment. 'It took me longer to get here than I expected. And the afternoon has just disappeared.'

Why had she spent so long talking? 'It has,' she said.

Damien's phone sounded. 'Just a message,' he said. 'I'd better check.'

He pulled the phone out of his pocket, glanced at it and was about to put it away, saying, 'It's not important,' when he went still. 'Ah,' he said, coming back to life. 'I'd forgotten.' He sounded excited. 'I took some pictures.' He was flicking through stuff on the screen.

'Yes, there, I thought I had. Look – she's in that one – can you see her?'

It was Celandine. Chani gasped, staring at the little screen. Could it be? She looked like Celandine, older, and as he'd said, very differently dressed, but was it her?

'I think I took more with her in them. Let me see.'

There were three more shots. The woman showed more clearly in these. Celandine, to the life. It had to be her. It couldn't be her.

'Here, sit down,' he said. 'You look a bit shaken. Can I get you anything?'

She sat, hardly realising she had, discovering they were in the kitchen. 'I can't believe it. I just can't ...' She held on to the phone, turning from shot to shot, her head whirling. When at last it began to clear she said, 'I don't suppose she told you anything about herself? Where she was living, or anything?'

He looked uncomfortable. 'She said very little about herself.' He seemed reluctant to tell her even that.

He took a few hesitant steps before half turning away. 'I ... there was a sort of arrangement to meet, later, some time.'

Of course. He would. She was an attractive woman. 'So you have her phone number?' she asked, turning practical. With a kind of sick excitement. 'Or email?'

'Well, no. She has mine. I'm really not sure, though, that she'll ...'

'No.' Should have known. But — 'But if she does, will you let me know? I mean, there's Jamie.'

'But of course. Definitely.'

Chani watched him drive away, thinking how wrong he looked in the big monster of a vehicle. And that she would probably never hear from him again.

One thing she did know, if this woman by some remote chance did contact Damien and he actually let her know, she would do anything she could to meet her. Just to prove it wasn't her.

But, what if, maybe, it was her? Could it be possible she could have her daughter back? There was a sort of fluttering round her midriff that didn't fit with the heaviness that shifted around in the region of her navel. Had there been something wrong with what she'd eaten? She pulled the high back chair near the stove and settled into its padding, rested her feet on a stool, took in a long, slow breath and just as slowly let it out. What a day.

In the comfort, warmth and quiet her eyes closed and her breathing slowed.

She dreamed, of Celandine. Celandine as a young girl, as a teenager, saying those curt, shattering things about leaving. And new scenes, of a woman dressed in long skirts and crystals, fully aware, smiling and reaching out to Chani.

She woke before their hands could touch, wrung-out and heavy-eyed. And shivering. Where was she? In the kitchen? What was she doing there? She shivered again.

The stove was nearly out. As she worked to bring it back to life she remembered the dream, all of it, and longed to be able to see Celandine again. Not the disturbing images from after she'd changed, but of the lovely child she'd been.   But – didn't she have some photographs? There were some,   somewhere. In a box, yes, she could see the box, but where was it? She searched everywhere she could think of, remembering at last about the loft.

The box was smaller than she'd thought, and very dusty. She had to wipe it with a damp cloth before she could take out the packs and spread their contents over the table.

There was her lovely girl, picture after picture, over the years from when she was about four or five.

Smiling, dancing, laughing. In one, in a field of flowers with other children and musicians playing guitars, drums, fiddles; one of them a sitar.

There she was, with Chani, on her birthday, on all her birthdays. Chani had always been there for them, even if she'd been travelling she'd made it back for Selly's birthday.

Her eyes misted over and the images blurred, except behind her eyes where Celandine was vividly alive.

She ached for the daughter she'd lost. Wanted her back so much the pain was more than she could bear. But she couldn't have that daughter back, not the girl she'd lost, that girl was gone for ever, was someone else now, someone who didn't want her.

She hugged herself and rocked, and moaned for Selly, her lovely little Selly.

Selly. She was only been able to call her that till she was been about eight. Chani could hear her voice.

'I'm a big girl, I want my big girl name.' Celandine, her big girl name, to go to the Big School, the juniors.

Such an active, curious child, she loved singing and dancing. Interested in everything, she really wanted to learn. She was glad then to be called Celandine.

What went wrong? Chani couldn't sit still, had to do something. She paced around the house, her mind, as restless as her body, firing out questions.

Had it been when they moved to Hebden Bridge and Celandine went to secondary school? She still enjoyed school and learning there, did well in everything except Science which she didn't like.

What did change was the way they lived. They weren't in this house at first, it was a smaller one,

360

further up the hill, a council house. A whole house, just for them, no other people to share with. Chani did all she could to make it good and she'd thought Celandine was happy. She made sure Celandine knew how to deal with boys, with sex and relationships, and Celandine brought her boyfriends home, and all her friends. Still, it must have been a huge change, more than Chani had realised at the time.

They'd been a single-parent family, hadn't they, but there were lots of them here. Lots of her friends didn't know their fathers, like Celandine. There were all sorts of families, conventional and anything but.

Before, in the communes, most of the relationships had been, well, fluid. Memories came of Chani's own parents: they'd called themselves free spirits, doing their own thing. Chani remembered a lot of freedom but always someone there. She'd called them Bo and Zee, like everyone did.

She'd chosen the name Chani Caladan when she was about fifteen and reading Frank Herbert's 'Dune' books. Bo liked those books too, she just smiled when Chani told her and nodded.

The memory jolted her into stillness – and a sort of semi-awareness of where she was, halfway up the stairs, but the scene in her mind was Celandine talking about calling herself Linda. For the first time, instead of this memory's focus being Celandine, Chani saw herself, so shocked she didn't know how to cope. Compared her reaction with Bo's and didn't like it. Yes, Celandine's choice had been terrible, boring, uncool, suburban, but had that been how Celandine had seen it? It had upset Chani badly, she'd thought it meant Celandine didn't share her beliefs any more. But why should she? Could it have been like when she'd changed from Selly to Celandine, to mark a new point in her life?

Oh, this was awful. She saw it now, the shock on Celandine's face, the hurt. And, she had to face it, the withdrawal. She, Chani, had caused it.

It was her fault Celandine had gone against her karma, that she'd tried to build a new karma with that Pomfret-Jones man; tried to create the sort of family she knew nothing about and Jamie was the result. Poor Jamie.

Poor Celandine. If only she could find her, she could try to make it up to her. She loved her, whatever sort of life she chose. If only she'd understood that at the time, if only she'd told Celandine that. If only she could find her and tell her now.

But what she could do now was try to make things better for Jamie, and she would. Sophie too.

She was shaking all over, her teeth chattering. Cold, it was really cold. Hell's teeth, she was outside. In her garden. No wonder she was shaking. The back door was wide open, the house would be freezing. Her legs trembled as she walked inside and made straight for the stove. Why the hell had she gone outside?

Even as the felt herself thawing, she still shook, her legs still trembled. On the edge of her mind the thought came – how seriously disturbed the flow of her chi must be. She became aware of a distant ringing sound. It was a nuisance, interfering with her thoughts. She shook her head. The sound stopped, but almost immediately started again. What was it? Of course – her phone. Where was it?

31

Still shivering though no longer cold, Chani found her phone in her bedroom. It had stopped ringing, but there was a message, from Damien.

'I just remembered something I think may be important. If you get chance after about 6 can you ring me?'

He might be there now. He was, she just caught him, about to go back after the afternoon break. He'd been thinking, he said, about Chani and Celandine.

'Something clicked in my mind. Selly said her son hated her, he told her he did, he'd hated his father and she was worse. I knew I had to get her to talk about that.'

Chani's insides were churning. Get on with it, she wanted to shout. 'Yes, good. And did she?'

'She said that was what had finished her. Said what a terrible strain it was, being mother and father to an ungrateful boy, more so because she hadn't liked his school or what it stood for. That was when she realised she needed more freedom and she knew she had to leave. So she made sure her son would be looked after and she organised money for him. She told me she didn't feel guilty, after all, he'd said he wished she were dead.'

'He said that?'

'Apparently, yes.'

So Celandine hadn't gone because of Mr Smith, or the five hundred pounds. But – what was that he'd said? 'Damien, what was it you called her?'

'Celandine?'

'Yes, but you used a different name just now.'

'Oh, yes, Selly. That's what everyone called her. Someone asked her if it was short for something and she said Celandine.'

Chani couldn't speak. Or see, for tears.

'Chani, are you all right?'

She coughed, to try to get past the huge lump in her throat. 'It is her,' she sobbed. 'She was always Selly.' That was all she could manage.

'Chani, I'm so sorry, you're so obviously upset. I'll ring you again this evening, if I can. But I have to say, and you won't want to hear it—' Even through her distress, Chani recognised the change to therapist-mode. 'Selly told me things she'll wish she hadn't. I really don't think she's going to contact me at all. I have to go, I'm really sorry, I will ring later.'

She couldn't answer him, couldn't hold back the tears and the heaving, tearing sobs. She fell onto her bed, the phone dropping to the floor, curled up and howled for a long, long time. She couldn't stop it – all the emotion she hadn't known was there poured out. All the time, like a refrain, knowing just as she'd all but found Celandine she'd lost her – again. How would she ever recover from that?

Chani was woken by yet another ringing noise. Not her phone this time, but her door bell. It went on and on. Through a sort of fog she made herself go to answer it, catching sight of herself as she passed the mirror. She looked tired, shadows round her eyes and strain lines at the sides of her mouth and between her eyebrows, she saw them deepen as the reason for them came back to her. The bell rang again and she hurried to do what she could to tame her wild hair, but before she could reach the stairs she heard the door open, and voices. Jamie and Brian.

She stood for a moment to ground herself, taking calming breaths until she felt ready to meet them.

'Sorry,' she said. 'I'd fallen asleep.'

Brian carried with him a strong sense of the solid, reasonable world of his life, which helped, and Jamie had what might possibly be a faint gleam of cheer. Temporary, probably. He was checking his phone.

'You do look a bit tired,' Brian said.

Sidestepping that, Chani turned to Jamie. 'Have you heard from Sophie?'

He shook his head and moved towards the kitchen.

'Tea, coffee ...? she asked Brian, robot-like, and told Jamie, 'there's teacakes in the fridge.'

'Coffee, great.'

The photographs were still there, where she'd left them, Jamie's eyes on them. She choked back a gasp.

'Who are these people?' Jamie asked, sounding casual, not all that interested.

'Why, it's Celandine, isn't it?' Brian said, moving for a closer look. 'Yes, I remember that one. You were in the other house then, weren't you?'

Chani nodded, afraid to speak.

Jamie was staring at the two of them and then at the photographs.

'It's your mum, Jamie,' Brian said. 'When she was little. Well, she's seventeen or eighteen on that one. I'd've been Year Eight or so then.'

'You knew her?' Jamie hadn't moved, was still staring. He sounded shaken.

'As much as any lad could know a stunner like your mum who was years older. By, she didn't know I existed!'

'Stunner?'

'Certainly was. Well, look. Have you never seen these before?'

Jamie shook his head. He moved slowly to gaze where Brian pointed.

'There she is with Chani,' Brian said.

Chani stood, paralysed by the need not to break down. Why wasn't Brian sensing an atmosphere that was charged like an electrical storm? She had to do something. Coffee, yes.

She'd never put so much effort and concentration into making coffee and buttering teacakes.

'Could you just make some room for these on the table, Brian,' she asked, not completely in charge of her voice.

Brian looked up, a frown appeared, his mouth opened as he read her face. He covered his mouth with his hand and moved quickly to push the photographs to one side and took the plates from her.

'That's great, Chani,' he said, in a hearty voice. 'It's a bit chilly outside.' He ate and drank fast. 'I'd best be off,' he said. 'I've to see Mum and Dad'

When Chani came back from seeing him off on the errand she knew didn't exist but grateful for it, Jamie was poring over the photographs.

'Where's this?' he asked. And, 'what's she doing there?' And, 'is it her birthday?' 'Is that you?'

Her answers were brief to start with, spoken through a raw, tight throat, but the more he asked the more she felt able to say, until she was offering information.

A text came from Sophie and he read it where he was. 'She's OK,' he said. 'So's her mum. She's been upset but she's all right now.'

He hadn't touched the teacakes.

He moved after a little while, in a vague sort of way, into the living room. Chani sank into the nearest chair, all her strength gone. The sound of the TV came, but after a few minutes it was overlaid by the sound of Jamie going upstairs. He was there all evening, his music drifting into Chani's consciousness. She offered him food when she felt strong enough. All he wanted was a sandwich.

She thought of ringing Vanessa to tell her what she'd learned from Damien, but didn't have the energy, or, yet, the courage. All she could do, after Jamie's sandwich, was push the photographs, unsorted, into the box.

She had forgotten Damien had said he'd ring later. She'd fallen asleep in the chair.

'Are you all right?' he asked, in full therapist voice. 'I'm sorry I had to tell you all that so quickly, I know it upset you but I couldn't say any more, or listen to you like I wanted to, I really did have to go back in.'

She couldn't work out what her reactions to him were, she was too tired.

There was real concern in his voice, it had the same effect on her as mulled wine: nice but fuzzy-edged and sort of weakening.

She was still exhausted, emotionally raw, with no resources left to help her cope but he deserved some sort of answer.

She dragged words from somewhere.

'I was upset of course, it's been pretty stressful recently. I really appreciate you going to all the trouble of telling me, it was important for me to know. You can imagine how I'm feeling, it's like I've found her but she's unreachable. You're very kind to ring me now, but I'm just too tired to deal with it. And we have to be out early tomorrow to pick Sophie up from the airport.' Not a bad effort.

'Do you have to drive to the airport tomorrow?' Even more concern.

'Not me, no, we've got a lift. But thank you. I'm all right, Damien, but I'm exhausted, I'll have to go to bed, if you don't mind.'

'Goodnight then. I'll be in touch soon.'

She was already asleep.

Brian rang in the morning. At nine thirty. Not his usual cheery self.

'I'm all right,' she said. 'Thanks.'

She was. Bit shaky, but she seemed to have found a strength from somewhere. Whatever the flow brought, she would deal with it.

'Good. Great.' He puffed out a breath and his tone of voice changed to more like his normal one.

'It's looking all right. Been no snow overnight and none expected today, I've checked and the roads are all clear. Checked the airport as well, they're all right. So

I'll see you at about half one, give us plenty of time.'

Chani relayed this to Jamie.

He was up and dressed, standing by the living room window, looking out.

'I'll make us a quick omelette. And some soup and sandwiches to take with us.'

She saw his face change, he seemed to be struggling with something. Oh no, please don't say you don't want to come, or you've rung Sophie and she's staying in France, or …

'Did you,' he said, in an odd, faltering voice, still facing the window, 'Er, did you tell Sophie she could come back here? To your house?'

So Sophie had told him. 'I did, yes.' She was finding it difficult to speak in a normal way. She had to breathe before she could add, 'She has nowhere else to go.'

Jamie nodded. He was clearly still struggling with something, didn't seem very sure of himself.

'She said something about going to the Sixth Form College here.' As if he were trying the idea out, as if it weren't quite real.

'Did she?' Chani aimed at non-committal.

'Would …' He cleared his throat and started again. 'Would you be cool with that?'

Cool, she thought, remembering her pleasure when Sophie had asked if she could stay. She thought how she'd longed for her life here, to have it back. It was beginning to look like she might get it, but not quite, not as it had been. Or not, if Jamie went back to Welwyn. What would happen then?

'Cool,' she said. 'Yes, that probably is the best word.'

Jamie shifted his feet around, half turned to look at her, still with glances to the outside. 'What about, what about if I did too?'

At first it didn't register, he'd spoken so fast and so quietly, so that the words took a moment to coalesce.

'If you did too?'

He faced her. 'Why not?' Belligerent. 'I mean, I could go there.' Mollifying.

'Go where?'

'The Sixth Form College.'

He'd almost taken her breath away. 'Could you? But what about your father's will and all that …?'

He scuffed his feet, watching them as if he'd only just discovered them. 'I … I don't, I don't want to go back there.'

'To Stokeley Manor?'

'Yes. No, I don't want to go there.'

Chani needed air. She wished Vanessa were there. 'See, I know you said you hated it, but how? I don't see what we can do?'

'Can that social worker do anything?'

Without thinking, Chani said, before she remembered about Nicola Harrison, 'Who – Lollipop Woman?'

Jamie laughed.

'Wow!' Chani said. 'I thought you laughed there.'

He laughed again and Chani chuckled. 'Do you really want to stay in Hebden Bridge?' she asked. 'Here?'

He lifted his head. 'Yes, I do. I think.'

Chani had to be sure. 'With me?'

Jamie nodded. 'Do you mind?'

She could see no trace of Roman Emperor. Nor did she know what to say or what to do. 'I'm … I don't know what to say.'

It seemed that nor did Jamie. For a while neither spoke.

Chani went to sort food out. It took the rest of the morning.

Jamie had just brought his jacket down when the doorbell went. It had to be Brian. She checked the time, five past one. He was early. And, she realised, there was something she had to make absolutely clear. She stood up. 'I'm not a granny, you know.'

Jamie almost smiled. 'I know.'

There was another silence, until Chani, on her way to the door, thought of something else. Something she didn't dare say, didn't want to think about, that she'd struggled to wrap up and put away but that, she saw now, was wrapped only in tissue paper. She clenched her hands. It had to be said.

'But, if you were up here, how would your mum get in touch with you?' There were other questions, but they'd have to wait. Like, what would happen to the house down there? How would the money be managed? She was so lost in all this she missed his reply.

'What, sorry?'

'I can email her.'

'Oh, right. Good.'

And it hit her. The bloody kid had her email address. She could only gape. But her shock burst from her in one explosive word.

'*What?*'

THANKS

Very many thanks to fellow writers who have read some or all of this book and given me their valuable insights: Nicky, Dave, Iris, Alison, Sarah, Paul; members of the SMWW, with particular thanks to David Beckler for his rugby-related advice.

My special thanks to Debz for her help, support and excellent editing; to Miles for all his advice and guidance, the staff at Choir Press, and especially to Phil, for all his support and for producing the cover images.

Thank you, as ever, to my family and friends for supporting and believing in me.

AUTHOR'S NOTE:

While Hebden Bridge and Welwyn Garden City are real places, I have used them as settings in outline only. The places and events I describe there are entirely fictional and any derogatory opinions expressed about them by the characters are not my opinions.

Ros Davis was born and grew up in Lancashire. She has worked in teaching, education management, child care and Social Services in this country and overseas. In between she has temped, travelled, danced, grown vegetables and still tries to play the piano She lives in north west England with her artist husband, Phil Davis.